The Summer Wives

ALSO BY BEATRIZ WILLIAMS

The
Summer
Wives

BEATRIZ WILLIAMS

WILLIAM MORROW
An Imprint of HarperCollins*Publishers*

Designed by Bonni Leon-Berman

ISBN 978-0-06-266034-3

To my husband and children
and to my in-laws, those cultural tour guides

The Summer Wives

FOREWORD: 1969

I RETURNED TO Winthrop Island on an unseasonably cold day in early May, one week after my tenth wedding anniversary. I missed the last ferry from New London—the schedule, not surprisingly, had changed in the eighteen years since I last climbed aboard—and hired an old tub of a fishing boat to carry me across from Stonington. I don't think the fellow recognized me, but I can't be sure. Fishermen are a stoic lot, you know. They don't emote. I paid him twenty dollars cash, and in return he didn't ask me any awkward questions, like my name and my business on the Island, though I wonder if it would have made any difference. What was he going to do, call the newspapers? Probably he'd never heard of me. Lots of people had never heard of me.

Because it was May, the sky was still light as we bumped across the few miles of Long Island Sound that separate the Island from Connecticut. I wore my sunglasses, which were black and extremely large, giving me the appearance of an exotic bug, and the spray soon coated the lenses with a film of salt. When I couldn't properly see any longer, I took them off, and the strength of the draft on my face surprised me, and the smell. I'd forgotten about the scent of the Sound, which had its own particular tang, different from anywhere else in the world, the English Channel or the Mediterranean or the South Pacific—or maybe it didn't, and that was all in my imagination. Still, it seemed to me as I stood near the bow of the fishing boat, leaning against the deckhouse, that the brine on that wind reached deep inside the wrinkles of my brain, penetrating the furthest regions of the hippocampus to lay its fingertip on certain tender memories therein. Bending over the stern of a lobster boat, hauling cages from a buoy line. Sitting next to a girl at the end of a midnight dock, sharing a bottle of cold champagne. Lying on a beach while the rain coursed upon me and a boy, kissing each other for the last time.

Ahead of me, the Island made a dark, flattened parabola, growing larger by the second until it dominated the horizon and the specks on its surface took on the character of houses. I saw the cluster of buildings around the harbor, the scattering of estates along the shore. I couldn't see Greyfriars from here—perched as it was on the southeastern corner of the Island—but I knew it still existed, overlooking Fleet Rock and its famous lighthouse. I knew this because of the letter in my pocketbook, which was written on Greyfriars notepaper and signed, in old-fashioned, reproachful copperplate, *Your Mother*. There was no mention of Isobel, but I knew she existed, too. There could be no Greyfriars without Isobel, could there?

Without thinking, I turned to address the fisherman, and his face went rigid with shock at the sight of me, now unhidden by sunglasses. "An accident," I said, touching the bruised flesh around my left eye and my cheekbone. "An automobile accident," remembering to use the American term—*accident*—instead of the British one, *smash*. A car smash, which is an interesting difference, you know. To call it an accident implies an absence of intent, nobody's fault, a tragic mistake. A smash is just that. Makes no judgment on how the thing happened, or why.

"I'm sorry, ma'am." He returned his attention to the direction of the boat. (Like I said, a stoic lot.)

"These things happen," I said. "I was going to ask you a question, if you don't mind."

"Fire away."

"Do you happen to know who keeps the Fleet Rock lighthouse, these days? I used to summer on the Island, many years ago, and I was just wondering."

"The Fleet Rock lighthouse? Why, that would be old Mrs. Vargas," said the fisherman, without changing expression, without turning his attention from the water before us.

"What about Mr. Vargas?"

"I'm afraid he's passed on, ma'am. Just a few months ago. One winter too many, I guess."

"I'm sorry to hear that."

"He was a good man. A good lobsterman."

I laughed politely. "Isn't that the same thing?"

He laughed too. "I guess it is, ma'am. I guess it is."

We said nothing more, all the way into the harbor, and I gave him another five dollars to keep quiet about the woman with the black eye and the sunglasses who was asking questions about Fleet Rock lighthouse. He put the Lincoln in his pocket and asked if he could help me with my suitcase. I said no, I was just heading into the general store across the street from the marina. He wouldn't take no for an answer, though, so I let him carry the suitcase anyway. Men sometimes like to make themselves useful that way, I've found, and you might as well humor them.

Inside the store, I absorbed the familiar, particular odor of dust and spices, and the scent gave me another jolt of exquisite pain to the solar plexus. There's something about the smells of your childhood, isn't there? Even when that childhood was short and flavored by bitterness and ended in catastrophe, in a disaster of devastating proportions, you still remember those small, sublime joys with an ache of longing. Because there's no getting it back, is there? You can't return to a state of innocence. So I waited patiently for the old woman behind the soda fountain to hustle and bustle her way around her shelves, her cabinets, her rows of merchandise, until at last she noticed my presence and apologized.

"It's no trouble at all," I said.

At the sound of my voice, her face changed, in much the same way as the fisherman's had. Her mouth made a perfect hole of surprise. "*Deus meu!* Miranda Schuyler?" she said in wonder.

"The prodigal returns." I removed my sunglasses.

"Oh dear! What is this thing that has happened to your face?"

"There was an accident. A car accident. I thought I might find someplace quiet to lick my wounds. I hope you don't mind."

Her voice was soft with pity. "No, of course. Of course not." She paused delicately. "Do they know you are coming? At Greyfriars? Your mother, she was here yesterday, and she said nothing to me."

"I thought I might surprise them. I don't suppose your husband still drives his delivery van, does he?"

"Ah, poor Manuelo, he is gone now."

"Oh! I'm so sorry. I didn't think."

"But I can drive you this far. My daughter Laura will keep the store for me. *Laura!* You remember Laura, don't you?"

"Naturally I remember Laura. I remember everybody and everything. How could I forget?"

We exchanged a look of deep, futile understanding that lasted as long as it took for Mrs. Medeiro's daughter, Miss Laura, scatter-haired and dumpy in a floral housedress, to emerge from some back room, clasp her hands, and express her absolute astonishment that the great Miranda Schuyler had returned to the Island at last, that she stood right here in the middle of their humble store.

"Or must we call you Miranda Thomas?" she asked, pretending not to eye the shiner that disfigured the left side of my face.

"Just Miranda will do. I'm here unofficially, you understand."

"Ah, I see." She smoothed her hair with one hand and looked at her mother, and some communication passed between them, to which Mrs. Medeiro replied with a small shrug. Miss Laura picked up a dishcloth and put it down again. I was opening my mouth to speak when she burst out, "What was it like to kiss Roger Moore?"

"*Laura!*" snapped her mother.

I slipped the sunglasses back over my eyes. "Just exactly as you might think," I said.

We were halfway to Greyfriars before I asked Mrs. Medeiro about her grandson, and she took her time to answer me.

"He's well," she said, "the last I heard."

"He never did answer any of my letters. I wrote and wrote."

"He thought this was best. There was no hope, you see."

I set my elbow on the edge of the window, which was rolled down all the way to allow the May breeze inside the fish-smelling cab. I might have looked out toward the sea, which was darkening into a purple twilight, but I didn't. I knew what was out there, the cliffs dropping away into the water, and Fleet Rock like a dream against the horizon.

Mrs. Medeiro changed gears to thrust the old van up the slope. "You *have* heard the news, yes?"

"That he escaped from prison? Yes, I heard."

"Is that—" She bit herself off and rattled her thumbs against the steering wheel.

"Is that why I've come back, you mean? Because of Joseph escaping from prison?"

"I'm sorry. It's your business, why you're here."

"It's a logical question. I don't blame you for asking. I mean, he's bolted from *his* prison, and now I've—well, here *I* am, fresh from London."

"So you *are* here for him?"

"I didn't say that."

"Oh." Mrs. Medeiro glanced at me. "I just—well, the police already came, the detectives, the marshals. I mean, they searched everywhere. They could not find him."

"I don't suppose you happen to know where he went?"

She shrugged. "Who really knows about Joseph? He always keeps his own mind."

"That's not an answer, Mrs. Medeiro," I said.

"No, I guess not."

I took off the sunglasses and folded them into my pocketbook. We had nearly reached the Greyfriars drive, and my fingers were shaking, shaking, my heart was thundering. I had thought, after so many years, I should approach the house like an old friend with whom you had quarreled long ago and since forgiven so far as to forget what the quarrel was about. But now I glimpsed the stone wall, crumbling to bits, and the gap through which I had walked so often, and the mighty, unkempt rhododendrons, and I was eighteen again—exactly half as old as my current age, now there's symmetry for you—and knew nothing about keeping your emotions in check, your spirit under exquisite control. I gripped the handles of my pocketbook and counted the pulse of my breathing, as my husband had once trained me to do, yet still the flutter remained and worsened into dizziness.

"Is everything okay, Miranda?" asked Mrs. Medeiro quietly. "Should I stop the car?"

"No, thank you. Drive right on up to the door, if you don't mind."

We turned down the drive and the tires crunched on the gravel, bounced over the ruts, dove into the potholes. In earlier days, the Greyfriars drive was an impeccable thing, almost as smooth as asphalt, and

Mrs. Medeiro, after one particularly bone-crunching jolt, was moved to apologize for the fall in standards, almost as if she had some responsibility for them.

"Things aren't the same at Greyfriars, you know," she said.

"I don't imagine they are."

"I think there is not much money now. You know they take in boarders."

"Do they? I didn't know that. Mother never mentioned it in her letters."

"She is proud. They don't call them boarders. It is—oh, what is it called? An artist colony."

"Oh, of course. How lovely. Artists. Shame they aren't gardeners, as well."

We passed the last, the largest rhododendron of all, from which I kept my eyes carefully averted. The sun was gone now anyway, and everything had disappeared into shadow. Even Greyfriars, as it slid into view, was an anticlimax: just a long, dark shape containing a few specks of light. I found I was able to breathe again. Mrs. Medeiro pulled around the semicircle and brought the van to a rusty stop.

"Should I wait?" she asked.

"There's no need." I plucked my suitcase from the back and waved her away. She must have understood me, because she obeyed, and I waited until the headlights had disappeared around the corner of the rhododendron before I turned to stand before the front step. The light was off, or else the bulb was gone, and I couldn't see much, just that the paint seemed to be peeling from that large front door, and I could no longer tell if it was black or green.

Then it swung open.

"My goodness! Who—"

Because of the light from the doorway, I couldn't see the face of the woman who stood before me. But I knew who it was. There could be no Greyfriars without her, after all.

"Isobel," I said. "It's Miranda."

JUNE

1930 (BIANCA MEDEIRO)

1.

HE IS THE most beautiful boy she's ever seen, more beautiful than Valentino or Errol Flynn or Lindbergh. She crosses herself when she sees him sailing his slim racing yacht up and down the Fleet Rock channel with Peter Dumont, because of the danger and because of the way the sun glints on his blond hair, an effect so brilliant she observes it all the way from the little bluff at the top of West Cliff Road, where she goes to watch them in the afternoon. In her imagination, the sun is anointing Mr. Fisher as its own, and only the devil himself could plant such a blasphemous thought in her head. So she crosses herself.

Today Tia Maria needs her in the store, however, so there is no need for guarding oneself against the devil. The Families have been arriving on Winthrop Island for the summer, one by one, by ferry and by private yacht, and so Bianca and her cousins must fill the shelves with the goods Tio Manuelo has ordered from the mainland: canned peas and canned peaches and canned sardines in olive oil, saltine crackers and Campbell's tomato soup, Ivory soap and Clorox bleach, Ovaltine and Quaker oats and cornflakes, cantaloupe and pippin apples and bananas, Morton salt

and Ceylon cinnamon, bags of flour and sugar and Calumet baking powder, Pond's cold cream and Listerine and aspirin (lots of aspirin), garden-
ing gloves and razor blades, distilled white vinegar that is really vinegar,
distilled white vinegar that is not really vinegar but kept on a shelf behind
the wooden counter for particular customers, whom Tio Manuelo serves
himself.

The weather turned hot this week, the first week of June, and even
though Tia Maria keeps the door wide open to usher in the salt breeze
from the harbor, the atmosphere remains stuffy and smells of sawdust.
Bianca stacks the soup cans in neat, long rows—tomato and vegetable
and cream of mushroom—because canned soup is very popular with the
Families, for some reason. She prefers the soups Tia Maria makes from
scratch and simmers all day in an iron pot on the stove, full of herbs and
vegetables and shellfish, whatever's fresh from the sea, but the Families
like their food bland, apparently. Bland and stale and rich, just like themselves. She crosses herself when she thinks this—the Families are the
Island's lifeblood, after all, and Tio Manuelo makes all his profit in the
summer from cans of soup and boxes of saltine crackers—but it's true.

Except for young Mr. Fisher, of course. There's nothing bland or stale
about him.

She knows all about him. He lives in a rambling house not far from the
village, all by itself overlooking Fleet Rock, and so new that—in certain
corners shielded from the weather, anyway—the cedar shingles haven't
yet faded to gray. The family is not quite so distinguished as those who
live at the other end of the Island, the eastern end, where the Winthrop
Island Club and its magnificent golf course stretch out over a hundred
precious green acres. The Fisher money is too new, Tio Manuelo says
sagely over dinner, but give it time. Money ages with remarkable speed.
Already Mr. Fisher has been to Harvard, where he became friends with
the sons of all the correct families, such as Peter Dumont. There's even a
rumor going about that Mr. Fisher became engaged over Easter to Peter's

sister, Abigail, but Bianca refuses to believe this. For one thing, Abigail Dumont is twenty-five, three years older than Mr. Fisher, and for another thing she's tall and wide-shouldered and has no breasts, no feminine qualities at all, a loud, braying voice like a well-bred donkey. While the newspapers call Miss Dumont things like *magnetic* and *incandescent*, Bianca's certain that Mr. Fisher has better taste than that. He spends his mornings on the cliffs between the village and Greyfriars—*Greyfriars* is the name given to the new Fisher house, for what reason nobody can imagine, other than the color of the cedar shingles as they fade—spends his mornings, that is, with his watercolors and his books, so beautiful that Bianca sometimes cannot even breathe when she sees him there, legs swinging dangerously over the cliff's edge, his perfect brow compressed in concentration.

She knows many other things. She knows his exact height (five feet eleven and a half inches) and the color of his eyes (as blue as the Mediterranean Sea) and his prowess at sailing, of course, but also at hockey (he was the team captain at Harvard) and at golf, at which he won the Winthrop Island Club championship last summer, the first summer of the Fisher family's membership. The Dumonts sponsored them. Bianca knows this because her cousin Laura happened to be stepping out with one of the Club caddies last year, at night and in secret, and *he* knew just about everything you ever wanted to know about the Families, because *they*, for some reason, thought the caddies had no ears in their heads except to receive commands. Or maybe they thought a ten-cent tip was enough to buy the loyalty of an impecunious college boy. (The Families were cheap tippers, it was part of their ethic.)

Not so Mr. Fisher. He once gave her cousin Manuelo a whole dollar for helping him push his Buick Battistini roadster back to Greyfriars from the village, where it broke down outside the ice cream parlor. How Bianca had envied Manuelo that magical day, as his manly shoulders strained side by side with Mr. Fisher's shoulders, even though the road ascended some hundred feet in total before it reached the summit on which Greyfriars was built, and the effort must have been enormous. When Manuelo returned, flushed and sweating, she had asked him what they talked about, and his face went carefully blank and he said, *Nothing*. So she knew Mr. Fisher had confided some secret in Manuelo, and that made her doubly jealous.

In fact, Bianca's thinking about that August afternoon right now, as she stacks her cans of soup in the hot, musty interior of the Medeiros' general store on Hemlock Street, right at the harbor's edge. She's remembering how Mr. Fisher took off his linen jacket and rolled up the sleeves of his shirt, and how strong his back seemed as he bent himself over the graceful rump of the Buick, how his shoulders formed the broad side of a damp, neat triangle that narrowed and then disappeared down the slim waistband of his trousers. She sets down another can of soup and crosses herself, and at that exact instant, by some arrangement of the universe, she hears none other than Hugh Fisher's young, enthusiastic, unmistakable voice calling out from the front of the store. The coincidence is so remarkable that at first she thinks she's imagined it.

"Hullo!" he calls again. "Anybody there?"

Bianca waits behind the tall shelf while her heart pounds and pounds, not breathing, waiting for Tia Maria to reply, for one of her cousins to reply. But nobody does.

"Hullo? Francisca? Anybody?"

He's going to leave. She lifts her hand to smooth her hair, but there's a can of soup stuck between her fingers, and she bumps her head with it instead. She shoves the soup on the shelf and darts out into the open, just as Mr. Fisher's turning to the open front door.

"Hello! Mr. Fisher!"

He swivels back, and all at once he's looking at her, her, Bianca Medeiro and nobody else, and the whole world lights up under the color of his gaze, the wattage of his smile.

"Well, hello," he says. "I was hoping to buy a bottle or two of vinegar."

2.

ANOTHER THING SHE knows about Hugh Fisher: last summer, he fell in love with her cousin Francisca, the third and the oldest of Tia Maria and Tio Manuelo's children, who's engaged to marry Pascoal Vargas in the autumn. Francisca, who was perfectly aware of Bianca's infatuation, tried to keep the affair secret for her sake, but Bianca knew almost from the first, when Francisca made some excuse about taking a walk one night last July, and came back flushed and bright-eyed an hour later, smelling of a particular kind of masculine soap that Tio Manuelo doesn't stock in his store. In truth, Bianca hadn't really minded. Francisca going to meet Hugh Fisher at night was almost as close as Bianca herself going to meet Hugh Fisher, and when she heard the back door open and squeakily close, she imagined Francisca running up the slope to the cliffs under the moonlight, Francisca embracing Hugh Fisher while the phosphorescent sea pounded beneath them, in a way she couldn't imagine Mr. Fisher embracing so distant an object as Miss Dumont. By touching Francisca's skin the next morning, Bianca felt she was somehow touching Mr. Fisher.

And another thing. Last summer Francisca was fully grown, nineteen years old, lush and beautiful, and Bianca was only sixteen, her period had just started the previous winter, and her face was round and spotty and childlike. As she lay throughout July and August in the little bedroom she shared with her cousins, listening to their clandestine comings and goings, she was happier imagining making love to Hugh Fisher as beautiful Francisca than she would have been to actually make love to him as herself. It was safer and infinitely more pleasant.

Then came the end of summer, when the Families all returned to their houses in New York and Boston and Providence and Philadelphia, including the Fishers. Francisca moped to devastating effect. She appeared at the dinner table tearstained and listless, eating nothing, and she completed her chores like one of those machines in a factory, without joy. When she accepted Pascoal Vargas's proposal at Christmas, everybody thought she finally saw sense, because the color returned to her cheeks, and her hips reacquired their old sway, and she plunged herself into the assembling of her trousseau, the most elaborate and comprehensive trousseau in the history of the Medeiro women, because Pascoal Vargas had made a great deal of money in his lobster boat during the past few years, a great deal, and now he has just received the appointment to keep the Fleet Rock lighthouse come October. Francisca will live in luxury, almost, so what if her devoted husband-to-be is past forty years old and resembles nothing so much as a leathery, dark-haired gnome? Who cares about romance when you've got a fiancé with money in the bank and a steady, respectable job?

But Bianca's not so sure.

Bianca hasn't missed the new brightness of her cousin's eyes, now that the Fishers have returned to Winthrop Island. She hasn't missed the way Francisca makes excuses to go walking in the cliffs above the village, or offers to help her brother Manuelo make the rounds throughout the Island in their father's old Model T delivery truck. And this summer is a whole new summer. Francisca's engaged, she's practically a matron, and Bianca has finally achieved that transformation of which young girls dream, from duckling into swan. Over the winter, her spots disappeared and her face became luminous and refined, her hair grew in thick and her small, dainty body rounded out in all those places men admire. As Easter passed and the blossoms came out and the harsh New England air turned soft and warm, as she prepared to graduate from the tiny Winthrop Island School and turn free, Bianca felt her hour had struck. Her blood sang in her veins, she woke restless every morning. She felt that something grand beckoned around the corner, the future for which she was destined.

All she needed was a sign.

3.

IS *THIS* THE sign? Hugh Fisher standing right there in the front of the store, a foot or two away from the wooden counter with the vinegar-not-vinegar hidden inside, wearing a blue seersucker suit that made his eyes even bluer than she remembered? Already his skin is golden with sunshine and pink with heat, and his shiny blond hair reminds her of the helmet of Apollo. (She will cross herself later.)

Bianca tucks a loose strand behind her ear. Tia Maria won't let them bob their hair, she absolutely refuses to let her girls turn fast like all the others, so Bianca arranges hers in a loose knot at the back of her head and then pulls out the dark, curling locks at the sides, so that the silhouette approximates that of Clara Bow.

"What kind of vinegar do you need, sir?" she asks politely, though her heart knocks like crazy next to her lungs, making speech difficult.

His smile turns sheepish. "Well, now. I've heard you stock a special kind of vinegar here, and I'm all out. Fellow was supposed to make a delivery at the Greyfriars boathouse last night and he never turned up."

Bianca glances anxiously at Tio Manuelo's sacred counter and back to Hugh Fisher's lips. (She can't quite meet his gaze, not until her nerves stop jumping like this, not until she can keep her eyes from filling with tears at the perfection of his beauty, so close as to be within reach.) "I'm afraid I don't know much about vinegar," she says.

"No, of course not. A sweet young thing like you. Is your father here?"

"My uncle," she says, hot with shame. A sweet young thing! Hasn't he seen she's a woman now, a swan? Hasn't he noticed her luminous skin and her shining hair, the glorious new curves to her breasts and her hips? All the boys are noticing her now, the men too, but she hasn't looked back at any of them, not one. This blossoming beauty of hers is meant for only one man in the world, and he stands before her now, and he won't *look*, he won't see.

"Your uncle. If he's in the back, I can find him."

"He's away."

"There's nobody else here? Just you?"

"Yes," Bianca says, though she's not quite sure on this point. Laura and Tia Maria were both here a moment ago. Where have they gone? Into the back garden to sneak a cigarette or two?

"I see." He looks at her kindly, as if she's a simple child, as if she's nothing more than the sweet young thing he called her, and reaches into the inside pocket of his seersucker jacket. "Then perhaps you can give him my card. Here, I'll write my telephone number on the back. Can you give this to him for me?"

He sticks the pencil stub back in his pocket and holds out the card with his strong, smooth fingers. Bianca reaches out and takes it, and when her fingertips inevitably brush against his fingertips, the sensation travels all the way up her arm and down her ribs and her stomach to her legs. She breathes in deeply to smell Mr. Fisher's particular shaving soap, which doesn't belong to any of the soap Tio Manuelo stocks on his shelves. The scent is like magic to her. She even wavers on her feet, so intoxicating is this flavor.

"Are you all right?" Mr. Fisher asks, in a voice of true concern.

"Yes, I'm all right." Fully drunk now, she opens her eyes, which were closed in appreciation of Mr. Fisher's soap, and this time she meets his gaze, his dazzling blue eyes, and she watches in triumph as they widen, like the flare of a match.

"I'm sorry," he says. "I don't believe I know your name."

"It's Bianca. Bianca Medeiro." She tucks the card into the pocket of her pinafore apron. "And I think I know where to find your vinegar, Mr. Fisher."

4.

HUGH FISHER WALKS away with two bottles and an order for more, whatever Tio Manuelo's got, and Bianca promises to deliver this merchandise herself. To the boathouse, he says. There's a hatch door on the ceiling, you'll find it. Before he leaves, he takes her hand and kisses it, first on the back and then—turning it reverently over—in the middle of her palm.

He curls her fist to trap the kiss inside, and he says, in a voice of deep sincerity, "It's been a pleasure, Miss Medeiro. Until we meet again?"

"Yes," she answers breathlessly, and for the rest of the day, at least six inches of air exist between Bianca's feet and the ground beneath them. When she settles into bed that night, she cannot sleep. She presses her palm to her lips—she hasn't washed that blessed hand, of course not—and thinks, *At last, at last, it's the sign that my life has truly begun.*

This time, she does not cross herself.

1951 (MIRANDA SCHUYLER)

1.

ON THE MORNING of my mother's wedding, I watched a pair of lobster boats crawl across the sea outside my bedroom window, setting their pots while the sun rose. They were some distance apart, one to the east of the Flood Rock lighthouse and one to the west, and I wouldn't have known they were lobstermen—I knew nothing about fishing in those days— except that I had a pair of binoculars, and I saw them dropping the pots, one by one, from the sterns of their boats. Each pot was attached to a rope, and at the end of the rope was a colored buoy that bobbed cheerfully in the water as the vessel pulled away.

Behind me, my mother stirred. "Is that you, Miranda?" she asked, in a slurred, sleepy voice.

"Yes."

"What *time* is it?"

"Only five thirty. Go back to sleep, Mama."

"What"—*mumbling*—"so early?"

"Watching the lobster boats."

She sighed and grunted, the way you do when you're still half-asleep, and you settle yourself gratefully back on a pillow and close your eyes. "*Strange* girl, Miranda," she muttered.

I wondered if she remembered she was getting married today. Sometimes when you sleep deeply enough, you forget everything you ever knew, even your own name, and Winthrop Island is possibly the quietest place in the world at night, except for the pulse of the ocean: so black and velvet that sleep comes as easy as that, as closing your eyes. You fall and fall, like an anchor that finds no bottom, and I don't believe I have ever again slept as I slept throughout that summer of 1951, in my bedroom at my stepfather's sprawling house on the Island.

Except, on that morning at the beginning of June, the morning of Mama's wedding, Hugh Fisher wasn't quite my stepfather. The fateful summer still lay before me, a reel of film waiting to unspool, and how could I know that I was right now witnessing its first momentous scene? I mean, you never do suspect what inconsequential event will change the course of your life. This particular morning, I only thought about the wedding to come. That was the affair of the day, wasn't it? The great occasion? Instead of sleeping deeply, I'd woken at dawn after a restless night, and now I knelt by the window, holding the binoculars to my eyes as the lobstermen labored on the water, and the sun climbed drowsily above the ocean.

I watched the lighthouse change color, from violet to palest pink to gold, and the surrounding rocks emerge from shadow, and the little buoys multiply in long, bobbing lines behind the boats. I watched the lobstermen shift about. In the easternmost boat, there were two of them: one short and broad-shouldered, wearing a striped shirt and a knitted cap; the other taller and leaner and bareheaded, hauling the wooden cages into the water while his shipmate baited them.

In the second boat, the one to the west, there was only one old man. He moved slowly, dropping maybe one trap for every three from the other boat, and as the light grew I saw the bulge of his tattooed arms, the silvery beard that grizzled around his face. He was nearly bald and chewed a pipe, and in my head I named him Popeye. I thought there was something awful and tragic about the way he baited each pot, attached line and buoy, and dragged it over the edge of the boat. Or maybe I only endowed him with those qualities in retrospect. Memory's funny that way. At any rate, the eastern boat ran out of pots or something, because it turned around and started back for the harbor, disappearing behind the Flood Rock lighthouse for an instant or two and then reappearing, its white sides brilliant in the glare of the sun. At the same time the boat flashed back into view, Popeye was swinging another lobster pot over the side of his boat, and maybe a wave jogged him, or maybe he lost his footing, I don't know. I'd returned my gaze to the other boat by then, and the lithe, bareheaded, carefree man who now stood at the wheel—a young man, arms and face richly tanned, curled hair whipping in the draft—so I never knew why Popeye went flying into the sea. I just saw the young man jolt, saw him turn his head and yell at his shipmate, saw him bend and yank off his rubber boots, and the next thing I knew he was diving into the water in a long, clean arc.

Now, I've heard many times that most fishermen don't know how to swim, as a matter of superstition or something. If that's true, this particular fisherman wasn't the superstitious kind. A hundred yards is a long way to swim, especially in the cold northern waters of early June, but he swam them just like he was stroking laps in the YMCA pool, regular and sure of arm, minding not the distance or the chill or the chop of waves. As I knelt there on the floorboards of my bedroom, frozen tight, following his progress through the glass of the binoculars, he made a final surge and dove under the surface, right where Popeye had just ceased to flail and resigned himself to sinking, and I thought, God save us, how is such a skinny fellow going to drag a stocky, solid artifact like Popeye back to fresh air?

I held my own breath in solidarity with the two of them. My arms began to shake, so I leaned forward and steadied my elbows on the window frame, keeping that patch of water in view, counting the giant thuds of my heart. When I reached too many, I abandoned numbers and started to whimper.

Please, please, please.

That carefree boy. That poor old man.

Please, Lord, please.

I still remember the silent glitter of the sun on that water. The particular musty-salty-linen smell of that bedroom, newly aired after the winter hibernation, a smell that still recalls the terror of that moment to my mind. And sometimes I think, well, what if they'd never come up again? What if *he'd* never come up again? What if those two lobstermen had drowned together on the morning of my mother's wedding, young and old, a terrible tragedy overclouding a day of promise, and I never knew either of them?

I guess there's no answer to that question. Because just as I started to panic, to lower the binoculars and rise from my knees and shout for help, they exploded together through the glittering waves like a single breaching whale. The younger man lunged for a rope hanging off near the stern of Popeye's boat, hauled Popeye over the side, hauled himself. Thwacked Popeye a good one right on the back, so Popeye vomited up a few gallons of cold salt water.

Then he grabbed the wheel of the boat with his left hand and the throttle with his right hand, and he made not for the harbor, a mile away on the sheltered side of the island, but for the nearest dock, Hugh Fisher's dock, my almost-stepfather's dock, the dock directly in line from my bedroom window.

Boy, did I rise then. I jumped straight up and ran for the door, ran down the stairs, ran to the kitchen, shouted at the kitchen maid to call the doctor, call the doctor, boat coming in, a man near drowned. A lobsterman.

Her pink face went round with amazement. "Who?" she cried.

"Some old fellow, out by himself!"

"Golly, that'll be Mr. Silva!" She spun for the telephone hanging on the wall, and I threw open the kitchen door and ran down the soft green lawn, past the swimming pool, past the big white tents awaiting the wedding, past the boathouse, and down the wooden dock, where the breeze blew on my cheeks and the sun drenched me, and the drone of the lobster boat's engine filled my ears like the sound of a thousand approaching honeybees.

2.

MY FATHER NAMED me Miranda. He was a teacher at a pureblood girls' boarding school in Virginia: not an English teacher, as you might expect from a name like that, but an art teacher. Painting, mostly, although he also taught sculpture, as the traffic allowed.

Still, he loved books, especially old ones. He taught me to read when I was very small, two or three years old, and by the time I was five we were decanting Shakespeare aloud to each other, each of us taking parts. We sat in his study, a fusty, tiny, comfortable room with large windows. I took the leather chesterfield sofa while he filled the armchair nearby. We drank cocoa and the air smelled of chocolate and leather and especially *books*—you know the smell I mean—I don't know if it's the ink or the paper or the glue in the bindings, but it's a very particular odor. I still smell it, somewhere in my memory, and it carries me back to that room and the sound of my father's voice as he began John of Gaunt's dying speech—

Methinks I am a prophet new inspired
And thus expiring do foretell of him . . .

He had a beautiful round baritone, and as he sat there in his arm-chair and spoke, one leg crossed over the other, wearing his soft shirt and tweed jacket and woolen vest while his blue eyes fixed not on the page—he knew the words—but upon or rather *through* the opposite wall of the study, I might have thought he really *was* the Duke of Lancaster, the great Plantagenet prince, splendid in his despair. To my mind, there was no man more heroic than my father.

This land of such dear souls, this dear dear land,
Dear for her reputation throughout the world,
Is now leased out, I die pronouncing it
　　(here his voice shook with agony)
Like to a tenement or pelting farm:
England, bound in with the triumphant sea
Whose rocky shore beats back the envious siege
Of watery Neptune, is now bound in with shame . . .

And he named me Miranda. Prospero's daughter, raised alone by her magician father on an uncharted island of fairies and strange creatures. I used to wonder why he chose that particular character, that particular daughter, that particular play. I think it had something to do with the sea, which he always loved, and with tempests, which also fascinated him. There may be more than that, but I'll never know. He embarked for England—"*This earth of majesty, this seat of Mars, this precious stone set in the silver sea*"—on the second day of November 1943, when I was ten years old, and I last glimpsed him waving at the rail of a gray-painted troop ship, before it dissolved like a ghost into the dark mist of New York Harbor. That was all.

Still, I don't think I've ever forgiven the sea for swallowing up my father like that. As I stood there at the end of the Greyfriars dock, watching the lobster boat tear toward me, the drone of its engine filled me with an unnamable thrill. Terror or joy, I couldn't tell. It just seemed to me that watery Neptune, having swallowed my father, was now spitting something back eight years later.

Something in the shape of a stripling boy with dark, curling hair and tanned skin, who could rescue a man from drowning.

3.

NOW, I DIDN'T know much about boats in those days, but I knew enough to grab the rope the young man tossed me and loop it tight around one of the bollards. The tide was high and slack, and the boat rode only a foot or two beneath the wooden planks. Inside the boat lay Popeye, coughing and wheezing, bleeding all over the place from I don't know where.

The young man lifted Popeye in his arms and hoisted him up toward the dock, where I hooked my arms around his shoulders and dragged him away from the edge. He was heavier than I thought, made of wet, compact bone and muscle, and my bare feet slipped against the wood. "Careful!" exclaimed the young man, leaping up beside me, and he tore open Popeye's shirt and checked his heart, his breath, because he'd stopped wheezing and now lay limp in my arms.

"The doctor's on his way!" I gasped out. "I saw you from the window."

"Ah, Jesus Mary. His arm."

I looked at Popeye's left arm, which was bent horribly, leaking blood.

"Here," said the youth, "hold it steady while I lift him. Can you do that? One, two, three."

I scrambled to my feet and bent to cradle Popeye's elbow while the young man scooped him carefully upward, lifting that weathered old fellow like—I don't know—like a knight would lift a damsel. Now I could see the bone sticking through the skin, through the wet plaid shirt, but

I wasn't going to be sick, oh no. I thought, the nurses in the war saw far worse, didn't they? Some nurse maybe tended my father. They hadn't flinched, and neither would I. I laid Popeye's arm across his middle as best I could, and we started down the dock to the lawn. Popeye remained still. I prayed he wasn't dead. The sun hit the side of my face as we loped up the slope of the lawn, past the boathouse and the tents, up the steps of the terrace and around back to the kitchen, where the maid was waving for us.

"Put him right here, Joseph! I cleared the kitchen table. Doctor'll be a minute. Oh Jesus Mary!" she cried. "Look at him! What happened?"

Down he went on the table. Joseph checked his chest again and swore. Bent over his face and pinched his nose and laid his mouth on Popeye's mouth, breathed the air of his own lungs into Popeye's lungs while the maid ran for kitchen towels or something. I just stood there, holding Popeye's arm together, not knowing what else to do. After a breath or two, Popeye started to heave, and Joseph rolled him quick on his side. Out came another quart or so of water, more sputtering, a groan of misery, and the doctor burst through the door right that second, dressing gown flapping around his legs, thank God.

4.

THERE HAS NEVER been any such thing as a hospital on Winthrop Island, as I later learned. Either you were sick enough to head for the hospital on the mainland, or you made do in your bed at home. This doctor—Dr. Huxley—didn't have a regular practice here. He was a summer resident who made himself available for emergencies on the understanding that he wasn't to be disturbed during cocktail hour or golf.

Lucky for Popeye, the good doctor was an early riser who just happened to live half a mile up Winthrop Road from Greyfriars. He set Popeye's broken arm and stitched up the holes in his hide, and Mr. Fisher had him put up in one of the guest bedrooms with strict instructions to watch for signs of pneumonia.

"What about his family?" I said. "Shouldn't we telephone them or something?"

Joseph looked down at me kindly. "He hasn't got any family. Wife died two years ago. Kids moved to the mainland."

"Oh, that's a shame."

"That's the way it is on the Island, I guess. Kids move away."

He was blushing a little, looking down at me, and I realized I still wore my old green flannel nightgown, which was wet with seawater and blood and stuck to my skin. I crossed my arms over my chest. Mr. Fisher and Dr. Huxley were upstairs with the maid, settling the patient in some spare bedroom or other. The kitchen was growing warm as the sun penetrated the window glass, and I noticed the smell of something baking, something sugary and vanilla-scented, something for the wedding, so I supposed the oven was on, too, adding to the general heat. I stared at the kitchen table, which Joseph had helped me clean up just now, dishcloths and hot water and vinegar that still stained the air. All immaculate, erased, you'd never know what happened. Just any old big kitchen on any old big summer estate. Two people standing in awkward proximity, like a pair of actors who've lost their place in the script.

Joseph started to turn away, toward the door.

"Want some coffee?" I said.

"Have you got any made? I mean you needn't make fresh."

"I think so." I went to the electric percolator on the counter and lifted it. Heavy. Behind me, there was a faint scrape of a chair leg on the linoleum. I opened up a few cabinets, looking for coffee cups.

Joseph cleared his throat. "You must be the daughter, then. Mrs. Schuyler's daughter."

"Yes, I am."

"Well, I'm sure sorry I ruined the big day for you."

"Oh gosh, that's nothing. I mean, he's alive, isn't he? That's got to be good luck. Thanks to you. The day's not ruined at all. Do you want cream or anything?"

"I'll get it."

The chair scraped again, and from the corner of my eye I saw him step to the icebox and open the door. He stood about an inch under six feet, and he still wore his yellow oilskin overalls atop his wet shirt, though his hair was beginning to dry in soft little waves around his ears. I turned toward him and offered the coffee cup.

"Thanks," he said, dribbling a bit of cream from a small blue pitcher. "You?"

"Yes, please."

He moved the pitcher over my cup and tilted it so the narrowest possible rope of yellow-white cream fell inside. "Say when."

"When."

He moved away, putting the cream back in the icebox, and I turned to the window so he wouldn't catch me looking at the place where his hair met the back of his neck. I didn't know much about boys, had hardly spent any time around a boy, and I couldn't tell how old he was. Twenty? Twenty-one? Older than me, for certain. Though his skin was fresh and unlined, there was something fully grown about his shoulders, something wide and weight-bearing. And his voice had an easy, mature timbre, not like a boy's voice at all.

Older than me. Maybe not all that much, but enough. Not a boy, after all, but a grown-up, a man who worked for his bread, whereas I was still a child, only just graduated from school. Eighteen last February. Eighteen going on eight, as unworldly as a kitten in a basket.

I stirred my coffee and sucked the spoon. Joseph came up next to me, not too close, and said, "How do you like the Island? You came up the other night, didn't you?"

"Oh, it's beautiful." I set the spoon on the saucer. "How did you know? When I came up, I mean."

"Miss Schuyler, here's the first thing you need to know about the Island. Everyone knows each other's business. All of it, about five minutes after it happens, if not sooner. Spreads through the air or something." He paused to sip his coffee. "Also, I saw Isobel driving you back from the ferry."

"Oh, of course."

The window overlooked the lawn and the tents. Sometime during the fuss of the past hour, an old rust-red Ford truck had driven onto the grass, and a couple of men were now unloading crates from the back. Crystal and china, I guessed. I could just see the edge of the dock, and the tip of Popeye's boat tethered up on the other side against the pale blue sky.

"It's got the whole island buzzing," Joseph said.

"What has?"

"Why, the wedding. Mr. Fisher's a big man around here."

I shifted my feet and looked down at the still, muddy surface of my coffee. "I don't really know him that well. He's been awfully nice to Mama."

"I hear they met at your school? Your mother and Mr. Fisher?"

"Yes. Last year." I paused, and the silence seemed so heavy and almost rude, given the tender, friendly way he'd asked the question, I rushed on. "At Isobel's graduation? One of the events. I don't really know which one, there's so many of them, ceremonies and parties and things. My mother was a secretary in the president's office, you see, ever since my father—well, since my father . . ." I stuttered to a stop, brought up short in the middle of all that flustered babbling by the thought of my father.

"Killed in the war, wasn't he?" Joseph said, without embarrassment.

"Why, how did you know?"

"Like I said, the Island's been talking about this for weeks, Miss Schuyler. Not that I listen to gossip much. But you can't help hearing a few things, even without trying. My grandmother, she runs the general store in town. There's nothing she doesn't know."

I glanced at him, and though he stared straight ahead, holding the cup to his lips like he was fascinated by the unloading of crystal and china, I thought he was smiling a little.

"Is that so?" I said. "What else have you heard?"

"Oh, just this and that."

You know, it's a funny thing. I didn't know this boy, this man. Just his name and face and approximate age, and the fact that he trapped lobsters for a living, that he could swim, that he was the kind of fellow who would jump in the sea to save another fellow from drowning. He was a stranger, but he wasn't. We'd held a bleeding, broken man between the two of us; we'd watched the eternity of life pass before us. Now we shared a pot of coffee. Stared out the same window, breathed the same air. So he wasn't a stranger, but he was.

I set down my cup and turned around to hop up and sit on the counter. The clock on the opposite wall pointed its sharp black hands to a quarter past seven. A quarter past seven! I thought I'd lived a lifetime. I crossed my arms over my disgraceful nightgown and said—not to Joseph but to the room at large—"He taught at Foxcroft for eleven years. My father. He took a leave of absence to join up, so when he was killed, Miss Charlotte gave Mama a job to make ends meet. She's like that, Miss Charlotte. Sort of tough and horsey, if you know what I mean, but heart of gold."

"What did he teach?"

"Art. That's why he volunteered, because he heard about what the Nazis were doing, looting and destroying all those treasures, and he couldn't just—couldn't stand by, he said . . ."

"A good man, then."

"He was. Oh, he was. Of course, I was only eleven years old when he died. So maybe I never saw him as a real person, as somebody ordinary and fallen."

"No," Joseph said. "He fought for something he believed in. That's a hero in anyone's book."

"Everybody fought. Mr. Fisher fought."

"Yes, he did. Lucky for your mother, he got out alive, though."

"Yes, lucky for her."

"They say she's a real beauty, your mother."

"Mama? Oh yes. Haven't you seen her?"

"Not up close, no. Just the photograph in the local rag."

"Sometimes I just stare at her, you know, thinking it's not possible anyone could be that beautiful. She was so young when she married Daddy. Only just eighteen. Can you imagine being a widow at twenty-nine? But she loved him so much, she just couldn't look at anyone else for ever so long."

He moved a little, turning his head to look at me. "What about you? Happy about all this?"

"Me? Of course I am. Why shouldn't I be?"

"No reason."

"Mama's happy, the happiest I've ever seen her, at least since Daddy died. You can't mourn forever, can you?"

"That's true."

"And I guess Mr. Fisher loves her back, because he's not marrying her for money, that's for certain."

"A real Cinderella story, then." He finished his coffee and moved to the sink. Rinsed out his cup. "Best be off. Got to take Silva's tub back to the harbor. And Pops'll be wondering where I am."

"Can't you signal him in or something? There's plenty of coffee left."

He smiled. "Pops'd never come in here. Not Greyfriars."

"Really? Why not? Mr. Fisher's not some kind of snob, is he?"

"A *snob*? No, nothing like that. I'll say this about the Island. The Families and the locals, they respect each other, which is more than you can say of a lot of places like this."

"The Families?"

"Summer residents. Like you." He wiped his fingers on a dishtowel and held his hand out to me. "Real nice to meet you, Miss Schuyler. Wish it could have been under friendlier circumstances, of course, but it's been a pleasure all the same."

I slid down from the counter and shook his hand. "It's Miranda."

"Miranda." He smiled again. *"Admired Miranda! Indeed the top of admiration! Worth what's dearest to the world."*

I snatched at the edge of the counter behind me. I think my mouth made an amazed circle. Outside the window, which was cracked open an inch or two, the birds sang like mad, thrilled to pieces at the beauty of the morning, and Joseph just stared at me like we were sharing a secret, and he was waiting for me to find out what it was.

Finally I said, "Why, how do you know—"

"Joseph! My goodness, what's going on?"

We turned to the doorway, where Isobel Fisher stood, long limbed and done up in curlers, her yellow dressing gown belted at the waist.

5.

I MET ISOBEL Fisher at the same instant I stepped onto Winthrop Island for the first time, two nights before the wedding. The morning storms had cleared away, and the breeze was cool and smelled of ozone, of the ocean. She had come to meet the ferry, and when I saw her, leaning against a massive, venerable Oldsmobile 98, wearing a checked shirt, rolled at the sleeves, and billowy white trousers, I waved from the railing. We might not have known each other, but I recognized her face and the pale, corn-silk shade of her hair. She wore no cosmetics that I could see, except for a swath of cherry-red lipstick, perfectly drawn. I remember she wasn't wearing a hat.

The ferry's engines ground and ground, shoving us alongside the dock in lazy, expert thrusts. Isobel's gaze slid along the line of passengers at the rail, and when she found me at last, still waving, she straightened from the car and waved back. I don't know if she actually recognized me. As the ferry knocked into place and the ferryman tossed the rope to the fellow on the dock, she swung her car keys from the index finger of her left hand, with no apparent regard for the monstrous diamond that perched a few digits down.

That was Thursday evening, and there weren't many other passengers. I came last down the ramp, staggering a little under the burden of the two old leather portmanteaus that contained nearly all I owned. My pocketbook banged between my wrist and the handle of the right-hand suitcase. As I reached the bottom and stepped onto the dock, Isobel went around to open up the back. "Just a minute!" she called, thrusting her head and shoulders inside, rummaging around. "I picked up the flowers from Mrs. Beardsley along the way. Was your journey perfectly horrible? I can't believe you made it all by yourself, you brave thing."

Her torso emerged from the back of the Oldsmobile. She pushed back her pale hair and reached for one of the suitcases, and without any effort at all she lifted it up and heaved it inside. Even at school, her lean, straight-hipped athleticism had awed me. Nearly all the girls brought their own horses to Foxcroft, but Isobel had brought two—great, rangy, bloodthirsty beasts—and hunted them both all autumn. Once she'd broken her arm in a bad fall, and the sling had somehow suited her.

Not to be outdone, I hauled the second suitcase myself, only more awkwardly. Isobel made a few adjustments, satisfied herself to the security of Mrs. Beardsley's flowers, and turned around at last. "Can you believe we're *sisters?*" she said, in that drawly voice of hers, always faintly amused at something or other. She stood back and held me at the shoulders. "*Miranda.* Little sister. I simply can't wait to show you Greyfriars. I can't wait to show you Winthrop and everything in it."

But that was two nights ago, and she hadn't had much time to show me anything yet, because of the wedding and because her fiancé arrived the next afternoon. Clayton Monk. (Yes, *those* Monks, the department store fortune.) His parents' house lay at the northeastern end of the Island, four miles away, and we'd all met for dinner at the Winthrop Island Club last night. Sort of a celebration. Mama's wedding and Isobel's betrothal, because they'd only just gotten engaged in May, when Clayton graduated from Harvard Law—*Hahvahd*, the Monks called it, short *a*, they're a Boston family—and this was the Club's first chance to properly congratulate the happy couple.

Well, it was a grand night, all right. Clay Monk was a clean, handsome, well-tailored fellow, you know the type, and Isobel wore a dress of such shimmery pale yellow satin, it looked gold and matched her hair. If I didn't know any better, I'd have said she was trying to outshine my mother—the actual bride, you'll recall—but then you haven't seen my mother, have you? I mean, not up close. Even at thirty-six she was more beautiful than Isobel. I say that without prejudice. Raven hair clean of even a single gray strand, eyes the color of twilight. Picture Elizabeth Taylor, I guess, and you're not far off. Isobel didn't stand a chance, even in her golden dress, and maybe she knew it. She laid low, stealing off with Clayton after dinner, and he must have driven her home afterward because when she walked into the Greyfriars kitchen at twenty minutes past seven o'clock on the morning of Mama's wedding, wearing her curlers and her yellow dressing gown, that was the first I'd seen of her since Clayton wiped a smear of crème anglaise from her chin the night before and led her out on the terrace, where the orchestra played "Sentimental Me."

Joseph greeted her with a smile you might call familiar. "Morning, Isobel. Nothing much. Just old Silva fell in the drink, and I had to haul him back out."

"Well, they're putting him to bed upstairs, awful fuss. I've got a terrible hung head. Is that coffee?" She yawned.

"Yes, ma'am."

She moved to the Welsh dresser that held all the everyday porcelain, planting a kiss on my cheek along the way. "Morning, sister dear. Did he wake you up too?"

I lifted my hand to return the caress, but she'd already slipped away. "I was already awake."

"Too excited to sleep, were you? What about your mother? I hope she got her beauty sleep, all right. Her wedding day!" Another yawn, and a wince. "I'm sure I'll be able to appreciate all that sunshine in an hour or two. Hit me, will you?"

She held out her cup to me and smiled. She wasn't wearing her lipstick yet, but her mouth was still pink. I took the cup and filled it with coffee from the percolator, added cream and sugar from the tin on the counter.

"Thanks, darling," Isobel said, taking the cup. "Shouldn't you be heading back to your boat now, Joseph? I'm sure you have plenty of lobsters left to catch this morning. Or maybe college boys are above that kind of thing?"

"*College?*" I said.

"Joseph's at Brown." Isobel looked over the rim of her cup, not at me but at Joseph, who stood before the icebox with his arms crossed. In her drawling, intimate voice, she said, "He's a rising junior. Isn't that right, Joseph?"

"Two years to go." He returned to her some kind of look, I didn't know what it was. Something warm and knowledgeable, something that connected the two of them, something that made me feel like an absolute stranger in that room, an intruder, an innocent. Which I was, of course. Still, whatever the frisson between them, it lasted only a second or two. Joseph uncrossed his arms and said cheerfully, "Like you said, best be heading back out on the water now. Nice to meet you, Miss Schuyler. Isobel."

He made a little salute with the first two fingers of his right hand and walked out the kitchen door, whistling a snatch of something, taking all the conversation with him inside a swirl of fresh June air. I watched the window until he came into view. Quick, jaunty stride. Sun striking his head. Isobel turned away.

"Oh, not you too."

"Me too what?"

She angled her head to the window. "That. Joseph. All the girls on the Island are crazy about him. He lives on the Rock, you know. Flood Rock."

I turned to her. "The lighthouse? Really? I can see it from my window!"

"His father's the lightkeeper. Of course, his wife does the actual work, so he can keep on lobstering. Nice little arrangement." She nodded again to the window, even though you couldn't see the lighthouse from this angle, tucked away at the side of the house, and I followed the gesture. Joseph was no bigger than a lobster himself by now, although considerably more graceful and less red, striding down the curve of the lawn toward the dock.

"It's nice they can afford the college tuition," I said.

"Well, why not? He hasn't got any siblings. And I guess old Vargas doesn't think so much of the lobster trade that he wants his son to follow in his footsteps. What about breakfast, do you think? Where's Esther?"

"Helping them put Mr. Silva to bed, I think."

She joined me at the window, cradling her coffee in her palms. She smelled of some kind of flower, maybe gardenias, and I thought it must be her soap or shampoo, because who wore perfume at this hour? Joseph had reached the dock. The tide had gone out a little, so the boat kicked against the pilings. He reached down and unwound the rope. Leapt nimbly from the dock to the boat and bent over the wheel, on the other side of the deckhouse, so we couldn't see him.

I had a thousand questions I wanted to ask Isobel. I wanted to ask about the Island, about her father, about Joseph. About college, about her own mother. Things I'd wanted to ask in the car from the ferry but couldn't, because Isobel gleamed like sunshine, because Isobel had graduated the year before me at Foxcroft and was therefore so untouchable as to be divine.

Yet there was something a little softer about Isobel this morning, as if her sleek, athletic edges had blurred with sleep in the night, as if the curlers in her hair had made her mortal. She leaned her elbows on the counter and sipped her coffee, staring, like me, at the lobster boat curving its way westward toward the harbor.

"Go ahead and look," she said. "Just don't touch."

"I don't know what you mean."

Isobel lifted herself back up and turned to me. She wore a wry little smile on her pink lips. "You and all the other girls. You can look all you like, I don't care. Just remember one thing, though." She leaned forward and spoke softly. "He's *mine*."

"Who's yours, darling?"

I spun toward the door, where Hugh Fisher stood in a dressing gown of his own—paisley, satin, blue, immaculate—and a helmet of gold hair the same shade as his daughter's, just slightly the worse for tarnish. For an instant, just that first flash of impression, I thought he looked a little like Clayton Monk.

Isobel went to him and set a kiss into the hollow beneath his cheekbone. "*You* are, Daddy, and you always will be. But thank God you've found a dear, lovely woman to marry this morning, and not some gimlet society goddess from the Club."

He chuckled and patted her back. "You know I've got better sense than that. Has young Vargas left already?"

"Yes, Daddy." Isobel moved to the Welsh dresser and rummaged for another cup and saucer. "Some poor fellows *do* have to work for a living, you know. Coffee?"

"Yes, please." He pulled a cigarette case from the pocket of his dressing gown. "Well, that's a shame. I wanted to shake his hand, after what he did this morning. He's a damned fine young man, that Vargas. A credit to the Island." He lit the cigarette, drew in a long, luxurious breath, and looked at me, smiling vaguely, as if he'd just perceived my existence in the corner by the window. "Ah, there you are, princess. Good morning. I believe you're wanted upstairs."

I started forward. "Mr. Silva?"

"Silva? What, what? You don't mean to say you've forgotten the main event of the day, have you?" He laughed, took his cup from Isobel, and beckoned me over. He'd already shaved, and his pink skin smelled of that masculine, expensive soap men use for the purpose, a scent that jolted me because it was exactly the same as my father's.

I stopped and stared at his left hand, holding the saucer, holding also the cigarette between the first and second fingers. His right hand curled in the air, motioning me closer.

I leaned my head toward him, trying not to breathe. I told myself it was the nearby smoke from his cigarette that repelled me, because I had always liked Mr. Fisher. He was so kind, always so perfectly courteous. He adored my mother, and he had charmed our lives over the course of the past year.

I don't know if he noticed my hesitation. He put his hand on my shoulder and said, in a confidential voice, "A certain blushing bride has need of her bridesmaid."

6.

I REMEMBER HOW Daddy used to describe the Foxcroft commencement ceremony. He liked to play this little game. As each girl's name was called, and she went forward in her white dress to claim her diploma, he would name the product from which her family had achieved its wealth. Miss Ames walked forward, and he thought, *Shovels*. Then Miss Kellogg—*Corn flakes*. Miss Vanderbilt, of course, recalled *Railroads*.

Now, no Fisher girls graduated from Foxcroft while my father taught there, so far as I know, but if they had, he would have said to himself, *Toilets*. It's true. Look closely at the throne in your bathroom, and you'll maybe see the Fisher logo, a stylized F bracketed by the word *FINE* on the left side and *FIXTURES* on the other. The company had been founded a hundred years earlier by Hugh Fisher's great-grandfather, expanded into kitchen and bathroom fixtures generally, and soon straddled the entire Western world by taking keen-eyed advantage of the Victorian hygiene craze. Of course, the Fishers themselves gave up management of the company some time ago—on the death of Hugh Fisher's father, I believe—and to save the blushes of later generations, the Fisher logo had diminished into that single, magnificent F I just mentioned. But still. Never forget where you came from, I always say.

Anyway, I don't know if Mama knew much about the source of the Fisher riches. To do her credit, I don't think she even thought about them, at first. She never did lust for wealth. After all, she'd married my father, hadn't she, when she could have married for money instead, and you just show me any other woman with her beauty who wasn't married to a rich man.

As I told Joseph, I don't remember exactly which tasteful affair on the commencement week calendar threw her together with Hugh Fisher, but I do remember the look on her face when she arrived home afterward. Dazed, smitten. Nothing came of it right away—summer intruded between them, summer and Winthrop Island—but come September, when school resumed again without Isobel Fisher, and Hugh Fisher should have no possible reason to visit Foxcroft Academy, visit he did. Drove right up to our small, shabby house in his graceful silver roadster, top down to reveal the sunshine of his hair, and off they went on a drive somewhere, laughing and gleaming. He stayed discreetly in a hotel nearby, but he took her out to dinner, and he took us both to lunch, and four months later, New Year's Eve, he asked her to marry him at some gala party in New York, while I stayed home in Virginia and heated up a can of split pea soup for dinner.

And now? Now June had arrived, that month of weddings and roses, and I was buttoning the back of Mama's tea-length lavender tulle dress, fixing the jaunty birdcage veil that just reached the bottom of her jaw. Downstairs, the guests were assembling in the drawing room, where the French doors had been thrown open to the salt breeze so you might almost be outside. There were only thirty of these guests, because Mr. Fisher's ex-wife apparently belonged to one of the other Families—as Joseph Vargas called them—and while the Island air wasn't exactly poisoned by ill will, there still persisted a sense of civilized discretion, without which these clubs and islands couldn't exist from generation to generation. The Dumonts and their allies, who mostly clustered on the northeastern end of the Island, pretended nothing was going on down along the southeastern end, and on the table in the foyer a few dozen wedding announcements lay stamped and addressed in a beautiful copperplate hand, which would, sometime during the course of tomorrow morning, delicately inform the absentees of today's doings. You see how it works?

"Dearest Mama," I said, stepping back. "You're the most beautiful bride. Mr. Fisher's just the luckiest fellow in the world."

"Oh, don't." She glanced in the mirror and hastily away. "I still can't believe it. I woke up pinching myself. I keep thinking it's all going to disappear. *He's* going to disappear."

"He's not going to disappear. He's waiting downstairs for you this minute to make you his wife. It's all real. *This* is your life, Mama. A whole new wonderful life for you."

"For us both, darling." She laid her hand on my arm, so fiercely I could feel the ridge of her engagement ring as it pressed against my skin.

I could smell the powdery, flowery, new-bride smell of her. She whispered, "Do you *mind?*"

"Mind? Mind what?"

"You know what I mean. We were just two, snug as could be, and now suddenly there's Hugh and—and Isobel, and everything else. Tell me the truth. If you mind at all, even the *smallest* bit . . ."

She left the sentence dangling, of course. No possible way she could articulate that terrible alternative.

I opened my mouth to tell her what I ought to tell her. What I meant to tell her, what I thought I felt, true and deep, bottom of my heart and all that. What a good daughter should say at a moment like this, as her mother stands before a shimmering dreamworld, waiting to enter. What Mama's violet eyes *implored* me to say.

I thought of something, just then, as my mouth hung open and the words formed in my throat. I thought of the moment I crawled into her bed after we learned about Daddy, into her hot, tiny bedroom that stank of July, and how bleak those violet eyes had seemed to me then. How wet and curling the lashes around them. She was hardly more than a child herself then; not just physically young at twenty-nine, but childlike. That's the word. In those days, Mama was one of God's childlike people, and I offer that as a compliment. Oh, she was clever, there was nothing diminished about her intellect. I guess I mean she was childlike in *spirit*, the way we're supposed to be and never really are, lamblike in her innocence, and my father's death was probably the first time this faith had betrayed her. I remember thinking I'd heard the cracking of her heart in the way her voice cracked and broke as she whispered to me in that terrible moment, and when I embraced her soft, small body, I embraced her more as a sister than a daughter. When we slept at last, we curled around each other for comfort. So it had gone on for seven more years. We had read each other's thoughts and dreamed often in each other's beds. We'd laughed and wept, we'd shared books and clothes. When we went to the seaside for a week each summer, everybody just assumed we were sisters, the especially close kind of sisters, by the way we giggled and ate ice cream and gamboled hand in hand in the surf.

So as the old lie formed in my throat, I recognized its untruth by the sting of bile, by the stiffness of my vocal cords as they labored and labored to give birth to the words. And then this gust of fury blew through my chest, stealing even the breath I needed to say them. I thought wildly, like a premonition, *This is the end, not the beginning. We'll never stand like this again, we two.*

But my God, I couldn't actually *say* such a thing! Not while her enormous violet eyes begged me to say something else. But I couldn't say *those* words either, so I just placed my two hands on her cheeks, atop the veil, and kissed her, and in that instant the right words came to me.

I said, "Daddy wouldn't have wanted you to pine away the rest of your life."

She nodded frantically. "He was so good."

"Don't cry, Mama. Here, have some champagne." I turned for the silver tray on the dresser, loaded down with bucket and champagne coupes of crystal etched in trailing leaves, and I refilled my glass and Mama's. Before I handed hers over, while I stood there holding them both in my fingers, fizzing sweetly between us, I said, "You really love him, don't you?"

"I do, Miranda. I truly love him."

I gave her the glass and clinked it with mine. "To true love."

Before I could sip, a soft knock sounded on the door, and Isobel slipped inside the room without waiting for an answer. She wore an identical dress to mine, pale blue and full-skirted to just below the knees, off-shoulder sleeves overlaid by sheer organza. Sweet floral cap nestled in her hair. "Everybody ready in here? Your groom awaits impatiently. Oh my! Don't you both look lovely. And champagne! Wait! Don't start without me!"

She rushed to the dresser and poured herself a glass, which finished off the bottle and nearly overflowed the wide, shallow bowl of the coupe. She smelled of cigarettes and flowers and champagne, and when she raised her glass, her eyes glinted with either mischief or wine, I wasn't sure. "What are we toasting, girls?" she said.

"To true love," I said.

"Oh yes. To love!"

We clinked and drank, giggling a little, and through the crack in the door came the sound of violins and a dignified cello. Isobel put her arm around Mama's shoulder and whispered something in her ear, and there was something so intimate about this gesture that I turned my head and stared through the window at the sea, at the Flood Rock lighthouse erupting in the exact center of the frame. A sailboat beat lazily across the channel behind, and in the violent sunshine, the whiteness of its canvas hurt my eyes.

7.

A CERTAIN NUMBNESS gripped me as I followed Isobel down the aisle between the rows of white chairs. I fixed my eyes on Mr. Fisher's shiny gold head, his hands twisting behind his back, and when a gasp seized the air behind me, as everybody caught sight of my mother in her lavender wedding dress, I heard it down the same narrow tunnel as I heard the *Figaro* wedding march, rendered delicately by a string quartet in the corner of the room.

Mr. Fisher shared no such reserve. Unable to stop himself, he turned to watch his bride approach, and you should have seen the way his face lit up when he glimpsed her. Oh, they were most certainly in love, the two of them. Even the minister couldn't help but grin. Mama's own parents were dead, there was no one to give her away, so she just put her own hand into Mr. Fisher's hand when she reached him, an act of flagrant self-determination, while I stood to her left and watched the minister's mouth move. Took Mama's bouquet of small pink roses when Mr. Fisher required her other hand as well. I don't remember a single thing anyone actually said. When I think about that wedding today, I remember the pastel colors, the smell of all those flowers, the scrape of impatient chairs, and the damp-ness of the minister's lips as he married my mother to Hugh Fisher, amen.

8.

MANY HOURS AFTERWARD—I won't bore you with the details, I mean a wedding's a wedding, right?—afterward we slouched on the edge of the dock, Isobel and I, swinging our legs above the twitching sea. A bot-tle of champagne sat between us, mostly finished. Overhead, a high and brilliant moon illuminated our identical pale blue dresses, illuminated the water and the line of the horizon, illuminated Flood Rock and the stocky lighthouse that thrust from its center.

"The way he carried her aboard." Isobel shook her head slowly, drunkenly, because she had swallowed twice as much champagne as I had, and I'd swallowed a great deal, I'm afraid. "I don't think I've ever seen anything half so romantic as that."

"Isn't it traditional?"

"Across the threshold of a *house*, Peaches. Not a yacht." She had a little trouble with the word *threshold*, but it came out all right in the end. *Peaches* had first appeared sometime around sunset, as we started the second bottle of vintage Pol Roger that someone had carelessly left out after the last guest had departed. *You're just as sweet as peaches, Miranda,* she told me, filling my unsteady glass, and I guess that's how nicknames happen, isn't it? In a strange new world like this, you need a new name, and someone gives you one. Peaches. Because she thinks you're sweet.

"Well, it was an awfully big yacht," I said. "Almost as big as a house."

"Yes. Almost as big as Vanderbilt's." She paused solemnly. "Do you know how he used to describe a yacht?"

"No."

"A hole in the water, into which you pour money."

"You've got to pour it somewhere, don't you? Otherwise it just sits there in the bank, getting bored and reproducing."

"Money's such a lovely thing to have. I don't know what I'd do without it. Work or something, I guess." She yawned. "Except what? I'm just like Daddy, no good for anything except decoration and conversation. And dancing. I'm a terrific dancer."

"Horses," I suggested.

"But I only know how to ride them. Not to care for them or feed them or anything useful." She lifted her left hand and admired the diamond on her finger, which glittered in the moonlight. "Can I confess something awful to you?"

I didn't think there was any need to reply—either way, she was going to tell me—but I said, *Of course*, just to fill the air.

Isobel wriggled the ring from her finger and held it out before us both. I hadn't seen it this close until now; I didn't want to be caught staring at such a thing, like a poor country cousin. Now it was a relief to indulge my curiosity. I saw the central diamond was round, or else slightly oval, about the size of an especially plump raisin and surrounded by smaller dark stones that must have been sapphires.

"I came out here last night, by myself," Isobel said. "Right on this very spot. Clay and I had a fight after dinner."

"Oh, I didn't know that."

"It was after you left. He drove me home from the Club, and we fought in the car. I can't remember what it was about. We were both rather drunk." She laughed. "Surely you noticed today?"

"Didn't you make up or something?"

"No, of course not. You've got to make them stew, Peaches, you've got to make them suffer for their sins. Anyway, I came out here last night, all drunk and wretched, and sat on this exact spot on the dock. I took off my ring just like this, and I held it above the water, just like this . . ."

In the instant before her fingers opened, I saw what she was going to do. I flung out my hand desperately, almost pitching myself into the water, just as her own left hand darted forward to catch the heavy, glittering fall of the ring. Our two hands bumped and the ring bounced from one of those eight outstretched fingers—I'm not sure which—and Isobel gasped. Together we fumbled, and for a terrible, infinite second, the ring crashed crazily between us like some kind of ping-pong ball, off my knuckle and her thumb, the round bone of my wrist, spinning in a strange, weightless midair suspension.

Then somehow, miraculously, Isobel's hand closed around it.

We both slumped forward over our knees, panting.

"Jesus Christ, Peaches! What the hell were you doing?"

"I thought—"

"For God's sake, I wasn't going to *drop* it!"

"But you did. You did drop it."

"Not for real." She straightened and opened her hand to reveal the panes of the diamond, sheltered from the moon by her curled fingers. "I was only imagining, Peaches. You know, picturing what it would be like. I'd never do it for real. What do you take me for? Some kind of dope?"

"Of course not. We're just—we're awfully drunk, aren't we?"

"Awfully. But not that drunk." She shoved the ring back on her finger. "Listen, Peaches. You mustn't ever try to save me, all right? I like to sail close to the wind, as close as I can, but I won't capsize. You know what that means, *capsize*?"

"Of course I do."

She laughed. "Don't be sore. I know you're not a sailor, that's all. *Capsize* means to flip the boat over, Peaches, to land yourself in the drink because you weren't careful enough. You didn't know how to save yourself. But I know how to save myself, never fear. I know what I'm doing."

"All right, then."

"Don't be sore," she said again. She placed her hands on the dock and hoisted herself up to her feet, wavering so deeply I thought she might topple, in the same way her engagement ring had hung above the brink of disaster. But she didn't. She just yawned. "I'm so dreadfully bored, now that it's all over. Aren't you bored, Peaches?"

"Not really. It's a beautiful night."

"Well, I haven't got your brains, I'm afraid. I need a little action to keep me happy." She turned and started down the dock.

"Where are you going?"

"To the boathouse," she called back. "For a flashlight."

She returned in a moment holding this flashlight, which she aimed out to sea in the direction of Flood Rock, switching it off and on in an irregular rhythm. The air was still warm, and a slight salt-laden breeze came off the water, lifting the edges of our dresses.

"Is that Morse code?" I asked.

"Silly. It's just a private signal." She lowered the flashlight and stared across the channel. The moon was not quite full, but the sky was so clear that the whole world seemed gilded in silver, and the rocks of the lighthouse etched by so fine a line, I couldn't breathe for the beauty of it. The light revolved slowly from the top of the building, streaking across our quadrant every ten or fifteen seconds. It arrived twice before Isobel lifted the flashlight and sent another signal.

"Maybe he's asleep," I said.

"No, he's not. He stays up late, reading Portuguese novels to his mother."

"That's nice of him."

"It's the only thing that puts her to sleep, apparently." She flashed the signal again and checked her watch. "She's a queer old bag. But I guess anyone would go a little nuts, living out there on a rock."

I cupped my elbows with my hands and watched the lighthouse. For what, I wasn't sure. Some kind of answering signal, I guessed. For some reason, the whole exercise came as not the slightest surprise, as if I'd been expecting some communication of this nature between Isobel and the vital young inhabitant of Fleet Rock, after all that had been said and not said in the kitchen that morning. My dress was damp and dirty and stained by the grass, thanks to a game of croquet that Isobel started up right after Mama and Mr. Fisher had disappeared in their yacht around the tip of Long Island. Headed all the way to Europe together, just the two of them and a silent, devoted crew. Mama wore a beautiful suit of sky-blue summer tweed, and as she'd waved goodbye from the railing, she looked almost too perfect, like somebody had painted her there as a kind of ideal, a magazine advertisement or something, sky-blue dress matching the sky-blue sky, while the deeper hue of the sea cast them in relief. The clean white railing. I imagined I presented a wholly different image, so stained and ragged as I had made myself during the course of the ensuing hours. Now it was almost midnight, and surely we were flashing our torch into a void. Surely the whole Island had gone to sleep, and Joseph Vargas too.

A tiny light flickered from the side of the lighthouse.

Isobel made a triumphant noise and grabbed my hand. "Quick," she said. "Before he says no."

9.

JOSEPH VARGAS STOOD on the edge of the small wooden platform that served as the Flood Rock quay. I couldn't see his face very well because the lighthouse blocked the moon, but I thought he was furious. His voice confirmed this. He called out, not loudly—I guess he didn't want to wake anyone—but with terrible force.

"What the hell do you think you're doing, Isobel? At this hour?"

"Hour, schmour. I've brought champagne!" She stood in the bow and held up two bottles, one in each hand.

"You don't need any more champagne."

"Maybe not, but I'll bet you do. Look, I've brought my new sister. You remember Peaches, don't you? From this morning?"

There was a little pause. "Of course I remember Peaches."

"Well, it turns out she can row. Lucky for me, because I do believe I'd have just gone round in circles, in my ineb—ineeber—in my condition."

During the course of this speech, I managed to maneuver the boat up to the quay, despite the swift, angry current that wanted to yank us in the opposite direction. Joseph reached in and grabbed the rope next to Isobel's feet, and with his other hand he lifted her safely to the dock.

"Well, you're a fool, that's all. Why'd you do such a crazy thing? Might've drowned you both."

"I'm bored," Isobel said simply, removing her shoes. She turned and started to scale the steps cut into the rock. The shoes dangled from her left hand. Joseph made a noise of frustration, torn between helping me out of the boat and helping Isobel mount the stairs. He must have figured I stood in greater danger, because he swiftly wound the rope around the bollard and held out his arms to me. I rose to my feet and did my best to appear steady and sober. I don't think he was fooled. He put his hands on either side of my waist and hauled me through the air to solid ground. I felt a brief sensation of weightlessness, of the world disappearing around me, and then his hands were gone and I stared at the ghostliness of his shirt as he went after Isobel. When he caught her, she laughed, as quicksilver as the moonshine around us.

"What a naughty pair we are," she said. "Don't send us back, though. Can't we just stay a little while?"

Joseph groaned in such a way that I knew this wasn't the first time they'd enacted this scene. I stood there on the dock and looked up at the pair of them. Took note of the stocky line of his shoulders, covered by the white T-shirt, while the darker color of his arms sort of melted into the rocks. Both hands sat on his hips. Isobel stood a step or two above him, her blond hair made white by the moon. On her face sat an expression of triumph, even though Joseph hadn't yet capitulated.

He lifted his right hand and dragged it through his hair. "Just a minute or two, all right? Then I'm rowing you back myself."

"Yes, do. I love watching you row."

Isobel turned and picked her way through the rocks around the other side of the lighthouse. Joseph turned to me and held out his hand. "Hold on. It's kind of tricky, if you don't know where you're going."

I slipped off my shoes and gathered them in my hand. "Where *are* we going?"

"The beach, it looks like."

"*Beach?*"

"It's not much, but it's ours."

I reached him on the steps and put my hand in his palm. His fingers closed around mine and he started through the rocks, the same way Isobel had gone. They were damp and slippery—the tide was on its way out—and I couldn't see the holes and gaps between them. Couldn't judge my steps so well. I didn't want to rely on Joseph's hand, but I had no choice. His palm was rough and strong, a fisherman's palm, and he kept a solid grip as we clambered through the silvery darkness to the other side of the lighthouse. Once my foot slipped, and he caught me by the elbow. "All right?" he asked, and I was surprised by the closeness of his face, the scent of his breath that suggested toothpaste.

"Yes," I gasped back.

He turned and led me forward, and over the corner of his shoulder the beach appeared. Beach. Just a scrap of pebble and sand, really, at the bottom of a sac formed by two outcroppings of rock, maybe fifteen feet apart. Isobel lay there, surrounded by the pale tulle waves of her brides-maid gown, and her shoes in a small pile near her hip. As we drew near, I saw that her stocking feet pointed out to sea, and her head rested on her folded hands.

"She's not asleep, is she?" I whispered.

"No, she's not," Isobel called out. "Just resting my eyes. Did you know your beach *moves*, Joseph?"

He released my hand and dropped into the sand beside her, propping himself up on his elbows. "I had no idea," he said.

"Well, it does. Sort of sways back and forth. Up and down. Baby in a cradle."

"Izzy—"

"No! That's not it. Not a cradle." Her voice had begun to slow and slur. "A magic carpet. That's it. I'm flying, Joseph, *flying*. Don't you feel it?"

"'Fraid not. Just good old solid ground for me."

"Oh, that—that's—such a shame . . ."

"Izzy."

No answer.

Joseph peered briefly over her face and laughed. "Out cold. How much booze've you two sucked inside today?"

"Just wedding champagne. A bottle or two."

"Between you? Then I guess Izzy must've taken more than her fair share." He patted the ground beside him. "Sit down. Let her sleep it off a bit. Come on, I don't bite."

I sank into the coarse sand and wrapped my arms around my legs. My stockings were wet, and the grit now stuck to them like a crust. I wished I had the nerve to take them off. Along the sea before us, the moon cast a wide, phosphorescent path that disappeared mysteriously over the edge of the horizon. I said, "You've known each other forever, haven't you? You and Isobel."

"Ever since I can remember. Born a few months apart."

"Who's older?"

Another soft chuckle. "Me. So how did everything go today?"

"Oh, the wedding? Fine. Just fine."

"Lobster all right?"

"Sure."

"Caught fresh just this morning. Your stepfather bought the whole catch from me and Pops."

"Oh, did he?" I cried. "That was *your* lobster?"

"Caught fresh," he said again.

"Oh. I wish I'd known." I paused. "It was wonderful. Best lobster I ever had."

"Aw, you're a good sport. Don't tell me it's the *only* lobster you've ever had?"

"Of course not! I've had lobster before." Honesty compelled me to add, in a grudging voice, "Not often, though."

"I guess we'll have to do a clambake for you, this summer. Like a baptism. Make a genuine New Englander out of you."

"I'd like that very much."

Joseph lifted himself upright from his elbows, so we sat side by side. His arm brushed against mine, warmer than I expected. "What's with *Peaches?*" he said.

"Oh gosh. Nothing, really. Isobel started calling me that today, just for fun."

"But why Peaches?"

"Ask Isobel, why don't you. She's the one who made it up."

He pointed his thumb. "Her? She's not going to remember a thing tomorrow."

"Then I guess you're just dumb out of luck, aren't you?"

He flung himself back on the sand, folding his hands behind his head, and for an instant I thought I'd angered him. Then I glanced over my shoulder and saw his chest was shaking, and a grin split his face from cheekbone to cheekbone.

"You're a peach, Peaches," he said. "A real peach."

"I don't see what's wrong with *Miranda*."

"Nothing's wrong with *Miranda*. It's a heck of a name. Suits you just fine in the winter months, I'll bet, sitting indoors with your books and your cocoa. Or dressing up for some party in your gown and long gloves. *Miranda*." He said it slowly, stretching out the vowels. "In Latin, it means 'worthy of admiration.' That's what Shakespeare was talking about, in that line I threw at you this morning."

"I know."

"Aw, of course you do. Sorry."

"My father used to tell me things like that, when I was little."

"Did he? I like your dad. In my head, I've been calling him Prospero. But I guess that's not his real name, is it?"

"No. It was Thomas. Thomas Schuyler."

"Thomas Schuyler. Warrior, teacher of art, father of Miranda. And maybe a bit of a Shakespeare nut, too. Right?"

I stretched out my legs and listened carefully to the rhythmic wash of the waves as they uncurled onto the beach. The air was so warm and so silvery, like a primordial dream, like we sat on a beach at the beginning of the world, and we were the only people in it. I said, out to sea: "We used to read plays out loud to each other."

"Did you? Now that's grand. Do you remember any of it?"

"Of course I do."

"Like what?"

"I don't know. A lot of things."

"Can you do *Once more unto the breach*?"

"That's a man's part."

"So what? You've got it in you, I'll bet. Thomas Schuyler didn't raise a sissy."

I straightened and crossed my legs, Indian-style. The tulle floated out over my knees, and as I gazed out over the gilded water, I thought, if I strained my eyes, I might actually see all the way to France. Harfleur. Did it still exist? Had anything happened there in the last five hundred years since the siege, or had it fallen into obscurity? Had my father maybe glimpsed it, in his last days? We'd received no letters from France. Any messages, any postcards he'd had time to write had disappeared along with his body, and yet I felt sure that if my father had seen Harfleur with his own eyes, he would have written to tell me.

"It's been a while," I said. "Since he left for the war."

"Say, you don't have to if you don't want to. I mean, if it hurts too much or something."

"No. It doesn't hurt anymore."

"All right. Whatever you want. I'm listening, that's all."

I lowered my voice and said,

Once more unto the breach, dear friends, once more,
Or close the wall up with our English dead!
In peace there's nothing so becomes a man
As modest stillness and humility,
But when the blast of war blows in our ears,
Then imitate the actions of the tiger:
Stiffen the sinews, conjure up the blood,
Disguise fair nature with hard-favored rage.

"Go on," said Joseph softly, from the sand.

I scrambled to my feet and shook out the grit from my dress. I had told Joseph the truth; I hadn't spoken those words since childhood, and yet—in the way of certain memories—they rose passionately from my throat. They burst from my mouth in my father's hard, warlike delivery. The blood hurtled into my fingers to grip an imaginary sword.

On, on, you noblest English,
Whose blood is fet from fathers of war-proof,
Fathers that, like so many Alexanders,
Have in these parts from morn till even fought
And sheathed their swords for lack of argument:
Dishonor not your mothers. Now attest
That those whom you called fathers did beget you.
Be copy now to men of grosser blood,
And teach them how to war. . . .

I didn't recognize myself. I was not Miranda but someone else, a man, a king, a warrior, a voice roaring. I heard its faint echo from the rocks.

The game's afoot.
Follow your spirit, and upon this charge
Cry "God for Harry, England, and Saint George!"

And there was silence, and my original soul sank back into my skin. Miranda resumed herself. My arm dropped to my side. I went down on my knees, one by one, shaking a little. Against my hot skin, the sand felt cool. Each grain made its individual impression on my nerves.

"That was something," said Joseph.

I shook my head and laughed.

"I mean it. You're something, you know that? You're something else."

I felt as if I'd just stepped off some boardwalk roller coaster. Been spat back ashore by some monstrous wave. Shaken and changed, muscles stiffened from the shock of metamorphosis. Joseph's gaze lay on my shoulders, on the back of my neck. I thought, *If I turn, if I look at him looking at me, I'll die.*

"Here, lie down," he said. "You can see the stars real good from here."

So I settled myself back in the sand, rigid, arms straight against my sides. Wanting and not wanting to come into contact with Joseph's shoulder, Joseph's arm, bare above the elbow in his white T-shirt. From this small distance, I could smell his soap. He must have been getting ready for bed when he saw our signal. That would explain the toothpaste, the soap, the T-shirt. I should have felt overdressed in my blue tulle, but I didn't. Maybe it was my stocking feet, crusted with sand, or the democratizing effect of moonlight and salt water.

"How well do you know your constellations?" Joseph asked.

"Pretty well." I was surprised to hear that my voice had returned to its ordinary timbre, not quivering at all. "But you must be an expert."

"Why's that?"

"Aren't sailors supposed to be experts on the stars?"

"Not anymore. The old explorers were, I guess. Back before we had clocks and instruments, and you only had the sky to tell you where you were. Skies and lighthouses. The old days." He made some movement with his hand, sliding it out from beneath his head to rub his brow. "Anyway, lobstermen fish by day, mostly."

"So what does that mean? Are you an astronomer, or not?"

"The answer to that, Peaches, is yes. I can map the night sky pretty well."

"Peaches," I said.

"It's your Island name. Don't you like it?"

"I don't know. I haven't decided yet. It's too new."

"Well, let me know what you decide." He lifted his hand and pointed. "There's Hercules. I've always liked him. Had to earn his place there in the sky. He wasn't just born with it, like the others."

"Me too. Makes me feel safer, somehow, knowing he's hanging there with his sword raised. Why don't *you* have an Island nickname?"

"Me? I don't know. Nobody ever gave me one."

"Maybe nobody ever dared."

"What's that supposed to mean?"

I turned on my side to face his profile. His nose was too big, his brow too ridged. His lips were full, though, which softened him a little. I wondered if the moonlight gilded my skin in the same way; whether his cheeks, if I were so unfathomably brave as to touch them, would feel as cool and smooth as they looked from here, a foot or two away. "That was something, this morning," I said. "What you did. Diving into the water and saving Popeye. You might have been killed."

He didn't turn toward me or anything. Just shrugged his shoulders a little, against the sand. "Popeye?" he said.

"That's what I called him, in my head. Watching you from the window. He had that shirt on, and he was chewing on a pipe—"

"Wait a second." He turned his head and squinted at me. "You saw his *pipe*?"

"I—well—"

"You were watching us with *binoculars*, weren't you?"

"Well—"

"*Miranda*! For how long?"

I rolled back to face the sky. "Just a minute or two. I was curious. Never saw anybody fishing for lobsters before."

"Aw, you're blushing."

"No I'm not. Anyway, how could you tell if I was?"

"I just can. I can feel your cheeks getting warm."

"No you can't. Not from over there."

"Yes I can."

I made to rise, and he caught my hand, and for a second or two we didn't move. The air grew heavy between us. His hand was calloused and hot, larger than I thought, so rough it seemed to scratch my skin. The hand of a lobsterman. I looked away, because I didn't know what was happening, because I'd never held a boy's hand before, certainly not a tough hand like that. The sea slapped against the rocks, the lighthouse beam swept above our heads. A fierce voice called out.

"Joseph! What's going on out there?"

Joseph turned toward the sound, but he didn't drop my hand. Instead his grip tightened, not uncomfortable, just snug. I looked, too, and saw a dark silhouette in the middle of a glowing rectangle, painted on the side of a squat, square building attached to the lighthouse.

Joseph called back to this apparition. "Nothing much, Mama. Izzy rowed over with a friend."

She said something back, something I couldn't understand, and Joseph replied in the same language, which I figured was Portuguese. Sounded a little like Spanish, but it went by too fast for me to pick out any words. The exchange ended with a noise of exasperation from the other side, the maternal kind of noise that means the same thing in any language, I guess, and the silhouette stepped forward from the doorway and became a woman, monochrome in the moonlight. She was small and sharp and graceful, and her dark hair was gathered in an old-fashioned bun at the nape of her neck. She made me think of a ballerina, only shorter. She was examining me, I knew. I felt the impact of her dislike like a blow. I shifted my feet and straightened my back, and when I realized Joseph still held my hand, I pulled it free and tucked my fingers deep into the folds of tulle that hung around my legs.

She turned her head to Joseph and said something in Portuguese.

He answered in English. "Don't worry. I'll row them back myself."

"You don't need to do that," I said. "I can row."

"Not on your life. That current's a killer when the tide's going out, and you'll be rowing against it." He bent over Isobel and shook her shoulder. "Izzy! Izzy, wake up!"

She moved her head, groaned, and went still.

"She's drunk," said Mrs. Vargas.

Joseph didn't reply to that. He didn't even sigh, as he might have done, annoyed as he must have been. Just lifted Isobel in his arms and said to me, "Can you make it across the rocks all right?"

"Sure I can."

He went ahead of me, carrying Isobel, and I followed his white T-shirt, phosphorescent as the ocean in the moonlight. My feet were steadier now. I wrapped my toes around the sharp, wet edges of the rocks and didn't slip once. When we reached the dock, I held the boat steady while Joseph bore Isobel aboard. "You better hold her while I row," he said, so I stepped inside and made my way to the bow seat and took Isobel's slack body against mine.

I don't think we said a word, the two of us, the entire distance from Flood Rock to the Fisher dock. I sat on the bench and held Isobel between my legs while she slumped against my left side. Joseph just rowed, steady and efficient, like a fellow who'd been rowing boats since he could walk, which was probably the case. He wasn't lying about the current. I watched as he fought the strength of the outgoing tide, hurtling through the narrow channel and out into the broad Atlantic; I watched the strain of his muscles, the movement of his shoulders, the pop of his biceps, and my bones filled with terror as I realized I couldn't have done this by myself, Isobel unconscious at my feet, however hard I pulled. The boat would have borne out past the Island to the open sea.

At one point, near the dock and the shelter of the small Fisher cove, our eyes met. I'd been looking over his shoulder and so had he, judging the distance to shore, and when he turned back his gaze made right for my face and stayed there, so that I couldn't help but succumb to its human gravitation. Instead of looking away, he smiled, as if we'd just shared a secret, the nature of which I couldn't have guessed, so young as I was in the early days of that summer. I only thought that he had a warm, beautiful smile, the most beautiful smile I'd ever seen, and in the instant before I ducked my head, I knew I was in love with him. Just imagine. As innocent, as uncomplicated as that. I still remember that moment, that sweet, shy revelation, remember it fondly, because it only comes once in your life, and then it's gone. You can't have it back. And it's only a second! Isn't that capricious?

One measly instant of clarity, tucked inside the reach of your livelong days. And then the boat touches the shore, and the moment flies, and your life—your real, murky, messy, incalculable life—your life resumes.

10.

AT EIGHT O'CLOCK the next morning, the morning after our parents' wedding, Isobel came into my room, dressed and fragrant, and told me we were going to church.

I hadn't exactly expected her, as you might imagine. I lay curled on the armchair in my dressing gown, comfortable as could be, staring through the window at the young, watery sunshine that drenched the Flood Rock lighthouse. A book spread open in my lap, unread. Last night, I'd fallen into bed, slept a sound, soundless six hours, and woken more refreshed than I ought, filled with an anticipation I couldn't yet name, and unable to concentrate on any words written on any page. I blinked at the shadows under Isobel's eyes and said, "*Church?*"

"Darling, it's *Sunday*," she said, as if the two ideas couldn't possibly exist without each other.

My father came from an old, intellectual family, and Mama from a young bohemian one. Neither viewed organized religion with uncritical awe; it was one of the few common territories between them. After my birth, nobody thought of baptizing me. When I asked about God—aged eight, mind you—Daddy told me solemnly that I should believe whatever my conscience held to be true. I asked him, what was a conscience? He said it was my inner voice that told me right from wrong, and from then on, when I thought of God at all, I thought of old Grandmama Schuyler, because for some reason her voice shrilled inside my head whenever I faced any kind of moral crisis. *Don't you take that second cookie!* or *Let the adults speak for a change!* and that kind of thing.

At the moment, and in her present condition, Isobel Fisher did bear an uncommon resemblance to Grandmama Schuyler, who was also long-boned and lean, and whose hair had been blond before it turned a rusty, streaked silver. I hadn't seen my stepsister since the previous night, when she'd stumbled onto dry land, vomited over the grass, and staggered into the house under Joseph's protection. His arm had held her shoulder, and his face wore an expression of stern pity, mixed with maybe a little remorse. He must have cleaned her up and put her to bed, but you could still read the history of the night before in that wan, tanned skin, in that dull hair, in those lavender half-moons beneath her eyes, which squinted against the sunshine. She wore an immaculate suit of dandelion yellow and a pair of matching shoes, and one hand rested against the doorframe to hold the whole act upright. The other hand contained her white gloves and pocketbook.

"What time does it start?" I asked feebly.

"Eight thirty." She glanced at her watch. "You'd better hurry. I'll get the car."

11.

"THE THING IS, everybody goes," Isobel called, above the roar of the engine, as we hurtled down the road toward St. Ann's Episcopal Church at the eastern end of the Island. "If you don't turn up, they'll wonder why."

"I don't care about that!" I called back.

"You will, believe me."

She drove wantonly, wastefully, rushing down the straight stretches and then slamming the brakes into the curves, so that the tires of her father's sleek Plymouth convertible whined and slid against the faded asphalt. All the while, she clutched a cigarette between the first two fingers of her right hand, and along the straightaways she sucked long currents of smoke between her clenched, red lips.

I kept my hands fixed in my lap. The sun packed its heat into the car's interior—Isobel had put the top up, in order to save our good hats from the draft—and my flesh still glowed from the haste of getting dressed. Underneath the suit and blouse, a trickle of perspiration ran down my left armpit and along my side. The smell of hot leather and cigarettes made me want to vomit. By the time we reached the neat white church, sitting against a field of green and surrounded by cars, I'd begun to feel faint for the first time since that terrible flu in my freshman year at Foxcroft. Isobel slammed to a stop in the grass and I threw open the door to inhale the clean, green-smelling air. The swollen chords of an organ billowed past.

"Damn it all to hell and back again." Isobel threw her cigarette into the grass and stomped it with her toe. "We're late."

We ran across the meadow, holding hands, weaving between cars until we reached the wooden steps of the church and slowed to a reverent pace. Isobel turned in the vestibule and ripped off her glove to fix my hat. By some strange trick of the sunlight, her engagement ring threw a shower of glitter on the wall just above the altar, and all the inhabitants of the packed pews started and turned, searching for the source of this otherworldly fireworks. They found us soon enough.

I don't know if you've ever had that experience, a churchful of well-dressed strangers all staring at you in astonished disapproval. I don't recommend it. Sometimes, in my nightmares, the image of those faces still returns to me, except I'm naked and grossly pregnant, and Isobel's left me to face them all alone, instead of clutching my hand in a firm grip—as she did then—and leading me to a pew in the last row, wedged up against the side aisle. The organ tootled on from above, oblivious, and the faces turned away, one by one, because the singing was about to start and none of those great ladies wanted to miss her cue. On Winthrop Island, as I learned, the singing of hymns was a competitive exercise, preferably in a high, godly soprano to reach Heaven itself and—coincidentally—drown out the efforts of both your neighbor and the choir in the small balcony above. (The choir, you understand, had room for just ten members, filled by a ritual of cordial, bitterly contested auditions at the beginning of each summer season.)

As for the men? I don't know. I don't think they cared as much. Even so innocent as I then was, I noticed how they kept slipping impious glances at Isobel and me, young and animal, glowing with perspiration in our shapely pastel suits. That space of ours at the end of the pew had lain empty for a good reason, because it stood square in the path of a block of sunlight, and as Isobel flipped hastily through the hymnal I found myself gasping for air once more. The notes and words swam before me. The hymn ended, the blessing began, the congregational responses, and at last—at last—we lowered ourselves to the hard wooden bench and allowed the service to swallow us.

12.

AFTERWARD, THE CONGREGATION gathered in the churchyard and greeted each other in the hot sun. Everybody was so nice. Said such pleasant, vague things about my mother and the wedding yesterday, how they wished Mr. and Mrs. Fisher all the happiness in the world, such a beautiful couple. I realized I must have been entirely mistaken about those hostile expressions at the beginning of the service.

Mrs. Monk invited us over for bridge. "Of course," said Isobel, kissing her cheek. "I'll drive Miranda."

Clay regarded Isobel with a slight frown. "I'd be happy to drive."

"But we'll be all squished in front, and I won't have Miranda in back all by herself."

"She wouldn't mind. Would you, Miranda?"

A word or two about Clayton Monk, as he aimed a respectful pair of eyes at me and awaited my reply. At the time, I thought he was too good for Isobel. Not too handsome and dashing and rich, I mean, but too *good*. She was probably going to ruin him. I thought he had no natural defense against her, no edge at all. I mean, just look at him as he then was, made of pleasant, bland good looks that would inevitably grow red and jowly in middle age, but not before he'd passed them on to a pair of sons, whom he taught to sail. (I could picture them all, father and sons and sailboat.) He wore a double-breasted navy jacket and tan slacks, a white shirt with a crisp collar, a sedate silk tie the color of hydrangeas. Looking at him, you wouldn't imagine that he'd once spent his days crisscrossing Europe in a B-17 Flying Fortress, dropping bombs all over the place, and that on a nice summer midnight in 1944 he'd crashed said Flying Fortress into a French field, so expertly that only one man was killed, and Clay himself had gotten away with a broken arm and a concussion. Afterward, as I said, he went to Harvard and then Harvard Law School, and he now occupied an office in some blueblood law firm or another, working his way toward the partnership, one dry, passive sentence at a time. Which might sound boring to you and me, but at least he was *doing* something, wasn't he? Earning his own living, instead of idling his days atop the Monk department store fortune. Anyway, in the summer of 1951, Clayton Monk was all that was pink and well-scrubbed. Just looking at him made you feel clean, inside and out, like a wholesome breakfast cereal.

I smiled back and said, "I don't mind a little squishing. My skirt's all creased anyway."

13.

ON THE WAY to the Monk estate, which was perched near the eastern tip of the Island, right next to the Winthrop Island Club and exactly opposite to Greyfriars, I asked Isobel whether she'd seen Joseph at church, because I hadn't.

There was a little silence. "Joseph?" said Clayton, who was driving. "Joseph who?"

Isobel said quickly, "Don't be silly, Peaches. Of course not."

"Didn't you say *everybody* goes to church on the Island?"

She started to laugh. "Darling, he goes to St. Mary's, in the village. The Catholic church."

"Oh, Joseph *Vargas*," said Clayton. "I didn't realize you'd met the locals yet."

"Yesterday morning. He brought in another lobsterman who'd fallen overboard. And then last night—"

Isobel's elbow met my ribs.

"What about last night?" asked Clay.

"Nothing." I looked out the window, toward the sea. "Of course, the Catholic church. I didn't think."

Isobel sat between us on the front seat, tilting her long legs at an acute angle to fit them under the dashboard. Clayton, a tall man, had taken down the top, and the draft blew warmly over our hats and ears. Isobel rummaged in her pocketbook for a cigarette and lit it clumsily. "Here's a funny thing about the Island, Peaches," she said, as she tried to get the lighter going in the middle of the crosswind. "I think it's telling. The Episcopal church only opens during the summer season, see, May to September, while the Catholic church runs all year round. Don't you think that's telling, Clay?"

"Telling what, darling?"

"I mean, the way things work around the Island. Who does what, and where, and when."

Clay propped his elbow on the doorframe and tilted his head to one side, so he could rub his left eyebrow. His right hand gripped the wheel at twelve o'clock. "I don't know what you're trying to say, Izzy. Sure, most of the fishermen happen to be Portuguese around here. Portuguese folks happen to be mostly Catholic."

"Exactly."

"Well, you're trying to make out like it's some kind of crime, that's all."

"It's not a crime," she said. She'd finally succeeded in lighting her cigarette, and she now smoked it with a peculiar ferocity.

"Well, we all get along, don't we? They've got their religion, and we've got ours—"

"And never the twain shall meet," Isobel said softly.

"—and everybody respects each other. Nobody's got a thing against Catholics, around here."

I spoke up timidly. "I think what Isobel's trying to say is that the summer residents, the ones with all the power and the money—"

"All right," Clay said. "All right. Fine. Look, it's a Sunday. Let's stay away from politics for one day, okay?" He straightened and reached for the radio dial.

Isobel, looking out the side, past my nose toward the blurry meadows, the occasional house, said, "Have you noticed there aren't any trees, Peaches? Old, native ones, I mean."

"Now that you mention it."

"It's because of some hurricane." She sucked on her cigarette. "Some hurricane, over a hundred years ago, that flattened everything. Now the Island's like a Scottish moor or something. Or Ireland. One of those. Isn't that right, Clay?"

"I guess so." He was still working the radio dial.

"Do you get any stations out here?" I asked.

"We get a couple out of Providence, when the wind's right. Sometimes Boston." He turned the dial millimeter by millimeter, listening carefully to the pattern of static.

"Oh, why bother?" said Isobel. "Honestly. We're almost there."

I waved away a stream of smoke. "This might be a good time to mention that I don't play bridge."

"What's that?" said Clay.

"She doesn't play bridge!" Isobel shouted in his ear.

"Not play bridge? But I thought all you girls played bridge."

"Miranda doesn't. She's an intellectual. Did you know she was named after a girl in Shakespeare?"

"Is that so? Now that's grand. Which one? Which play, I mean?"

Isobel turned to me. "Which one, Peaches?"

"*The Tempest*," I said, just as the car slowed and began its turn down a long, slender, curving drive toward a house plucked right out of the half-timbered Elizabethan countryside and onto a cliff overlooking the entrance to Long Island Sound. At that instant, whether by design or coincidence, a bank of black clouds swallowed up the sun.

14.

WHEN IT COMES to bridge, the punishment for ignorance is apparently banishment, which suited me well enough. For a short while, I hung around the well-appointed drawing room, holding my iced tea, watching the rain shatter violently against the French windows while the Monks, unconcerned, set up the bridge table. Lucky for them—or again, maybe by design—there were two other guests, a mother and daughter, who made up the other sides. They were the Huxleys, Mrs. Huxley and her daughter, Livy, and Isobel explained that it was Dr. Huxley, husband and father of same, who had come to Popeye's rescue in the Fisher kitchen yesterday. We exchanged the usual bland pleasantries. Livy and her mother were perfectly nice, perfectly pretty, like two round, full scoops of vanilla ice cream, the younger one wearing a dress like a lemon meringue. I remember thinking, at the time, how utterly harmless they seemed, how absent of tooth and claw. Clay had disappeared somewhere with his father. Isobel had mixed herself a drink from the liquor cabinet and now sat in her bridge chair, next to Mrs. Monk, wearing an expression of sharklike intensity.

When the rain died away to a drizzle, I called over my shoulder that I was going for a walk to see the cliffs and I slipped through one of the French doors to the bluestone terrace and the lawn beyond. The wet grass soaked my shoes and stockings. When I reached the cliff's edge, I took them off and laid the stockings to dry across a large, white rock, and then I sat down on a neighboring rock and watched the clouds storm angrily away to the northeast. The cliffs weren't especially high, maybe forty or fifty feet, but they were steep and rugged, and the path snaked carefully down the least forbidding side to end in a pale beach. Out to sea, a lone sailboat picked its way along the coast, about a hundred yards from shore.

Now that the sun shone unobstructed, the heat built once more, sinking into my skin and bones and the rough surface of the rock beneath me. I removed my jacket—I'd left my hat and gloves indoors—and thought I should really find some shade, before I burned. But I didn't want to move. There was just enough breeze to make it bearable. The air was rich and damp with the smell of the sea, and there was something hypnotic about the movements of that lone, brave sailboat, something graceful and eternal. I could just make out the man who sat in the stern, next to the tiller. He had dark hair that flashed from time to time against the white of the triangular sail, and at some point, as I watched, I began to realize that the sailor was Joseph. Or maybe I was only hoping it was Joseph? Maybe it was just longing.

I straightened and squinted, and as if he felt my scrutiny, the sailor turned his head toward shore.

Joseph.

I raised my hand and waved, even though he couldn't possibly recognize me from there, not sitting as I was on the opposite corner of the Island from the house where I was supposed to be sitting. Up went Joseph's arm, returning the wave, and then he rose from his seat at the tiller and reached for a rope. A *sheet*—wasn't that what they called ropes on boats? Sort of confusing, if you asked me, because something you called a *sheet* ought logically to be a sail. Whatever it was, Joseph did something to it, adjusting its pitch against the wind. When he turned back, his arm lifted again, in such a way that he seemed to be beckoning me toward the water.

I stood and glanced at my shoes and stockings, drying on the nearby rock. I glanced at the path, snaking its way to the beach below. My skin was flushed and damp, my skirt creased, my blouse stained with perspiration. The salt breeze tumbled my hair.

"Miranda. There you are."

I pitched forward. Clayton's arm shot out to catch me.

"Careful!" he said.

"Sorry! I didn't hear you come up."

"No need to apologize. Shouldn't have snuck up like that. Gosh, who's that crazy fellow out there?"

"Just some sailboat," I said.

"He's not afraid of a little squall, I guess." Clay stuck his hands in his trouser pockets. He'd taken off his jacket and stood there in his shirt-sleeves, rolled halfway up his forearms. A considerable concession to the heat, for a man like him. He rolled onto his toes and back down again. "Say. Do you have a moment, Miranda?" he asked.

"Sure I do."

"Can we sit?"

I took the larger rock, next to my shoes and stockings, while Clay propped himself on the smaller one and crossed his legs at the ankles. His feet looked hot and uncomfortable, encased in brown argyle socks and leather shoes. I tucked my bare white toes against the rock and said, "Anything in particular?"

"Actually," he said, as if the idea had just occurred to him, "I wanted to ask you about Izzy."

"What about Izzy?"

He uncrossed his ankles and crossed them again, putting the other foot on top. His hands twiddled together against his thighs. "That was some party, yesterday, wasn't it? A big day for you both. A happy day. We're all—well, we couldn't be happier for Mr. Fisher. Your mother's everything we might have hoped for in a—a new mother for Izzy."

"She's already got a mother, hasn't she?"

"Well, of course that depends on whom you ask. I don't like to speak ill of people. You haven't met her, have you? The ex Mrs. Fisher?"

"No."

"I don't suppose there's any reason you should. She lives in . . . is it Nice? Somewhere in the south of France, I understand. She remarried a few years ago, some old French aristocrat she met during the war. Lost all his dough, I guess, and wanted hers. They say he's a—well . . ."

"A what?"

"Nothing. Nothing you need to know about. Let's just say they both go their own ways, the two of them. That's what I hear, anyway."

"Then why did they marry?"

"People marry for all kinds of reasons, Miranda. I don't know, maybe she wanted the title. She's a funny old bird. Always was. Restless, you know, wanted to go abroad all the time, spend her time with that international set—you know who I mean—instead of summering on the Island."

At the time, I didn't know whom he meant. Clay pronounced the words *international set* with distaste, as if it were some disease that had no cure, but to me it sounded exotic and wonderful. So I said innocently, "What's wrong with that? I'd like to go abroad."

"I mean make a habit of it. Socialize with those people, artists and aristocrats and hangers-on, new money, all the time having affairs and divorcing and God knows what else. Anyway, she's never shown much interest in poor Izzy, even when she was a baby. So I think we were all hoping—when we heard the news—and then we met you and your mother—"

"Maybe she'd be an improvement?"

He nodded vigorously. "Oh, she is. I mean, you've got to be careful what you say, because Mrs. Fisher—the *former* Mrs. Fisher, I mean, the Countess whatever she is now—her family still summers here. The Dumonts?" The end of the sentence turned up inquisitively, as if there were some kind of chance I knew the Dumonts personally.

"I've heard about them," I said. Before us, the sailboat had started another tack. The sun caught the brilliant white of the canvas, so sharp against the dark blue sea that I had to look away.

"Anyway, that's all behind us now," said Clay. "What's important is that Izzy has someone to look out for her now."

"You're her fiancé. Aren't you supposed to be doing that?"

"But we won't be married until next June." He sprang from the rock and stepped forward, right to the edge of the cliff. He had a nice trim backside, a narrow waist. A pair of old-fashioned braces held up his trousers. "Last night . . . ," he said.

I waited a moment and said, "What about last night?"

"I don't know what happened with you two. Maybe I don't want to know. She had a little too much to drink, didn't she? She gets carried away, you see."

He seemed to be starting another sentence, which he bit off. I had the feeling he was struggling with something, groping, juggling words in his head. He fiddled with his sleeves, took out his handkerchief, wiped away the perspiration on his temples.

"For what it's worth, I like that about her," I said. "I like her high spirits."

"Yes. Of course. Look. I don't know—I don't usually—Miranda—you don't mind me calling you that?"

"Of course not."

"Do you mind if I tell you something private? Just between you and me, Miranda, because I can tell you aren't the gossiping type."

"You can tell me whatever you like, Mr. Monk."

"Clay. Look. The truth is, the night before last, the night before the wedding, we'd had a bit of a—a—I don't know what to call it . . ."

"Clay, you don't—"

"—a lovers' quarrel."

The words burst out almost in a shout—*lovers' quarrel!*—followed by a delicate silence, expecting my reply. When I didn't say anything, Clay looked down and toed the dirt.

"I'm sorry. I shouldn't have said that. I haven't told anyone, not even Mother."

"You've got to talk to someone, don't you? You can't keep everything bottled inside."

Clay made a dry noise. "Can't I? That's what we do, Miranda. Keep it all bottled. Don't burden anybody with your private troubles. We don't talk, certainly not to strangers. I sometimes wish . . ."

He let the sentence dangle, the wish unexpressed. I tucked my legs against my chest and wrapped my arms around them. A few feet away, Clayton shifted his feet and noticed the handkerchief in his hand. He shoved it back in his pocket.

I said, "If there's anything I can do to help—"

It was as if I'd pulled the cork from his mouth. Clayton started to burble. "She's a terrific girl, Izzy. She's the one, I mean there's never been anyone else. But she's got a restless streak, always has, all this bottled-up energy like some kind of Fourth of July firework. Don't get me wrong, it's one of the things I love about her. Maybe she gets it from her mother, I don't know. You just can't take your eyes off her, wondering what crazy, wonderful thing she's going to do next."

I pressed my thumbs together. I think I was trying not to say something rash, trying to hold back this immense surge of pity I felt for Clayton Monk in that moment. He leaned down and picked up a rock from the dirt near his feet. Turned that rock around again and again between his fingers, examining every last ridge, every facet, each tiny grain that made up the whole.

He went on in a quiet voice, talking not to me, but to the rock in his hand. "The trouble is, she gets temperamental, she gets in these moods sometimes, and I just can't—I can't—I don't know what to do. Honestly, I don't know *what* I said the other night, I mean I don't have the slightest clue what upset her so much."

Clay dropped the rock suddenly and put his hand to the back of his neck. His fingers were long, his nails well-trimmed, his forearm dusted with light hair. His other hand sat on his hip. I looked past him toward the sea, but his body now blocked my view of Joseph in his sailboat, and I didn't want to rise and startle him, so close as he stood to the edge of the cliff.

I said, "It was probably just the excitement of the day. She loves you very much."

"Does she? Did she say that?"

"Well . . . not in so many words."

He made a mournful laugh. "Thanks for the honesty."

I didn't know what to say. I hardly knew him at all, him or Isobel. I had the feeling I'd walked onto the stage of a play, sometime in the middle of the second act, and assumed a leading role. And I had no script, no story. I didn't even know the name of this play. Was probably wearing the wrong costume. I leaned back on my hands and stared at the long, vertical creases down the back of Clay's shirt. The sun burned the top of my head, my hands, the back of my neck. A gull screamed from the rocks down below.

"Vargas!" Clay exclaimed.

I startled up. "What? Where?"

"The lighthouse keeper's son. Fellow who was with you last night. Don't deny it. Vargas?"

"Joseph. Yes."

"I think he's in love with her."

The sentence struck in the middle of my chest. I stepped to one side, in order to find Joseph's sailboat on the stretch of empty sea before us. For a second or two, I thought he'd been swallowed by the water, but when I shielded my eyes and looked farther, I saw he had only angled around the eastern tip of the Island to tack down the other side. The boat was smaller now. You couldn't make out Joseph himself, just the white, triangular sail against the navy water, as it began to disappear behind the land's edge. I caught my breath again and said, "How do you know?"

"Oh, he's always been crazy about her. Used to hang around the house when they were small. Take the dinghy back and forth. They had some kind of signal they used to send each other, through the windows."

"But she doesn't feel the same way. She's engaged to you, not to him."

"Another man's ring isn't going to stop a fellow like that."

"I don't think—" I checked myself.

"Don't think what?"

"I just think he's more honorable than that."

"Do you? Well, I've known him all my life, and I wouldn't put it past him. Not the way he's been pining for her all these years. Sitting there in his lighthouse, watching her from the window, beckoning her over to see him."

The tip of the sail winked out past the edge of the cliff.

"Then Isobel should put a stop to it," I said. "Especially if it hurts you."

"Oh, it doesn't *hurt* me. Not a bit. A fellow like that . . ." Clay turned to face me, and his expression was so haggard, the lines so deep and painful in his fresh, young face, I forgot my anger. He took my shoulder under his hand. "It's Izzy I'm worried about. She's impulsive, she's—she trusts him, God knows why. It's because he's not one of us. He's—well, she knows she can't marry him, and you know how it is with girls—" He broke off and—perhaps realizing how tightly he was gripping my shoulder—let his hand drop to his side, where he shoved it into his pocket. "And he loves her. He's crazy about her. Last night. I should've—man, I should've gone over there myself, I should've socked him. If I'd known, I would have."

"I'm glad you didn't. Nothing happened, Clay, nothing at all. She was—we were both a little tipsy, from the champagne and all, and he was worried about us and rowed us back home. That's all. Joseph did a good thing."

"He could have telephoned me. I would've fetched her back."

"Do they have a telephone out there?"

"Sure they do. Underground cable."

"I didn't realize."

"There's a lot you don't realize." He swiveled back to the sea. Ran a hand through his hair and shoved it in his pocket, like the other hand, good and deep. "Mr. Fisher—God bless him—he's indulged her all these years. I don't blame him. She's had it tough, with that mother of hers, and—well and everything else. But he's not here to protect her just now, and I hope— I don't mean to ask you to sneak around for me, nothing like that, but I just— If you could let me know if she's in trouble, that's all. If she's about to do something stupid."

I pictured that engagement ring, three or four carats dangling above the sapphire water. "She's not going to do anything stupid," I said. "And if she is, I don't think I could stop her."

"I could. I could stop her. If you just let me know how she's doing, *what* she's doing." He pulled his left hand out of the pocket and checked his watch. "I've got to be back at the firm tomorrow, but I'll be back up here as often as I can, believe me. I'll give you my number in the city. Call me at any time. Collect, if you need to."

"I'm sure that won't be necessary."

Clay reached out and took my hand, very gently, the way he'd been taught.

"I'm just grateful you're here, Miranda. I'm just grateful Izzy's got someone like you around at last, a proper female influence, someone steady and sensible."

"Thank you," I said dryly.

Clay leaned forward and pressed my hand hard and kissed my cheek, cutting me off. He smelled of sunshine and perspiration, and his cheek, brushing mine, was hot and damp.

"Just keep her busy, all right?" he said. "For God's sake, just keep her away from that Vargas."

15.

ISOBEL DROVE HOME from the Monks' house at a crawl, because she'd drunk so much gin and tonic over bridge, and the road, I think, was playing tricks on her. Overhead, the sky was gray and troubled, and a few fat drops of rain smacked against the windshield. Isobel switched the wipers on and off and peered up to check the state of the clouds.

"Peaches, darling," she said. "Do you know what I hate most about the Island and everybody in it? Except you, I suppose."

"What's that?"

"Nobody ever says what they really mean. There is this vast fabric of tender little lies, and all the important things are unspoken. Boiling there underneath. We only bother telling the truth when it's too small to count."

"I don't think that's true at all."

"You haven't been here long enough. It's like a sport, it's the only real sport they know, and because I love sports I play them at their game, but I hate it. If I had my horses, now . . ."

"Why don't you?"

"There isn't room. Poor dears, they're on Long Island, getting fat." She paused to negotiate a sharp curve, surging and slowing the Plymouth as if she couldn't decide her approach. She was a wholly different driver when drunk, I thought, and as I watched the bony grip of her hands on the wheel, fighting the turn, I wondered if I should offer to take over. Before I could work up the nerve, she straightened out the car and said, "Don't you ever miss Foxcroft?"

I turned my head to stare out the window at the meadow passing by, the occasional driveway marked by stone pillars. The air was growing purple with some impending downpour, and I felt its approach in my gut. "I haven't been gone long enough."

"I do. When I was there, I couldn't wait to leave. All those books and rules and studying. But now I think, at least there was something new every day. Here, everything's the same. The same damned summer, over and over, the same day, the same people, the same small talk, the same small sports and parlor games and lies, of course. There's no escape."

"It's only a few months. Sometimes it's nice to spend a few months doing nothing."

"But then in September we go back to the city and do nothing there. What *hope* is there? Tell me, Miranda. I really want to know."

I turned to stare at her sharp profile, and for the first time I noticed a tiny bump along the bridge of her nose, as if she'd broken it some time ago. "You might have gone to college," I said.

"That's just putting off the inevitable. Beside, I'm not like you. Books bore me. All your Shakespeare and Dickens and old men like that. Marriage is going to bore me even more." She opened the window a few inches and tossed her spent cigarette into the draft. "My God, I should've been born ten years earlier."

"Why?"

"Why, because of the war. I'd have trained as a nurse or a Resistance agent, I'd have been splendid at that. I'd have made some use of myself, some purpose. It would have transformed me. I'd never have been the same, I would have had no tolerance at all for this." She waved her hand at the Island. "I don't understand how everybody could come back from the war and just sit there with a gin and tonic and play bridge. God, what a drag. It's like they've all gone to *sleep*."

"Because it wasn't an adventure, Isobel. It was hell. People died."

"Oh, that's right. I'm sorry. Your father." She paused respectfully. We had reached the Greyfriars drive, and she began to slow in preparation for the turn. Another handful of raindrops smacked the windshield. The drive was bordered with giant, mature rhododendrons, transported at great cost from the mainland—Isobel had told me how much as we drove away this morning—so that you couldn't see the house until you rounded the last curve, so that you found yourself straining and straining as you approached your destination. Now Isobel drove even more slowly, a walking pace, while I checked the sky and the windshield and clenched the muscles of my abdomen.

Isobel waited until she began the last turn before she continued. "Still. You'd think they couldn't stand all this shallow hypocrisy, after what they'd been through. And yet they embrace it. They want it to stretch on into infinity, never changing, never deviating one square inch from the old, dull, habitual ways. Marrying suitable boys you don't really love, having children you don't really want. I tell you, I can't stand it any longer. I'm about to explode, Miranda, but nobody knows it yet. Nobody but you. Just watch. I'm going to . . ."

Her sentence drifted off, as if she'd lost her train of thought. I looked up and followed her gaze, and at first I saw nothing amiss, nothing out of order. Greyfriars rambled before us in its immaculate, elegant way, not a window out of place, gray shingle meeting white trim and green lawn. The grass, the young trees, the rosebushes, the neatly fenced kitchen garden, the tall boxwoods guarding the swimming pool—all these features as tidy as money could make them. Only the gathering rhythm of the rain disturbed the expensive Fisher tranquillity.

Then I noticed the front door, which was open, and the person leaning against the doorway, smoking a cigarette attached to a long black holder. A woman wearing a magenta dress, a towering hairdo, and a large white flower pinned above her right ear.

"My God. Who's that?" I asked.

Isobel switched off the ignition and rested her arms on the top of the steering wheel. A prolonged rumble of thunder shook the windows. The woman straightened from the doorway and beckoned us with her cigarette in its holder.

In a voice of wonder, Isobel said, "It's my mother."

16.

"CALL ME ABIGAIL," the Countess said, as I stumbled over her foreign title, which I couldn't quite remember. "Everybody else does. Even my children."

"Do they really?"

"Just watch." She turned to Isobel, who had hung behind me as we raced across the gravel and ascended the steps in the gathering deluge, and now rolled her eyes as her mother embraced her dripping body. "Hello, darling. You look as beautiful as ever, of course. Except you really must eat more. People who don't eat are simply boring, and it's far better to be fat than boring, believe me."

"Hello, Abigail," Isobel said. "What a delightful surprise."

Up close, the Countess was even more extraordinary than from across the driveway. There was nothing dainty about her. She was tall and broad-shouldered, and her dress of magenta silk billowed down her heavy bones to sweep the ground, interrupted only by a sash at her waist, which— somewhat contradicting her earlier injunction—was not fat but certainly sturdy. She wore several glittering necklaces and her hair, swept up in a pompadour, had already turned silver, though her face was still smooth. I think it hardly needs saying that her lipstick was the same color as her dress, and that a glass of gin and tonic rested in her other hand—the one not occupied with cigarettes—bearing a neat half-crescent of said lipstick on its rim. When she turned, as she did now, leading us from the foyer and down the hall, she revealed a narrow, gathered cape of magenta silk that drifted from the swooping neck of her gown to form a train behind her.

"I've taken the liberty of reserving a table at the Club for dinner," she said, over her shoulder, "but that's not for ages, so I've ordered tea on the terrace."

"I expected nothing less."

"I've taken my old room, of course, which doesn't seem to be occu-pied. Where has all the staff gone, darling? We used to have three times as many housemaids running around. I had to shout for help, and I dis-like shouting. It's barbaric."

"Housemaids don't grow on trees anymore, Abigail," Isobel said, walking past her mother to burst through the doors to the terrace, where a table and chairs had been arranged under the shelter of the porch while the rain poured beyond. A newspaper and a jeweled cigarette case lay next to the tea tray, and Isobel snatched up the case and flipped it open. "You can't imagine how much servants cost. Especially on the Island."

"In France, they're dirt cheap. Everything's dirt cheap. You ought to move there with me, as I've told you a thousand times."

Isobel lit her cigarette and turned. "My French is terrible, Abigail."

The Countess snorted and turned to me. "Tell me about yourself, dear. You're Francine's daughter, of course. Lovely Francine, I couldn't ask for a better wife for Hugh."

"She's a dear," Isobel said.

The Countess waved her hand at Isobel. "No. I want to hear from Miranda. You and me, we have a way of drowning out other women who aren't as self-absorbed. And Miranda's not self-absorbed, are you, darling?"

"She is," Isobel said, "just in a different way. But everybody's self-absorbed in his own way. Being charitable is just its own form of self-absorption."

"Quiet!" thundered her mother, and Isobel plopped onto a wicker chair and gave me a droll look.

"I don't know what to say, actually," I said. "What do you want to know?"

"What do you like to do, child? What do you like to read?"

"Shakespeare," supplied Isobel.

The Countess whipped around. "Go inside. Just go inside. Or else remain absolutely, positively silent."

Isobel lifted her hand, zipped her lips, and stuck a cigarette between them.

The Countess turned back to me. "I apologize. I'm afraid I had very little to do with her upbringing, which was not my choice. Now it's too late. And you're laughing at us, how despicable. Not that I blame you."

I collapsed on another of the wicker chairs. "I'm sorry."

"No, don't apologize. You must never apologize unless absolutely necessary, although if you *must* apologize, do it properly. You like Shakespeare, do you?"

"Among other things."

"What other things? Speak up, I can't hear you above all that deluge."

I raised my voice. "Books. Art."

"Yes, but *which* books? *Which* art? This is terribly important. Do you prefer the Greeks or the Romans?"

"The Greeks."

"Middle Ages or Renaissance?"

"Renaissance, but I like some bits of the Middle Ages. The Plantagenets."

"Yes! Brutal but decisive, most of them. Chock full of sex appeal. I approve. Trollope or Dickens?"

"Trollope."

"Chinese art or Japanese?"

"Japanese."

"Verdi or Wagner?"

"Verdi. I can't bear Wagner's women. He doesn't understand them."

"What about Isolde?"

"She's only there to exalt Tristan."

"Brünnhilde?"

"That's the exception. The only woman he actually makes wiser than the men. Except she ends up dead like the others. At least the music is revolutionary."

The Countess turned to Isobel. "There, you see? I'll bet I've found out more about her in two minutes than you've discovered in all those years at school."

Isobel gestured to her lips.

"You may speak."

"I was just going to say that I don't give a damn about any of those things."

The Countess frowned. "Why are you wearing that awful suit?"

"This? Because we went to church this morning, Peaches and I."

"*Peaches?*"

"That's her nickname. I gave it to her."

"But why *ever?*"

"Because she's sweet and round and delicious, of course. Just look at her."

The Countess spun back to study me. She gave the business her whole attention, crossing her left arm under her breasts and propping her right elbow on the knuckles while she sucked thoughtfully on her cigarette. I tried to decide whether she was beautiful or not—certainly her face had the symmetry of beauty, the shapely eyes—but really she was something else. Not handsome or pretty or attractive, something beyond description, so that she held your attention, your dumbstruck admiration, without the slightest effort. *Striking*, that's the closest word. You could say she was striking.

As she studied me studying her, she didn't give any sign of what she was thinking, or what conclusions she drew from whatever figure I presented to her, in my ragged hair and ill-tailored suit and sunburnt face. The cigarette languished and died. She plucked the stub from the holder and tossed it into the ashtray and said to her daughter, "Whatever she is, she's certainly not *Peaches*. Are we absolutely certain you're mine, darling? It's impossible to believe I've borne a daughter with so little penetration."

Isobel sprang from her chair and stalked to the French doors. "I'm going to take a shower and change clothes. Are you coming, Peaches?"

"She's not answering to *Peaches* anymore," called back the Countess. "I forbid it."

Isobel didn't pause, and I rose and followed her, because I did need to bathe and change before dinner, there was no question of that. As I passed the Countess, she took me gently by the elbow.

"Before dinner," she whispered, "we've got to talk."

17.

"DON'T DO IT," said Isobel. "Don't let her pounce on you. She will, you know. She's a terrible pouncer." Isobel made claws with her hands as she paced across my bedroom floor in her bathrobe, smoking fiercely.

"Why not? I like her."

"Oh, everybody adores Abigail. That's how she does it. Look." She stopped and spun to me. "I need you to do me a favor, Peaches. A really big favor."

"A favor? What kind of favor? Don't I have to get dressed for dinner?"

She glanced at her wristwatch. "You've got an hour. I need you to go into the village, quick-quick. It's only a mile. You've got to go to the harbor and deliver a little message for me."

"Can't you do it yourself?"

"No, stupid child. I can't do it myself. *She's* watching me." Isobel pointed her finger straight down to the rug and the floorboards beneath, presumably in the direction of her mother.

I was curled up on the window seat in my own bathrobe, my knees pulled up to my chin, my arms wrapped around my legs, still damp from bathing. As soon as I'd emerged from the bathroom, Isobel yanked me down the hall to my room and closed the door and began her pacing, and I contracted into this little ball in which I now found myself, like one of those insects. If I could've grown a shell, I would have, because Isobel's skin positively radiated waves of reckless, crackling electromagnetic energy, and I knew they meant trouble for yours truly. I turned my head and glanced out the window, where the Fleet Rock lighthouse perched atop the water, washed in some kind of unearthly light as the rain sheeted away to the east.

"Yes, that's right," Isobel whispered.

"What's right?"

She darted forward and knelt before me, clutching my knees. "Joseph. I need you to give him a message."

"Oh, Isobel—"

"Please, Peaches. *Darling* Peaches. You know why she's here, don't you? She's my chaperone."

"Of course she is. She's your mother, isn't she?"

Isobel's fingers dig into my skin. "Listen to me. She hates Joseph. She hates all of them, the Vargases."

"Surely she doesn't hate them?"

"Oh, she does. She does. It's why they divorced, don't you know that? One of the reasons, any way. She's the worst kind of snob, the old-money kind, and she hated seeing me play with Joseph when I was little because he's not the right sort, is he? A lobsterman's son. So when Daddy went away one summer, just before the war, she forbade me to play with him, forbade Joseph to come here, and when Daddy came home and found out, he absolutely blew up, and that's when she left him. And I *know* that's why she's here now. I know it."

"But that's ridiculous."

"Oh, it isn't. Believe me. You have no idea, Peaches, no idea what bigots they are. She tried to get me to leave with her, but I wouldn't. I put my foot down. I wasn't going to give him up."

I released my arms from around my legs, forcing her hands away. She rose quickly and stepped back, but her wide, excited eyes didn't leave my face. "The thing is," I said, "aren't you engaged to marry someone else?"

"It's not that, Peaches. It's the principle. I'm taking a stand, that's all." She stuck her hand in the pocket of her bathrobe and brought out a piece of folded paper. "Just give him that, all right? He's down in the harbor right now, waiting for his mother to come out of church so he can take her home in the boat."

I looked down at the paper in her shaking hand. "Can't you just telephone him?"

"Abigail will overhear. She'll pick up the extension in the library."

"Then deliver the note yourself!"

"She'll see me leaving. She'll see me headed for the harbor and stop me."

"So what? You're all grown-up. You can take a stand, like you said."

"She'll find a way to punish me for it, believe me. She's marvelously subtle, our Abigail. She'll say something to the Monks."

"Well, shouldn't she? If you're running around behind Clay's back?"

Isobel's arm dropped. "Why, Miranda Schuyler. What a prig you are. You're no better than *she* is, aren't you? Girls should be locked up and spied on, it's for their own good, gracious me, God *forbid* the precious flower should speak to a boy she isn't married to, especially if he's some dirty Catholic boy—"

I snatched the paper from her hand. "All right. Just this once. But I don't like it, Isobel, not one bit. Not because he's a lobsterman, but because it's sneaky, it's dishonest."

"I know, I'm terrible." She enfolded me in an enormous embrace. "You're such a darling for putting up with me. I can't tell you how grateful I am."

I stared over her shoulder at the pastel wall, the framed watercolor exactly above the bed on the right and the matching watercolor above the one to the left. Her cigarette still burned from between her fingers, perilously close to the pale pink fluff of my bathrobe. The scent made me sick, or maybe it was something else. Maybe I was already sick.

"Just this once," I said.

Isobel pulled back and held me by the shoulders. "Just this once," she promised, in a voice so sincere I knew it was a lie.

18.

I FOUND JOSEPH right away, reading a book from a puddle of sunshine on the bow deck of a sailboat. The same sailboat, I imagined, he'd taken about the Island earlier that afternoon. I said his name and he scrambled upright, brushing his hair with his hand.

"I'm sorry. I didn't mean to startle you."

"Not at all." He glanced over my shoulder, across the street fronting the harbor. "Are you—what are you doing here? Don't you have dinner at the Club or something?"

"Not for another hour." I had all these words, all these clever things I was going to say to him. I'd worked out my lines as I walked down West Cliff Road toward the harbor, jumping over the pockets of mud and water left behind by the squalls, and now I couldn't remember a single one. So I just pulled Isobel's note from the pocket of my cardigan and said, "Here. This is for you."

He reached forward and took it. "What's this?"

"From Isobel."

He glanced up at me. "From Izzy? What's it about?"

I shrugged. "How should I know? She asked me to bring it to you. Her mother just arrived and she couldn't get away herself."

"I see." He still held the book in his left hand, folded over his thumb to mark his place. From this angle, I couldn't see the title, and I didn't want to act as if I were curious. He was frowning at me, and I tried not to frown back, but the intent quality of his gaze started the blood to rise up my throat and into my cheeks. I shoved my hands in my pockets and started to turn.

"Well, goodbye then," I said.

"Wait! I mean, does she want some kind of reply?"

"She didn't say."

"So hold on a minute." He scrambled down from the bow and set down the book. I glanced at the cover and saw it was *A Handbook of Practical Ship-Building*. I hadn't lied to him; I really didn't know what Isobel wrote to him. I told myself I was just being honorable and decent, not reading other people's private messages, but the truth was I didn't want to know. Had no desire to see the words inscribed on that page in Isobel's dashing handwriting. Even now, I waited miserably as Joseph read the note, as he stood there in the middle of the sailboat, perfectly balanced against the gentle lapping of the water, holding Isobel's sentences between his fingers. Instead of looking at his face, I stared with fascination at his neck and the intersection of his white collar and tanned skin. He swallowed briefly, and his Adam's apple slid up and down. "All right," he muttered. "All right."

"Can I go now?" I asked. "I've got to walk back to Greyfriars so I can change for dinner."

"I can drop you off on my way back to the lighthouse. Mama's coming out of church any minute."

"No, thanks. I'll walk."

"Are you headed to the Club to eat?"

"Yes."

"When will you be back?"

"I don't know. Ten o'clock, maybe?"

Joseph folded up the note and stuck it in the pocket of his trousers. His Sunday trousers, I supposed, tan and neatly creased, topped by a white shirt and starched collar and no tie. The kind of clothes you wore to take your mother to afternoon Mass, even if you weren't going inside the church yourself, but lying back in the sunshine to read about shipbuilding and to intercept clandestine letters from your lady friend.

"Tell her it's all right with me," he said. "If you don't mind, that is."

"What's all right?"

He lifted his chin and looked out across the harbor, toward the dark line of the Connecticut shore on the western horizon. His eyes squinted, and his face caught the full sunshine of late afternoon. "What she said in the note," he said, and looked at me. "You'll tell her that?"

"Sure." I turned away. "Have a nice evening."

"Miranda, wait. Is everything okay?"

"Sure it is."

"You look frosted. Are you sore at me?"

"I'm not sore."

"It's no trouble, is it?"

"No trouble at all. Enjoy your book. It's one of my favorites."

"Thanks, I will." He glanced at the cover and grinned. "One of your favorites, huh?"

"To each his own."

"Kind of an obsession, I guess. You've got your Shakespeare and your imagination, I've got the sea." The unexpected warmth in his voice held me there on the dock, not moving, while the sun struck my back. The rains had cleared the atmosphere, had cleared the air of haze and heat. A breeze touched my hair. I heard him say my name, like a question.

"I'm sorry. I've really got to get going, or they'll wonder where I am."

"You're sure I can't take you back?"

I thought, *I won't turn.* Anyway, I knew how he looked, standing there in his slim little sailboat, one foot braced on the side, wearing his good Sunday clothes. I wondered why he didn't go to afternoon Mass with his mother, and waited instead on his sailboat, studying shipbuilding. As I wondered this, I noticed a delicate, black-clad woman making her way down Hemlock Street from the direction of the white church on the corner, and I pinned my gaze in fascination upon her figure. She wore something on her head, a hat that was not quite a hat, and a black veil that trembled in the breeze, as if she'd come from a funeral.

"That's Mama," said Joseph. "You're sure? I can have you home in a jiffy. The wind's just right."

"No, thank you."

I started back down the dock, moving quickly so I wouldn't be obliged to stop and speak to Mrs. Vargas. She seemed to have the same reluctance. She slowed her pace a tiny degree, so I was stepping off the dock in the opposite direction while she was still a dozen yards away. I waved nonetheless, to be polite. She stared at me and nodded, and I thought her face was a little like Queen Victoria's, only not as plump: round and dour, hung with some pious, deep-felt grief.

19.

WE WENT TO dinner and came home a little drunk—naturally the Countess's arrival at the Club had caused the kind of excitement ordinarily reserved for foxes on the fairway, or lobster thermidor on the menu, and everybody came up to greet her, a blur of faces and names made fuzzier by all those bottles of vintage champagne the Countess kept ordering to toast them. So we were drunk, as I said, deliberately on my part, and Isobel made a great show of going to bed, but I wasn't fooled. I sat awake reading until I heard the infinitesimal creak of her door, the faint disturbance of the back staircase, and I laid aside my book and went to the window.

Of course, there was nothing but shadows, except for the regular sweep of the Fleet Rock lighthouse. But during one of those brief flights of light, I thought I saw a boat moored at the end of the Fisher dock, and I thought I saw two people embracing on the bench near the water's edge.

But it might have been a trick of my eyesight, seeing the thing it expected to see. The mind's funny that way. In any case, I couldn't say for certain, and I rose from the window because I didn't really want to know. I didn't want to know the answer.

1969 (MIRANDA THOMAS)

1.

I DON'T REMEMBER much about that first month back at Greyfriars, not until the morning of what would have been my mother's eighteenth wedding anniversary with Hugh Fisher, if my stepfather had still been alive.

I didn't especially want to sleep in my old bedroom at Greyfriars, but Mama insisted. An elderly watercolorist named Brigitte occupied one bed, and Mama convinced her to allow me the other one, the one I used to sleep in. *It's the best I can do for you, Miranda*, she told me, and I tried to explain that I would much rather sleep by myself in one of the smaller, northwest-facing bedrooms—the ones that didn't overlook the Fleet Rock lighthouse, say—but she closed her ears in that particular way of mothers, and I was stuck with Brigitte and a vista most people would kill for.

But maybe that was no better than I deserved, no more than I'd asked for when I returned to Greyfriars as I had, clandestine and without explanation, like some kind of fugitive. In any case, Brigitte was deaf and had no interest in cinema at all, no regard for actors and fame and gossip, so she kept an amicable silence and never asked a single awkward question. Nor did the sea view trouble me in those early weeks. For most of May the weather was so terrible, rain after rain, you couldn't see much of the lighthouse, except for the dull, long beam of the light itself. These were mercies, and I was grateful for them. But the fourth of June dawned clear, and the pink glitter of the sunrise woke me in a strange, unquiet mood. I listened to the gentle rumble of Brigitte's snore until I couldn't stand it any longer and slipped free from the worn white bedspread, the sagging mattress, to make my way to the window and a sight that puzzled me.

There was the lighthouse, of course. Your eyes couldn't help going straight to the lighthouse, sticking up out of that plucky, rocky little island, its white walls all pink with dawn. The tide hung low, exposing the underside of the rocks, and in that flat, uncertain light, a lobster boat seemed to draw away from the ramshackle dock that lay in the lee of the narrow, vicious channel between Winthrop Island and Fleet Rock.

I suppose my heart stopped, or something like that. Certainly I felt the shock right in my chest, right where everything vital lives, and I couldn't seem to move. The boat churned quickly to the west, pulling a delicate white wake behind its stern, and as the distance grew between vessel and lighthouse, the life returned to me. I dove for the shelf where I used to keep a pair of binoculars, but of course the binoculars were no longer there, and I went from drawer to shelf to cabinet, searching desperately for binoculars, telescope, anything. In all the fuss, Brigitte woke and demanded to know what was the matter.

"Nothing," I said, though I knew she couldn't hear me. Like I said, she was mostly deaf. I went back to the window, but of course the boat was gone. Not even the foam of its passing remained, and I wondered if I had simply imagined it. A hallucination, a ghost, because it was the fourth of June, after all, the anniversary of my mother's wedding to Hugh Fisher.

2.

THERE WAS NO going back to bed after all that, so I put on my bathing suit and went to the pool to swim before breakfast, as I did every morning, even in inclement weather. When I first met my husband, he informed me—in that kind, embarrassed voice of an Englishman telling you an intimate fact—that I needed to lose ten pounds for the camera, and in order to help me achieve this feat he drew up a regular program of exercise that I'd maintained ever since, even while pregnant. I did this not to please him, but because it gave me a strength I thought I'd lost, a strength I couldn't find elsewhere. I liked swimming most. I felt fleet in the water, weightless, without substance. I felt as if I had distilled myself back to the essential Miranda. I felt as if I were eighteen again, and a boy I worshipped was leaning in close to kiss me.

This was especially true inside the swimming pool at Greyfriars, which was filled—now as before—with salt water, not that chlorinated stuff they call fresh. How I relished the pungent, saline tang. I counted off thirty laps, long and steady, and I was just pausing at one end, considering the position of the sun in the sky and wondering if I ought to add on another five, maybe ten, when I noticed the tall, blond fellow who stood by the cabana in his swimming trunks, arms crossed against his bare chest, observing me.

"Excuse me," I said. "Am I in your way?"

He unfolded his arms and walked toward me. He had a tremendous young physique, a sturdy, masculine skeleton not quite filled out, limbs straight and golden, and he was smiling. I adjusted the side of my bathing cap and summoned my dignity.

"It's Miranda, isn't it?" he said, coming to kneel by the pool's edge, about three yards away. A respectful distance, and yet familiar.

"I'm afraid I don't know whom you mean."

"Aw, Miranda. It's me." He held out his hand. "It's your brother. It's Hugh."

3.

I REMEMBER EXACTLY where I was when I first learned I had a baby brother. I knew he was arriving, of course—or rather *it*, I knew *it* was arriving—but still I felt a shock when the Countess laid the newspaper on my breakfast tray and pointed to the relevant item. We were staying in Paris at the time, the Ritz. It was the end of March and the weather outside the window was bleak and terrible, and I'd caught a nasty cold on the liner. Hadn't been out of bed since we arrived, almost. I remember the soft sheets and the elegant blues and yellows of the room, and the Countess's anxious face as she watched me read the few lines.

> To Mrs. Hugh P. Fisher of Winthrop Island, New York, and the late Mr. Hugh P. Fisher, a boy, Hugh Percival Fisher, Junior, at the Rhode Island Hospital in Providence, Rhode Island.

"It's a boy," she said, quite unnecessarily.

"My brother," I said, in the throaty, rough voice of a bad cold.

She took the newspaper back. "I hope everything went well. It doesn't say anything about their health, mother and baby."

"And they're not going to tell us, are they? Isobel or Mama."

The Countess folded the newspaper, refilled my coffee cup, and kissed my forehead. "I'll find out the details, don't you worry. Just rest and get better."

I drank my coffee and sat back on the pillow and thought about this new fact, this new human being, squalling in some bassinet across the ocean, who belonged to me. It didn't seem real. Maybe because I was sick, maybe because I had endured so much in the previous seven months, calamity after calamity, until I was simply numb. I could not seem to create a place for him in my brain, in my heart, this living bundle of humanity. He was a theory. My brother, Hugh Fisher Junior. Of course they named him after my stepfather; they could hardly name him anything else, after what happened. I wondered what he looked like and what kind of personality he had, what kind of man he would be. I remember turning my head to gaze at the rain crawling down the window, the gray Paris landscape beyond, and wondering if I would ever find out.

And now here he was. *This* was what he looked like, this was who he was. A living human being. A teenager.

I lost my grip on the pool's edge and flailed to right myself. Hugh dove forward and caught my arm and sort of slid into the pool right next to me. A silly young grin split his face.

"Sorry to sneak up on you like that," he said. "I only just got back last night."

"Got back from where?" I gasped.

"School. St. Paul's. You knew that, didn't you? I know you and Mom write letters."

"Of course I knew that. I understand—I understand you're doing well there."

"One more year to go."

"My goodness. I suppose so. You're—you're seventeen now."

He leaned forward and kissed my cheek. "Nice to meet you, sister. If you don't mind my saying so, you look a hell of a lot different inside a swimming pool than you do on screen."

"Oh my goodness," I said. "*Hugh.*"

"Aw, don't cry. It's all right."

There was absolutely no way to embrace him, as I clung to the crumbling stone edge of the Greyfriars swimming pool, mastering my shock. For some reason, I still pictured my brother as a kid, about eight years old, grinning and towheaded as he appeared in one of the photographs Mama dutifully sent me, once we had begun to write to each other again. Now the white hair had darkened to gold, and only the grin remained of the picture in my head.

"Now you're getting it," he said, rubbing away a tear from my cheek. "Take a deep breath."

"You look like your father."

"So they tell me. C'mon, let's get out of the water." He turned and stroked to the ladder. I watched his confident arms and my eyes began to sting again, so I launched myself after him before I could think, I followed him in a daze, took his hand to help me up, and at last our arms went around each other, an embrace that would have been awkward if Hugh hadn't hugged quite so tight, so wholehearted, as if I really were his long-lost sister.

Well, Christ. *I was*, I thought. *I am*.

"Can't believe it," he said, pulling away to beam at me. "Mom didn't say anything. It was Isobel. She said I could go down to the pool this morning, they'd filled it up finally."

"*I* filled it up," I said.

"Did you? Hasn't been filled in years. Not since the Fisher stock stopped paying dividends. Mr. Monk told Mom she oughta sell out before the whole company went belly-up, but she wouldn't." He picked up a towel from one of the lounge chairs and tossed it at me, and then he proceeded to the cabana to fetch himself a towel of his own. "Anyway, Isobel had the old gleam in her eye, if you know what I mean, so I figured something was up. As soon as I saw you, I knew what it was."

"I thought you said I looked different offscreen."

"Well, you do, but you're still Miranda Thomas, you know? Nobody else like you, especially around here. You've got that glow."

"That's just the makeup they give you."

"No, it's not." He whistled as he toweled himself off. "The fellows at school don't believe me when I tell them you're my sister. Just wait till I—"

"No! You can't tell them."

"What's the matter?"

I laid my finger on my lips. "I'm not here."

Up went his eyebrows. "Ah! I got you. Incognito. What about the rest of the Island, though? Don't they know you're here?"

"I haven't been out yet. I've stayed at Greyfriars."

"Well, I guess if you wanted to hide out somewhere, you couldn't find a better place. Still. No one's going to tell if you head to the Club for dinner or something. This *is* the Island, after all."

"Do you still belong to the Club? I thought—"

"Mom keeps up the membership somehow, though she never goes."

"Oh. Of course. I should've known she would." I tucked the towel around the top of my breasts and sat down on one of the chairs, while Hugh lit himself a cigarette from the pack he seemed to have fetched from the cabana, along with his towel. "Should you be smoking that, at your age?"

"Aw, you won't tell, will you?"

"That depends."

He waggled the pack at me. "Want one?"

"No, thank you. They're bad for your health."

Hugh flung himself on the neighboring lounge chair. "Everything's bad for your health. You might as well live a little. Anyway, I don't do it that often. Just sneak a couple, here and there. What's the matter?"

"I can't believe it's you, that's all. I can't believe you're sitting there."

"Neither can I. I mean, I can't believe *you're* sitting there. Look at you, in the flesh. And I just hugged you."

"You were just a theoretical brother. Your mother and I—"

"*Our* mother, sis."

"We fell out for a few years, around the time you were born. As you know."

"Yeah, I know. At least you patched things up a little. Passed the old olive branch between you. And now you're here." He turned on his side, and he looked so much like his father in that instant, smiling and golden, it shocked me. I had to curl my fingers into my palm, the way I did sometimes, on camera or at home, when I thought I could no longer bear the strain of everything.

"I'm here," I said.

"And I'm here. And Mom, and Isobel, and all the dear old crazies with their easels and pottery wheels. So maybe we can pretend to be a real family, for once. At least for the summer, anyway."

"We *are* a real family." I reached out and touched his arm. "It's wonderful to meet you at last, Hugh Fisher Junior. In the flesh."

"Same to you, Miranda. Miranda Thomas. My famous sister."

"Oh, that. It's just a show, Hugh. Just some stupid films."

"Not stupid at all. It's how I got to know you. I've seen your movies about a million times, you know that?"

I turned away and pulled my legs up to my chin. Above the boxwoods, the sky was fresh and blue, absent of any clouds. "That's not really me, Hugh. We'll have to do better than that."

"Well, it was the best I could do at the time. I thought about writing, but then I figured—I didn't want to bother you or anything—just some fan of yours . . ."

"Hugh, my God. You're not—you're my *brother*. I'd have been delighted, I really would. I wish you had. I'd have written too, but I thought—well, Mama . . ."

"Yeah. Mom."

"She's done a wonderful job raising you. I can see you've grown into a fine boy."

"That's what they tell me." He voiced deepened. *"You're a fine young man, Hugh Fisher, a credit to your father."*

I turned my head and saw that he was still looking at me, or maybe beyond me, past the top of my forehead to land on the boxwoods, or the cabana, or the ragged rooftops of Greyfriars looming above all. He had a certain faraway expression. My God, he was handsome. I thought I was used to handsome, I was used to men whose looks arrived from some different universe, some territory of the gods, like Valhalla, but young Hugh Fisher might have had them all beat, and he was just seventeen.

I reached over the gap between us to pluck the cigarette from between his fingers and drop it on the paving stones. "Just leave off the cancer sticks, all right?"

Hugh rolled his lean blue eyes, in the way of teenagers everywhere, and flopped on his back to take in the sun. "Whatever you say, sis."

4.

I MUST HAVE dozed off, because I found myself startling awake, sometime later, to discover the empty chair by my side. According to the sun, only a short time had passed, and yet I had the disquieting feeling that I'd lost the entire morning somehow, that I had possibly dreamed the whole episode. That I had imagined Hugh as well, like the lobster boat at dawn. But when I looked down at the paving stone, I saw the spent cigarette lying there where I'd dropped it. I picked it up and ran my finger around the end, where his mouth had been, and I thought, *My brother.*

I rose from the chair and tossed the cigarette end into the hedge of enormous, overgrown boxwoods that enclosed the pool from view. Eighteen years ago—as I well remembered—those bushes had been trained into immaculate, square-edged perfection by a fleet of gardeners. Not one of those gardeners remained now. The green lawn, the fragrant roses, the careful perennial borders—all wilderness. I had spent my own money to fill this pool, to pay for the fellow who came once a week to clean it. One patch of cultivation existed, and that was a new patch altogether, a kitchen garden, where Mama and Isobel grew the vegetables and herbs that had once come from the grocer in town.

Imagine my surprise, then, when I emerged from the cabana, showered and dressed in my caftan, and discovered a small clutch of new June roses on the lounge chair, where just a moment ago I'd been sleeping.

5.

ALSO IN THE way of teenaged boys, Hugh Fisher slept all afternoon and woke at five o'clock, wanting to go to the Club for dinner and to see his friends.

"Certainly you may," said Mama, without looking up from her easel. "Are they expecting you?"

"'Course they are. It's summer, after all. Everyone's back on the Island." He bent and kissed the top of her head. "What're you painting?"

"That." She pointed her brush at Brigitte, who perched naked on the low stone wall bordering the terrace, clasping her arms around her legs, leaning her cheek against her bony knees. Brigitte, I should add, was about seventy years old, but she displayed not the slightest sign of embarrassment at her nakedness, as if her sagging, imperfect body did not belong to her at all, or else belonged to all women. Whereas I, in every photograph—not the films, mind you, just the photographs—felt the weight of the camera lens like a brand against each precious inch of exposed skin.

Hugh peered at the canvas. "Not bad this time. The angle of her arm, that shadow. You need to work on her face, though."

"Faces are the hardest."

Hugh straightened and turned to me. The sun hadn't yet fallen behind the ridge of the Greyfriars roof, and he stood there like Apollo with his blond hair and his tanned face, bathed in light. Sometimes it's astounding, the inequitable distribution of genetic material, those fateful, chemical spirals locked in our cells, and the worst thing, or else the best thing, was that he had no idea. No conscious knowledge whatsoever that he, Hugh Fisher, had received such an unfairly vast largesse from nature while the rest of us made do with less. He just smiled, without guile. "Miranda? You coming?"

There was a shattering little silence. Even the two chattering sisters on the nearby lawn—oil paint, both of them—seemed to arrest their conversation, and in the quiet, I became aware that Brigitte was humming to herself: a wandering, tuneless tune. Isobel, on the other side of the terrace, looked up from her pile of knitting.

"*What* did you say, Hugh?"

"I thought Miranda should come to the Club with me for dinner tonight."

"Miranda? The Club?"

"Yeah, the Club. Where else can you go for dinner around here?"

"She can't," Isobel said. "Her bruises."

"What bruises?"

"On her face."

Hugh stared at me. "She hasn't got any bruises."

"Isobel's right," said Mama. "Of course Miranda can't go to the Club."

"Why not?"

I tucked my thumb into the crease of my book and said, "Because I'm persona non grata around here, don't you know that? I don't dare show my face inside the sacred walls of the Club."

"*Miranda*. Don't use that tone," said my mother.

"She *ought* to use that tone. It's stupid. Why shouldn't she go to the Club?"

"She's not a member."

"She's with me. She's my sister."

"For God's sake, Hugh. Give it a rest," said Isobel, picking up her knitting again. "She can't go, that's all. Maybe it's stupid. But people have long memories around here, and—well. It's the Club."

"To hell with them," said Hugh. "It happened eighteen years ago. It was before I was born. She was a kid. And anyway, I don't see what she did that was so bad."

"*Hugh*," snapped my mother. "He was your *father*."

"C'mon, I've read the old newspapers. I've read the transcripts. I don't get it. What's the big deal? She spent the night with a boy, that's all. It was 1951, not the Middle Ages. You can't blame her for what happened after."

"You don't understand," Isobel said.

Mama threw down her brush. "Do you know that the marshals were here again today? Asking about the Vargas boy?"

"Marshals?" I whispered, but nobody heard me.

Hugh made a noise of interest. "Were they, now? Any news?"

"No. But I'm sure they'll be knocking on all the other doors, disturbing the entire Island with their terrible questions, and Miranda's the last person anybody will want to see at dinner after *that* ordeal."

"Aw, Mom," said Hugh. "That's not fair. It's not *her* fault Vargas awarded himself an early release."

"Don't be flippant!"

I stood up. The world tilted, and then righted itself. I glanced out to sea—I couldn't help it—and toward Isobel, staring watchfully, and then my mother. "You're sure there's no news?" I said.

My mother pressed her lips together and frowned in Isobel's direction. "No news. There's no sign of him."

I breathed out slowly and smiled. "If you'll excuse me, I'll just go get dressed for dinner."

"Miranda!" my mother said, agonized.

"Hugh, you'll meet me at the front door in—oh, fifteen minutes?"

He jumped to attention and saluted me. "Right on."

On my way back inside, toward the one set of French doors that still opened properly, I crossed behind Mama. As I did, I turned my head to regard the canvas. Like all my mother's paintings, it was abstract and somewhat derivative, borrowing the perspective of a more original mind. Brigitte's body had been rendered in a series of blurred triangles, and the only clear detail was the line of numbers tattooed on her wrist, which Mama painted larger than life.

6.

HUGH FISHER MIGHT have inherited his father's thick, golden hair, but he wore it longer, looser, without all that pomade I remembered, and it tumbled around his head as we sped around the long, sunlit curves of Winthrop Road.

"So what was Isobel talking about back there?" he said. "The bruises, I mean."

"Nothing. It was nothing. I had a little accident just before I arrived, that's all."

"An accident, huh? What kind of accident?"

"A car accident."

"Jesus. Are you all right?"

"I am, obviously. All better now."

"Because if that husband of yours gave you those bruises, I'd—I'd knock his lights out."

"Well, the car gave me the bruises, and I'm afraid its lights are already knocked out."

"Jesus," he said again. "You *are* all right, aren't you?"

"Perfectly fine."

"And the husband? Where's he?"

"Back home in London, as far as I know."

"As far as you *know*?"

"I have a marvelous idea, Hugh. Let's talk about all your girlfriends, every single one."

He laughed. "That would be a short conversation."

"Not as short as this one."

Hugh whistled. "All right, all right. I can take a hint. Film director husband is off limits. At least until I can get you loaded enough to spill the beans."

"In which case I'll get you drunk enough that you don't remember a word I said."

"What? Gosh, Miranda, I'm not even eighteen yet. I might have to report you to the police for corrupting the morals of a minor."

"From what I've seen so far, there's not much left to corrupt."

"Aw, Miranda. Stop busting my chops."

"I'm your sister, darling. I'm supposed to bust your chops."

Hugh laughed—he seemed to have a sunny nature, my kid brother, God knew why—and reached over to land a swift pat on my knee. "You know what? I think I like it."

I made a noise of dismissal and crossed my legs, so that the knee he'd patted was covered over by the other. I wore a simple dress—simpler is always better, my husband used to tell me, and he was right about that—a short, well-cut sheath of sapphire blue and a pair of low matching heels, so the knees in question were bare. I'd hesitated upstairs before putting it on. Maybe the dress was too short for the Winthrop Island Club, maybe the Families weren't keeping up with the times. Maybe all the matrons would sneer at me, and all the debutantes would narrow their eyes. Well, they were going to do that anyway, weren't they? Might as well give them something to sneer at. I stared at the gray road ahead, pale in the late sunshine, and I thought I could taste the sea at the back of my throat.

"Do you ever think about it?" Hugh asked. "Or do you just push it out of your mind?"

"Think about what?"

"The murder," he said.

I closed my eyes and concentrated on the draft blowing past my cheeks. Hugh's car was a Ford convertible, ten years old, noisy and fast, most un-Island like. I wondered where he got it and how he'd paid for it. I turned the words over in my head—*the murder*—and I said, "You say that like it wasn't your own father."

"Well, I never met him, did I? I have his genes, that's all. I mean, I love him, I guess. The idea of him. But I didn't know him at all." He paused to shift gears. "How well did *you* know him?"

"Not very well. I only met him a few times, actually. When he was courting my mother, and then the wedding. Then they went away on their honeymoon and didn't come back until the end of the summer."

"When Vargas killed him."

I turned away to stare at the passing bushes, the young trees, far more of them than there were eighteen years ago. I'd mentioned this to Isobel a week or so ago, and she said that the seeds apparently blew in during the hurricane of 1938, that's what the scientists said, and now the new growth was finally starting to take hold and spread. One hurricane taketh away, and another hurricane giveth.

"Didn't he?" Hugh said. "Come on. Lay it on me. You were there at the lighthouse when it happened."

"I don't know. I was asleep. As you must know, if you read those transcripts."

"But were you really? Asleep? I always wondered."

"I testified under oath, didn't I?"

"But you were in love with him, right? So maybe you were trying to protect him. You *said* you were asleep, but you really saw everything."

"Who says that?"

He shrugged his shoulders. "Everyone around here. They say you nearly got him off. When you went public, gave all those interviews and said you didn't believe Vargas could have killed anyone, a lot of people believed you. You were pretty convincing, even then."

"Well, I didn't get him off, did I?"

"Only because he pled guilty."

I didn't reply.

"I'm sorry," said Hugh. "We can talk about something else. I'm just curious, that's all. I always wondered."

"Of course you did. He's your father."

"But you're not going to tell me any more?"

"I've already said everything that needs to be said," I told him, and I opened my pocketbook and put down the sun visor, so I could touch up my lipstick in the mirror. "Thanks for the roses, by the way. Where on earth did you find them?"

"Roses?" he said. "What roses?"

7.

THEY LOVE A little excitement at the Winthrop Island Club, and don't let them tell you any differently. When Hugh Fisher and I appeared at the entrance of the dining room, arm in arm—he insisted—you could see the disturbance pass from table to table, the way the waves ripple away when you drop a stone into a pond of still water. Quick, flickering glances and furtive words and turned shoulders, that kind of thing. People reached for their cocktails and drank.

Hugh leaned into my ear. "We're sitting with the Huxleys, by the way. Did I mention that?"

"Are you certain?"

"Mrs. Huxley telephoned to beg me an hour ago."

"But she didn't know I was coming too."

"I thought it would be a terrific surprise. Come along."

I kept my gaze straight ahead as I walked through that dining room, my arm linked with that of my sturdy young brother, the same way I might at a film premiere or an awards dinner, when everyone's catching a glimpse of you, everyone's examining the cut of your dress and your hair, the color of your lipstick, your posture, your stride, your cleavage, your everything. But this was different. You might encounter a little jealousy in those crowds, a dagger look or two, but the gazes are largely admiring, even worshipful, especially when your husband walks by your side, and he's their most revered of all gods, legend of all legends, whom nobody dares to cross.

The Families, on the other hand. The members of the Winthrop Island Club. That's a different crowd altogether, the toughest crowd in the world. I don't think a single one of my famous London friends could have got himself into the Club, not for a million dollars, and especially if he were so gauche as to actually *offer* a million dollars. And this brother of mine, Hugh Fisher Junior, he might possess a great deal of goodwill on the strength of his good looks and his tragic upbringing—the Families are nothing if not loyal to their own—but I knew and he knew that he was crossing an uncrossable line, as he escorted his notorious half sister into that dining room overlooking the magnificent links and the cliffs beyond, and the hazy blue sky of a June evening. The difference was, he was enjoying it.

I recalled that eighteen years ago, the Huxleys always ate at the table in the far northwest corner of the room, adjacent to the famous sixth hole, and I'll be damned if my brother didn't steer me in that direction now. Horses in a pasture couldn't have been more habitual, and indeed the fellow who lifted his martini glass as we approached, hiding an expression of horrified astonishment, had something of the look of a horse. Long face, large, dark eyes set a little too far apart. Rather like his sister, Livy.

"Hugh," he said helplessly, starting to rise, because I *was* a woman, after all, even if I was *that* woman.

"Mr. Huxley," said Hugh. "I've brought a little surprise with me. I hope you don't mind. My sister, Miranda. Miranda, Dick Huxley."

I held out my hand. "Of course. I remember Dick very well. You were just eleven or twelve when I last saw you, isn't that right?"

Dick looked at the woman who must have been his wife, and then he looked at me, and at last he reached out one shaking hand and touched mine, briefly. "Miss—Mrs.—"

"Just Miranda. We're all friends here, aren't we? Is this your wife?"

"Y—Yes. Candy. Candy, this is—this is—"

"I know who it is," the woman said coolly. She was slim and dark-haired, altogether too pretty for Dick Huxley, which meant she wasn't from one of the Families. She'd married in, I guessed, on the strength of her looks and her ambition. "How funny of you to bring her along tonight, Hugh. I'm not sure we have room at the table for her."

God, the nerve of her. I had to admire her nerve. I glanced around the table, which was large and round, laid for seven, one seat empty. I judged plenty of space between settings, but maybe the family liked its elbow room. There were four more Huxleys, two children and an older couple that I recognized instantly as the grayed, wrinkled versions of Dr. and Mrs. Huxley, Livy's parents. Mrs. Huxley was looking at her daughter-in-law, wearing an expression of faint approval, and Dr. Huxley was studying the ice in his gin and tonic. The children—aged just below their teens, a boy and a girl—were bouncing from their seats with excitement, bless them.

"Oh, look. Your lovely children." I bent down to look at them on their level, the way you absolutely must with young ones. "Do you know something? You're just about the age your father was, when I last saw him."

"You're Miranda Thomas, aren't you?" the girl said, in awe.

"Can I have your autograph?" asked the boy.

"*Children.*"

They snapped to attention. Candy Huxley had that look on her face, the rage of a betrayed mother, flushed cheeks and fierce eyes, and now I knew for certain she wasn't from one of the Families. They don't do rage, they don't do passion. They drink quietly, copiously, to wash it all out of their systems. I also knew that I wouldn't be forgiven for this small act of seduction, that I had just destroyed any chance of redemption, and maybe I'd done it on purpose. Maybe I wanted to drive myself out of the pale right away, a single stroke, so I wouldn't have to stalk across this damned dining room again in my life. And yet I had come here willingly.

I turned to Hugh. "Perhaps we might—"

"What, no room for my sister?" My brother looked directly at Candy. "I see plenty of room. There's always a place for family, isn't there, Dick?"

"Hugh, I think—"

"Dr. Huxley? Mrs. Huxley? I'm sure you remember my sister, Miranda. I'm sure you'd like to welcome her back, after all these years."

Mrs. Huxley's face turned to granite. Dr. Huxley frowned at my ear.

"I heard a story once," Hugh said, "I heard a story that you were one of the first people Miranda met on the Island, Dr. Huxley. I think Isobel told me. Old Mr. Silva fell off his boat and they brought him into my father's house, and you raced over to stitch him back together on the kitchen table."

"That was Joseph who saved Mr. Silva, you know," I said. "Dove into the water after he fell from his boat. Joseph Vargas."

The name dropped like a cannonball into the middle of that table, as I knew it would, and in that instant I realized that everyone around us had gone quiet, that a gargantuan silence filled that dining room as nothing had ever filled it before, at least in my brief experience there. Not a clink of glassware, not a nervy chuckle, not a single rheumy cough. Just the smell of perfume and cigarettes, just the strain of two hundred ears.

"Did he?" said Hugh. "Isobel didn't say. How about that."

Candy Huxley turned to her husband. "Dick. Say something."

Poor Dick. He fiddled with his napkin and babbled a little. "Now, Hugh, now—let's—you know, Hugh—the marshals were just here—and, uh—"

Hugh, who was more than a decade younger, displayed considerably more composure. He set his hand on Huxley's shoulder and said quietly, "Dick."

And I thought in that second that Hugh Fisher's son and namesake was maybe born for the wrong age, that he would have made an excellent army lieutenant, a leader of men, absolutely certain of himself at the moment of crisis. I thought that his father, whatever his faults, would be terribly proud of this young man, of whose existence he scarcely even knew before he died.

I touched my brother's elbow. "You stay and eat, Hugh. I'll just—"

"No, Miranda. You'll just what? Drive home alone? If there's one thing that makes me mad, it's a fellow who won't stand by a lady." He removed his hand from Huxley's shoulder and took my arm. "We'll both leave. Good night, *ladies. Gentlemen.*"

The words about groaned with irony, but before anybody could stiffen his back at this unspeakable slur, before Hugh could even steer me around for our departure, another voice reached us.

"Hugh Fisher. Look at you, young man. Back from school, are you?"

I tilted my head to regard the man before me, dressed in the eternal Club uniform of jacket and tie and slacks, and I knew he was familiar. I knew that face, that voice, and I can't really say why I didn't immediately recognize him.

He recognized me, however. He turned his bland, tanned face toward me and smiled broadly. Held out his hand and said, "Miranda Schuyler, as lovely as ever. You're always welcome at my table."

I took his hand, and the name came out before I even knew it. "Why, Clay! Clayton Monk. You haven't changed a bit."

8.

I CONSIDERED THIS little lie as we sat on the little stone bench overlooking the eighth hole green a couple of hours later, Clay and I, taking in the fragrant, salty twilight as we watched Hugh instruct Clay's pretty daughter Lucy on the art of sinking a long putt.

Because of course Clay had changed; everyone changes, and why would you want to stay the same? God knew *I* wasn't the same round, pink child who had stood on these links eighteen years ago to be kissed for the first time. And Clay? Clay was no taut war hero of twenty-six, pining for a wife. Clay had grown a bit of jowl, and his nose was starting to take on the rosy, middle-aged sponginess common to his tribe, and naturally he had put on weight around the middle. That longed-for wife now stood at the edge of the nearby green, dangling a cigarette, sipping a cocktail, observing their daughter's progress. And I don't mean the golf.

All the same, he was still a handsome fellow. He wore his age better than most of the men around here. Maybe he drank less, maybe he ate less. Maybe he spent more time exercising. He sat leaning forward, elbows on his knees, and smoked a quiet cigarette. The glass was empty on the bench next to him, but he hadn't gone for more. I gazed across the darkened course, made silver by the rising moon, and the monumental, rambling clubhouse to our right, and I thought that maybe I hadn't lied that much after all, that Clay remained the same in everything essential. Certainly the Club was the same, the Island itself had altered by not one hair in eighteen years. I said this aloud to Clay.

"I guess you're right," he said. "Summer after summer, we stick to our ways around here. It's our own world."

"That's the appeal of an island, I suppose. You get to evolve all by yourselves, like Madagascar. Or not evolve at all."

Clay gestured with his cigarette toward the nearby mansion. "That's going to change, though. Did you hear? We're finally going to build a new clubhouse."

"A new clubhouse? Why?"

"Well, look at it. It's a dinosaur. Too big, too grand, too expensive to keep up."

"Too expensive? Haven't you got all the money in the world?"

"Oh, we're just thrifty New Englanders at heart. That old place was never really our style. We're not Newport, after all. Nobody's here to show off."

"Still, it seems like a waste. It's not that old, is it? It only went up in the twenties. And didn't some famous architect design it?"

"Well, it's too late now. The contract's signed. At the end of the season, Tom Donnelly's going to knock it down and build us something smaller, a little less flashy. A family sort of place."

"I hope he's got a big enough wrecking ball. It's going to take weeks. Wouldn't it be easier just to blow it up?"

"Residents won't have it. It's in the contract, he's got to dismantle it piece by piece, without explosives or fire or wrecking balls or anything like that. He wasn't too pleased, but he wanted the contract." Clay paused to smoke. "A good man, Tom Donnelly."

"I never met him."

"He lives down at your end of the Island. A year-rounder. Does most of the construction work around here. People trust him."

I stared at the yellow-lit clubhouse, as gargantuan and indiscreet as they come, turrets and gables and half-timbering, a vast cliché of olde English vernacular, and I supposed he was right. It was the kind of architecture that pretended to old age, a false birth certificate, a pedigree where none existed, and the Islanders didn't need that kind of clubhouse. They had their own pedigrees.

Clay coughed and went on. "If you're thinking of making any repairs at Greyfriars while you're there—fixing the place up a bit, I mean—he's the right fellow to call. I'd be happy to introduce you. The house could use some work."

"Yes, I noticed."

"Your poor mother, left without any money. First the taxes on the estate, and the mortgages—she had to sell the New York apartment, not that she ever lived there—and then the Fisher company stock. I told her to sell it all, but she had this faith." He shook his head. "Hugh Fisher. He sure knew how to spend money, that fellow. Remember that damned yacht of his? Twenty crew, all on salary. That was the first thing she sold, after he died, and even that just went toward the tax bill."

"Were the taxes so bad?"

"Seventy-seven percent. She had to sell everything she could, and all she had left was the Fisher stock. She lived on the dividends until those went dry, and a year later the whole company went bankrupt, and she had just about nothing to live on. Terrible situation. We'd help out if we could, but she'd never take it. You, on the other hand."

"Me?"

"You could fix things up, while you're here. I think she'd appreciate it. She's done everything she could to hang on to Greyfriars, because of your father. She wants to keep it for young Hugh."

"It's going to cost an awful lot of money to fix up Greyfriars," I said. "It's fallen to pieces, almost."

"Well, but—I don't mean to be vulgar—but . . ."

"You can be vulgar with me, Clay. We're old friends."

"Well, surely money's no trouble. That husband of yours, he's made a lot of movies, hasn't he?"

"Ah. Yes, of course," I said. "He certainly has."

"I'd be happy to put you in touch with Donnelly. He's a good man."

"Please do."

"It would give you something to do while you're here. A project. I know we're a little dull here on the Island, for a movie star like you."

I returned my attention to the three figures on the green, and to Clay's wife, languid in the moonlight. She was not beautiful, too long-nosed and sharp-boned, but she didn't need to be beautiful, did she?

"So you married Livy Huxley," I said. "I hadn't heard."

"Yes, I did. Sixteen years now, can you believe it?"

"No, I can't. I really can't."

There was a terrible pause. Livy's giggle carried across the grass, Hugh's patient murmur.

Clay said, "Well, a fellow's got to marry somebody." He paused lengthily, while we both digested the meaning in that sentence, and whether it required further explanation, and whether I had a right to hear that explanation. Apparently he decided I did, because when he spoke again, his voice had lowered to a burr. "I waited a year for Izzy to come around, but she didn't. She wouldn't. Then Livy—I don't know. After a while, it just seemed right. We've been happy. She's been a good wife, a good mother."

"You have two other daughters, isn't that right? I think that's what she said."

"Yep. Jacqueline and Barbara. They're back home with the nanny. Livy doesn't want them having dinner at the Club until they're ready."

"That's sensible. We can't have kids running amok at cocktail hour."

He laughed briefly. "No, we can't. Anyway, the old guard's had enough excitement for one evening. Can you believe Dick Huxley? He's always been a damn sissy. That wife of his."

"It wasn't just Dick. They were all against us. *Me*, I should say."

"Not all of them. Maybe not even most of them. They're good people, you know, but when a few people set their minds against you—well." He lifted his cigarette. "Anyway, like I said, you're welcome at our table. Hugh's a solid young man. We've always liked him around here."

I looked across the ten or fifteen yards to the green, where Hugh was shaking his head, laughing, taking the club from Lucy's inept hands. I said, "He's a terrific kid. I wish I'd had the chance to know him sooner."

"You know, Miranda, I've looked on him like a son. I've tried to treat him like one. It's a bum hand he was dealt, and only the women to raise him. They sent him to the local school for years, until a few of us got up the nerve to—well, the thing is, we took up a collection. Don't tell your mother. She thinks it was a scholarship, that St. Paul's thought he showed a lot of promise—well, he *did*, he's a smart kid—but that wasn't it. We just didn't want him to fall through, you know? So he could go to the right school, meet the right people."

"Of course. The right people are so important."

"Don't, Miranda. Don't be like that. They're decent people. You never got to know them, that's all. Livy's dad, you know what he did? He was forty-five when the war started, and he convinced the army board to give him a commission. He spent two years in Europe, Miranda, two years. First as a battlefield medic, then a base hospital surgeon. Forty-five years old with a wife and kids, and he landed on the beaches on D-Day and spent the next forty-eight hours amputating arms and legs and whatever else. For two days he didn't sleep. He won't talk about it, but it's true."

"I didn't know that."

"You have to understand how shook up people were, when it happened. What happened to your stepfather, I mean. And there you were, giving interviews, talking publicly about the whole thing. Defending Vargas."

"I was only telling the truth. I only wanted justice."

"You don't think he killed Mr. Fisher?"

"I didn't say that. I just think—whatever happened, it wasn't Joseph's fault. It couldn't have been."

"Whatever happened." Clay finished his cigarette and crushed it out carefully on the bench, dropped the stub in the empty glass. Bad form to leave cigarette butts on the sacred course, I supposed. "I always thought you were the one who could answer that, Miranda."

"I already have. I told the police everything I knew."

He placed his hands on the edge of the bench and leaned back a little. "It divided the whole Island. The locals thought one thing, the summer families thought another thing. I don't think anyone's gotten over it. We come here to relax, you know, to escape things like that. Murders and what have you. To live quietly. And the whole thing happens, and you're in the middle of it. And maybe they could have forgiven you for that—I mean, it wasn't your fault, you were just a kid—but when you *talked*, Miranda, when you spoke to the newspapers, *that* was the real crime. You know, murdering someone is one thing, but talking to the newspapers?" He made a cutting motion to his throat.

"I didn't *want* to. But nobody would listen, everybody just wanted the whole thing to go away, *Joseph* to go away—"

"And now he's escaped from prison. Christ. He's got some nerve, I'll say that."

"Nobody knows where he is?"

"I don't know, Miranda. Maybe you can tell me the answer to that."

I spread my hands. "I'm afraid I can't."

There was a fractional pause, and then Clay leaned his head back and chuckled. "Damn it all, Miranda, listen to you! Anybody'd think you were an Islander now. Well, maybe you were right to stay away. It's done wonders for you. Our Miranda, a movie star! Say, where's that husband of yours? I'd like to meet that fellow. He's a genius."

"Back in London, I'm afraid."

"Is he going to pay us a visit? Or maybe you're not staying that long."

I turned to face him. The lights from the Club just reached his face, and for a moment it seemed I was facing him eighteen years ago, and we were both still kids, in love with other people. "Can you do me a favor, Clay?"

"Anything."

"Let's not mention my husband. In fact, let's not mention anything. I'd rather the whole world didn't know I was here this summer, if you know what I mean."

"Something wrong?"

I put my hand around his elbow. "Just spread the word for me, please? I know they don't like me, but—"

Clay shook his head and laughed. "Nobody's going to rat on you, trust me. This is the Island we're talking about."

I considered the expression on his face, and I turned my head to consider Livy, who had finished her cigarette and set her empty glass on the edge of the green, and now stood between Hugh's arms in her short, dark cocktail dress, nested together like two spoons, his hands wrapped around her hands wrapped around the handle of the club. Livy was giggling, and so was Lucy, standing at Hugh's left elbow, and Hugh was imploring them both to be serious. A delicate business, putting a golf ball. You couldn't laugh and putt at the same time, not if you wanted to sink the ball in the hole.

"Yes, I know," I said. "That's why I came here."

Clay reached into his pocket and lit another cigarette, rather slowly, because his attention lay also on the scene before us. I smelled the warm, pungent smoke, the comfortable bite of whisky that clung to him. The wind blew in cool Canadian gusts from the northwest, making me shiver a little, and Clay must have noticed because he took off his jacket without a word and laid it over my shoulders. "Anyway," he said, returning to his old position, flicking the ash from the tip of his cigarette, "you know the last thing anyone wants around here is a bunch of newspapermen pitching tents on the grass again. Brings down the tone."

"I'll say. Almost as bad as a United States Marshal."

We sat there without speaking. Livy sank her putt at last, and it was Lucy's turn. Clay's hand crept under the hem of the jacket and clasped my hand.

"How is she? Izzy?"

"She's fine. At first I thought she'd changed completely—you wouldn't recognize her—and then I thought maybe she's just who she always was. Who she always wanted to be. But maybe I'm wrong."

"You'll tell her hello for me?"

I gave Clay's hand a last squeeze, stood up, and removed his jacket from my shoulders. As I turned to hand it back to him—he was rising too, Clayton Monk would never remain seated in a woman's presence—I saw how bereft he looked, how vulnerable in the indigo twilight. So I kissed his cheek and spoke softly.

"I think maybe you should tell her yourself, sometime."

9.

WE DROVE HOME an hour later, Hugh and I, under a watchful moon. As we passed the sentry gate that marked the private eastern end of the Island—there was never a sentry, it was just for show—I turned to Hugh and said, "So Clay Monk married Livy Huxley. You know he was engaged to Isobel once."

"No way. Are you serious? Mr. Monk and Isobel?"

"He was desperately in love with her that summer. She was such a minx, she kept breaking it off and then taking him back."

"Really?" He laughed. "Old Isobel was a manslayer, huh? You wouldn't guess now."

"Well, she's changed a great deal since those days."

"I'll say. Man, oh man. Isobel and Mr. Monk."

"Don't tell her I told you. I think she's put all of those things behind her. The things that used to belong to her."

"Yeah, she's good at that."

Without warning, he slammed on the brakes and veered off the road, into one of the giant meadows adjoining the sea. I braced myself on the dashboard and screamed. "What the hell are you doing?"

"Sorry." He threw the car into park and switched off the engine. "C'mon. I want to show you something."

"You might have warned me."

Poor boy, he was still so young, he didn't know what I meant. What it was like to have brakes squeal and wheels swerve so soon after experiencing a terrible smashup like I had experienced. The papers had kept it quiet, of course. My husband had seen to that. He'd made sure that the nurses in the hospital hadn't talked, and the doctors hadn't talked, and the police hadn't talked. Not one detail had crept out into that vast, teeming, insatiable public curiosity, such that I sometimes wondered if it had really happened at all. Whether I'd dreamt the whole evening.

Then I looked down at my flat stomach, the way my dress hung from my hips, and I knew it wasn't a dream.

I sat in the passenger seat of Hugh's Ford convertible, catching my breath and my nerves, while Hugh got out and went around to open my door.

"Say, you're all right, aren't you? I didn't stop too fast?"

I took his hand and lifted myself out of the car. "Quite all right. Just what did you have in mind?"

"You'll see."

He stuffed his hands in his trouser pockets and started off to the east, toward the sea. The field had been recently mowed, the hay gathered up and baled, and the smell of dry, warm grass lay everywhere. I couldn't re-

member who owned it. Some local farmer, I thought, not one of the Families. But maybe it had changed hands since then, maybe I was mistaken.
The stubble scratched my shoes and my delicate stockings. I called out to
Hugh to wait a minute while I took everything off, stuffed stockings into
shoes, and he obeyed me, though I could see he was impatient, animated,
all covered in silver by the moon. Hands twitching in his pockets.

My feet were too tender, and the rough grass hurt the soles as I walked,
but I welcomed the pain. It was good to feel things again, to experience a
pain that you had inflicted on yourself with conscious intent. In any case,
it didn't last long. The field was narrow, maybe two hundred yards from
road to sea, and the end came abruptly. My toes encountered pebbles
among the grass, then rocks. Hugh stopped, and I stopped, and when I
looked up there it was, dark and still except for a long, white path cast by
the moon. The sea.

We stood on a little ridge, about fifteen feet up. Below us, the waves
washed gently along a small, U-shaped beach. "The Islanders call it
Horseshoe Beach," said Hugh. "Want to climb down?"

"Why not?"

He clambered down the rocks a bit and turned, hand outstretched, to
help me. I grasped his fingers for balance, because the rocks were damp,
but my bare feet gripped the surface pretty well. I curled my toes into the
granite and felt rather strong. The last jump into the sand, I released my
brother's hand and let fly, dropped my shoes, ran straight into the edge
of the surf and splashed around while he stripped off his own shoes and
socks and rolled up his trousers to wade in beside me.

"Now I *know* you're my sister," he said.

"I always was."

"Don't you love this place? Nobody ever comes here. You can't get
in so easy from the road, and you can't just walk over from the other
beaches. You'd have to sail in. Or row."

I looked from side to side and saw the curve of the inlet, the two opposite points covered in rocks, and a chill passed over me. "I see what you mean. You'd have to know it was there."

Hugh was kicking around at an incoming wave. "I like to come here to be alone, you know? Sit and think. Sometimes I take my boat out at night and sail right in, and it's like I'm the only person in the world."

"I like that feeling, too." I smiled at him. "What do you think about?"

"Oh, you know."

"No, I don't know. I wish I did. What do you like to think about, Hugh? What kind of books do you read? What do you like to study at school?"

"Me? Everything, sis. I want to read it all, I want to play it all, see it all. That world out there." He waved his hand. "What's it like?"

"It's pretty grand, sometimes. But sometimes it disappoints you too. People disappoint you."

"Who's disappointed you?"

"Not you, that's for sure," I said. "I liked the way you stood up to Dick Huxley. Not a lot of boys your age would stick up for their sisters like that."

He shrugged. "What else was I going to do? Anyway, we had a good time with the Monks, didn't we?"

I nearly opened my mouth to say what I really thought—that the Monks, while decent to invite us back into the pale, were also about as scintillating in their dinner conversation as a lump of tapioca pudding—before I remembered that my brother was, after all, only seventeen. "I'm sure we did," I said. "One Monk in particular seemed to be enjoying your company. Lucy?"

"Aw." He kicked again, ducked his head. "She's a good sport."

"She's very pretty."

"She's all right."

"She's how old? Fifteen?"

"I guess so. Fifteen last February."

"She certainly enjoyed her golf lesson," I said, and I added silently, *As her mother did*.

Hugh bent to pick up a stone and send it skidding across the surface of the water, which was placid this evening, more lake than sea. "She's nice," he said, "but she's a little dull. You know. Not much curiosity."

"She's young."

"No excuse. Anyone can read a book, you know? I don't get it. All these people who just want to stay on the Island, summer after summer. Don't they want to see the world? Do new things? Meet new people?"

"Is that what you want to do?"

He picked up another stone and turned it over, hefted it, bent sideways to send it skidding forcefully out to sea. He had an easy swing to his arm, like a boy who played baseball or football. "Feel like I'm going to explode sometimes," he said. "Just . . . *kerpow*. You know what I thought last night, standing there on the ferry? I thought I might want to just dive overboard and swim to shore and—I don't know—get in a car and drive west. South, north. Anything but Greyfriars. Mom with her paints and Isobel with her fucking knitting—aw, geez, I'm sorry."

"Oh, I've heard worse, believe me."

"I love them. I do. They mean the world to me. But I used to watch you up there on that movie screen and think, how did she do it? How did she escape?"

"I had help from a friend, for one thing. Isobel's mother helped me. When the papers came out and nobody else would speak to me, not even Isobel and Mama, she picked me up in her car and took me straight to New York. We sailed to Paris the next day, on the old *Ile de France*."

"But only because you dared. You took a stand. Against them." He nodded to the left, in the direction of the Club. "You know how the Fishers got in, don't you? The founders wouldn't let them buy one of the original plots in the development, the ones around the Club, so my grandfather picked up that whole section on the southern end, overlooking the lighthouse—used to be a farm—and built Greyfriars. And they ignored him for a couple of years, until the Crash hit, and Peter Dumont nearly went under. He'd invested in some risky securities, it turned out. And nobody had the bread—liquid, I mean—to bail him out. Nobody but good old August Fisher."

I started to laugh. "Is that so? I never knew. Poor Peter, how humiliating."

"That's what Mr. Monk told me once."

"So you really *can* buy your way into the Winthrop Island Club."

"And once you're in, you're in. You couldn't get out if you tried." He held up his arms to the sky. "One more year. One more year of school, and I'm free."

"What about college?"

"What *about* college?"

"Aren't you going to Harvard, like your father?"

"Not me. Another four years of all this? No way, Jose. I'm not going to college, Miranda. I'll be eighteen years old by then. I've got plans."

"What kind of plans?"

"I've been saving up, caddying every summer. Going to sell my old ragtop and buy myself a sailboat and take off for a whole year." He picked up another stone and examined it for seaworthiness. "Promise you won't tell Mom, though. She's got her heart set on— I don't know. Me following in Dad's footsteps. Being the fellow he was supposed to be, winning back all the dough he lost, so she and Isobel can—you know, all that." He waved his hand once more in the direction of the Club.

"And you don't want that?"

"Heck no. I want to see the world. I want to do what you did."

"Acting? Well, you've got the looks for it, I suppose."

He dropped the stone in his hand and picked up another. "Shucks, sis.

I don't want to *act*. I want to *be*. I want to *do*. I want to—well, like I said, you'll find out. Next spring, just watch. What?"

"Nothing. You remind me of someone, that's all."

He threw the stone—a decent toss, four or five skips—and picked up another one. "Now you tell me something."

"What's that?"

"Why did you come back? And don't tell me you were bored or between films or anything like that."

"I was bored," I said. "I was between films."

He threw the stone, but it didn't take. Sank without a trace at the second bounce. Hugh swore and shook his head, staring at the black, lapping sea, hands on hips. When he turned back to me, he was grinning from one side of his mouth. "So maybe you've come back to save us, have you? Stir up the pot? Get Mom and Isobel to put on their glad rags and have dinner at the Club? Hire a few builders to patch up Greyfriars and throw a great big party?"

"That's not a bad idea."

"But it's not the real reason, is it?"

"Maybe I just wanted to see you. Maybe I wanted to visit my mother and sister and brother, after all these years. Heal the wounds."

"That's a nice story," he said, "but I'm not buying it. Why this summer, of all summers? Was it Vargas?"

"No, of course not."

"Oh, come on."

"It's true. I didn't find out about—I didn't know he'd escaped until after I'd—after I'd decided to leave England."

"So what was it? What's the tale, nightingale?"

I opened my mouth to make some snappy remark, some denial of the obvious, but his face was absolutely earnest as he looked down at me, like the face of a thirty year old, and I remembered he had no father. He was a boy with no father who stood on the edge of manhood, and this was something we shared. The two of us, we knew how that void in your heart, that father-shaped hole, might lead you down paths of terrible sorrow, in search of something to fill it.

"Okay, I know it's not the Winthrop way," he said. "We don't ask questions. We pretend everything's just fine and then drink ourselves to death. Or get murdered by the son of the lighthouse keeper, for some reason nobody on this damned Island is ever going to talk about."

I put my arms around my brother's back and drew him close, and I felt the comfort of his own arms around my waist, holding me there. The beat of his enormous heart. He smelled of cigarettes and soap and green youth, of everything lost. When I opened my eyes again, the sea lay before me, over the crest of his shoulder. I thought, if I tried, I could peer across the tip of Long Island and see all the way to England.

"I came because I lost a baby," I said.

The jolt of shock went right through his middle. I had to clamp my arms to keep him from jumping apart.

"Oh, sis. Oh my God. *When?*"

"In the accident. I was about six months along. They couldn't save her."

"Her," said Hugh. "It was a girl. Jeez, my niece."

"Yes."

"So what about your husband? Why isn't he here with you?" Hugh loosened his arms and pulled away to look down at me, and this time I let him. "My God, he *does* know about it, doesn't he?"

"Of course he knows about it," I said. "He was driving the car."

10.

NATURALLY I DIDN'T tell him the whole story. How could I tell him everything, a boy like that? I mean, there were no words anyway, no possible means to express the details of that awful night, the quantity of vodka Carroll had drunk, the vile things he had said to me. Besides, why should Hugh believe me? As far as anyone else knew, Carroll was a man of urbanity, of sophisticated reserve, a gentleman, a genius. Certainly not a man given to fits of rage and jealousy, given to consuming, on an almost nightly basis, a favored, potent mixture of barbiturates and vodka to keep what he was pleased to call his demons at bay. His demons. As if they were something outside himself, something that did not belong to him, but instead tormented the poor, suffering genius and made him *do* things, Miranda, made him do things he would not ordinarily do. Terrible things, of course, but not things he had himself committed. It was the demons, Miranda.

Oh, those demons. Those demons who flew from the netherworld in such power and strength, who assumed control of Carroll Goring's body back in April, for example, when we went for drinks to the Mayfair flat of his dear friend Victor. Victor, you see, was celebrating the Academy Award he'd just won for Carroll's film *The Paradox*—Best Actor, as you might recall—for which Carroll had also been nominated for Best Director and lost. (Carroll Goring, as you might also recall—the press certainly makes hay of it, in every article and interview—has been nominated for eight Academy Awards and never taken home the statuette.) Now, Carroll *himself* was deeply happy for Victor—they share a long and complicated history, Carroll and Victor, having once been lovers—but the demons, I understand, were not pleased at all. The demons saw me sitting on the sofa with Victor toward the end of the evening, enjoying a laugh, and decided that Victor must be the father of my unborn child, not Carroll. After all, Carroll had undergone a vasectomy ten years ago, just before we were married, and therefore there was no possibility whatsoever that he had fathered my child, was there? It must be Victor.

There was a terrible fight. A *row*, as Englishmen call it. Victor went to call the police, and Carroll locked the door to the library and forced me on the sofa and pulled up my dress. I told him no and pushed him off and ran for the door, but he caught me and slammed me on my stomach over the sofa arm. The violence of it shocked me. He had never struck me before; his weapons of choice had, until that moment, been words.

He didn't actually penetrate me. I don't think he could manage any sort of erection, any genuine sexual arousal, because he'd had too much to drink, too many pills. But his powerlessness only made him more determined to hurt me. I knew at once that something was wrong, that the brutality with which he rammed and rammed, pounding me against the sofa arm in a fruitless pantomime, had done some irreparable damage. I remember trying not to scream, though he seemed to go on forever in a paroxysm of frustration, though the tears ran down my face and onto the dark, stained leather of Victor's sofa. Even now, the smell of leather starts a panic inside me.

At last he gave up and hauled me downstairs to the empty lobby and out through the service entrance. I didn't make a fuss because of the police, you see, the newspapers and their vicious columns, and because I was so shocked and so battered, so utterly without strength after a difficult pregnancy. I thought I'd let him take me home and then when he was asleep at last, knocked out by his pills and his vodka and his demons, I would actually leave him this time. He had crossed a final, uncrossable line, and I would pack my things and go before he woke up.

The car was parked on the corner of Curzon Street. The air was damp and full of fine drizzle that choked me as I tried to hold back my sobs. Carroll made sure no one was looking—it was two o'clock in the morning—before he threw me in the car and told me more vile things, what a cheap whore I was, how I owed him everything, how I was a fraud, a bimbo with no talent, how he was going to tell the world what I'd done. I kept silent as we swerved around the empty London streets, because I was in terrible pain by now, my insides cramped and cramped, I simply thought I was going to die, there was no point in arguing.

Instead of driving to our flat in Kensington, Carroll headed straight out of London toward Bath, where we had a country house, keeping up a manic simmering of bile. He described every film we had made together and each specific instance in which I had disappointed him, each scene I had ruined, so that his failure to win those Academy Awards was really *my* fault, the sacrifice he had made for *my* sake, and *look* how I had repaid him. I *knew* he hadn't wanted a child—he'd made that clear from the beginning—and I had gone out anyway and slept with Victor, hadn't I, gotten myself pregnant by Victor, admit it, Miranda, just admit it, for God's sake! GOD DAMN IT, MIRANDA! ADMIT THAT YOU FUCKED MY FRIEND! ADMIT YOU'RE CARRYING HIS CHILD, YOU BLOODY TART, YOU FUCKING WHORE!

By then, I think I was almost delirious with pain. I would have said anything to make him stop.

All right, I screamed back. I admit it. I slept with Victor, I was pregnant by Victor. We started an affair right under your nose during the filming of *The Paradox*, we carried on right through the premiere and the promotion and the week in Los Angeles for the Oscars, we fucked two or three times a day, he was insatiable, he was magnificent, he was a god.

Carroll jerked the wheel once, and we careened right off the Bath Road and into a tree. When I woke up, I was in hospital, in a white, dreary room in the middle of Wiltshire, and the baby was dead. Carroll, of course, was unharmed and full of remorse. The demons had done it, he said, weeping in my lap. It was the demons.

11.

SO YOU SEE what I mean, how I couldn't tell my green seventeen-year-old brother about these things. Instead we lay on the beach, side by side, and stared up at the dainty stars without speaking. The tide came and went. At one point I rose and clasped my knees, and I thought I saw the white flash of a sail on the horizon. But when I stood up and ran to the edge of the water, it was gone.

The house was dark by the time we returned, and as I crept up the back stairs I couldn't see the shabbiness, the peeling paint and missing bulbs, and I realized that without these signs of decay, Greyfriars felt just the same as it had before, smelled exactly the same. I had the sudden, unnerving conviction that I had traveled through time, that I was creeping up those same stairs as a guilty seventeen-year-old virgin, afraid of being found out for my transgressions. Then I heard the creak of Hugh's footsteps behind me, and the present world returned, my husband, my dead child, the weight of every year that had passed since I first saw Joseph Vargas dive into the water from his lobster boat and save a man from drowning.

We whispered good night on the landing and I slipped into my old bedroom, the one I shared with Brigitte, who snored quietly from her bed. On the window seat was a bowl of roses, the same June roses I had found on my lounge chair that morning, and I went on my knees and stared at them, and the lighthouse that grew between the small, pink buds.

JULY

1930 (BIANCA MEDEIRO)

1.

ON THE FOURTH of July, in the middle of a tremendous display of fireworks on the lawn, old Mr. Fisher dies.

Bianca hears the story over breakfast the next morning from her cousin Manuelo, who heard it from one of the Fisher housemaids, who's sweet on him. He collapsed with some kind of heart attack, apparently, and because of the darkness, nobody even noticed until after the fireworks were exhausted and the party began to file inside. His wife found him first and began to scream for a doctor, and luckily there *was* a doctor among that crowd of people, but he came too late. Old Mr. Fisher was already gone.

Nobody sees Bianca's face as Manuelo relates this information, between bites of Tia Maria's good sweet bread. Nobody notices how the blood falls away from her cheeks, and her lips part in agony. When she rises from the table and begins to clear the plates, hastily and without sound, nobody bothers to thank her.

And nobody pays any attention when she slips out the back door afterward and runs along the warm, empty streets toward West Cliff Road.

2.

SHE FINDS HIM in the swimming pool, slicing up and down the clear blue rectangle in a businesslike way, like Johnny Weissmuller. She calls his name several times before he interrupts his movements and spins, startled, searching for the source of her voice.

"Here," she says. "In the boxwoods."

"Well, come on out."

"Won't they see me?"

"Mama's had enough pills to knock out a racehorse. And the housemaids won't tell, believe me."

Bianca steps free of the bush and stands, quivering a little, on the terrace that surrounds the pool. The sun's already met the surface, paved in genteel Connecticut bluestone, and its warmth seeps through the soles of her shoes.

Hugh holds out his arms. "Come swimming with me."

She shakes her head. "Can't swim."

"I'll teach you."

She steps closer. "I'm awfully sorry about your father. I only just heard."

He turns and launches himself back down the length of the pool, but this time he finds the ladder at the end and hoists himself out. He's wearing the latest style of bathing suit, snug and brief, and his chest runs with water. Bianca spins away and starts to cross herself, but before she even touches her right shoulder, her hand falls away to her side.

"Drink?" says Hugh.

"No, thank you."

"Come on. There's plenty. Why are you standing like that?"

Bianca feels like a fool and turns. On the other side of the pool, Hugh stands next to a table topped with glass, pouring a drink from a pitcher.

No—two drinks, clear as water, into which he drops a pair of lemon slices from a small bowl of cut glass. The sun strikes his shoulders, making them glisten. His hair is sleek and disordered from the water. A small breeze wanders in from the south, smelling of brine, which Bianca inhales in shallow, cautious breaths, as if the air itself contains the raw ingredients of this new mood that shimmers between them. Something is coming to her, some momentous fate. She can feel its approach like a giant wave, like a thunderstorm tearing across the sky to engulf her.

"Well, come here, then." Hugh straightens from the table. "I'm not going to bite you, am I?"

Strange that he tacked on that question at the end of his declaration, she thinks, but she walks obediently around the end of the pool anyway, conscious of her thin, cheap dress and worn sandals. She stops a couple of yards away, just out of reach, relying on her rigid spine to keep her upright in the face of all that impossible glamour.

He holds out one of the glasses. "Here you are. My special recipe."

"I don't want it."

"Why not?"

"Because I shouldn't."

"Yes you should." He waggles the glass, making the ice clink. "I'm in grief, little one. You've got to go along with my whims."

Bianca reaches out and snatches the glass. In her haste, she spills the contents over her fingers. She lifts her hand and sucks the drops from her skin, and while of course she's not exactly expecting water—she's not *that* innocent—the pungency of it, the sharpness, still stuns her.

Hugh observes her actions with a steady, attentive expression. He holds up his own glass. "To the old man, may he rot in Hades."

"Oh no!" exclaims Bianca.

"What's this? Shocked you, have I? Sweet little one. Sweet Bianca. She knows no evil, does she? God protect her darling heart." He raises the glass again, a little higher this time. "Let's try again. To my dear, departed pater. May his soul—now, let me think—may his soul find the eternal reward it so richly deserves. Amen."

His beautiful blue eyes are a little wild, a little pink, and Bianca hesitates.

"Little one," he says, more softly, "it's just gin. It's not going to hurt you, you know. Nothing could hurt *you*."

She steps forward and gently meets his glass with her own, and she waits until he drinks before she lifts the rim to her lips and sips. The earlier taste has acclimatized her tongue, however, and it's not quite so powerful as she fears. She tries again, more deeply, and this time notices the flavor, and the peculiar fragrance of the fumes, the scent of juniper berries, and the way the gin burns down her throat and numbs the contours of her brain.

Hugh holds himself still, watching her. "What a beauty you are, Bianca. A fresh, marvelous, hypnotic beauty. Your face amazes me every time I see you. Have I ever told you that?"

"Many times."

"Many times, *Hugh*. Say my name."

"Many times, Hugh."

"That's better. You say it so well." He drinks again and takes her hand. "Let's sit down together."

He leads her to the edge of the pool and kneels to remove her sandals, one by one. His touch is so cool and so delicate, Bianca shivers in pleasure. When he's done, he sits, dangling his legs into the water, and tugs her down beside him, not quite close enough to touch, though he keeps her hand in his.

"How old were you when you lost your parents, little one?" he asks.

"I was three. I don't even remember them."

"It was a plague of some kind, wasn't it?"

"Yes, the typhoid. I had it too, but I survived. So they sent me to live with Tia Maria and Tio Manuelo, and a year later we came to America, and—" She shrugs her shoulders, because that's all there is to tell, really. She has scarcely any memories of Portugal, just heat and dryness and pungent, spicy air, of a wide, blue ocean and people of tremendous size. Of course, their great size was only relative to her own childlike frame, but still she has this idea of Portugal as a land of giants.

"Maybe you're lucky," says Hugh. "Maybe you never had the chance to learn that your parents were human beings instead of gods."

"I don't know. I don't think about them. Tia Maria and Tio Manuelo are like mother and father to me."

"They're good to you?"

"Very good," she says swiftly, firmly.

He lifts her hand and kisses it. "I'm glad to hear that. I won't have my little one mistreated by anybody."

Bianca keeps absolutely still. She knows she ought to be saying something comforting just now, but she can't imagine what. He's lost his father, in sudden and terrible circumstances, but Hugh and his father did not share some simple, uncomplicated filial love of the kind she understands. Underneath his skin, he's teeming with the desire to tell her all about it—she can feel this desire, she can sense the awful words roiling in his throat—and she doesn't want to hear them. But she must. If Hugh bears any burden, however grotesque, she must share it with him. It's the only way, when you love someone. You must find whatever ugliness there exists within him and have the courage to extract it, like a bad tooth, or if it cannot be extracted to actually journey inside him and gather this ugliness in your arms for metamorphosis, by the strength and the purity of your love to make him beautiful again. This she believes with all her heart.

The sun beats against their skin, side by side. The salt water laps against their legs and stings the pores of Bianca's skin.

"Bianca, perhaps—"

"Your father," she bursts out. "What was he like?"

Hugh reaches for the glass of special recipe gin, which rests next to his right thigh, sweating copiously into the stone. "Don't ask. You don't need to know about these things."

"Tell me. I want to know. I want to know everything about you."

"You already know everything that matters. We're linked, Bianca, linked by fate and by your beautiful brown eyes. These little details are too small for your notice."

"Nothing's too small. If it matters to you, it matters to me."

"Believe me, little one—"

"Believe *me*," she says fiercely, "I can take anything, anything at all if it belongs to you. We are made from the same soul, you said it yourself."

He finishes the drink and hurls the glass into the boxwoods, where it disappears without a sound. Bianca stares at the tiny, startled leaves, the dark scar where the glass burst through. Hugh's fingers dig into her palm, making her eyes sting with tears.

He begins in a casual voice.

"He was a drunkard, a philanderer. Used to beat my mother, from time to time, when she raised any objections. A scoundrel of a business-man, I'm told, though that's just hearsay, so you can decide for yourself if it's true. He never let me near the company. Sold it last year—took it public, I mean, sold off most of the shares on the stock market—just so I couldn't ever get my hands on the keys of power. I guess he knew what was coming. He saw all these doctors, took all these pills, but a fellow's got to know when his time's running out." Hugh pauses to kick a little water with his long, strong legs. "When I was young, he used to take out his belt and whip me for any little thing, any excuse to lay out his rage on some innocent hide that couldn't hit back. He shot my dog dead when I was nine, because it made a mess on the stairs. That's what he was like."

"Oh, Hugh, I'm so sorry—"

"I'm glad he's dead." Hugh drops her hand and scrambles to his feet.

"I saw his body lying there in the grass last night, and I thought, *I hope to God he's dead, I hope to God they can't save him.*" By now he's weeping, his shoulders are heaving, his breath comes in terrible spasms. "Do you know what he said to me, before he died? His last words? He said, *Go take that pretty face of yours and find some girl to fuck. That's all you're good for, isn't it? Drinking and fucking.*"

Bianca jumps up and puts her arms around his waist and lays her head on his shaking chest. "It's all right, Hugh, it's all right, he was wrong, it's all right."

"But that's it. He wasn't wrong. God forever damn the bastard, he was dead right. I'm a cad, Bianca, a drunkard and a cad. I'm no good at business. I'm no good for anything."

Bianca, who suspects but isn't quite sure what this word *fucking* means, still insists, "No, no. There's so much more to you, you're an artist, you're a dreamer, you're a thousand times better than him. It's all right, you can cry, come, Hugh, you can be sad and angry both, it's all right."

He wraps his arms around her and weeps into her hair, and she's so happy, absorbing his tears and his grief, Bianca alone among all women, that she knows she ought to cross herself. But her arms are otherwise occupied, holding Hugh with all her might, his bare skin beneath her palms, his scent laying itself upon her, his precious bones and sinews cradled by hers. After a while, he pulls back and tilts her chin up with his finger and starts to kiss her, slowly.

3.

IN ALL THE hours they have spent together, Hugh Fisher and Bianca Medeiro, they have never kissed on the mouth, and this is because of Abigail Dumont.

"I'm engaged to be married, little one," he told her sadly, the first time they met alone, as twilight settled over the cliffs to the west of Greyfriars. "The wedding's set for Labor Day. Do you mind?"

"Of course not," she replied. "I don't even know you, do I?"

"But we can be friends, can't we? I feel as if you and I can be friends. Lifelong friends. Tell each other things we can't tell other people. Everyone needs a friend like that, a friend you can sit with and be silent together and just understand each other. Made from the same soul. Do you know what I mean?"

"Of course I do."

"Good, then. I think you'll find I'm an excellent friend. If there's anything you need, just come to me. And if anyone tries to hurt you, Bianca, anyone at all, why, he'll have me to answer to."

She hadn't replied to that because her heart was so full, all words and even thoughts were crowded out. She only leaned her head against his shoulder, tentatively, amazed at her own boldness, and he curled his arm about her and laid his hand on her hair, and with his other hand took her fingers and laced them together with his fingers, there upon his lap. They sat like this for many minutes, perhaps even an hour, and watched the sunset without saying a single word. At last he lifted their linked hands and kissed the seam where they joined, and said he would drive her back into the village now. She said no, because someone would see, and so they walked instead, all the way down the hill, and said goodbye where West Cliff Road met Hemlock Street. He always said goodbye the same way, kissing the palm of her right hand, and she always closed her fist and ran down the street to the general store and the room she shared with her cousin Francisca on the third floor, knowing he kept watch until the darkness took her back, until the light in the window winked out.

So it went all through the month of June; not every night, but three or four times a week. She knew when to slip out the door because he would find a way to get her a note of some kind, hidden by mysterious means among the soup cans in the store or tucked into the book she was reading and once even inside the pocket of her pinafore apron. She thrilled to those clandestine messages, written in beautiful purple-black lettering, those signs of his cleverness and his all-powerful ways, and his regard for her and her reputation most of all. Because of course her aunt and uncle and cousins would not understand. They would think he was taking advantage of her, that she was giving herself sinfully to Hugh Fisher, that there was something sordid and unclean in these meetings.

But Bianca knew otherwise. She believed in the purity of their love because he never kissed her on the lips, not once, nor touched her in any way that was not reverent and guiltless.

And she believed something else. She believed one day, when their love grew strong enough to overcome the demands of his family and his social station, he would renounce Miss Dumont and declare himself to Bianca, by word and deed. He would seal this promise with his lips. Then they would be married, and consummate their vows as God ordained. In her deepest heart, Bianca knew this to be true, and she prayed to God on her knees all June that this day would arrive soon, before the yearning inside her blood grew too clamorous to hold in check.

4.

AND NOW IT'S July and he's kissing her at last, his mouth on her mouth. He finally understands how much he loves her, how he needs her and only her, how only Bianca among all women truly understands him. Tragedy has peeled the scales from his eyes and his heart.

Having never kissed anyone on the lips before, she's startled at first by the strange taste of a man's mouth, by the silken quality, by the intimacy. Still, she accepts all these unfamiliar sensations without restraint or even doubt, because these are Hugh's lips she's receiving, Hugh's tongue, Hugh's love, and she and Hugh are made from the same soul, they are linked by fate and by God. She lifts her arms to encircle his neck, and he makes this groan like she's hurting him in some terrible way. In the next second, he lifts her into the air and carries her into the shade of the cabana, where he sets her gently on a cushion and sits back on his heels. The material of her dress falls away from her neck, and Bianca looks down and realizes that somehow, in the midst of their embrace, her buttons have come apart. She gasps and raises her hand, but Hugh pulls it away.

"No, let me see you, little one. I just want to see you, that's all. I won't hurt you, I promise."

He slides her arms from their sleeves and allows her bodice to fall around her waist. Beneath her camisole, her breasts are tight and swollen, and she crosses her arms over them. But he will have none of this modesty of hers. He takes each hand by the wrist and pulls them apart, sighing a little, or maybe that's just the heightened pace of his breath. He slides his thumbs across her bosom and up to her shoulders, and one by one he takes the straps of her camisole and eases them down her arms, as he did with the sleeves of her dress, and just like that, Bianca finds herself absolutely bare before him, all the way to her waist. She looks down in dismay. Her breasts are so naked, so sinfully large and round, and Hugh's gaping at them, mouth parted. Bianca has to fist her hands behind her back to stop her own arms from shielding against his gaze, and in doing so her spine arches, creating the exact opposite effect, as if she's offering herself up to him. So Hugh takes one in each hand and sort of weighs them, like fruit, and says, in an awed whisper, "Do you know, Bianca, do you have any idea how perfect you are?"

Bianca shakes her head slowly.

"It's like I've never seen a woman before now. Are you actually Eve, my love? Are you Eve, and I'm Adam, and this is Eden?"

She tries to laugh at this blasphemy, although Hugh's face is heavy and serious. He reaches forward and takes her hands between his fingers.

"Do you love me, little one?"

"Yes, Hugh. I love you."

"You trust me?"

"Yes, yes!"

"I am sort of drunk, you know. Been drinking since dawn. Fell asleep drinking the night before."

"I know." She slips her hand from his fingers, lays it on the back of his head, and looks steadily into his unsteady eyes.

There is an instant of connection, of understanding and perhaps forgiveness, before he lowers his mouth to the tips of her breasts, kissing and then suckling like an infant, how strange, hard and then gentle and then hard again, pulling, as if he's trying to draw milk from her. She doesn't object when he puts his hand under her dress and climbs like a spider up her leg, although she jumps as his finger reaches the edge of her knickers and slides right up underneath them to touch the wicked place at the junction of her legs, where the Devil lives.

Hugh lifts his head from her breast and whispers, "Shh. Let me touch you a little, just touch you, you're so soft in there, little one, little love, you feel so good on my finger."

She stares into his eyes, which seem to be having trouble focusing. She cannot stop him, she realizes. She doesn't even want to stop him. After all, this is Hugh's finger touching her, and isn't he made from the sun, isn't he her Apollo on earth? Doesn't she trust Hugh more than anyone in the world? Can he not, by the divinity of his touch, drive away the Devil from between her legs and turn sin into sacrament? All her life she's wanted this, she has craved some Apollo to anoint her with his love, to anoint her and only her. She has prayed to God on her knees, and now God is answering her prayer at last. She kisses Hugh's forehead because she can't reach his lips, and he starts to fold her dress with both hands— her thin, cheap dress of clumsily printed flowers, orange and pink—all the way up her legs in wide, deliberate tucks, until they form a kind of sash around her waist. From there, it's only a small distance to her belly, against which the ribbons of her knickers lie, waiting to be untied, which he does. The knickers are then discarded, without ceremony, and he lifts himself above her and fumbles with his swimming trunks.

"Hold still," he says. "Hold still a second."

Bianca stiffens in panic under his looming weight. She digs her fingernails into his shoulders and thinks, *Wait a moment, wait a moment, what is this?*

"Hold still," Hugh says again, and his fingers lodge between her legs, his knees spread her apart, and Bianca tries vainly to close herself.

"Please," she says. "Please."

"Please, no? Or please, yes?"

"Please, God!" Somehow, in the dizziness of her mind, they have become the same, God and Hugh, two faces of a single sun.

"Should I stop?" he pants.

She sinks her hips fearfully into the cushion and puts her hands on his bare, damp shoulders, either to push him away or to embrace him, she isn't sure. *Be brave,* she thinks. *It's God's will, whatever happens, it is God's will. God is answering your prayer.*

"That's right. Just for a second, darling," Hugh says. "I promise I won't—ah, little one—I shouldn't—I shouldn't—oh Christ—I can't stop—don't *move* . . ."

His speech descends into insensate mumbling. His fingers slip and pry, and then a blunt, thick, searing pressure assails her. Bianca gasps and tries to draw away, but there's nowhere to go, no possible escape, his hands have clamped on her hips, holding her in place against the cushion, and she screams as he pushes, grunts, pushes harder, and slides deeply into her, actually *into* her, so this forbidden part of his body is crammed tight into that forbidden part of her body, locking them together. Bianca feels like she might faint. A few minutes ago, she was standing in the boxwoods, and now she's pinned on her back, virginity ruptured, in the very act of immoral intercourse with Hugh Fisher. Hugh Fisher! She's probably dreaming, that's it. She lies in shock beneath him and digs her fingers into his shoulders.

But it can't be a dream, she thinks. He's too real. This thing between my legs, it's incontestable. It's the rest of my life that's the dream, everything else I have dreamed, until now.

"Ah, little one, Bianca. Sweet little love, I'm so sorry, did I hurt you?"

"No!" she shouts ferociously.

"How does it feel?"

She moves her lips, but there are no words for this sensation, to be so full and frightened and conscious of sin, to feel as if your world has overturned, to feel as if your love has transformed from a filmy, childish, fanciful thing into something carnal and solid that strains everything inside you until you might burst apart. So she just nods.

"That's right." He bends his neck and kisses her. "You're all right, it's just me, that's all. It's *love*, Bianca, this is what love is."

Still she can't speak, so she makes a noise that sounds a little like a meowing cat. He starts to rock his hips against her hips, to slide out of her and then inside again. She tries not to cry out—she now understands it's a test, a sacrifice demanded by God, so she must acquit herself bravely and prove herself worthy of Hugh's love—but she can't help a little moan each time he pushes back in. After a minute or two, the rhythm builds to a furious pace like the stroke of a hammer, splitting her apart, and another scream builds in her throat, because it's too much to bear, whatever it is, too much pressure, too much pain, too much everything. But before the scream bursts free, Hugh shouts, *Ah Christ!* and goes rigid, closes his eyes and locks his elbows. Like a statue he arches above her, perfect in all respects, gleaming with sweat, wearing an expression of exquisite agony and so utterly magnificent, so *triumphant* she cannot breathe or think or feel, she cannot decide if she hates him or loves him. But this lasts only a few seconds before he crumples to her chest.

"Shh, it's all right," he gasps in her ear, "it's over now, it's done, Bianca, forgive me, it's all right."

She strokes his hair. The joints of her pelvis ache with his weight, spreading her open. He is hot, scorching hot, boiling over with a heat that astounds her.

Hugh mumbles, "God, I needed that." Then he lifts his head. "You're all right, little one?"

"Yes," she whispers.

"Don't be frightened. I'll take care of you, I promise. It's happened, that's all. It was always going to happen, I guess. You and me, Bianca. Fate." He kisses her. "Was I an awful beast? Do you still love me, little one?"

"Yes!"

"Well, I love you too. I'm crazy about you, I'm demented. Now more than ever. You must have known that already. I'll take care of you always, I promise. Whatever happens. You'll have anything you want, just ask. You won't ever have to leave me."

Another kiss, and he lifts himself up on his hands. Their skin sticks briefly, as if reluctant to part, before the cool air rushes at last over Bianca's breasts and wet belly. He pulls himself out of her and rolls over on the cushion with a noise of immense relief. The sun strikes the cabana at such an angle as to cut him exactly in half, sunlit and shaded. Bianca supposes the same is true of her. She tries to move and cannot, she's too stiff and stunned, but she can at least turn her head to stare at Hugh, whose face addresses the stripes of the cabana's top, though his eyes are closed.

For some time, they are both still, side by side on the cushion, recovering breath. Bianca feels something wet trickling between her legs, but she's too numb to comprehend its meaning entirely, except that it belongs to Hugh, that it endows their love with some kind of substance, with a permanence that cannot be undone.

"We're bound together now," Hugh says. "That's it."

"Yes," Bianca says, for the third time.

He turns his head to face hers. His expression is earnest, though his eyes are still unsteady. He touches her hair, her cheek, and tells her softly, "You must promise never to leave me, Bianca. You must let me care for you always."

"Always," she agrees, and she means it.

5.

AFTERWARD, HUGH WALKS Bianca almost to her doorstep and kisses her softly, lingeringly, behind the shelter of a young elm. She slips through the garden door and into the back of Tio Manuelo's shop, thinking not that she is engaged to marry Hugh Fisher, but that they are now actually man and wife before God, who hears the secret vows between lovers, who witnesses the ritual of their consummation and who blesses them with the fruits of sacred union.

This she believes with all her heart.

1951 (MIRANDA SCHUYLER)

1.

OVER BREAKFAST ON the terrace, Isobel decided we should go to the festival. It was Sunday, the twenty-second of July. I remember the date well.

"What festival?" I naturally asked.

She looked at me, eyebrows raised, as if I'd committed some act of unforgivable ignorance. The Countess answered for her.

"The Festival of the Holy Spirit, my dear. Down in the village. The church puts it on each year. St. Mary's, I mean."

"Are you sure we'll be welcome?"

"I doubt it," said the Countess. "It's the last thing in the world they'd welcome, us turning up like tourists to gawp at them."

Isobel buttered her toast from a pot buried in a bowl of ice. "Oh, they won't care. It's not some kind of religious ritual, in case you're afraid of being made to kiss the pope's ring or something. Just the part about the blessing of the fleet, but the rest is all fun and games."

"Blessing of the fleet? Do you mean the fishing fleet? They bless the *boats*?"

Isobel shrugged and looked out to sea. With her right hand she reached for the cigarette case, and her gold bracelets clinked against the wrought iron table. "Fishermen are superstitious."

We had breakfast on the terrace most mornings, when it wasn't raining, which it usually wasn't. The weather through June continued warm and fair except for the occasional drenching cloudburst, each day melting into the next, and when I think of those placid weeks between the wedding and the Festival of the Holy Spirit, I remember it as a rhythm, the beats of which consisted of breakfast and lunch and dinner, of morning tennis and afternoon swimming, of evening cocktails, of sunshine and moonshine, repeated at the same pace, the same speed, sunrise to sunrise. On weekends, the rhythm altered slightly, as new instruments joined us and the whole piece moved into a different key, but—well, you get the idea. That was the Island's appeal. Human beings love rhythm, they love a beat to which they can tap their toes and dance sedately.

So we danced, and we danced, and we drank, my God. As if the effects of rhythm were not stupefying enough, we pickled ourselves too, in careful, steady doses that maintained a certain desirable state of just-lucid intoxication throughout the day. Maybe you couldn't have one without the other, I don't know. Maybe the rhythm would drive you crazy without the drink, and vice versa. At first, I tried to resist the allure of a fresh, zinging Bloody Mary to move your blood in the morning, followed by regular injections of gin and tonic to keep you thriving throughout the day, followed by champagne cocktails, followed by wine at dinner, followed by some kind of nightcap, but it was like trying to resist the phases of the moon. They happened without your trying, half the time without your even noticing, carried along by the unceasing beat of mealtimes. The only thing I ever managed to resist that summer was bridge. Oh, and cigarettes. That was because of loyalty to my father, who had always hated the smell of tobacco smoke.

Isobel had no such loyalties. She plucked a cigarette from its case—her fourth already this morning—and lit it swiftly with a gold lighter that matched her bracelet. The air was heavy and still, and she had to wave away a cloud of smoke in order to find me again. "Well?" she asked.

"It's a silly idea," said the Countess. "In this heat. We could go sailing instead. Clay will take us out in his yacht, I'm sure."

"I wasn't asking you, Abigail. I was asking Peaches."

Her blue eyes contained a familiar energy, which I tried to ignore. I poured myself another Bloody Mary from the glass pitcher. "I think your mother's right. It's too hot. Let's going sailing or swimming instead."

Isobel tossed down her toast and rose. The skin beneath her eyes was tired and bruised, and her mouth seemed to strain for words. "Then I guess I'll just have to go on my own, won't I?"

"Sit down," said the Countess. "We're going sailing with the Monks."

"Not me. Not unless you're planning to kidnap me."

The Countess tapped each corner of her mouth with a napkin, sipped her coffee, and lit a cigarette. She liked a full breakfast, even in this heat, porridge followed by eggs and toast and fried ham, whereas Isobel ate only fruit in the morning. Fruit and coffee, that was all. Her mother frowned briefly at the end of her cigarette and looked across the water, toward the Fleet Rock lighthouse, sticking up from the still, blue sea as if to anchor the water to the sky.

"Very well," she said at last. "If you're so determined to make a fool of yourself. I'll just ring up the Monks and see if Clay doesn't mind joining us there."

2.

SO THAT WAS how we came to put on our sundresses and our straw hats and our espadrille sandals and head down to the harbor that day. It was because of Isobel, who had probably made some arrangement with Joseph in the note I'd carried to him the day before, or during their clandestine meeting sometime past midnight at the swimming pool, which was shielded by boxwoods and therefore suitable for such rendezvous. I only knew because I'd kept my window open, such was the heat, and heard the tell-tale splashing, the suppressed giggles, the deep voice imploring quiet.

At the time, I wondered how the Countess could possibly have remained ignorant. Maybe she wasn't, but she was also wise enough not to say anything. Isobel might have been in love with Joseph, but she was also addicted to the thrill of disobedience. She sent me as go-between because it enhanced this thrill, and I obeyed her because I couldn't say no. I told myself that this was for Isobel's sake—better for me to remain inside this secret than out of it, the one sensible person to check their recklessness—but in truth I was selfish. Joseph and I might spend only a few minutes talking when I delivered Isobel's notes, fragrant with her peculiar scent, but those few minutes were the truest minutes I spent all week. The instance of clarity amid the slumberous haze of an Island summer, the moment I was truly awake, possibly even alive.

And though I might have begged off this expedition to the Blessing of the Fleet, remaining at Greyfriars on principle, I did not. I chose to go too. I told myself that the Countess would need all the help she could get.

When I arrived at the car, Isobel was already inside, applying her scarlet lipstick in confident strokes by the reflection of the rearview mirror. She caught my approach over her shoulder and smiled.

"Well, jump in," she said. "Don't want to miss all the fun, do we?"

"Where's your mother?"

"Here." The Countess came up behind me, dressed in a tangerine caftan and a hat so broad-brimmed and floppy, I had to peer underneath to see her face, which was tense and resigned. "I'll sit in the back, dear ones. I'm feeling a trifle *malade*."

How lithe we were, how tanned as we sped down the pale, curving road toward the village and the main harbor. The wind tumbling our hair, the sun striking the chrome points of Hugh Fisher's silver convertible. Isobel parked in the grass outside somebody's house and reached for her pocketbook and hat in the back seat—the Countess handed them to her—and I noticed as she fumbled to pluck another cigarette from its case, to light and to stick it in her mouth, that her fingers were unsteady. I opened the car door and pushed up the seat so the Countess could extract herself from the tiny space behind. I don't know how she fit to begin with. She had put on a pair of tinted glasses so I couldn't see the expression in her eyes, but I felt she was looking at me as she grabbed my hand to lever herself free from all the white leather and polished wood. She kept her grip as we started down the sidewalk, in the direction of the noise and the music nearer the water's edge, while Isobel walked slightly in front of us, in a quick, eager stride. The hot air rose in waves from the ground; I think it might have been the hottest day of the year, and the marina had taken on a faintly rotten, salty odor, overcome now by the reek of frying fish. I saw the first clusters of men and women, the first stalls, and my pulse thumped in my neck. Isobel's stride lengthened, and I hurried to catch up with her. The Countess made a noise of exasperation. Somebody turned and saw us, a woman wearing a strange, colorful dress and headscarf, and she started and took the elbow of the man standing next to her, who wore a billowing white shirt and black knee breeches and a scarlet sash around his waist. So he looked too, and pretty soon the whole group of them had fallen silent and staring, while Isobel and I made our way down the street toward the tendrils of smoke and the small brass band playing a tune I didn't recognize.

As we passed the knot of men and women, Isobel raised her hand. "Hello, there! Scorching day, isn't it?"

There were answering nods and waves. We turned the corner of Hemlock Street, which ran along the scattered docks and shops that made up the marina of West Harbor, and everything had transformed from when I had seen it last, just a couple of days ago. Picnic tables covered the green, and stalls rose up alongside the road selling refreshments and wares, and everybody milled around in what I supposed to be some kind of Portuguese national costume. At the other end of the street, the docks and moorings were crammed with fishing boats, with fishermen laughing and talking and drinking. Now I felt the full weight of our intrusion, the hot shame of it. I walked bravely onward next to Isobel, weaving my way between knots of astonished people, children in ruffled clothes, elaborately embroidered, women radiant in red. And the men, baggy and vibrant, who nodded and smiled.

Isobel greeted everybody by name, like they were old pals, like they came over daily for tennis or bridge. She hurried us toward a stall selling wine from wooden barrels and also homemade ice cream, and she bought two strawberry cones—her mother refused one, the first time I had ever seen the Countess turn down something edible—which we ate on the bench outside the tackle shop. The awning overhead cast us partly in shade, and Isobel stretched out her golden legs to catch the sun. I licked the ice cream and asked her how she knew everybody so well.

"Let me see." She ran her tongue around the edge of the cone, where the ice cream melted away in long, pink trickles. "There's Mrs. Menzies, who runs the post office. Her husband's that drunk fellow climbing into the boat, off the dock to the left. She's got a couple of sons, I don't know where they are. And that's old Santana with him, he runs the ferry on this side, his wife sells the tickets in summer. They had seven or eight children and the last one moved to the mainland last year, I think. Becky Santana. Nice girl. Met a fellow working on the Island for the summer and married him. That's Mrs. Costa and Mrs. Sweeney, gossiping together as usual. Their husbands are lobstermen. Frank Costa, that's her son, he gets seasick, so he's a groundskeeper over at the Club. You get to know everybody, that's all. When you've lived here long enough."

The ice cream was melting all over my hand, faster than I could lap it up, requiring a certain amount of strategic concentration. I lost the train of names and made some kind of assenting noise to cover the lapse.

"Why, what do you think, Peaches? You think we just lounge about in our pretty houses and ignore everybody else? We're all family here on the Island, you know. We're all in this together. If a hurricane strikes, why, you'd better hope you've got friends among the fishing fleet, because nobody at the Club has the least idea how to survive without electricity for a month, let alone rescue some poor soul washed out to sea."

"Like Vargas," I said, under my breath, but she heard me anyway.

"Yes, like Joseph."

She said his name in such a way that I forgot my ice cream and glanced to my side. Isobel slouched back against the bench, red-striped sundress hanging from her long, straight legs, while her narrowed eyes peered over the curve of her pink ice cream scoop to some point in the distance. I followed the line of her vision to its object, all the way down the wide wooden dock directly opposite, in the center of the harbor, where a group of men stood in resplendent costume, and the most resplendent of all was a slim, wiry, long-legged man who stood just to the side, wiping the wooden trim of his lobster boat with a white kerchief. His hat and his short black jacket were lavishly embroidered in gold, and the scarlet sash dangled from his waist like a spill of blood. As I watched—as we both watched, Isobel and I, while the ice cream melted down our hands and made them sticky—he straightened and turned to the man nearest him and made some joke to which they both laughed. I thought how hot he must feel, under the blazing sun in that black woolen jacket. All of them, those men wearing their quaint, breathtaking costumes. They must have been sweating through their shirts. In the middle of their laughter, a woman started down the dock and approached them, dressed in black and scarlet like the others, gold embroidery, looking like she meant to scold them for irreverence. I couldn't see her face; I thought it must be Vargas's wife, Joseph's mother.

"And that old woman over there," Isobel continued, reading my mind, "the one coming up to Joseph right now, that's his grandmother."

"His grandmother! He never mentioned a grandmother," I said, without thinking.

The Countess, who'd sat quietly throughout all this, looking extraordinarily ill-placed in her bright, flowing florals, put down her cigarette and drawled, "Oh, he *didn't*, did he?"

"I mean—"

"In all those times you snuck down to the harbor to see him?" She stuck the cigarette back in her mouth, sucked briefly, and said, "Don't think I didn't see you, sweetheart. I see everything."

"How very naughty of you, Peaches. I'm shocked to the core."

"Tell me about this grandmother," I said. "She looks formidable."

"She is. Why, she's the one who started this little affair, nine or ten years ago. Isn't that right, Abigail?"

"I don't remember. I was too busy divorcing your father, at the time."

"No, it was before that. It was the summer after the war started. Started for America, I mean. And all the young men had joined up, and only the fathers and grandfathers were left on the boats. Her own son was in basic training somewhere, as I remember. So she thought this would lift everybody's spirits, and also bring good luck, you know, God's blessing upon us all and that kind of thing."

"It was a dark time," said the Countess. "A very dark time."

"Did it work?" I asked.

"No. We lost two boats in a storm that summer. And then her son was killed on some Pacific island or another, I don't remember which one. He must have been too old to join up but he went anyway. They all want to get off the Island, you know, all the boys, most of the girls, and I guess he thought this was his chance. And then the Japs blew him apart on an island on the other side of the world. So you can't say God doesn't have a sense of irony, can you?"

The woman was kissing Joseph's cheek. He had to stoop a little so she could reach, and he put his hand at her back to hold her steady, while she touched his face with her fingers. "How terrible for her," I said.

"She runs the general store. Her husband had a heart attack a few years ago. He's been laid up ever since. Old Medeiro. Her daughter helps her."

"Mrs. Vargas?"

"Oh no. The older one. I can't remember her name. Do you know her name, Abigail?"

"I can't recall," the Countess said.

"Well, whatever her name is. There was another daughter, too, but she killed herself."

"*Killed* herself! Why? When?"

"Oh, a long time ago. Around the time I was born, I guess. Do you remember, Abigail?"

"Not really."

"Well, I heard it was for love. She and her sister were both in love with Joseph's father, old Vargas—impossible to believe, I know, but it was twenty years ago—and when Vargas married the other one, she drowned herself. Jumped off the cliff, not far from Greyfriars."

"Now where did you hear that nonsense?" the Countess said scornfully.

"From Livy. She heard it from her mother. Livy says the girl was pregnant, too. Pregnant with Vargas's baby, and that's why she did it." Isobel shuddered. "Look at him. Can you imagine making a baby with *that*?"

"She did, however. Mrs. Vargas made a beautiful son with him," said the Countess.

I glanced at her in surprise. "Do you mean Joseph? *Beautiful*?"

"Don't you think? A little rough-edged, maybe, but that's to be expected."

"I just don't think *beautiful* is the word I'd use."

"*I* think he's beautiful," Isobel said.

"*You're* an idiot," said the Countess. "Anyway, she didn't jump off the damned cliff. My God, out of the mouths of silly young girls. It was a boat. A boating accident in the Fleet Rock channel. You know the currents there. She was on her way to the lighthouse, because her sister was having the baby—Joseph, it was—and there was an accident."

"I thought you said you didn't remember anything," said Isobel.

"I remember *that* much. Now be quiet. Here comes the bishop."

As she spoke, the band stopped playing, the conversation and the horseplay went still. One by one, everybody turned in the direction of the western end of the harbor, where St. Mary's Church stood on the corner of Hemlock Street and Grace Street. Everybody except me. I went on staring at Joseph, as I turned over this new information in my mind, the terrible story of his birth, and maybe Isobel was looking at him, too. I think she must have been. In the dry, nerve-wracking silence, Joseph felt our observation and tilted his still-grinning face toward the tackle shop and the bench outside, and the smile dropped away. His head turned hastily back. Isobel tossed the remainder of her ice cream cone on the grass and stood up.

"Come on." Isobel snatched my hand and tugged it.

I resisted, turning to the Countess, who flipped her cigarette on the sidewalk and settled her hands on her knees to rise from the bench.

"No, go with her," she said. "I'm going to find the Monks. I'm sure they'll be here any minute."

So I rose, stuffing the rest of the ice cream and the cone into my mouth, licking my fingers. Isobel dragged me across the crumbled street as the trumpets struck up, something triumphant, and I craned my neck to see the white-robed priest emerge from the church doorway, flanked by acolytes, carrying a large silver jug. A rush of organ music followed him down the steps to merge with the trumpets. The mood changed so swiftly from anticipation to reverence, I stopped on the edge of the dock and pulled my hand away from Isobel's.

"What's the matter?" she hissed.

I didn't answer. I knotted my sticky fingers behind my back and stood, perspiring, to watch the solemn procession down Hemlock Road toward the docks. The sun burned through the crown of my hat. A woman stood just ahead of me, rolling a perambulator back and forth, humming faintly. She had beautiful golden skin, unlined, and dark hair beneath her scarlet headdress, and her fingers gripped the handle of the perambulator with great strength as she observed the approach of the priest and his men in their embroidered robes. In her other hand she held a rosary, which she slid carefully between her fingers, and I realized she wasn't humming. She was praying.

I lost track of Isobel. The priest reached the dock and the crowd parted. The trumpets made a final, reverent flourish and fell silent, so that you could hear the click of the priest's shoes on the wooden dock, the shuffle of the acolytes' robes, the water slapping against the pilings.

The priest lifted the pitcher and tilted it above the prow of the first boat, which was painted white and hung with flowers. I could have sworn that the drops hung in the air for an instant, refracting all that hot, white sunshine into something glittering and holy. But maybe that was just my imagination. The water fell and scattered on the new-painted wood, and the priest said, "Bless this ship and all who sail in her, in the name of the Father and the Son and the Holy Ghost, amen." He turned to the young man standing next to the boat, cap in hand, and he laid his palm on the dark curls atop the fellow's head and blessed him, too.

Next to me, the woman with the rosary let out a deep sigh, and the baby started to fuss because she'd stopped rocking the perambulator while the priest was speaking. She bent over the nest of blankets and lifted him out to hold him against her shoulder, and I felt her relief, the release of her tension in soft waves from her skin. The baby must have felt it, too. He nestled into the curve of her breast and went quiet, as if he were listening for the beat of his mother's heart.

The priest moved on, blessing the next boat and the next. There were no women on the dock, just the fishermen in their costumes of black and white and scarlet, and the gold embroidery that glittered in the sun. With tremendous discipline, I kept my eyes aimed strictly at the priest. I thought of Popeye, and all the blood, the gallons of salt water in his lungs, and how I never even noticed when he fell into the water. Never knew by what vicious, instantaneous accident he'd nearly met his end. I watched the sway of the priest's white robes and began to feel dizzy, began to feel as if it were Joseph's face on Popeye's body in my memory, Joseph who had fallen instead of Joseph who had saved. I curled my fingernails into my palms and made a bargain with God, this same God in whom I had placed so little trust before. I pledged that if I didn't carry any more messages, if I played no more part in the clandestine correspondence between Joseph and Isobel, if I made no more journeys to a certain lobster boat in the harbor, then God would allow Joseph to survive whole and intact by the end of summer, and send him safely off to college. Surely that was fair? For an all-powerful God, who giveth and taketh away at a whim, who had already taken away my father seven years before, that was surely a fair bargain, wasn't it? *Lord, hear our prayer.*

The priest reached Joseph's boat. From this distance, I couldn't hear the words, but the ritual was the same. The fall of glittering water from the pitcher, the ripple of the priest's white robes. When he lifted his hand to bless Joseph's head, Joseph closed his eyes and bent his neck, because the priest was a few inches shorter and somewhat stout. The priest then turned to the thick-shouldered, gray-haired fellow standing next to Joseph—Mr. Vargas, I assumed—and repeated the blessing. And I released a lungful of warm, salt air I hadn't realized I'd been holding, a sigh that sounded very much like the sigh of the young mother standing next to me with her perambulator.

3.

THE PRIEST MADE his way up one side of the dock and came down the other side, and when he stepped back to shore and traveled up the street to disappear through the open doorway of St. Mary's Church, surrounded by his acolytes, the friends and relatives of the fishermen streamed into a giddy mass. The women tore the flowers from the boats and pinned them in their headdresses, and the men took out beer and wine and began to drink. I saw Isobel making straight for the Vargases, and instead of following her I turned away. There was no sign anywhere of the Countess, no bright floral dress, no Monks either. I was alone.

I walked up Hemlock Street, without any kind of aim, and when I came to St. Mary's Church I paused. I felt a rush of cool air on my burnt skin, pouring forth from the shaded interior, and I thought about Mrs. Vargas in her black clothes.

I turned and went up the steps and into the church.

4.

THE INTERIOR OF St. Mary's Church was cool and empty. Priest and acolytes must have gone into the vestry or something, changing out of their ceremonial robes. I slid into the pew in the rear corner on the right-hand side of the nave, and sat there without moving, without thinking. I was just there to cool off, after all. Just to have a minute to myself.

I don't know exactly how long I stayed. You know how it is, when you slip into a trance of some kind, a form of Eastern meditation. You lose track of the passing of minutes. Time escapes its neat structure, its clock rhythm, and just sort of breathes along with you. I do know that I only noticed the small, dark-clad woman in the front pew when, moved by an unknown impulse, an inner timepiece I suppose, I at last prepared my stiffened legs to rise.

She knelt at the end of the pew, in the shadows, half-hidden by the back of the next pew and by a wooden pillar, which was probably why I hadn't seen her at first. Though her hands were clasped, she didn't bow her head. Instead she stared, without moving, at the altar, until the rustle of my clothes seemed to stir her. She turned her head a little and called out softly, "Joseph?"

I gripped the pew before me. My throat was dry with thirst, and I couldn't seem to speak. The woman rose and turned her body, and I saw that it was Mrs. Vargas, which I guess I already knew. Our gazes fastened upon each other, and I squeaked out, "No, it's just me," as if she should somehow know who I was.

"What are you doing here?" she asked.

"I—I was hot. It's hot outside, so I came in to rest."

She glanced at the door. "And the rest of your family?"

"Still out there, I guess."

Her eyes returned to my face. She seemed to think she had the right to study me. She stared without embarrassment, like she was cataloging my features, like she was trying to decipher a code I'd hidden there. I had the idea that her muscles were tense, that her nerves lay taut and fine under her skin, but maybe that was only me. Maybe I was the tense one. After a minute or two, she nodded at the door.

"If you're waiting for my son, he'll be here any minute."

"Oh!" I turned reflexively and then back, ashamed. "No, I wasn't, actually. I didn't realize—I didn't know you were here."

She made a noise that sounded like a good, old-fashioned *hmph* and sat back down in the pew, staring forward, from which I concluded that the conversation was over. I glanced down and saw that somebody had left a hymnal on the bench. I picked it up and put it in the pocket on the back of the pew, and I edged sideways down the row until I reached the aisle and turned to the open doors, just as a man hurried up the last step and rushed through the doorway, like he was late for a meeting. Joseph Vargas.

He saw me and stopped. "Good Lord. *There* you are."

"*Joseph*!" came his mother's sharp voice from the direction of the altar.

Joseph glanced over my shoulder and crossed himself. "Sorry, Mama. Are you all right?" (This to me.)

"Of course."

"Everyone's looking for you. It's a bit—there's been a—" He looked again over my shoulder, grabbed my elbow, and leaned to my ear. "Can you come to the dock later?"

"I—I don't know."

He straightened away, and an instant later Mrs. Vargas appeared at my side, holding out her hand.

"Joseph," she said again.

"Mama, we can't just leave her here. They're worried sick up at Greyfriars."

"Then telephone them."

I stepped back. "It's all right. I can telephone them. Go on ahead, I'll walk back."

"Not in this heat," he said firmly. "Not this time. We're taking you back in the boat."

"But—" I began.

"Joseph, don't be ridiculous," said Mrs. Vargas. "You know they won't like it."

"I don't give a—" He bit off the word and glanced at the altar. "I don't honestly care if they like it or not. Not after that circus this afternoon. I'll use the telephone in the vestry. Wait here, the two of you."

He hurried up the aisle and to the left, disappearing through a plain wooden door. I looked at Mrs. Vargas's round, frowning face as she watched him go. "Tell him I walked home after all," I said, and I turned away.

Like the head of a snake, her hand came out to snatch my arm. I stared in shock at her white fingers upon my skin.

"My son said to wait," she told me. "So we will wait."

5.

OUTSIDE, THE SUN had fallen deep in the sky, and the street was empty of people. Just trodden flowers and beer bottles and candy wrappers, the detritus of human happiness. The air was warm and drowsy, the tide had gone out. For an instant, I panicked and wondered if I'd lost track of days altogether, if I'd fallen asleep and this was tomorrow, or next week, or another life. But it couldn't be; the boats still bobbed at their moorings, strewn with petals, and when I looked down the street I saw a man in a blue mechanic's jumpsuit picking up the trash in slow, resigned movements.

We walked all the way down Hemlock Street to the last dock in the harbor, where Joseph's little sailboat was moored away from all the lobster boats, the working boats, newly blessed. Mrs. Vargas walked between us, silent and rigid, her arm inside the crook of Joseph's elbow. When we reached the boat, he helped her inside and then turned to me, but I was already climbing over the edge and settled myself near the bow while he raised the sail and threw off the mooring rope.

Now there is something about sailing, isn't there? They say all living creatures evolved from the sea, and maybe that's why my heart thrilled at the way the sail, freed at last, billowed out and filled with air, the way the boat surged beneath my bones and carried us around the harbor point. Joseph kept the tiller in one hand and the jib sheet in the other, and the direction of the wind was so sweet he didn't need to tack as we skimmed along the cliffs toward Fleet Rock. I leaned back on my hands and turned my face to the dropping sun.

"Tide's starting to come in," said Joseph. "I'll take us into the Rock and row you across the channel to Greyfriars."

I glanced at him in surprise, but his expression contained nothing but concentration on the job at hand. His mother sat by his side, carefully avoiding the swing of the boom, looking not at me but at the cliffs, which ranged high and rugged before they tumbled down toward Greyfriars, presently hidden behind the outcropping.

The tide might have been going in, but we avoided the force of the current in the channel and swung into the Fleet Rock landing from the south. Joseph secured the boat and handed his mother to shore, and without a word to either of us Mrs. Vargas made straight for the door of the lighthouse. Joseph jumped out and offered his hand to me, and this time I took it. "The dinghy's on the other side," he said, and we climbed in, first him and then me. He shipped the oars and turned his head to judge the shore.

"The current's not too strong, is it?" I asked.

"It's fine. The moon's past full."

I glanced up at the sky, as if I could actually see this phenomenon for myself, but of course the whole of the universe above me contained nothing but hazy blue, and a sun growing white and heavy to the west. I turned back to Joseph and said, "What do you mean, circus?"

He shook his head. "They're crazy, you know that? The Families."

"I'm one of them, remember?"

"No you're not. You know you're not."

"What am I, then?"

"You're Miranda," he said. He looked over his shoulder, judging distance and direction, and pulled on the left oar. "You know what the problem is? They're bored, that's it. Their daddies and granddaddies did all the work, building some business or another, and they've got all the money they need. The war's over and won. They've got no purpose left. Just watch the world race on while they turn to stone."

"Well, what about you? What's your purpose?"

He looked at me. "You know the answer to that."

"Me? How should I know?"

"Think about it."

I shrugged.

"Aw, come on. I'll give you a hint. Remember that book I was reading, that first day you came down to the harbor?"

I frowned. "You want to build ships?"

"Not just ships. Yachts, the way they used to. Some for racing, some for pleasure. One by one, designed and made by hand."

"That sounds wonderful."

He was staring out to sea, even though his arms continued the same steady rhythm on the oars. "It's the most beautiful thing in the world, a good, sweet ship skimming her way along the water. I mean it gets in your soul."

"Then do it," I said. "Build yourself a sailboat."

"I already have, Miranda. You just sailed in it."

I twisted to look back at Fleet Rock, at the boat moored on its dock. "*That*? You built that yourself?"

"Me and Pops. But I designed it."

"Oh," I said. "Oh." I turned back to face him, and I didn't know what to say. He had taken on a whole new dimension; he had acquired a skill and a capability that made me feel like a child. He stroked along in silence, staring at some point above my shoulder, frowning. Eventually he spoke.

"It's got to stop, you know."

"What's got to stop?"

He nodded over his shoulder. "*That*'s got to stop."

I curled my fingers around the edge of my seat and said, "You and Isobel?"

"What? Me and *Isobel*? I mean Isobel and Clay. She's got to figure out what she wants. You know what I mean."

"You mean break off the engagement?"

"Maybe I do. She can't marry him the way things are. For one thing, she's too young. But you know that, right?"

I fixed my gaze on Greyfriars, bobbing above his shoulder. "I guess I do."

"I don't know what she was thinking, saying yes to that starched shirt, at her age. I guess she thought it would make her father happy. You have to talk to her, Miranda. You have to make her see sense. Miranda? Are you listening?"

I returned to his face, which was now thunderous, deeply creased with some intent, violent emotion. "Yes, I'm listening."

"Don't you agree?"

The boat crossed a wake or something, pitching hard. I threw out my hand and gripped the edge; Joseph didn't seem to notice. We were in mid-channel now, and I could feel the strength of the current, even though the tide was still low. The muscles of Joseph's arms popped and strained, plowing the water with the oars.

"What's the other thing?" I asked.

"What other thing?"

"You said, *For one thing*. For one thing, she's too young. What's the other thing?"

"She'd make him miserable," Joseph said. "She *is* making him miserable, poor fellow. She's not right for him, and he's not right for her. She needs a fellow with a little more guts to him, guts to match hers. Fellow who can handle her moods and not try to keep her in some kind of glass box. Fellow who appreciates what he's got with her."

"A fellow like you, then?"

His head shot up. For an instant, he looked amazed, and then his teeth appeared. "Yeah, as a matter of fact. Now that you mention it. Maybe that's just the kind of fellow I had in mind. Say, what's going on with you? What's the matter?"

"Nothing. I'll speak to her."

"What's that?"

I lifted one hand and cupped my mouth. "I'll speak to her!"

"Good!"

Joseph focused his attention on navigating us across the rest of the channel, and I gripped the boat and tried not to be seasick. When we swung at last against the Greyfriars dock, I was glad to take Joseph's hand, glad for the support of his arm as I stepped from the shifting hull onto dry, immovable land.

"So what happened today?" I asked. "The circus, I mean."

He dropped my hand and grabbed the rope. "Isobel came over to chat, after the blessing, and the Monks turned up. I guess they don't like to see her spending time with a bunch of bum locals."

"Was there a scene?"

"I'll say." He dragged a hand through his hair, which was damp and curling from the spray and the salt air. "To be square, it wasn't Monk who started the argument. Isobel laid into him first. He's a gentleman, I'll give him that. He didn't yell or anything. But Izzy could yell for two."

He was shaking his head, and I couldn't tell if he was proud of her or ashamed. "So how did it end?" I asked.

"I walked away, is how it ended. I told her she ought to go home with her mother. With her *mother*, mind you, not Monk. But by then we'd caused a real stir. I'll bet the whole Island knows about it." He stepped back into the boat and settled between the oars. "You'll be all right? You'll speak to her?"

"I don't know what I can say. You know how determined she is."

"Determined is right. Determined to throw herself off a goddamned cliff. Could you toss that rope for me?"

I lifted the rope from the bollard and dropped it into the boat, and Joseph dipped the oars. The water swam around the wooden hull. I felt an instant of panic, thinking of all the things I meant to say to him, the vastness of what was unsaid, but it was too late. The wedge of sea grew between us. Joseph looked up and smiled, and the panic dissolved.

"Going to the Club tonight? I hear there's a swell party going on."

"Yes."

"Well, have fun." He maneuvered the boat a little, getting a line on the lighthouse, and looked back at me, still grinning. I remember thinking how white his teeth were in his tanned face. "Just not too much fun, all right? And keep our girl out of trouble for me, will you?"

"I'll do my best," I said, but he was already pulling out of earshot. I waved once and turned toward Greyfriars, where a committee of two—Isobel and her mother—ran down the grass to meet me.

6.

ACTUALLY, I'D FORGOTTEN all about the party at the Club tonight, until Joseph mentioned it. It was a Hawaiian luau theme, and Isobel had made us both muumuus out of some garish floral fabric—much like that worn by the Countess today—she'd ordered from the mainland, having been talked out of her original idea for grass skirts and coconut shells.

Mind you, these weren't ordinary muumuus—you might say they weren't exactly muumuus at all—and Isobel hadn't exactly made them herself. She'd found a pattern somewhere, Butterick or something, and had a seamstress in the village stitch them up. They had arrived yesterday, wrapped in brown parcel paper, and Isobel hadn't let me see them before she whisked the package upstairs. They were a surprise, she said. Just you wait.

Now I sat in the back of the silver convertible in my muumuu that wasn't a muumuu, thinking I should maybe pitch myself out of the car before I arrived, because surely that would prove less painful than walking into the clubhouse wearing . . . well, I don't know how to describe it. You might say that while the grass and the coconuts were out of the picture, the general idea remained. I looked down at my bosom and tried to tug up the neckline—such as it was—but that only exposed more of my midriff to general view. At least the evening air was still warm. If I had to walk into the Winthrop Island Club wearing a few scraps of floral costume fabric, I wasn't going to leave with pneumonia.

And there was Isobel, dressed as briefly as I was, but with far more panache. A giant hibiscus nestled in her hair, and she drove with one hand while the other held a forgotten cigarette. I think she was too animated to smoke. Her mother sat beside her so they could continue to argue about what had happened that afternoon. I wasn't listening, mostly because the draft thundered against my ears, leaving me in blissful ignorance of the exact sequence, the words that were said, Isobel's opinions of both men, the Countess's opinion of her. By the time we pulled up to the clubhouse, where a swarm of scholarship boys in bow ties were parking the cars, the Countess had belatedly turned to the subject of Isobel's costume. To my surprise, she approved.

"At least it'll remind that poor boy why he fell in love with you in the first place," she said, pitching her cigarette into the impatiens. "And Miranda looks divine. Why doesn't she have a hibiscus?"

Isobel spun to look at me for the first time. "Why, where's your hibiscus, Peaches?"

"I don't know. I don't have one."

She smacked her forehead. "My God! I forgot! Here, have mine."

"No, really—"

"No, you must. It's my fault."

She reached for her hair, but I stopped her hand. "Really. I don't want it."

"You must, Peaches. It's pink, and pink looks better on you than it does on me, trust me." She unpinned the flower and turned my head. "Hold still. See? Sitting pretty in those lovely dark curls of yours. Much better."

"I feel silly. You can pull it off, but I can't."

Isobel pulled back, took my shoulders, and angled me back and forth for examination. A smile grew on her mouth. "You're wrong, my precious. You can pull off anything if you just stop trying."

"Come along," said the Countess, "before Mrs. Monk drinks up all the mai tais."

At the door, the members of the Luau Committee dropped fragrant leis over our heads, handed us cocktails in coconut shells, and wished us aloha or something. A cloud of thick, sweet-smelling smoke drifted in from the open doors to the terrace, lending authenticity to the rumor about the suckling pig. I plucked a coconut hair from the surface of my drink and said to Isobel, "Do you have a minute?"

"*Now*, Peaches?"

"Yes."

She sighed a little and turned to her mother. "Abigail, I'm going to take Peaches into the powder room to fix her lipstick. Run along and chitchat, will you?"

The Countess lifted one of her sculptural eyebrows, not at Isobel but at me. I tried to return her some kind of knowing gaze, and I guess she noticed, because she made a small nod and shrugged her shoulders. "I don't chitchat," she said to Isobel, and she walked off in the direction of the terrace, holding her coconut in the middle of her palm.

Now, the ladies' powder room at the Winthrop Island Club—the old clubhouse, I mean, not the one they rebuilt after the fire—that powder room was something. First you walked into a kind of anteroom, with a long white marble counter and a row of lighted mirrors and red velvet stools, and intimate little sofas upholstered in the same soft red velvet, and then—if you actually needed to answer the call of nature, that is, not just the call of vanity—you stepped through a doorway into the business

side of things. Lucky for us, the place was empty. Isobel stalked to one
of the velvet stools, motioned me into the one next door, and opened her
pocketbook.

"What are you doing?" I asked.

"Why, fixing your lipstick. Come on, sit down."

"I don't need you to fix my lipstick. I need to talk to you."

"Well, talk, then. Just do like this." She made a purse of her mouth.

"Isobel, about what happened this afternoon—"

"You don't know anything about it, Peaches, so shut your trap and
let me put this on you. I've been meaning to tell you for ages that coral
doesn't suit you. *Pink*, Peaches. You may not want to hear this, but pink's
just right for you, with your dark hair and fair skin."

"Pink's too frivolous."

"Not the *right* kind of pink. Now, hold your lips still and listen to me. I
know what you're going to say. Shh! Lips still. I know what you're going
to say, and it won't make any difference. I've made up my mind." She
leaned back to scrutinize her work, and turned me to the mirror. "What
do you think?"

I stared back at my reflection, lit to brilliance by twelve low-wattage
incandescent bulbs, and said, "Made up your mind about what?"

"I can't tell you, can I? That wouldn't be fair. I can tell you what I
think, though. Clayton Monk doesn't love me, not the way I want to be
loved. He doesn't understand me the way I want to be understood. And
I guess I knew that already, but I thought it didn't matter, because there
was always—I could always—"

"Joseph," I said.

We were speaking to each other in the mirror, our faces laid out side
by side in perfect contrast. Mine, round and fair and large-eyed, pointed
at the chin, framed by dark hair; hers, lean and blond and oval, anchored
by a pair of small, hooded eyes. But there were symmetries, too. Our
hair, light and dark, curled in the same short style around our ears, and

our lips were the same wide shape, except she had colored hers in their usual scintillating red, and mine were magenta. They matched the hibiscus in my hair, just above my left ear, which was the other obvious difference between the two of us.

Now Isobel laid her finger over her scarlet lips and winked at me in the mirror. "Not a word about *that*, precious. That's private, all right? Now let's go get nice and drunk together, shall we? I'm going to need a few more of these to work up my courage."

She lifted her coconut from the counter and I lifted mine, and together we walked to the entrance just as the door flung open to reveal Livy Huxley in a grass skirt.

"Livy! You nearly spilled my drink, darling," Isobel said.

But Livy was staring at me. "Why, is that *you*, Miranda?"

"Isn't she beautiful? I had a feeling that muumuu would suit her."

"It's not really a muumuu," I said modestly.

Livy made a tiny, vicious smile. "Whatever it is, it certainly does *some*thing for her. Did you put that lipstick on her, too?"

"She's like a different girl with it, isn't she? Like a movie star." Isobel wrapped her arm around my shoulders. "When you're famous, Peaches, I'm going to give an interview to *Life* magazine and say it was all my doing."

7.

IN LATER DAYS—OR SO I understand—that luau party of 1951 took on a legendary reputation among the Families. Everybody agreed that the committee carried off the theme so well and so thoroughly, nobody could ever host a luau party on the Island again, because this one couldn't be topped. I don't know if that's true. I do know we got nicely drunk, as Isobel wanted, and we sat down at round tables on the terrace and ate our pineapple and our suckling pig and various other dishes I can't remember. The orchestra played all the usual numbers, except with a Polynesian twist, and I later learned that the committee—isn't this just the *most*?—the committee actually brought in musicians all the way from Hawaii itself to play that evening. Yes, by ship and by train, seven thousand miles just to entertain the Families for dinner and dancing on a single hot July night in the summer of 1951.

Or maybe the luau's legendary status came about not because of the food and the coconuts and the Polynesian music, but because of what happened on the lawn below the terrace a half hour before midnight, when Isobel Fisher finally swallowed enough fruity cocktails to break off her engagement with Clayton Monk in the middle of "Some Enchanted Evening." It was what they call a *scene*, I believe. The Countess lifted her skirts above her knees—she was wearing an actual muumuu, not Isobel's version—and ran down the steps to take her daughter into custody, and when we had maneuvered her safely into the shelter of the tennis dressing room, the Countess turned to me and said, "Go find Clay."

"Clay? Me? Why?"

"Make sure he doesn't throw himself off a cliff or anything. Make sure he doesn't get himself engaged to somebody else. I don't know. I saw him heading off toward the sixth hole."

I thought it was pointless to argue at such a moment. I looked at her and at Isobel, who was waltzing herself dreamily around the lockers, and I turned around and walked back across the lawn toward the golf course, while every single pair of silent, well-bred eyes in the joint that evening traced my progress.

The Countess happened to be an avid golfer, as familiar with the Club course as she was with her own living room, and she was exactly right about Clay. I found him on the green at the sixth hole, practicing his long putt with an imaginary club. Maybe she was right to be worried, because the sixth hole was one of the most dramatic on the entire course, bordering the steepest part of the cliffs that formed the northern edge of the Island, such that the green itself was only a few yards from catastrophe and the flag looked as if it marked the end of the world. A lot of golf balls lay half-buried on the narrow beach below, let me tell you.

The dense, short grass swallowed my footsteps, and I knew I should make some kind of noise so I wouldn't startle him. I stopped a few yards from the green, cleared my throat, and said his name softly.

He didn't so much as flinch. "Miranda? That you?"

"Yes."

"How is she?"

"Pretty tight, I'd say."

"Well, we're all a little tight, aren't we? That's the trouble." He lined up his putt just so and swung his club made of air, and the figurative ball must have gone straight in the hole because he straightened and turned toward me. The moon was about three-quarters full and the sky was clear, and I could see him pretty well because he was wearing a pale, tropical suit. I stepped forward onto the green.

"She didn't mean it," I said, and the words probably sounded every bit as insincere to him as they did to me.

"Of course she meant it. She's been meaning it all summer. I could see her simmering with it since Memorial Day; I'm surprised she held back so long."

"It's just nerves. She's still so young to get married."

"Not that young. She's twenty, plenty of girls get married sooner."

"Yes, but Isobel's different."

Clay turned back to the hole and lined up another putt. "Yes, she is. She certainly is. That's why I love her, because she's different from the other girls, she's strong and wild, and I thought I could love her enough to—to make her—to calm her a little, just enough to—" He bent suddenly to the grass and came up with a bottle of something he must've purloined from the bar.

"You should tell her that. You should tell her what you've just told me. She wants to be worshipped, Clay, she wants to be a goddess to you. She doesn't want to be a wife, she wants to be a—a—I don't know, a fellow adventurer. She wants adventure."

"But I want to settle down, Miranda. I want to settle down and have kids. My mother's been dying for grandkids. You know my brother, couple of years older, paratrooper, he was killed in Holland. So I'm her last chance, she's been waiting and waiting . . ." He lowered the bottle from his lips and held it between his hands as he settled into his stance again. "She told me a month ago to break it off with Isobel and find some other girl, but I wouldn't do it. I can't imagine being with anyone but Izzy. She's the only adventure I want."

"Oh, Clay."

He swung the bottle like a club. "Aw, it's all right, Miranda. Here I am, dumping all my heartache on you. You don't mind, do you?"

"Of course not."

"You're like a sister to me. Izzy's little sister."

There was a sad lilt to his voice that drew me closer. His shoulders were still bent, but he wasn't looking at the hole. He was staring down the neck of the bottle. Like I said, he was dressed in a tropical suit of white linen, according to the theme of the evening, although he had discarded the jacket and stood there in his shirtsleeves, rolled up to the elbow, like they'd been when we first talked like this above the cliffs at his own house, not far away. I took the bottle from his fingers and poured out the rest of the contents on the green.

"Thanks," he said. "I'm glad someone had the nerve to do that."

"Any time."

"You look sensational tonight, by the by. In case nobody's told you. You've got a kind of bloom, these past weeks. Maybe the Island agrees with you, or something."

"Oh, you know. It's just this lipstick Isobel gave me."

"You're going off to college in September, isn't that right?"

"Yes. Mount Holyoke."

"Good for you, good for you. You're going to blossom. You'll make some—some Amherst kid a very lucky—lucky man—"

His voice broke a little, and it seemed natural, because his arms had spread open, to step inside the circumference of those arms and hug him, the way a kid sister would comfort her big brother when some girl broke his heart. He wrapped his arms around me and bent his head to cry into my hair, and we stood there while the wind blew softly over us and the smell of whisky made a snug, pleasant, pungent knot binding us together. He stroked my hair a time or two, smoothing away his own tears, and I happened to look up at that instant. "You're so beautiful, Miranda," he whispered, and he kissed me on the cheek.

I didn't know what to say. The embrace turned awkward. I started to pull away just as he went to kiss my other cheek, and somehow the kiss ended up on my lips, and we were kissing each other, my first kiss.

At first I was too shocked to move. I just stood there while his mouth moved mine and his hands slipped against my back, which was bare in most places, remember, because of the provocative design of Isobel's muumuu. Then, because I'd drunk a cocktail or two myself, and because he kissed so gently—because the kiss surprised me, because I didn't want to wound him, because I didn't know what else to do when a boy kissed you—I started to kiss him back. He groaned a little, the way boys do when they're overcome by the taste of a girl's mouth, though of course I didn't know that yet. I'd never heard a boy groan before. I felt his tongue slip through the seam of my lips, at the same time as his right hand crawled up and grasped the bandeau top of my muumuu-that-wasn't-a-muumuu and pulled it down, so my breast spilled out into the bare, warm air, to be captured at once by Clay's spread fingers.

There was a gasp that I thought was my own, but which actually came from Livy Huxley, who stood at the edge of the green, about ten yards away, wearing her grass skirt and an expression of outrage.

"Livy!" Clay exclaimed, but she was already gone, running back toward the clubhouse, grass skirt whisking into darkness. He looked back at me, down at my naked breast, and said, "Oh, hell."

I turned away and stuffed my bosom back into place, shocked and throbbing with shame.

"I'm sorry, I'm sorry," he said. "I don't know what came over me."

"Me either."

"It was the whisky. I'm so sorry. I don't usually—well, I shouldn't've—aw, damn. Are you all right?"

"Of course, of course."

"I'm sorry. Geez, Miranda. I'm sorry, I was so low, and you—you *do* look sensational—that dress—oh, Jesus *Christ*, what have I done? What am I *thinking?*"

"I don't know. I don't know."

"Aw, geez. Geez. Livy, of all people. I could just—God, what a heel I am. The damned whisky. I'm so sorry. I'll walk you back, all right? I'll find Livy and make sure she understands."

Understood what, exactly, he didn't say. He didn't say anything at all, in fact, and neither did I. He snatched up his jacket and we walked back swiftly, hot-faced, not touching, not speaking, and parted on the lawn, just outside the spill of light from the clubhouse. I think we were both shaking. Certainly *I* was shaking. I thought I felt the vibration of Clay's nerves alongside mine.

"I'll find Isobel," I said.

"Yes."

That was all. We had kissed, my first kiss, and he had pulled down my dress and put his hand on my breast, and that was all we had to say to each other about that. I guess the groundskeepers must've found the whisky bottle on the sixth-hole green the next morning, but they probably found a lot of things that day. Like I said, it was a hell of a luau, a legendary party.

8.

I FOUND ISOBEL alone, sitting on a bench in the rose garden. She stood up when she saw me, lean and disheveled, and I thought, *I have just been kissing Clay Monk.* I clasped my shivering hands behind my back and tried to speak.

"Let's go home," she said.

"Home? Now?"

"God, yes. I can't stand it any longer. Can you?"

"I'll go find your mother. You're in no condition to drive."

"No, don't. I can't face her. We'll walk."

"Walk? It's four miles!"

"Four miles is nothing, Peaches. We could use the exercise after all that lousy suckling pig. And pineapple, Jesus. I never want to see another pineapple."

Well, what was I going to say? I had no more desire to face the interested gazes in the clubhouse than she did. We crossed the lawn and the flowerbeds to Winthrop Road, gray in the hazy moonlight. The air was still warm, but the breeze from the sea made me shiver. Or maybe it was my conscience that made me shiver, my conscience that woke and trembled as the shock of kissing wore away. I wrapped my arms around each other and followed the silvery bob of Isobel's shoulder. In my mind I saw Clay Monk's face leaning toward mine, eyes closed, and I felt sick. Our feet crunched in the gravel at the side of the road.

"You aren't cold, are you?" Isobel asked. "In this heat?"

"Maybe a little. It's the breeze."

"Really? I love it. I'm hot as blazes."

We walked another half mile or so, and Isobel stopped. "My feet are killing me," she said.

"Mine too."

"Damned sandals." She reached down and took one off, balancing miraculously on the other foot, and then she removed the other one with a deep sigh. "Go ahead, Peaches. I won't tell."

"But the gravel."

"We'll walk on the grass. Come on."

So I took off my sandals and discovered the ecstasy of the crisp grass beneath the soles of my feet, and my skin began to warm again, and I didn't feel quite as sick, just dizzy and tired from all those fruit-tasting rum cocktails in coconut halves. I saw Clay's face again, but this time, just before he kissed me, he turned into Joseph. Isobel and I were walking Indian file now, and I stared at the back of her neck and thought, *She's kissed them both, she kisses them both, back and forth.* How do they stand it? Do they know? Joseph knew, but did Clay? Probably he did. Probably that was why he had kissed me at the sixth hole, because of some subconscious need for revenge on Isobel. That was what the shrinks would say, wouldn't they? Oh, a shrink would have his hands full with all of us. Me with my dead, beloved father, and Isobel with all these men who adored her, worshipped her, forgave her—

She turned suddenly. "Let's sit down. I'm pooped."

"You? Pooped?"

"It's been a long night, sister."

She threw herself on the grass and grabbed my hand to pull me with her, so we lay staring at the charcoal sky, the pale patch surrounding the moon, listening to the shrieks of a thousand crickets. A few stars glimmered through the blur. The grass still smelled of sunshine, of hay and gold.

"Have I made a stupid mistake, Peaches?"

"Well," I said, "he loves you, you know. He adores you more than anything in the world."

"*Does* he love me? Or just some ideal of me? Some woman he's made up in his imagination who happens to look like me."

I picked at the grass next to my leg. "No, it's you, all right. He knows who you are. But he needs to settle down, because of the war and because of his brother—"

"Poor Bingo."

"His name was Bingo?"

"No, it was Benjamin. But everyone called him Bingo. He landed all right, but a sniper got him on one of those narrow Dutch roads. Mrs. Monk got the telegram and still went to dinner that night. Isn't that awful? Not because she wasn't upset, but because she was."

"My mother didn't even come out of the bedroom for weeks after Daddy died."

"There's the difference, you see. The difference between us and everybody else." Her hand found mine in the grass. I felt her chest shudder through the bones of her arm and fingers. "Daddy's going to be so upset."

"Don't cry."

"I'm so drunk, you know."

"Everybody's drunk tonight," I said. "A real swell party."

"I want something, Miranda, and I don't know what it is—I don't know how to get it—I just know that I can't live like *them*, like corpses. I haven't even *lived* yet—"

"I'd say you were doing a pretty good job of it."

"This? *This?* Oh, this is nothing. Petty rebellion."

"You have it in you, though."

"You know what my trouble is? I was born for the wrong age, Peaches. That's it, that's the problem. I should have been a flapper or something, and instead I happened along after they had all the fun, after they had all the adventure, and now everybody wants to settle down in nice, dull families, everybody wants to be a square, everybody but me—poor, sweet Clay—"

"Then just go off and do something. Live. Nobody's dragging you to the Island every summer, nobody's forcing you to marry Clay. You can do whatever you want—"

"But then I'd be poor. I'd be nobody." She rolled on her side. "Don't you see? They've got us trapped. We can't live without this, it's what makes us special. What makes us better than everybody else. We don't like to admit it, it's un-American to admit it, but it's true. When you have money and prestige—*especially* prestige—you think you deserve it, somehow, and everybody else is just—ordinary. Nobody else matters. Why do you think Daddy married Abigail? To be one of them, to be part of their little club. He'll be so crushed that I—"

A noise rumbled faintly from the road, the sound of an engine. In the two miles we'd walked from the Club, we hadn't heard or seen a single car. Most of the Families lived in the other direction; only the Fishers had bought their land and built their house so close to the business end of the Island, apart from everybody else.

"It's Clay," Isobel said dully.

"How do you know?"

"It's Clay." She put her hand on my shoulder. "Lie still."

We breathed quietly against each other. I closed my eyes, as if by not seeing anything, I could not myself be seen. I whispered, "We should have worn those grass skirts after all."

"Why?" she whispered back.

"Camouflage."

Isobel started to giggle. The engine roared closer, drowning out the sound of the crickets, and I thought I could smell gasoline, could smell the sultry automobile exhaust, the rubber burning against the pavement. Isobel snatched my hand and held it tight. The ground vibrated softly beneath my back. The noise grew and grew, intolerable, and the air whooshed as the great beast flew past us and slammed on its brakes in a tremendous squeal.

"Damn," said Isobel.

Clay came running. "Izzy! Izzy! Oh God! God, *no!*"

She sat up suddenly. "I'm just fine, darling. Just lying here with Peaches, soaking up the moonlight."

In the next instant, he had reached us, he had snatched up Isobel with a cry of incoherent relief.

"I thought—I thought—saw you lying there by the road—what the *hell*, Izzy, what the devil were you—"

"Hush, hush," she said, laughing, clinging to him. "I'm all right."

"I'd have killed myself, Izzy, *killed* myself if anything happened to you."

"I know, darling, I know. You're such a dear, faithful boy, and I'm so mean to you."

"I don't care. I only care that you're safe, Izzy. You can't scare me like that, you don't know what I thought just now—lying there by the road—if it hadn't been for the crazy color of your dress—"

Clay kissed her forehead and her cheeks, everywhere but her lips, and Isobel tilted back her head and just drank it in, his idolization of her, the cinematic quality of his adoration. She was smiling still, absolutely delighted with herself and with the way things had turned out, and I thought, amazed, *Maybe she did it all on purpose.* All of this, the whole day, the whole evening, just to amuse herself, to wake herself up, to make her feel alive.

Without so much as a glance at me, Clay picked her up and started for the car. I don't think he even saw me, I don't think I made the slightest impression on his conscious mind, even though an hour earlier he had kissed me and fondled my breast and said I looked sensational. Isobel peeped over his arm and met my gaze and winked, before she slapped his chest and said, "Darling, what about Peaches?"

He spun back, still holding her, and searched for me in the grassy moonlight. I was sitting up by now, arms clasped around my knees. "Miranda! I didn't—I'm sorry."

I rose from the grass and dusted off my dress, what there was of it. "Think nothing of it," I said.

9.

CLAYTON MONK DROVE a four-seater Lincoln with a hardtop roof, plain black, the kind that could go fast if the driver wanted, only the driver never did. I climbed in the back without being told and lay down promptly on the plush cloth seat that smelled of dog. Isobel nestled in front under the protection of Clay's arm. I stared at his shoulder, bent to accommodate her, and at his worried face in the rearview mirror, which kept trying to capture my gaze and ask me, without asking, what I'd said to Isobel.

Let him wonder.

The rumble of the car lulled me. A minute later, my eyes turned heavy and dark, and I guess I must have fallen asleep, because I became conscious of the car having stopped, the engine having cut; of the rhythmic squeak of the seat springs, counterpointed by small, suppressed grunts. I kept my eyes closed, even though there was nothing to see. The car was dark. The squeaking came faster, faster, faster; Isobel shrieked once like a bobcat; *squeak*ing *squeak*ing *squeak*ing et cetera and then nothing, just a moan from Clay that lasted only a second before it seemed to choke off in his throat, followed by an absolute, heavy silence that was thick enough to draw your name in. I waited and waited for somebody to move, somebody to say something, but they had done each other to death, it seemed.

After what felt like a decent interval, I found the door handle with my fingers and crept out as quietly as I could, leaving the door open so they could get some fresh air, at least. When I looked up, I saw I was in the Greyfriars driveway, parked neatly by a rhododendron. The moon was still out, and instead of walking straight through the front door I went around the side, past the kitchen entrance, down the long, dark lawn toward the Greyfriars dock. Two hundred yards away, the moonlight touched the squat top of the Fleet Rock lighthouse, and the light made its lazy revolution around the sea. I made out the foam striking the rocks at the base, and the dock with its shelter for the two boats, the sailboat and the dinghy. A few lamps were lit inside, small golden specks at the bottom of the tower, and I wondered which one belonged to Joseph. Whether he was inside, and what he was doing. What his bedroom looked like. What color was his bedspread, how many pillows, what books inhabited his nightstand and his bookshelf.

The crickets clamored around me. There was no sound from the driveway, no sign that Clay and Isobel had roused from their stupor. I thought maybe I was the only person awake on the Island. My lips felt strange and swollen from Clay's kiss, my first kiss, and yet when I put my fingers to the seam of my mouth, there was no difference. The same old lips as always. Maybe it hadn't happened after all; maybe I had dreamt it, maybe it was all mixed up in my half-drunk memory. I turned and found my way inside the darkened boathouse, felt the shelves with my hands until I found the flashlight. I walked back outside into the moonlight and down onto the end of the dock, where the water slapped against the pilings. I sat down at the end, exactly where Isobel and I had sat on the evening after our parents' wedding, and held the flashlight in my lap, secured by my two hands, while my legs dangled above the water.

1969 (MIRANDA THOMAS)

1.

MOST MORNINGS, THERE were roses of various colors, whites and pinks and yellows and occasionally even red. I remember they were not always fragrant—each variety of rose has its own personality, you know, and some are bred for looks alone—but occasionally, like the day of the moon landing, the twentieth of July, their perfume so saturated the air, sultry and delicate all at once, I thought I was drunk. I buried my face in the middle of the bouquet, disregarding the possibility of thorns, and—as I did every morning—I looked around for some sign of my clandestine admirer. An article of clothing left behind, maybe, or a footprint or a scent left hanging in the air, or the movement of some swift body in the boxwoods.

But I discovered no trace of another human being, except the Burbridge sisters on the lawn with their easels and oil paints, capturing the intrusion of dawn on the lighthouse.

2.

AFTER SWIMMING, I crossed the grass to the kitchen door, intending to head upstairs for a shower. Already I could hear the hammering of Donnelly's men as they repaired the French doors from the terrace to the dining room, as they installed the new bathrooms upstairs. The landscapers were due to dig up the lawn for resodding next week, but for now the grass was still in terrible shape, choked with weeds. I picked a careful path between the pricklier sorts, and when I was about halfway to the house, I stopped and turned to the sea, where Miss Felicity and Miss Patricia still sat on their camp stools, stabbing away with their brushes. I tucked my towel a little more firmly around my head and went to them.

"What lovely work," I said.

"Thank you," said Miss Felicity. Miss Patty ignored me; she was concentrating too fiercely on her art. They both wore headscarves in violent gemstone colors; to keep their hair in check, they said, when the sea breeze kicked up.

"How long have you been painting this morning?" I asked.

"Before dawn," said Miss Felicity.

"Really? How energetic of you." I pretended to examine the canvasses, which were curiously opposite—Miss Felicity an Impressionist who favored timid pastels, and Miss Patty a hard, unforgiving realist. "I don't suppose you happened to see anyone on the lawn this morning?" I asked. "Near the swimming pool?"

"No, dear," said Miss Felicity.

"No," snapped Miss Patty.

I turned to leave. On the grass before me, Brigitte had just laid out her blanket to sunbathe in the nude, which she liked to do for an hour each morning after breakfast, before the sun grew too hot.

"But I did see a fellow rowing away on his boat, while I set up my easel," Miss Patty added grudgingly.

"Did you?" said her sister. "I didn't see any such thing."

"That's because you won't wear your spectacles. Look at that rot you've painted." Miss Patty pointed a condescending brush at Miss Felicity's efforts. "There isn't a single line anywhere. It's not a painting, it's a blur."

"The boat," I said. "Where did it go? Which direction?"

"Couldn't tell. Facing east. Lost him in the sun. Anyway . . ." Miss Patty leaned closer to her easel, drew back, leaned close again. She looked down and examined her palette.

"Anyway what?"

"Hmm? What?"

"The man," I said. "The man in the boat. You said you couldn't tell which direction he was headed, but there was something else."

"Oh, nothing else. Just had the feeling he didn't want to be seen." She daubed her palette and resumed stabbing at the canvas, which depicted the lighthouse in a strange, harsh glow, each line appearing as if refracted in a prism.

The towel around my head became loose. I pulled it free from my hair and stood there, staring at the dock, thinking that I must have a glass of water, I was feeling dizzy.

"Unless it wasn't a man," said Miss Felicity. "Are you sure it was a man? We only have Otto here at Greyfriars. Otto and Hugh. And Leonard, but he's a queer."

"Of course it wasn't Otto. I would have said if it was Otto."

"What about little Hugh?"

"It wasn't Hugh, either. Will you be quiet, Felicity? I'm rendering the light."

"Rendering the light," Miss Felicity muttered. "Rendering the light, if you will."

"Although now that I think of it, it might have been a woman," said Miss Patty. "A woman in trousers. As I said, I was facing the sun."

3.

WHEN I ARRIVED at the general store at a quarter past nine, Miss Laura was keeping the counter. She was so surprised to see me, she went so far as to raise her eyebrows a millimeter or two. She asked if I wanted a cup of coffee, and I said no, I wanted a pair of binoculars. After an instant's consideration, I said I'd take the coffee, too.

You would think that a pair of binoculars might be a longshot for a small, old-fashioned general store on Winthrop Island, but Miss Laura poured the coffee and went right into the back. She returned about five minutes later with a cardboard box. "You're in luck," she said. "My father must've stocked these before he died."

"Thanks. How much?"

"Ten dollars sound fair?"

I opened the box and pulled out the binoculars. They weren't much to look at, just plain black, no fancy dials or levers or anything. "Do you mind if I try them out in the harbor?" I asked.

"Suit yourself."

I splashed a little more coffee down my throat and went outside, where the sunshine had finally tumbled over the crest of the hill and filled the harbor with light. The early ferry was just putting in at the dock. I raised the binoculars to my eyes, and the magnification shocked me. I stared in fascination at the face before me, a middle-aged man wearing a felt hat and an expression of intense anticipation as he observed the rituals of docking. I could see the stubble on his chin, the small, diagonal scar disfiguring the middle of his forehead, the three vertical lines between his squinting eyebrows, each detail rendered in bright, sunlit color.

I lowered the binoculars and went back into the general store, which seemed much darker and plainer than when I left it. I finished the coffee and opened my pocketbook. "Ten dollars is more than fair," I said.

"Plus twenty-five cents for the coffee," she said.

I dug out a quarter. "Can I ask you a question, Miss Laura?"

"If you like."

"How's your sister doing, all by herself at the lighthouse?"

If I was hoping to shock some information out of her by the suddenness of my question, I was surely underestimating—and not for the first time—the stoic Islander nature. A very slight, very discreet vibration passed over her skin. She took away my coffee cup, and when her face was turned to the side, she said, "No idea."

"Miss Laura, I wish you'd trust me. God knows I've suffered my share in all this. I think I deserve your confidence by now, don't you?"

She set the cup and saucer in the wide, deep sink and asked me if there would be anything else.

"For God's sake," I said. "Don't be such an Islander."

Miss Laura whipped around. "What do you know about that? What do you know about living here? About making a living off the crumbs of rich folks? You think you have a right to us. You and the Fishers. Suffered your share? You're the *cause* of all this misery. And now you've come back, for what? To ruin us all over again?"

"I don't understand," I said. "What have I done?"

"You just use us when you need us, and you never care about the mess left behind. Bianca and Francisca and poor Joseph. You stay away, do you hear me?"

My nerves were jumping now, my heart hammering. I felt as I did in that hospital in Wiltshire, packing my things at three o'clock in the morning. I pressed my fingertips into that worn counter, which had once been so new and shining. "Joseph. What about Joseph? Tell me!"

She came to stand before me, across the counter, and she leaned her own hands against the surface and said, "Never you mind. Never you mind about any of us. I swear, if they burned Greyfriars to the ground, I'd dance on the ashes. I would."

"*Laura!*"

Miss Laura jumped guiltily and turned to the stockroom door, where her mother stood akimbo in a neat blue dress and cardigan sweater, unbuttoned.

I said, "Stay away from what, Laura? Tell me!"

"*Deus meu,* Laura. What's that fly in your eye? Miranda has nothing to do with our troubles."

"But—"

"We have all got our misery, rich and poor and in between. And we each bring our own shame upon ourselves, and God alone can judge us." She pointed to the storeroom. "Go. They are bringing some boxes from the ferry, I need you to unpack them."

She was the kind of woman who must be obeyed, and Miss Laura, after a brief, resentful mutiny, pushed herself away from the counter and followed the path laid for her by that single finger. When she was gone, Mrs. Medeiro turned to me.

"I am so sorry, Miranda. Girls can be so impertinent." She glanced down at the binoculars on the counter. "Is that for the moon tonight?"

She seemed perfectly serious, as if she actually thought I was going to observe, with a pair of bird-watching binoculars, a couple of astronauts prowling the Sea of Tranquility. I tucked them back into the box with my trembling fingers. "I don't think the weather's going to cooperate. We're headed up to the Monks' instead, to watch the landing on television."

"It's so exciting. I remember riding in a donkey cart back in Portugal, when I was a girl. I never saw a car until I was sixteen. Now we are walking on the moon. The moon!"

"It hardly seems possible, does it? I've got my fingers crossed that everything goes well."

"I will say ten Hail Marys tonight. I have been praying all week since they started up their rockets." She nodded at the box. "Did you get everything you needed?"

"I did, thank you," I said, as if my heart were not still pounding, as if I didn't hear Laura's voice knocking in my head—*stay away, stay away*—and because I couldn't sustain another word of conversation, I wished her a good morning and left, to the faint jingling of bells, out into the familiar salt atmosphere of the harbor. The passengers were now disembarking the ferry, and I spied the man I'd observed earlier at ten or twenty times magnification, who now strode across the landing toward a plain white Chevrolet idling on Hemlock Street. As I watched, mesmerized, he unbuttoned the front of his suit jacket, which was far too heavy for summer, and maybe he felt the weight of my stare, because he turned his head and found me, and his eyes widened in recognition.

"Miss Schuyler!"

I whipped around. "Oh! Tom, you startled me. You shouldn't sneak up on a girl."

"My apologies. I was just on my way up to Greyfriars. You've saved me the trouble."

"Your men are doing a terrific job, if that's what you're checking on. The bathrooms are almost finished, and the plasterwork in the dining room—"

"Oh, I wasn't going to ask about that. I had a look-in yesterday, while you were out swimming. No, it's something else. Kind of a favor." He eyeballed the harbor and adjusted his hat. Tom Donnelly was a man of old habits and persisted in topping off his ensemble with a straw panama hat, an article more typical of one of the summer scions than a year-rounder, but then again he and his father had made a great deal of money building and repairing houses on the Island. I guess he had a right to a panama hat, if he wanted to wear one.

"What sort of favor?" I asked cautiously.

"Well, you might've heard I'm throwing a little party on Horseshoe Beach at the end of summer. Everyone on the Island's invited. I thought it might be a nice idea, with the clubhouse closing early for the demolition, and—well, I've always liked the way the summer folks and the year-rounders got along on Winthrop. If we could all come together, have a few drinks, a little music, some good times together, it's just good for the Island."

"I think it's a wonderful idea."

He stuck his fingers in his belt loops and sort of rocked back and forth, from heel to toe to heel again. Looked back at me and smiled, and now my hackles were truly raised, my inner radar was on high alert. So many people want favors, you know; it's one of the things they don't tell you about having your face on magazines and movie posters. Everybody believes you owe him a little piece of yourself.

"So I was wondering," he said, "I was hoping you might help us out a little."

"Donate something, you mean?"

"No. I was thinking you might provide a little entertainment for the evening."

"Entertainment? And just what did you have in mind?"

A fine red flush overtook his face. "Oh! Nothing fancy, of course not. I thought—you've got all those artists living under your roof—I thought you might organize a little theatrical production for us. Raise the tone of things. It doesn't have to be long—a half hour or so would be ideal."

"I see," I said slowly.

"Will you consider it, then? Everyone'd be tickled pink."

"Oh, I'm sure they would. Certainly I'll consider it. Of course it depends on the cast. Whether I can get enough of the residents to pitch in."

"Excellent, excellent. You'll let me know?"

"I will."

He touched his hat. "Thank you. Thank you so much. I do want everyone to have a good time. And Miss Schuyler?"

"Hmm?"

"Something with an island theme, you know? Like *South Pacific* or—or—I don't know. Since we'll be on the beach, and we're an island."

I smiled and tucked my cardboard box under my arm. "I'm sure I can think of something, don't worry."

4.

THE MORNING AFTER I first returned to Greyfriars, I walked all the way down to the harbor and back again, even though the weather was gray and terrible. I wanted to get it over with, to tread that path right away and chase off any ghosts that might be lurking along its curves and slopes. When I reached the cliffs, I went off the road itself and stood in the damp, lengthening grass to gaze out over the Fleet Rock channel, the Sound, the lighthouse, and that was where Isobel found me.

She'd hardly said a word when I arrived at Greyfriars the evening before, had shown no surprise or curiosity. She'd called for my mother, who hustled and bustled and made space for me, as she might for any artist arriving for a summer's residency at the Greyfriars Colony—almost as if she'd expected me, come to think of it—and the three of us hadn't said a word about the past, or the future. Only the immediate present necessity.

Isobel didn't speak much on the cliffs, either. We'd stood together, a few feet distant, because our limbs seemed to flinch apart if we tried to approach any closer. The freshness of youth was gone from her face; she was as slender as ever, skinny even, the old athleticism just an echo along her arms and legs. She wore no cosmetics, not even her old swipe of red lipstick, and her straight blond hair had faded and thinned. The sea wind whipped us hard, but neither of us was going to be the one who backed down first. At last she made some remark about the weather, and I replied in kind.

Then she said, as we stared together across the channel to the lighthouse, "Remember how we rowed out to Fleet Rock, after the wedding?"

"I remember."

"I sometimes wonder if everything would have gone differently. If I hadn't rowed you out, and you hadn't fallen in love with Joseph."

"It was too late," I said. "I was already in love with him."

"But he wasn't in love with *you* yet. It was the Shakespeare that did it, you know. I heard you. You thought I was asleep, but I wasn't. I heard you speaking in that voice of yours, and I nearly fell in love with you myself."

I couldn't think of any reply to that. Anyway, my heart was too full, standing there in that familiar grass, watching Long Island Sound twitch below me. Eventually she turned me to face her and ran her fingers along the enormous bruise that disfigured the side of my face, and I willed myself to stand there and let her do it, though my skin shied away from her skin.

I don't know how long we stood there, while she examined my wounds. I stared at her critical face and thought how plain she was, and how I had once thought her the most beautiful creature alive. At some point, I reached up and pulled her hand from my cheek.

"Whose idea was it, anyway?" I asked. "The colony."

"Mine. I knew she wouldn't take in boarders, she's too proud. So I thought, let's call it something else. Something with prestige. Artists command respect, you know, even when they're terrible."

"Yes, that's true. Even when they're terrible."

Her eyes slid back to regard the bruise. "I was also the one who told her to write to you. I thought you ought to know about your brother. He ought to know about you."

"Thank you for that."

She was still staring at the shiner. Without pity, which was a good thing, because I might have socked her if she gave me pity. She just said, shaking her head, "You sure know how to pick them, don't you?" And she walked away, just like that. In my relief I nearly fell. I'd thought she was going to ask me how I got that bruise, and I would have had to tell her the truth. I couldn't lie to Isobel.

But she hadn't asked me then, and she still hadn't asked me. For two months, we had lived under the same crumbling roof, and we had shared no further confidences of any kind. Most of the time, she looked past me or—if absolutely necessary—through me, which was why I was so surprised to see her stalk down the driveway, on the twentieth of July, as I returned from the village with my binoculars.

"What's the matter?" I asked.

"The television! That's what's the matter!"

"What television?"

"As if you didn't know!"

"I don't know."

She set her hands on her hips. "Somebody set up a television in the library."

"A television! Who?"

"Who? Who?" Isobel snapped her fingers. "I know, maybe it's Brigitte. I'm sure she's rolling in dough. She could buy twenty TV sets."

"Well, it wasn't me. I don't know what you're talking about. Hugh and I are headed to the Monks' tonight to watch the landing. You should come along, you and Mama. I'm sure they wouldn't mind."

"Aren't you just full of clever ideas. No, thank you."

"I'm serious. You should. You can't hide yourself from the world forever."

"I'm not hiding myself from the world."

"What would you call it, then?"

"I don't know, Miranda. What do you call what you're doing? Because I don't see that husband of yours anywhere around here. I don't see him calling, or sending postcards, or writing messages in the sky. I've been wondering if he even knows you're here."

Her eyes, for the first time since my arrival, gazed directly into mine, and for an instant that fierce blue gaze looked exactly as it did in my memory. We stood next to the giant rhododendron that served as a final barrier before you turned the corner and saw Greyfriars, and in the flat, overcast light the lines of her face disappeared. She was ablaze with life.

"I don't know anything about the television," I said, and I walked past her down the drive, around the corner, cutting across the circle of the driveway—the fountain long since dry—toward the door.

She caught up in long, lithe strides. "You've come here to fix us, have you? Come here to make amends, maybe? Lavish all your stinking money on this place and buy some kind of forgiveness?"

"I don't need your forgiveness."

"If it's Hugh you want, you can't have him. He's ours."

"Hugh belongs to Hugh, Isobel. Not to any of us. If you try to hold him here, you're going to lose him altogether."

"How dare you," she said.

"Oh, I dare. He's my brother, too. If you can't see how badly he wants to break free—"

"Is that why you bought that sailboat? So he could just take off and leave us, whenever he wanted?"

I was climbing the front steps. At the top, I turned and looked over my shoulder. Isobel stood at the edge of the driveway, where it met the steps, and her face was defiant.

"How do you know about that?" I said.

"My uncle Peter told me yesterday. Dr. Huxley's been trying to unload that ship for years, and then *you*, out of the blue—"

"Yes," I said. "That's exactly why I bought Hugh that sailboat. And

I'm having it refitted and stocked it with food and water and maps, ready to sail whenever he wants. Because a boy like that needs to make his own adventures."

"A boy like that needs to understand who his friends are."

"Don't, Isobel. Don't play the matriarch. You of all people should know what I mean."

"Oh, I understand, believe me. I understand a hell of a lot more than you do."

Her expression was so angry, and her voice was so bitter. The driveway stood behind her, the unkempt gravel and the wilderness of rhododendrons. That first week in May, I had gone down on my hands and knees and pulled up all the weeds, starting from the front door and working my way outward, weed by weed, to the road. But they came back. That's the thing about weeds, you can't let up. As soon as you've finished pulling out the last ugly, persistent plant, you have to start right back at the beginning again.

"What happened, Isobel?" I said softly. "What happened to you? You were so full of life. You were going to escape, you were going to *do* something."

"That was you. *You* left. Someone had to stay and take care of them."

"I had no choice."

"Neither did I." She paused and looked away. "He was my *brother*."

"She was my mother. My own mother, and she wouldn't speak to me. *You* wouldn't speak to me. I would have given anything—"

"Oh, stop. You took *my* mother, didn't you? I'd say that was a fair trade."

"Your mother took *me*. She took me when nobody else would."

Isobel turned back to me. Her cheeks were pink, and the tip of her nose. "I don't know why she's letting you do this. I don't know why she's letting you take over the damned household with your money and workmen and your charm. As far as I'm concerned, you can just fly back to London." She made a motion with her hands, as of wings. "Go on. Fly."

I set my hand on the doorknob and stared at it. My thumbnail was short and bare of varnish, almost childlike, and I liked the change. "No, thanks. I might stay for a while, in fact," I said, and I was just starting to turn the doorknob, to push open the heavy door, when Isobel's voice stopped me again.

"Unless you're hoping Joseph turns up. Unless you're hoping to catch a little adulterous adventure from an escaped con. Sail off with him in that yacht you say you bought for Hugh. Are you?"

"What a question. As if I even knew where to find him."

"You'd better hope you don't," Isobel called after me. "Because if *I* find out where he's hiding, I'll kill him."

5.

NOW, DON'T LET Isobel fool you. I wasn't in charge of the Greyfriars refurbishment; my mother was, right from the start. She had laid out a number of stipulations when we first sat down with Mr. Donnelly, but they all boiled down to this: we couldn't do anything that would alter the appearance of Greyfriars from that of eighteen years ago. Instead of replacing any fixtures in the bathroom or kitchen, Mr. Donnelly's men had to take out the old ones, clean and repair them, and reinstall; only the rotting wood could be taken away and rebuilt with new; each new bucket of paint had to be carefully matched to the existing color. I gazed at her in tremendous admiration as we sat at the dining room table with our blueprints. She was made of steel. Someone had taken my exquisite mother and tempered her in a forge of some kind, and this was the result: stainless, unbendable. The blueprints went in the dustbin. Work began the next morning.

As anyone knows, however, the idea of a renovation is far more appealing than the reality. The hammering, the mysterious white powder settling on every surface, the bathrooms in squalor: my God, it was awful. I made my way around the furniture piled in the foyer—that once-grand hall of perfect proportion, of checkerboard marble, of staircase curving elegantly to the second floor—in the direction of the library, which happened to be the only room downstairs still untouched by Mr. Donnelly's men.

Inside, the furniture had been cleared to the sides, and right in the center of the great Oriental rug stood a modest box on a tripod, on which Hugh and Brigitte were operating like a pair of surgeons.

"My God," I said. "She wasn't kidding."

Hugh looked up. "Who wasn't kidding?"

"Isobel. How did *this* get here?"

"Borrowed it from a friend." Hugh stepped over the snaking electrical cable and turned for a loving gaze. He cupped his hands around his mouth and said loudly, "Switch it on, Brigitte!"

Brigitte turned the switch at the bottom, and instantly the square screen filled with loud, livid static. Hugh dashed forward and turned down the volume. A pair of long antennae stretched from the back; he grasped hold of each one and started moving them around. "Any better?" he called, over his shoulder.

"No. What's it for? I thought we were going over to the Monks' to watch the landing."

Brigitte, observing from a few feet away, uncrossed her bare arms and pushed Hugh gently aside. She was so tiny, he was like a blond giant next to her. He stepped back politely while she reached for the channel knob and turned it, and the messy gray lines on the screen resolved into a clear monochrome picture of a grinning Hoss Cartwright. Hugh smacked his forehead.

"Is that *Bonanza*?" asked a querulous voice from the doorway. It belonged to Miss Patty, carrying her paints under one arm and the easel under another, hair seized by the kind of disorder that only a damp sea breeze could bring.

"I believe so," I answered, "but don't worry, we're just testing it out. We'll turn it off in a moment—"

She turned around and bellowed, "Felicity! *Bonanza*'s on!"

"Wonderful," I said. "Exactly why did you bring this thing into the house again?"

Hugh turned to me with one of his thousand-watt grins. "Because there's been a change of plans, sis. Clay and Livy're coming here tonight. I invited them over at church this morning."

6.

LIKE ANY GOOD ship, we all pulled together in times of crisis. Miss Felicity made a crumb cake, I made cocktail sauce for the shrimp Hugh brought in from the harbor and steamed in a large, battered pot on the Garland range. Miss Patty threw open the doors to the old liquor cabinet and Brigitte coaxed the icebox to produce ice. Otto the sculptor produced a delicious pimento cheese recipe from his old nanny. Then Leonard, who'd been writing poetry on the beach all day, blew in through the kitchen door and started whipping up a ham loaf. There was pineapple salad and a noodle ring with a crabmeat center, and somebody carved a watermelon basket and filled it with melon balls. We spread it all out on the sideboard in the dining room with the good china, like the company buffet in a Betty Crocker cookbook, and I stood there before it all and thought, *Maybe it just might work.*

Although I wasn't thinking about the food. I was thinking about Tom Donnelly's party.

The Monks arrived promptly at one minute past five o'clock. The younger girls stayed home; Lucy had gone to the moon party at the Club. With an air of indecorous curiosity, Livy glanced around the room and asked, "Where's Mrs. Fisher?"

I kissed each of her cheeks. "She's upstairs with Isobel. They're a little under the weather." Well, I didn't exactly lie, did I? There *was* weather, after all, and they certainly existed beneath it.

"Both of them together," said Livy. "How strange."

Clay was concerned. "They didn't eat something, did they?"

"I think it was just the excitement. Won't you come in? Miss Patty's made a champagne punch from Old Mr. Fisher's vintage Pol Roger, unless you'd prefer something mixed."

The verdict came in unanimous in favor of Miss Patty's champagne punch—a dozen or so bottles poured over a trove of frozen strawberries, age unknown, rescued from the depths of the icebox—and we migrated out to the terrace. The sky was overcast, the air unseasonably cool. As we filed through the French doors, each person looked up reflexively, searching for the moon.

"A shame about the clouds," said Clay.

"It's only a crescent, anyway," I said. "Nothing much to look at."

"You'd think they might have waited for a full moon," said Livy. "Wouldn't it be easier to land?"

I stared at her over the rim of my champagne glass—darling little crystal coupe, excavated from the dust in the butler's pantry—but her square, sharp face was perfectly serious. She held a cigarette between her fingers as she sipped her punch, and as I watched, she glanced at Hugh, who had struck up a nearby conversation with Brigitte about televisions. He spoke loudly in her ear, and her expression was so animated, so unlike its usual flat apathy, I thought for an instant she was somebody new.

Livy leaned toward me. "Is that one of your artists?" she asked, forming the word *artists* as if it were a vocabulary lesson.

"That's Brigitte. She works in watercolor, mostly. She's my roommate."

"Roommate?"

"She was sleeping in my old room, and my mother didn't have the heart to kick her out."

"I see." Livy paused to sip her punch, to suck her cigarette. "She speaks with a touch of an accent, doesn't she?"

"I think she's Austrian."

"*Austrian. I see.* And now she's come here to America, how nice. I've always thought your mother such a heroine to take them all in and give them a home. Like strays." She laughed faintly.

"Actually, Brigitte has talent," I said. "Some of them are really quite skilled."

"Are they? Well, I suppose a view like this would inspire anybody. The Island is such a haven, I've always said."

"Such magical properties, the Island."

"They ought to put on an exhibition at the Club. Wouldn't that be fun? So many of the members are patrons, after all."

"I can't imagine anything I'd enjoy more."

She turned her head—all this time, you see, she'd been speaking sideways to me, fixing her attention on the other guests, on the view across the disgraceful lawn—and lifted her eyebrow. The same skepticism I suppose I expressed earlier, when she asked about the full moon.

"I'll be happy to put in a word with the events committee," she said. "Although I'm afraid we'd have to leave your name out of it. I'm sure you understand."

"I understand perfectly."

"Mind you, we're up to our eyeballs right now with the flower show. My God, it gets worse every year."

"Not enough flowers?"

She snorted, if such a sound could be said to originate from the nose of Livy Monk. "The opposite. Everybody trying to outdo each other. It's really too much. And this year, of course, there's the rose problem."

"The rose problem?"

"All the prize roses are just disappearing during the night. First one garden, then another. Clipped and gone in the morning. A rose thief! Can you believe it? The lengths some women will go to."

I choked back a little champagne.

"Are you all right?" asked Livy.

"Yes. Just caught a bit of strawberry. If you'll excuse me. I think your husband's run out of punch already."

Now, Carroll and I had done a great deal of entertaining during the course of our marriage, and I learned the essential trick of it early on. Being a hostess was like acting, it was like taking on the role of somebody else, somebody who was gregarious and solicitous, somebody who could listen to a narcissist and a raconteur with equal delight, somebody who drank just the right amount as she ensured her guests drank just a little too much. There was also the art of matching unlikely pairs, and the art of discovering useful secrets, at which Carroll excelled. We made an excellent team in that respect. Oh, you should have seen our parties, before it all fell apart. You should have seen who came, and who left, and when. You should have seen Sinatra standing on Carroll's Steinway and belting out "It Had to Be You," or Laurence and Vivien igniting an unholy row when he caught her screwing one of the hired waiters in the kitchen. (Actually, it might have been two at once—that woman had the libido of a Thoroughbred stud.) But the main thing about our parties, the essential thing, is that we never invited anybody boring. They sinned freely, Carroll's friends, and they were often mean and mercurial and faithless, and they were always, always high, but by God they entertained. That was their job, after all, the only thing of genuine value they brought to this world, and they knew it too well. When I think about those years, I think about what a show it was, an endless, shallow, brilliant, pitiable vaudeville.

On the night of the moon landing, though, as I carried Clay's glass to the Waterford punch bowl and refilled it, as I passed the Burbridge sisters along the way and directed them mischievously to Livy, I hadn't yet begun to reflect on my life with Carroll. It was too raw and recent, and I had only this party to compare it to. This strange intermingling of the Greyfriars art colony with Mrs. and Mrs. Clayton Monk of Boston and Winthrop Island, and the way we were brought together by the moon, a waxing crescent that lay hidden behind a bank of sturdy clouds. I refilled my own glass for good measure, and when I turned to make my way back to Clay, I saw a flash of light from one of the windows of the Fleet Rock lighthouse, and I sort of froze, I guess, while Hugh called my name from across the terrace, near the doors.

"Miranda!" he said again. "Miranda! Hello!"

The light was gone. Did not reappear. I rotated my body in the direction of Hugh's voice. "Right here," I said.

He came up to me swiftly, and I was surprised by the expression on his face, which had nothing to do with his pleasure in discussing circuitry and diode tubes with Brigitte.

"Is something the matter?" I asked.

He spoke in a low, confidential voice. "Not too bad. I just thought you'd want to know that a pair of U.S. Marshals turned up a moment ago, wanting to speak to Mom. They're in the library talking, right now."

7.

I REMEMBER EXACTLY nothing of the next hour or so, just that I kept away from that corner where the library window overlooked the terrace—not because I didn't want to see what was going on in there, but because I didn't want them to recognize my face. My damned face, which had appeared on billboards and movie screens, magazines and newspapers, and was safe from the vulgar consequences of that exposure only on Winthrop Island. Or so I'd thought, anyway. At some point, somebody—I think it was Clay—stuck a cigarette in my hand, and I believe I actually smoked it. Like I said, I don't exactly remember.

I do recall that after an hour or so, I couldn't bear the strain any longer, so I set my empty glass next to the punch bowl and stole into the morning room, where I peered between the curtains into the driveway. The intruding vehicle—a white Chevrolet Corvair parked at a rakish angle next to the sad, dry fountain—seemed to hook my memory. I'd seen a car like that recently, hadn't I? I'd seen something like it just that morning on Hemlock Street, in fact, as the felt-hatted man from the ferry approached the passenger door.

I drew away from the window and sat on the seat, panting a little, holding my hand to my chest. The room was papered in oppressive florals, which Mama refused to take down; they matched the chintz upholstery, they provided a bucolic setting for all the china shepherdesses. I thought I was going to suffocate in those flowers. I thought my chest was going to crumple under the weight of all those knickknacks. I heard the floorboards creak, and I turned automatically to the door, which I had stupidly left open, and where a man now stood, leaning to get a view inside the room. He wore a pale suit and held a straw hat between his hands. I thought I saw another man behind him, bending his shoulders to light a cigarette.

The first man stepped inside the doorway, quite tall and narrow-chested. "Mrs. Goring?" he said respectfully.

I stood and smoothed my dress, which didn't take much smoothing, being short and white and made of a thin, stiff fabric. "I'm afraid I am not receiving visitors, just now," I said, and I walked to the door on the opposite wall the way they had taught me at Foxcroft, a book balanced on your head, and found myself in the library, where Brigitte was coaxing the television back to life.

"Is my mother upstairs?" I asked, leaning back against the closed door, as if that could stop a pair of United States Marshals who wished to have a word with me.

Brigitte showed no sign of having heard me. She made some adjustments to the rabbit ears and looked back down at the screen, which remained fuzzy. I walked to the television and touched her shoulder, and she startled so boldly, she nearly knocked me to the floor.

"Sorry," she said.

Sorry, I said at the same time.

We stared at each other for a second or two. I leaned toward her ear. "My mother! Is she upstairs!"

"I think so."

I turned to go, and she took my arm. "What did the police want?"

There was a peculiar tenor to her voice. I reached for her hand that clutched my elbow and covered it gently. "I'm sure it's nothing," I said.

From her expression, she didn't believe me, but she let me go anyway. I hurried across the hallway to the back stairs and went up two at a time, staggering a little as I reached the warm air of the landing and turned left, toward the master bedroom, which Mama and Isobel now shared. When I burst in, they jumped from the window, through which they had both been staring in the direction of the lighthouse.

"What did they want?" I asked.

"You should knock first."

"What did they want, damn it?"

Isobel said, "They want to set up a listening post in the attic."

"A what?"

"They want to keep watch on the lighthouse. Station an officer upstairs with binoculars and a—I don't know—some kind of special microphone for spying on people."

My legs gave way. I found a pink slipper chair just in time.

"What did you say? You didn't agree, did you?"

"Of course not," Mama said. "The idea."

"But why here? Why a listening post? Have they learned something?"

Isobel went to the bureau and lifted the pack of cigarettes that rested there. "I don't know, Peaches. What do you think? Is there something you need to tell us?"

"Nothing."

"It seems they think he's visiting the lighthouse from time to time," Mama said. "Visiting his mother. Possibly even staying there."

"If that's true, then why won't you agree to the listening post?"

"Because it's my home. It's not a—a police stakeout."

Isobel lit her cigarette and turned to me. "We play fair around here, Peaches. Never forget that. You have to give the man a sporting chance." She blew out a little smoke. "Besides, they can watch Fleet Rock from somewhere else just as easily. From a boat in the water, maybe, or the cliffs."

"It's not a direct line from the cliffs," I said, "and if they station a boat out there, Joseph will notice it."

"So he's Joseph, is he?"

"If he's really there, I mean. Which is almost impossible."

"Why? Why is it impossible?"

"Because somebody would know, wouldn't they? Somebody in the village. His family and friends."

Isobel laughed. "Oh, for God's sake. You know an Islander would never rat him out to a mainlander. It's simply not done. He might be a despicable murderer, but he's our murderer." She took a long drag on her cigarette and wandered back to the window. The dull twilight shadowed her face. She rested her elbow on one hand and said, "*Your* murderer."

"He's not mine. I haven't seen him in eighteen years, not since I left."

"Oh, he's yours, all right. You're the reason he went to prison, and I wouldn't be surprised if you're the reason he left. I used to wonder why.

I used to think, why on earth did he confess like that? Plead guilty, go straight to prison without a trial. I used to wonder if maybe he was covering for someone, and then I wondered—well, whom?"

"Isobel!" Mama snapped.

"Didn't it ever cross your mind, Mother?" She turned her head to me and smiled. "Peaches? What about you?"

"I don't know what happened that night. I was asleep."

"Yes, you were asleep. Sleepy Miranda. It was the talk of the Island, how asleep you were that night. Must've been some evening."

"Stop, Isobel," Mama said, more wearily, sinking into a chair and staring at her hands.

"Oh, I'm just having a little fun. It's all academic, isn't it? Vargas confessed, he saved himself from hanging with his terribly convincing description of the crime—murder in the second degree, my father was only *sort of* murdered. So comforting."

I rose from the chair. "Poor Isobel. Poor tragic Isobel. How utterly awful for you. What must it be like, I wonder, to lose a father? So suddenly, so violently, right when you need him most—"

Mama jumped from her chair. "Stop it, both of you! My God, I lost them both, I lost everything! For God's sake, stop!"

I hung there without speaking, staring toward the window, to Isobel's cigarette against the smudged outdoors.

"Just stop," Mama said. She wandered across the room and through the door to the bedroom itself. For an instant, I thought I smelled her old perfume, but it must have been a trick of my senses, because I knew she never wore it anymore.

Isobel stubbed out her cigarette on the window frame. "Say. I wonder if we've landed yet."

"Landed?" I said stupidly.

"On the moon, Peaches. Landed on the moon, remember?"

8.

SHE ACTUALLY CAME down with me. Isobel actually took my hand and walked down the stairs by my side—the main stairs, not the back stairs—and into the library, where everybody had assembled on the rug in front of that little television. Brigitte had got it working, had found the channel. They'd gone through the buffet line and sat Indian-style on the rug, like kindergartners, holding their plates in their laps, their pretty coupes of champagne punch next to their toes. Not one of them glanced up when we entered.

Isobel called out, "Well, have they landed yet?"

Livy spilled her punch. Clay set aside his plate and rose to his feet.

"Landed yet? They landed hours ago!" said Miss Patty.

"Just past four o'clock," Miss Felicity said. "We missed it."

Hugh rose too. "My fault. I got my times mixed up. But they haven't come out of the module yet. I think they're sleeping or something."

"Sleeping?" said Miss Patty. "You mean land on the moon and then lie down for a nap?"

"That's what the schedule says."

She turned up her head to take in the ceiling, a dozen feet above. "*Scientists.*"

Isobel and Clay were staring at each other. Clay looked away first. "Can I get you some dinner?" he asked the library shelves. "It's all laid out in the dining room."

"I can get it myself. Come along, Peaches. Aren't you famished? I'm famished."

We loaded our plates and returned to the library. By now it was nine o'clock. Livy announced she was bored and went off somewhere; the blurred, gray images on the television screen didn't seem real. I ate and listened to the droning voice of the announcer for as long as I could, until at last I turned to Clay and asked how much longer.

"About an hour or two," he said cheerfully. "Aren't you listening? Fascinating stuff. I always wanted to be a scientist."

I gathered up a few plates and returned them to the kitchen, and instead of going back to the television in the library I went outside, right through the kitchen door onto the lawn. My heeled shoes sank into the turf. I took them off, took off my stockings too. The air was so cool I was almost chilled, a strange sensation at this time of year, as if the world were upside down. I considered doubling back and digging up a cardigan from my bedroom, but the journey was too far, the object too small, and anyway I didn't want to be inside Greyfriars. I wanted to be here. The breeze struck my face, thick and sharp with the sea. I started toward the dock, and then I thought better of it, I don't know why, some premonition maybe. I went to the swimming pool instead.

The feral grass scratched my feet. I stepped right on one of those prickling weeds and swore in a whisper. There was a trace of fragrance in the air, some hidden thing blooming. In the darkness, I ran straight into one of the boxwoods, but this time I swallowed the word that rose in my throat. Again, I don't know why. Some premonition. Instead, I felt along the foliage until I reached the gap, slipped through the gap, listened to the quiet lap of the swimming pool water, moved by the breeze. And a voice, a murmur. From the cabana.

The fear I felt then, I can't describe it. Just cold, you know, and paralyzing. And yet I forced myself silently forward, my bare feet absolutely noiseless against the stones, my breath blocking my throat. On the cabana itself there fell some light from the house. I made out the shape of it, the stripes on the awning. I stopped at the corner and peered inside. Two bodies, not one. A woman sitting upright and unclothed on the cushions, facing the wall, somebody beneath her. She was moaning. Her breasts caught some flicker of light from inside the cabana, a candle or something, and as they swayed in a particular, universal rhythm, she said, to the same beat, *Hugh, Hugh*.

I stumbled back and fell. The moaning stopped.

"Who's there?" said a woman's voice. "Clay?"

A man's voice made a muffled curse.

Run, I thought. Run.

But I didn't run. I could not run away from this. I stood up and stepped forward, so they could see me, they could see who I was, though I kept my own gaze fixed on the single, short candle sputtering on the shelf.

"Get off my brother," I said. "Get out of my house. Now."

9.

WHEN I RETURNED alone to the library, the room had the limp, eerie air of a failed party. Leonard lay asleep on the sofa by the wall. Miss Felicity lay with her head on Miss Patty's lap. Isobel reclined on her side, idling her fork around her untouched food. Only Brigitte still sat in her original pose, one hand on each knee, staring keenly at the images on the screen. Clay glanced up from a cross-armed stance before the television. "Where is everybody?" he asked.

"Livy's gone home, I'm afraid. She's not feeling well."

"Hugh driving her?"

"No. Hugh's gone for a nice, cold swim in the pool, I think."

Clay looked into my eyes, and I looked into his. The elegant, vaguely British voice of the announcer droned nearby. Miss Patty said something about moving out of the way.

Clay lifted his hand and rubbed his thumb against his brow. He was holding a cigarette, and a crumb of ash dropped away from the end and landed on the rug, unnoticed, as if he'd forgotten he was still smoking. "Then I guess I'd better head home," he said softly.

"Probably you'd better."

He swore. "But she's got the car."

"I'll drive you home," I said.

"Are you sure? I can ask Hugh."

"No, I'll drive."

We exchanged another look, absent of expression. Isobel, sitting up, wore a slight smile, though she directed all her attention to the television screen. Clay picked up her glass and her plate, picked up his glass and his plate from the side table nearby, and carried them all into the dining room and stacked them on the sideboard. He patted his pockets, as if he'd forgotten something. "Ready?" he said.

"Ready."

We said not one word as we drove to the Monks' house, on the other end of the Island. I drove Hugh's car with its noisy engine, for which I thanked God, because it covered the silence so admirably. A nice, cold swim in the pool, I'd said, which was the honest truth. I mean, what else could he do? Livy sprinting away, carrying her shoes. Hugh—sweating, bare-chested—torn between sprinting after her and making some kind of explanation to me first. I made it easy for him. I grabbed his arm and asked him what the hell was going on.

It was my fault, he said manfully. I went for a swim, and she happened by, and she—

He stopped and turned red.

She what? I asked.

He said he didn't know how it happened, one minute she was standing there with her cigarette, asking him about football, and the next moment she dived in naked, and Jesus, Miranda, she just—I couldn't just—she came right up under the water and started—I didn't even—

All right, all right, I said. I think I get it.

He lowered himself to the edge of the pool and sat there, head in hands.

The air was black, I couldn't see him very well, but I thought he might be forcing back tears. What have I done, he said. What the hell have I done.

I put my hand on his shoulder. I mean, he was my brother, my only sibling. Like me, he had no father, no strong fellow to put him straight in such matters. I thought about that first time with Carroll, and how I woke up the next morning with a terrible headache and saw his gray-speckled hair and thought, in panic, *What the hell have I done?*

You made a mistake, that's all, I said. Just promise me you won't make it again.

He whispered, Jesus. Mrs. *Monk*. Jesus.

And that was when he dove into the pool. It wasn't my idea, I assure you. It was his.

Anyway, I wasn't going to tell Clay these little details. I wasn't going to tell Clay anything at all, and I wouldn't have said another word on the topic, I would've just dropped Clay off at his own front door if he hadn't taken hold of my hand as I reached for the gear shift and spoke, for the first time in a quarter of an hour.

"Keep going to the guesthouse. It's where I sleep."

I looked at his hand on mine, and for some reason I remembered that story about the B-17 over Germany. I thought, *This hand once ditched a crippled Flying Fortress in the middle of a French field, saving the lives of several men.* Funny how life works out.

"All right," I said, as if this were a perfectly ordinary request, and instead of shifting into neutral I popped the clutch and proceeded down the long, curving gravel drive, not quite certain what I was looking for, until Clay said, *Stop.*

So I stopped. Put the car in neutral.

We sat there. Clay rolled down the window, and the noise of the sea rushed in, much bolder here than in our corner of Winthrop because the Monks had some ocean exposure, facing Rhode Island instead of Long

Island. He put his elbow on the doorframe and said, "Livy's not really sick, is she?"

"Not sick, no. She just wanted to go home."

"All right. All right." He reached for a cigarette, checked his wristwatch, and swore. "The astronauts! You're going to miss it."

"Oh, it's all right."

"I've got a television inside."

"I really should get back, Clay."

"C'mon. It's history, Miranda. You can't miss history. What are you going to tell your grandkids? You had to get home and take an Alka-Seltzer so you missed the astronauts walking on the moon?"

I laughed a little. "I can catch it on rerun."

"Aw, hold on a second. You can't be serious. You're not really going to leave me alone to watch history all by myself, are you?"

He said it lightly, but I thought he meant it. Sometimes the words you say lightly are the ones you feel the most. I reached for the ignition. "Fine, then. Only for a minute, though. Just until they—you know—"

"Walk on the fucking *moon*, Miranda? Just that?"

I laughed again, harder now, because the weight of the evening was beginning to strain the tendons of my throat. "You win, you win. Let's go."

A fine drizzle was filling the air, so we hurried across the drive and ducked inside. The house had no porch, seemed to be some kind of modern structure, lean and boxy and constructed mostly of windows overlooking the sea. Clay flipped on the lights and went for the television in the corner. It was a new, space-age model, blinding white like the furniture. I had the feeling that the main house looked much different, was decorated according to Livy's taste. "Care for a drink?" asked Clay, and I opened my mouth to say *No*, but what came out was *Yes*! Almost a shout. Yes, my God, I needed a drink right now. Miss Patty's champagne punch belonged to a distant and more innocent past. If such a thing still existed.

"Coming right up," Clay said, without asking what I wanted. There was a liquor cabinet, of course there was, well-stocked and convenient, paneled in walnut. I stared at the television screen, warming up slowly, and listened to the clink of glass behind me. My nerves spun, my head felt a little uncertain. Clay came up behind me and nudged my hand with a glass.

"What is it?" I asked.

"Oh, just a little something I improvised. Secret recipe. We'll call it the Moon Landing."

"Not very original."

"The Moon over Winthrop? The Waxing Crescent? The Sweet Miranda?"

"How about the Buzz Aldrin?" I said. "Emphasis on the buzz."

"Done. Cheers."

I clinked his glass with mine, and we drank in unison. "My God!" I sputtered. "It's a little strong, isn't it?"

"The primary ingredient in the secret recipe is vodka."

"I'll say." I sipped more slowly. The screen was coming into focus now, such as it was, and the announcer's voice came through clearly, if faintly. Clay leaned forward, turned up the volume, and invited me onto the sofa. The vodka had already begun to roar in my ears. I didn't say yes, I just stepped back and sank onto the cushion. Clay sank next to me.

We watched the screen without a word, waiting and waiting for the hatch to open, for somebody's boot to appear, for history to occur before us. Armstrong was going first, the announcer said, and he read off the message inscribed on the plaque they were going to leave behind. Something about coming in peace for all mankind, a nice pleasant sentiment. Nobody could argue with peace for all mankind. By now I was sort of floating above the sofa on a vodka cloud, a secret recipe cloud, a Buzz Aldrin cloud, emphasis on the buzz. I'd emptied the glass somehow. Clay pried it from my hand and rose to pour me another, pour himself another.

I remember thinking, when he sat back down again, he was closer than before, and that he lit a cigarette. Or maybe I'm just remembering it that way because it fits, you know, fits the narrative of what happened that evening, that night, the night of the moon landing, when the whole world was holding its breath and watching its television set.

Of course, you already know *that* story. The hatch opened just after eleven post meridiem on the East Coast of the United States. We all leaned forward, clutching our vodka and our cigarettes, and watched a blurry Neil Armstrong make his way down the ladder and utter his famous words, *One small step* and all that. I recall the instant of that step, his boot touching the dust, because for that instant it all fell away, Joseph and Isobel and Hugh and Livy, Carroll and my sweet, dead baby who never lived to see a human being step on the moon. For that instant I was made of wonder. I set the glass on the floor and wept.

"That was something," Clay said, rubbing my back.

I nodded and wiped my eyes with my thumbs.

"You know, it actually happened a few minutes ago. Isn't that a gas? I mean, we're all hanging by our fingernails but it's over and done with, this isn't actually happening right now."

"Because the radio signal takes so long to reach us."

"Not that long. It's because—well, if something happened"—Clay's hand began to slide downward to my waist—"if he missed a step and fell on his ass, for example."

"Oh, stop."

"I'm sorry. I didn't mean that. It's just a—a hell of a day."

I leaned back, causing his arm to fall along my shoulder, and I was too loaded and too listless to shake it off. Anyway, it was just Clay. Clayton Monk, my old friend, almost like family. Why, just an hour ago, his wife had been screwing my kid brother inside the Greyfriars cabana. We were practically related.

"Livy . . ." he said.

"What about Livy?"

"She was with Hugh, wasn't she?"

I didn't answer. Clay swore.

"She does this," he said. "She's been doing it since—I don't know—after Barbara was born, I guess."

"She's your third?"

"Our second," he said. "I took an early train home one evening and found her in bed with the neighbor's son, college kid, mowed our lawn in the spring. Mowed more than that."

"My God."

"She made up some story, I forget what it was. Lucy was at a friend's house, the baby was asleep in the other room. I forgave her—all right, you know, I'm not perfect myself—and things got better. We had Jackie. Then they got worse again. I won't bore you." He heaved himself up from the sofa and went to refill his drink. "Once Jackie's in college, we're going to divorce. Until then, we live cheerfully in hell together. The show must go on." He toasted himself in the mirror above the liquor cabinet.

"I'm so sorry, Clay."

"The thing is, the kind of comic relief in all this, irony, whatever," he said, staring at himself, his pink eyes in the mirror, "I thought this was what I wanted. Wife and kids and a nice, quiet life. Flying out there at night, you know, when I was overseas, Germany, freezing to death, flack shooting up my ass, it was all I dreamed about. Isobel and a house in Brookline, summers on the Island, every day like the one before, all the traditions, all the—the stuff we did as kids, forever and ever."

"I remember."

"Then, you know, the reality." He finished the drink and turned. "I'll have a word with Livy about Hugh. That's just—that's sick, she's sick, she needs to see a shrink or something. Is he all right?"

"He wasn't exactly himself, if that's what you mean. He feels terrible.

He's a good kid, he feels guilty. I don't know if he's—if he's ever done that kind of thing before, or if she—"

"Aw, Jesus. Jesus Christ. I never should have taken her to Greyfriars tonight. I knew she was taking notice of him, but I thought—I mean, my God, *Hugh*. He's like a son to us. Are you sure he's all right?"

I stared down at the glass on the floor, half empty or half full or whatever it was. Both at once. I picked it up and said, "He will be. I thought it was best to give him some time to himself. I'll speak to him in the morning." And I finished off the rest of my Buzz Aldrin in one gulp.

"Don't tell Isobel," Clay said. "She thinks the sun rises and sets on that boy."

"Of course I won't."

"She'd never forgive me."

"Wouldn't she? You've done everything for Hugh, and it's all for Isobel's sake, isn't it? It was all for her."

"Doesn't matter. You know Isobel. It's all or nothing. The way she changed after that night—the way everything changed."

"Oh, Clay. Things change anyway. You try to keep everything the same around here, fixed in amber, but it's no use. You can't stop the tide."

"The world," Clay said. "The fucking world. Spinning out of control. Everything—everything changes—even the Island—and you try to grab something, and it just—it just—it disappears in your hand."

"Yes," I said.

"I don't know what to believe in anymore."

"There's plenty to believe in."

"We're irrelevant. Fishers and Monks and Dumonts, we used to be kings, we built the country, we fought a goddamned war, and now—and now—I don't even know who the kings are anymore. Not us." He nodded at the television. "Fellows who can put a man on the moon, I guess."

I stood up. "I think it's time for me to go."

Clay checked his watch. "You want to stay here a little longer? You're a little the worse for wear to be out driving."

"No, I should get back."

"Then I'll drive you."

"You're as loaded as I am, brother."

"Then stay, Miranda. Don't be stupid. Those cliffs—"

"I'll be fine. I'll drive slowly."

Clay set down his empty glass and walked toward me. The television flickered behind him, some reporter on scene in Houston, filled with joy. "Don't leave," he said.

"Clay, I'm married."

"I'd say you were about as married as I am. Isn't that right?"

"Maybe. More or less."

He put his hands on my back. I saw the kiss coming, felt the weight of his vodka breath falling on my vodka breath, and I thought, *I don't want this, I should put a stop to this*. But I didn't. It just seemed easier to kiss him.

10.

I FIRST MET my husband at a party in Paris, where the Countess—*la chère Comtesse*, as they called her there—kept an apartment. It was spring, and we had been living there together for a year. The Countess said Europe was the place for me, that I was wasted on those Puritans back home—she was referring, I think, to Mount Holyoke, which had delicately required me to resign my place in its freshman class, on the grounds of my having displayed both the immoral character and the bad taste to admit publicly to spending the night with a boy, a confessed murderer—and she immediately set about broadening my mind, as she called it, and refining my style. I allowed her to do this; it was something, after all. Something to give shape to the days, to give occupation to my thoughts. For that terrible year, I was happy to be the Countess's new toy, her doll, to be dressed and educated and placed about Paris according to her desire. At Christmas, struck by the impulse to become someone else entirely, rehearsing over and over the events of that August day on Winthrop Island, I asked her if I could take acting lessons. The idea entranced her.

So it was not by accident, I think, that Carroll turned up at one of the Countess's parties that April, when I had just turned nineteen and begun to grow out of my girlish roundness into a more sophisticated silhouette, elegantly draped by the Countess's favorite couturier. Carroll was then in his middle forties, handsome and well-groomed, fresh off the success of his brilliant adaptation of the Robert Langford spy novel *Night Train to Berlin* and lionized everywhere. He had at least two lovers, who also attended the party that evening, spitting barbs at each other. I could hardly bring myself to speak to him, but of course he was used to stuttering starlets, and with kind condescension offered me a small part in his next film. On set, he took a tremendous interest in me one day—I still can't determine what particular thing intrigued him, what particular spark set off his obsession—and began to develop me, as he called it. To teach me not only how to act, but how to be. (They were quite the same thing, after all, he said.) For hours and hours he coached me, sometimes late into the night. Pygmalion could not have been more devoted. My voice, my expressions, my movement, my posture; the various unconscious details of human behavior, the enormous mental concentration required to slip without friction inside the skin of another human being—all these things he coaxed lovingly to life inside me, and for that, for this career I might never have experienced without him, for this extraordinary mineral he discovered and extracted from my soul to give brilliance to my days, I shall always be grateful to Carroll Goring.

But for all the intimacy of our friendship, for all his charisma and his genius and his famous libido, we did not so much as kiss for nearly six years. It was not until the Countess's sudden death on New Year's Day of 1959—a heart attack on the stairway of the Ritz Paris, sending her tumbling down to the bottom with a broken neck—left me so altogether bereft that he offered me a temporary home in the guest room of his Kensington flat. For a week, he treated me with the utmost compassion. He brought me breakfast, he presented me with small, thoughtful gifts. (Carroll Goring was far too subtle to offer jewels.) On the sixth evening, he said it would do me good to go out, to have a lovely dinner somewhere and get drunk. We went to Scott's, of course—where else?—and left at two o'clock in the morning, having accounted for at least three bottles of vintage champagne, although I may have lost track. In the taxi, as we rounded Hyde Park Corner, Carroll leaned over and kissed me for the first time, and because I had drunk so deeply after such a long abstinence, this came as no surprise. I put my hand around the back of his neck and kissed him back.

Upon our arrival, he led me directly into his bedroom and said he had been waiting for years to make love to me, only I hadn't been ready until now. He asked me to take off my clothes, and by God, I was so used to taking physical direction from him, I simply obeyed. Isn't that shameful? For a long time, he stared at me, the way he stared at a set, at a scene, deciding precisely how he was going to film it. I remember how the pupils dilated inside his blue eyes. I remember wanting to cover my breasts, my stomach, and yet at the same time I wanted him to see them, to touch them, to approve of them. I wanted desperately to belong to him, this man who had taught me how to act, how to be, who had nurtured me so carefully for so long, lest he should walk away and leave me too. When he asked me to turn around slowly, so he could inspect the curve of my back and my arse, I did. When he asked me to sit on the edge of the bed and spread my legs apart, I did. When he reached into the drawer of his bedside table, produced a condom, and asked me to unzip his trousers, I did. After that, he stopped asking. He pushed me gently back on the bed and told me to relax, told me I would enjoy intercourse very much, told me he knew from the beginning he was going to teach me how to make love, like everything else. And all this seemed, after six years acting under his masterful direction, after the death of the Countess, after three shared bottles of champagne, the most natural thing in the world.

The next morning, as I said, I woke before Carroll and stared through the arms of a throbbing headache at his thin, straight, shining hair on the pillow, and panicked. I thought, *What the hell have I done?*, and the question was genuine. I did not quite remember everything that happened, just the hazy beginning when he first penetrated me, and so I was surprised, when I swung my legs out of bed and stared at the white carpet, to find two foil wrappers lying on the floor, two limp rubbers, a smear of blood disfiguring the creamy wool. I ran to the toilet and vomited. When I returned to the bedroom, Carroll was awake, smoking a cigarette, his thin arms crossed behind his back. His face was soft and tired. He gazed at me warmly, with genuine love, and asked how I was feeling. He said he was going to ring for a hot bath and a pot of strong, black coffee to set me right.

And then, he said, he supposed we should get married.

11.

SO PERHAPS IT was inevitable that I followed Clay into the bedroom of his guesthouse overlooking the sea. They say human beings are creatures of habit, that we are wont to follow the scripts already written in our heads, the stories we have learned to believe, over and over again in the same implacable, brutal cycle, however much we long to write our own, original verses. I only replaced one lead actor with another, Carroll with Clay, but the story remained the same, the performers hit their marks. In despair, our heroine swallows poison, and reaches for some older, sturdier fellow to heal her, only to discover that she cannot absorb sturdiness through her skin, she cannot replace one person with another. She cannot actually make love by making love.

We took off our clothes. The drizzle fell against the windows. Clay's hands moved awkwardly against my skin, the kind of man who didn't really understand how to touch a woman, just wanted to rub her breasts until she caught fire like a pair of sticks. I took his fingers and tried to show him, but he was too drunk to learn, and I was too drunk to have any patience, so we tumbled onto the bedspread and he climbed on top of me, lifted himself on the palms of his hands. We met for an instant, my blurry eyes and his blurry eyes, poised on some brink, and his face held the same grief it wore on that long-ago golf course, when Isobel had broken his heart. Maybe he was thinking along the same lines. "Oh God, you feel so good," he said, and he started to weep. He rolled off, and I stared for a moment at his shuddering shoulders, the back of his head. I sat up against the pillow and laid my hand on the back of his neck, and I believe I wept, too, only without any sound or movement, just the tears.

12.

I DROVE HOME some time later at about five miles an hour, following the beam of the headlights. There were no other cars, thank God, everybody was home or at the Club, celebrating the genius and the daring of American manhood. I'd hardly eaten anything all day, had only picked at that courageous buffet in the Greyfriars dining room, and now the hollowness inside seemed to swallow me. The pitiless road just curved and curved, without end. To the left, I saw a familiar field, and I pulled over. Or maybe the car pulled over all on its own; it was Hugh's Ford, after all. It knew where to go.

Now that I think about it, I may have left the door open and the keys in the ignition. I'm pretty sure I turned off the engine. I walked slowly so I wouldn't fall. The grass had recovered since the June mowing, and the long stalks itched my bare shins. In the darkness, I ran straight into a bush that covered my arms in scratches. If it hadn't been for the booze, I'd have screamed in pain, but I think I hardly felt it. I don't remember hurting, at least on the outside. When I reached the edge, where the meadow met the wet rocks that tumbled down the twelve or fifteen feet to the beach below, I stopped and went into a safe, sensible crab position. Made my way along the rocks with tremendous precision while the drizzle ran down my hair and my face. When I reached the sand, I just collapsed. Crawled forward a few paces. Rose to my feet and stumbled into the surf, which was frisky tonight, invisible under the heavy clouds and the rain, and let the cold waves wash me to the chest.

I don't remember thinking I should step back a little. I didn't want to leave, even though the water chilled me, the rain choked me. I realized I was sobbing. I was thinking about the baby, and everything that had left me when my child slipped from my womb, and how I had hoped to see my father's eyes again and now would not. I was thirty-six, I had left my husband. How could a woman start again at thirty-six? Say to herself, I want to go back to the beginning, I want to do things over, I want to have that new, shining chance back in my hands again, and this time not to break it.

The tide, I think, was coming in. The waves were starting to overwhelm me, and I wasn't backing down. For some reason I wasn't backing down. I don't know why. The instinct for self-preservation had fled. The hollowness had swallowed me. I lifted my hands above my head and closed my eyes, reaching for the moon maybe, even though that moon had set long ago, silent and invisible behind the clouds, population two. My feet left the ground. I think—I hope—I was going to swim. I think I would have swum, but I never did find out for certain, because at that moment a pair of arms enclosed me from behind.

I didn't resist. I allowed my body to be dragged gently from the water, floating, until we reached the sand and the arms lifted me, carried me, settled me in some hollow above the high tide, where we sat together, shivering.

13.

FOR SOME TIME, I thought it was a dream. It was the kind of thing that happened inside your head, and anyway I had stupidly drunk two glasses of Clay Monk's secret recipe, which was mostly vodka, and I had that feeling you sometimes get when you're drunk, which is that everything happening to you is happening to someone else, some drunk person, and you are experiencing all these sensations, the wetness of your skin, the chill of the wind, the salt in your nose, the warm slab of human flesh at your back, the arms enclosing your arms, at some remove. Like a dream.

Also, in dreams as in drunkenness, the impossible becomes possible, becomes even ordinary, matter of course, like turkey on Thanksgiving Day. You hear the deep, familiar sound of someone's breath in your ear, and you smell his smell, and you think, *Oh, it's you*, without considering how he got there, or why, or whether it's really him. Of course it's him. Who else?

For some time, I continued to shake. I sobbed and shivered together, I was a mess. The drizzle came down upon us. So great was my shuddering, I couldn't tell if he shivered too, or whether he had grown impervious to such trifling discomforts as the cold after seventeen years in the state penitentiary, which I understood was not the kind of place you went for recreational purposes. I became aware that I sat between his knees, that he was possibly kissing the top of my head, and there seemed nothing untoward or unexpected about these facts. He said nothing, and neither did I. He didn't ask me why I was sobbing, or what I was doing on this beach, floating on this perilous sea at midnight. He didn't ask about my sorrow, and I didn't ask about his.

14.

I WOKE IN my own bed, sometime past nine o'clock the next morning, with a pounding headache and no memory of having arrived there. I wore a nightgown, and my hair was brushed and dry. A bowl of fresh roses sat on the nightstand. When I looked outside the front window, Hugh's car was parked in its usual place, absorbing the sunshine.

I went downstairs and asked Brigitte if she remembered my coming in last night and going to bed, but she said she didn't hear a thing. Of course, she was nearly deaf.

AUGUST

1930 (BIANCA MEDEIRO)

1.

FRANCISCA AND TIA Maria have been away all week on the mainland, shopping for Francisca's trousseau and for the furnishing of her new home with Pascoal Vargas in the Fleet Rock lighthouse, so Bianca has indulged herself in a perilous habit. Each night, when Tio Manuelo and Laura and cousin Manuelo have gone to bed, she slips out the garden door and steals up Hemlock Street to the dark corner of West Cliff Road, where Hugh Fisher waits to lead her to Greyfriars and the small cottage built for guests.

This cottage has lain empty most of the summer, because once the Fishers returned to the Island from the funeral and interment on Long Island, they lived quietly, in mourning, without visitors. Except Bianca. Bianca has stolen over to Greyfriars whenever she can to comfort Hugh Fisher, to ease his filial grief by the solace of her embrace, in the pool and the boathouse and summerhouse, even once in the rose garden surrounded by perfume—really, wherever they can find space and privacy, as a good wife should. She understands the strength of a man's needs, and she loves him so much and so wholly, she wants always to give him this thing that only a wife can give him, this rapture he craves so desperately. And there is rapture for her too, salve for the clamor in her young blood, in ways she has never dreamed of. Hugh has shown her how. First he showed her certain ways she might please him, and then he showed the ways in which she could be pleased *by* him, and since God has created man in his image, and ordained that man and woman should marry and be fruitful together, these acts of consummation are surely sacred, are they not? They are holy sacraments. This she believes with all her heart.

And now, for this precious week, they have a real house and a real bedroom, just like any other husband and wife, and Bianca lies snug in Hugh's arms and feels the beat of his heart enter through her back and across her bone and muscle and lungs to invade her own heart. It is four o'clock in the morning and they have made love twice already, twice he has poured his sperm into the vessel of her womb, and if history serves he will likely want to repeat this ritual a third time before she steals back down West Cliff Road to Tio Manuelo's general store, which is not her home anymore but simply a place where she boards until Hugh can claim her as his own, as his wife before God, mistress of Greyfriars and of his own heart. It will have to be soon.

Now Bianca's exhausted and wants to sleep, but her nerves are too wrought. Her mind spins round and round, trying to grasp an idea that lies just outside her comprehension. Another portent, she thinks. Something new occurred between them tonight, some heightened frenzy that delighted her at first. The very moment she arrived in her best blue dress, scrubbed and curled and perfumed, Hugh swept her through the doorway, actually lifted her into the air and laid her on the edge of the bed, lifted away her dress and made love to her right there. He finished so quickly, with such shattering energy, that he lay senseless afterward, and she slipped from beneath his tranquilized limbs and went into the kitchen to make him tea, flavored with gin the way he likes it. Thus revived, he reached for her once more, and now he took his sweet time, he went on for ages, all around the cottage, the floor and sofa and window seat, the kitchen table and against the wall, every position, every which way you could fit two bodies together, perspiring freely from the vigor and the August heat, and all the bones in Bianca's body are now flaccid, dissolving into the mattress, dissolving into Hugh and the hot, still night that surrounds them.

Still she finds the strength to turn on the damp sheets and ask him if he's awake.

"Yes," he says. "What's the matter, little one? Have I been too rough?"

"You know that's not true. You know you can do whatever you like with me."

"Lusty little angel, you." He strokes her hip and stretches luxuriously. "I'm about done for, though, even if you're not. I've got a ten o'clock tee time tomorrow morning and I don't know how I'm going to find the strength to lift a club, let alone survive through eighteen holes."

"Then maybe you should have been more careful just now."

"Ah, but I couldn't. I can't hold back with you, little one, you know that. All I have to do is look at you and I'm lost."

"Yes, I know. But it was different tonight," she suggests gently, making the declaration a little like a question.

He hesitates. His hand involves itself in her hair while he considers how to answer her. He looks not into her eyes but her forehead, as if he's trying to read some sentence, some line in a script that's written on the smooth skin that meets her hair.

"A little different, yes," he says. "Bianca, I have to tell you something. This may be our last time together for a while. A *short* while."

She swallows. "Because Tia Maria and Francisca are coming back from Providence?"

"No. Because I'm getting married next week."

And there it is, the thing causing her mind to spin, the portent hanging in the air in the midst of all that frantic copulation. For an instant, she lies rigid, and then she bolts upright in the bed.

"Married?" she howls.

Hugh sits up too and takes her by the elbows. "Sweetheart, you know that. I told you already."

"Who? *Who?*"

"You know whom. Bianca, don't. You knew this already. I told you, the first time we met, how it was."

"I thought—but I thought—" She's crying now, hiccupping, beating his chest while he holds her arms.

"We talked about postponing the service because of Father, but in the end—it's what he wanted so much—"

"But you *hate* your father!"

"Bianca, stop. What's wrong? You know this has nothing to do with us. You and I, we're sacred, I can't live without you, but you know a man in my position—"

"A man in your *position?* We are bound together in God's eyes, you and me. We are made from the same soul, we're linked forever. You said it yourself. Not you and that stupid girl, that—"

"Bianca! She's not stupid, she's a nice girl, you don't understand how it is—what I meant by *bound*—"

"Oh, I understand, all right."

Bianca jumps from the bed and grabs her dress from the floor.

"My God! What's the matter with you? I thought you understood, I thought we understood each other—"

"It seems I did not understand you at all, Hugh Fisher. It seems I thought you were a man of honor."

He startles as if she's slapped him. His eyes open wide. He leaps from the bed and takes her by the shoulders, and she pushes him away, so hard he falls backward on the floor.

"You thought I would be your *mistress*, is that it? *That's* what you meant? *This* is our wonderful fate together? Mistress, do they even do that anymore? I guess they do. You and your damned Families. You can afford anything, can't you? One wife for the summer, and another wife for the rest of the year. My God, I am an *idiot!*"

Hugh scrambles to his feet and stands before her, panting, while she puts on her clothes, her dress first and then her knickers, everything out of order. He lowers his voice and speaks with forced calm.

"Bianca, stop for just a moment. Stop and listen to me. When I told you these things, when my father died, when we first—you know, what we did by the pool, I meant what I said then, what I've said to you every day since. I love you, little one, I can't live without you. You know that. I want you here with me, always. We don't need to live apart, not ever."

She stops and stares in horror at his face, which is absolutely sincere and wracked with misery. His immaculate hair flops all over his forehead, and his beautiful features are transfigured into some grotesque of longing.

"I can't believe it," she whispers. "You thought—you thought that I—that we would just—"

"Bianca, don't," he whispers.

"Because I am just a nobody girl from the village. A nice Portuguese girl for good times in the summer."

"That's not true."

"Now you have covered me in sin. You have covered me in shame."

"In *love*, Bianca."

"It's a mortal sin, what we've done. You just remember that, Hugh Fisher. You just remember that when you stand on your altar and say your vows to that Abigail. You just remember that when God empties his vengeance on your head and my head."

"Bianca, don't. Don't leave."

But she does. Turns away and runs out the door and across the wet grass, thinking it must be a dream.

2.

BIANCA DOESN'T REMEMBER anything about her parents, but she does remember the day she came to live with Tia Maria and Tio Manuelo, who welcomed her with tears and great love, and at night tucked her into the dark, queer-smelling room she was to share with her cousins Francisca and Laura.

Laura went right to sleep, snoring peacefully, but Bianca lay awake in misery and knew that Francisca was awake too. Sure enough, a hiss came from the bed nearby.

"Psst! Bianca! You awake?"

Bianca must have said *Yes*, because Francisca continued.

"Mama says Tia and Tio died and that's why you're living here now."

For a moment, Bianca was confused, and then she remembered that her mother and father had been Francisca's aunt and uncle.

"Yes," she said again.

"Mama says we have to be nice to you, because you're an orphan now."

Bianca just stared at the ceiling. The word *orphan* seemed very strange to her, and also lonely and sort of bleak. Not a word that belonged to her, surely?

"Just remember," says Francisca, "they're not your real parents, okay? You are a charity child, Bianca. You don't belong to anybody. I'm sorry."

Bianca stared at a small black spider, making its way along the edge of the window by some dim light outdoors, the moon or maybe a street-light, and felt a kind of kinship with him, small and alone like that, trudging along a precipice.

"I'll tell you what. If you're very good and obedient, then when I'm married, you can come and live with me and help me with the housework and take care of my kids," Francisca said generously. "How does that sound?"

"Okay," Bianca said, and for some time she listened to the creaks and groans of the strange house, the bedsprings of Tia Maria and Tio Manuelo making music in the room next door, until eventually she must have gone to sleep.

To this day, it's the only distinct memory she has of Portugal, perhaps because it is so raw and painful, because it turns her heart cold, because each time she remembers that night she is made to endure its misery anew. She once recalled the conversation to Francisca—not long ago, in fact—but Francisca just laughed and said she didn't remember saying any such thing.

But she did remember what a funny, skinny, grave child Bianca was, how scrawny and unlikable, and how it was some time before anyone thought of her as part of the family.

3.

FOR SOME REASON, Bianca's mind returns to that night, to Francisca's words—*If you're good, if you're good, when I'm married, when I'm married, don't belong, don't belong*—as she races across the garden to the small door she keeps unlatched. When she reaches her room, she finds Laura sitting on Francisca's bed in her dressing gown, arms crossed, taking in Bianca's crumpled dress and bare legs.

"Why are you here?" Bianca asks stupidly.

"A little birdie whispered in my ear. Jesus Mary, you silly girl. What do you think you're doing?"

"Nothing. Nothing at all."

Laura throws herself back on the bed. "What are we going to do, huh? What are we going to do?"

"We're not going to do anything."

"It's Hugh Fisher, isn't it? Merciful God. That *pig*. Not again."

Bianca goes to the washstand and peers at her face in the mirror. The lamp's off, but the sun has already begun to crest the horizon, and the room contains just enough gray, humid light to reveal how haggard she looks, how guilty. She looks upon this face as a stranger's face, belonging to somebody else. Inside, she feels nothing like Bianca. She is cold, and hard, and frozen, and entirely foreign. Her mind hears the echo of Laura's words from a distance, and at first she's confused by the word *Again*. Then she remembers.

"You mean Francisca? Last summer?" She turns away from the mirror and stares at her cousin, flat on her back in Francisca's bed. "She seems to have made out all right."

"*Made out all right*. Don't you know? She had an operation last October. He got her in trouble, the pig, and Francisca was too scared to tell Mama and Papa, so we went to the mainland together—you remember—and went to this place in Providence and got rid of it."

Bianca hears these words as a whooshing in her ears, as the sound of a different language. Laura crosses herself, sits up again, and braces her hands on either side of her legs at the edge of Francisca's bed.

"And we got lucky, because that dumb cluck Pascoal Vargas was so sweet on her, and thank God she's going to be married and have a nice life. He's going to give up the bootlegging and they're going to keep the lighthouse together and raise a nice family. But she's paid for her sins, Bianca, and so will you if you don't watch out, and dumb clucks like Pascoal don't grow on the trees around here. Even if you don't get in trouble, sooner or later word gets around, and no nice Catholic boy is going to touch you, that's for sure."

Bianca stands straight in the middle of the room, listening, arms rigid against her waist and hips and thighs. So hard and frozen as she is, she imagines she is really an icicle, hanging from somebody's roof, and at some proximate instant she will drop and shatter all over the place, what a terrible mess, too bad about that poor fool Bianca, but she got what she deserved, didn't she? The wages of sin.

"Bianca? Are you listening to me? What's wrong with you?"

"Nothing's wrong." Bianca turns and wriggles out of her dress and her wet knickers, wet with Hugh's vile sperm that leaked from her womb as she ran. She knows Laura's staring enviously at her nakedness, at Bianca's astonishing, voluptuous beauty, and she doesn't care. Her body is a hateful thing to her now, obscene, unclean, it doesn't even belong to her. She pulls her thin summer nightgown from the drawer and drops it over her head. "I'm going to sleep, that's all."

4.

THE NEXT AFTERNOON, when the fishing boats come into the harbor, Bianca picks out Pascoal Vargas and just so happens to be walking the same direction. She's wearing a dress from last year, too small, and her woman's body nearly bursts its seams. Pascoal, flushed to his ears, nervously offers her a cool drink when they reach his house at the end of Primrose Lane. She accepts.

It takes less than a quarter of an hour before he succumbs, even though she lets him think it was all his idea, that he's seduced her, she has surrendered her virtue to the force of some unstoppable attraction that binds her fate to his. Men are all alike in their vanity, she realizes as he climbs aboard, bedsprings creaking, absolutely identical in their propensity to carnal weakness. Pascoal shoves and sweats and slobbers gratefully atop her, rolls and twists her breasts like the dials of a goddamned radio while the skies open up outside the window in a typical August downpour. She remembers to scream in pain when he first prods his thing inside her, in that wicked place where the Devil lives, and to weep when he lets out a long, ecstatic howl and collapses on her belly like a wet sack. Then he cries too and tells her he's sorry, he doesn't know what came over him, and he begs her not to tell her cousin. He tells her this cannot happen again, they must stay away from each other and never, ever speak of it.

On the following afternoon, she waits inside his cottage and makes him tea, and when he arrives home she cries and throws herself on his barrel chest and tells him she cannot sleep or eat, she cannot think of anything but him. Overpowered by her weakness, he takes her on the kitchen table, finishing within seconds because—as he tells her, gasping—he has been thinking shamefully of her all day on his boat, thinking all day of what occurred the previous afternoon, thinking of her beautiful virgin's body yielding to his. Then he slides to the floor and shuts his eyes, muttering some prayer in Portuguese. Bianca brings him his tea, which he drinks in large, desperate gulps. He yells at her to go, to leave him alone, and Bianca crumples and sobs on the kitchen floor in her too-small petticoat, her bare feet and arms, sobs and shivers until her ripe, vulnerable beauty sends him mad once more, until he hurls the teacup against the wall and tears away her petticoat and mounts her, right there on the linoleum, calling her a witch and an angel as he pumps his hips wildly against hers. She closes her eyes and curls her fists, she makes herself ride this grunting, heaving friction into release, as Hugh taught her to do, because she wants that too, because she wants to take back that gift from Hugh as well. She wants to take back everything. Without pity she uses Pascoal's anatomy, until—drained at last—he buries his weeping, exhausted face between her breasts and implores mercy from God, from his mother's soul, from Bianca herself.

For the next three days, she and Pascoal meet like this in dirty secrecy, until Pascoal is a mere husk of a man, his will worn down and stripped away by an endless cycle of temptation and copulation and remorse. For her part, Bianca is both disgusted and fascinated by Pascoal, by the difference between her beautiful first lover and her gnomish second, by the expression of abject, ugly rapture on his face as he humps away between her legs, and by the feeling of power with which this drenches her.

When Tia Maria and Francisca arrive home at last on the Thursday afternoon ferry, Pascoal—his trousers buttoned only minutes before— bursts into tears at the sight of them, and everybody is amazed except Bianca.

1951 (MIRANDA SCHUYLER)

1.

AT FIVE O'CLOCK in the morning, the whole world was deserted. I walked down West Cliff Road into the harbor almost by memory, because the sun still lay below the horizon, still and gray, and the moon was just a tiny sliver of a thing hidden behind the fog. My footsteps crunched softly in the gravel, the only noise except for the wash of water against the bottom of the cliffs, which was so faint I had to strain my ears for it. A calm, auspicious sea for a lobsterman.

I wasn't sure how early the fishing boats set out from the harbor. I hoped I wasn't too late. I thought surely they couldn't set out until sunrise, especially in this fog, but what did I know? As long as the Fleet Rock light guided them away from the rocks and the channel, they ought to take advantage of the peace and quiet and haul up all the lobsters they could before lunchtime. Before the cooks and the housekeepers went down to the market for supplies, before the delivery vans started up their engines and trundled down the Island's dignified lanes to its waiting kitchens.

So I quickened my steps, until the white dust settled on the straps of my sandals and my breath and my heartbeat churned in my chest. The road curled downhill, but when your legs are moving that rapidly, your circulation has to keep up. Alongside, the grass thickened into brush, but there were no trees, not until the road met Hemlock Lane and the elms planted there by human hands.

Down in the village, the fog was even thicker, and a feeling of disorientation came upon me, like I had walked into a dream. I stopped in the middle of Hemlock Street, unable to see even the trees that lined the road, and luckily I caught the faint sound of somebody shouting a command, some lobsterman in the harbor, that drew me back to this earth. I followed the noise and the heavy brine smell and the road—what I could see of it— and a moment later the harbor rushed up to meet me, my feet found the wood of the docks, the sound of my name carried through the fog.

"Joseph?" I said, turning my head.

"Miranda. What're you doing here? You didn't walk down in this peasouper, did you? The sun's not even up."

I couldn't understand how he saw me, but he did. I saw his hair first, dark against the pale fog, and then his hand found my shoulder. "Note from Isobel," I said, quietly so the other lobstermen wouldn't hear, because of course they were listening, all of them, their eardrums strained mightily as they readied their boats for the day's work. Nobody more curious than a fisherman.

"Is something wrong?" he asked, snatching the note.

"No. She left for the mainland yesterday with her mother, that's all. A shopping trip to Providence, I think. She wanted you to have this early."

"And you listened to her? You might've walked off a cliff!"

"I wasn't going to walk off a cliff. I'm not blind."

He stuck the note in his pocket. "So why didn't *you* go shopping in Providence?"

"I don't like shopping much. Anyway . . ."

"Anyway what?"

"Anyway nothing." I turned back. "So long, then."

"Wait a second. You're not walking back, are you?"

"I made it down all right."

"By God's mercy. Come on, into the boat with you. Chop-chop."

"Now how is that any safer than walking?"

"Because Pops and I know this harbor better'n we know our own kitchen, all right? Anyway, it's faster. Now get in."

We were speaking in quick, quiet whispers that sank into the haze around us. The air was full of Joseph's smell, of the essence of the sea, of the interested gazes of the lobstermen hiding in their foggy boats. I thought of Isobel, who had handed me this note after lunch yesterday, as she fussed with her pocketbook getting ready to leave, and said, "You don't mind, do you? The sooner the better." She was dressed for the mainland, natty in a yellow frock that reminded me of buttercups and a hat like a small daisy. She was thrilled to get off the Island, you could feel it shimmering off her skin.

Now, according to my vow, I hadn't delivered any more notes to Joseph since that day in July, and Isobel hadn't asked me. She and Clay seemed to have reached some kind of equilibrium, some understanding, the nature of which I didn't dare to guess, although I imagined it had something to do with those squeaking springs in the front seat of the Lincoln, something to do with Clay's adoration and Isobel's lust for danger. So the sudden appearance of this note surprised me, after a month of silence. I stared at the white square in my hand, and I glanced back up at Isobel's animated face, and I thought, *Well, it's the end of summer, isn't it? What trouble could possibly arise?*

I tucked the note in the pocket of my sundress and said, *Of course not.*

But I hadn't gone out to meet the incoming fleet that afternoon, and I hadn't waited for Joseph to bring his mother to church, and I hadn't sent any signal with my flashlight from the dock at midnight. Instead I'd risen before dawn to carry Isobel's message to him now, at the beginning of a fresh, whole new day. Joseph, as a matter of courtesy, now offered me a lift home in his lobster boat. The fog curled the hair around my hot face and dampened my skin. I pushed back a few strands and tucked them behind my ear and said, *Okay*.

2.

SO MAYBE, DEEP inside the unconscious matter of my brain, I had it all planned out. Or maybe I just felt it was inevitable, what happened that day; that some tide had arrived in my affairs which I must take at the flood, *or remain bound*—I heard my father's solemn voice among the dust motes of the study—*in shallows and in miseries*. I guess, like everything else on this earth, the nature of the affair depends on how you look at it.

Joseph led me to the boat, though I knew exactly where it lay at its mooring. Could have reached it blindfolded, which I almost was, stuck inside this swirling mist. Joseph called out to his father and helped me aboard, while the slow, grinding thud of the engine filled the air with exhaust. At the wheel, Vargas stood without expression, clenching a cigarette between his lips, not even looking at us. He was shorter than I thought, not much taller than I was, and his face was as lined and as deeply tanned as an old saddle. In the strange dawn light, I couldn't tell if the shirt beneath his yellow oilskin was blue or gray or white. His stumpy arms, covered with coarse black hair, gripped the wheel. As soon as my second foot touched the deck, he shoved back the throttle and yanked the vessel away from the dock. I lost my balance, and Joseph, still holding my elbow, pulled me upright.

"Steady," he said, and I stepped away, burning, to stand near the bow, away from all the lobster cages stacked in the stern. Joseph turned to his father. "We're going to give Miranda a lift back home, all right?"

"All right," said Vargas.

"Unless you want to stay out with us." Joseph raised his voice to me. "Do you?"

"Do I what?"

"Want to stay out on the water. Fog'll burn off soon. Be a nice day."

"I don't know. You'll be out for hours, won't you?"

"What, have you got better plans? Bridge and iced tea at the Club or something?"

He was grinning, swirled by mist, and I grinned back. "I guess not."

"Well, then."

"I'm not exactly dressed for hard labor, though." I gestured to my sundress.

"That's all right. We'll handle the lobsters. You just sit back and look pretty, that's enough for two old salts like us. Enjoy the cruise. Right, Pops?"

Vargas shifted the cigarette to the corner of his mouth and said something that sounded like Portuguese. He wasn't looking at me, he was clearly concentrating on the intricate problem of navigation, the buoys and the lights from the other boats, all of us puttering for the harbor point and the wider sea beyond. Now the sun was nudging upward, rendering the thinnest possible line of pink on the horizon, and though the air was still cool, the streaming fog more chill than I imagined, my insides were warmed by the simple ignition of the word *pretty*. Of course he didn't really mean it, of course he was just tossing out a friendly compliment. I wore no lipstick this morning, no brief Polynesian garment; I was plain and untidy in a white dress and navy cardigan, I wasn't sensational by any rational description. Nonetheless, the word ignited me. We rounded the harbor point, and the first thing I saw to the east was the Fleet Rock light, penetrating the gray-pink haze, though I couldn't see the lighthouse itself.

I folded my knees up to my chin and said, "Where are we headed today, Mr. Vargas?"

Mr. Vargas tossed his cigarette stub into the water. "East."

Joseph had settled down to bait the wooden traps in the stern. He laughed and said, "Pops means we're headed to the eastern end of the grounds, off Orient Point."

"Don't the Long Island lobstermen mind?"

"We have a little arrangement between us."

"Because I don't want to get myself harpooned."

Joseph glanced at me, still grinning a little. "You know I'd never let that happen."

I unfolded my legs and rested my elbows on the wooden bow while the wind tossed my short hair about my face. As if by design, the sun edged higher, brightening the air, and I closed my eyes and smiled. I had spent this past month in perpetual motion, spinning from sport to sport in Isobel's restless wake, swimming, dancing, locked in tennis combat. I felt strong; I felt as if my firm, tanned limbs were ready for any adventure.

Under the fog, the water was so still as to be made of thick, gray glass. The boat skimmed across its surface, passing Fleet Rock to the right, making for the unseen point of Long Island that lay between us and the broad Atlantic. The salt air rushed up my nose and stung my lips. When I closed my eyes, I thought I was flying, I thought I was free.

"There's coffee in the thermos," Joseph called from the stern. "Sandwiches, if you're hungry."

"What kind of sandwiches?" I asked. "Lobster rolls?"

"Not us. Ham and cheese all right?"

"Maybe later, when I'm hungry. I wouldn't mind some coffee, though. Where's the thermos?"

Joseph put down the trap he was holding and started for the deckhouse. "I'll get it."

"No, don't get up," I said, too late, and for an instant we faced each other, Joseph and I, in some kind of standoff I didn't quite understand. He wore a plain white T-shirt over his dungarees and his oilskins, stained work gloves on his hands, no hat, and his arms reminded me of ropes, plaited with lean, strong muscle. The draft kicked at his hair, but he was otherwise still, legs braced slightly against the rhythm of the boat.

"No trouble." Joseph continued to the deckhouse, shucking off his gloves, and poured coffee from a large, battered thermos into a pair of tin mugs, which he handed to each of us, me first and then his father, no ceremony. As he did so, he said something to Vargas in a low voice, and a moment later the boat began to slow and curve to the northeast. Joseph returned to the traps, put his gloves back on, and resumed the baiting from a large metal bucket full of fish guts or something. I drank my coffee for a minute, watching the deft movement of his gloved hands, and then I stepped forward, leaned against the deckhouse wall, and addressed Mr. Vargas at the wheel.

"How long have you been lobstering?" I asked.

He reached for the battered cardboard pack of cigarettes on the deckhouse ledge. "About twenty years now, I guess."

He spoke with an accent. I supposed it was Portuguese, and so I asked him when he arrived in this country. He waited until he'd lit the cigarette and taken a long first drag before he replied.

"After the war," he said. "The first one."

"Oh, so you didn't start fishing right away."

He shifted the cigarette to the other side of his mouth and didn't reply.

Joseph called from the back of the boat. "Go on, Pops. Tell her."

"I messed around a little first," he said. "Before I got married."

"C'mon. You were a rumrunner, isn't that right?" said Joseph. "That's what Tia Laura told me. But you gave it up when you got the lighthouse appointment."

Mr. Vargas shrugged and grunted.

Joseph turned to me. "He used to take his boat out to Rum Row at night and haul in booze to order, for everyone on the Island. Champagne, whisky, gin, whatever you wanted, direct delivery. Greyfriars had a nice hidey-hole in the boathouse. Isn't that right, Pops? You kept the Families nicely pickled throughout the Scourge. Or at least until you met Mama and went clean."

"That's a terrific story," I said. "I'll bet you could tell us a lot of adventures."

"Nah, he won't do it. I've tried to drag it out of him, but the lips are sealed. Huh, Pops?"

Vargas shrugged his shoulders. "Not much to tell."

"Sure there isn't. Just dodging the Coast Guard every night, the supply gangs, the pirates. Anyway, it was a living," Joseph said cheerfully. "A nice nest egg to live on when the trade went south in the thirties."

"Was it that bad?"

"It was bad everywhere. A lot of lobstermen left the Island back then, according to Pops. I don't know, maybe they were just looking for an excuse. Winters are rough in the best of times."

"At least you had the lighthouse," I said. "Doesn't that pay some kind of salary?"

"Some, I guess." Joseph turned back to his traps. "It sure helps."

I warmed my hands around the coffee cup and looked at Vargas. I thought he wore a little smile around his dwindling cigarette. "Are you sure you didn't take in a little trade afterward? I mean, a lighthouse makes for good storage, doesn't it? And the location is just about ideal."

"No. I gave it up," he said.

"Mama made him," Joseph said. "She didn't want to take any chances. They had me right away, and you don't want unsavory types coming and going when you've got a baby around the place."

I opened my mouth to ask whether he'd had any brothers or sisters, but my gaze happened to fall on Vargas's stocky shoulders, his jaw locked, his cigarette burning from his mouth, and the question died. Instead, I turned back to Joseph and asked if he wanted coffee.

"Sure, thanks. More cups in the deckhouse."

I went inside and found the cup on the shelf, which had a slat along the open side to keep all the dishes from tumbling out. When I emerged a moment later, I noticed that the fog was thinning. The shadow of Long Island appeared on the horizon, and the climbing sun stretched out its rays to burn through the mist.

"The other thing was Mama," Joseph continued, matter-of-fact, taking the coffee from me. "She had a hard time with me. Nearly died. There was a storm and they couldn't get to the mainland, so Pops had to deliver me."

It took me a moment to absorb this sudden information. "Oh my goodness!" I said softly, looking at Vargas.

"He did all right. Didn't you, Pops? All's well that ends well. But she was sick for a long while. Couldn't get out of bed. Pops took care of us both, kept the lighthouse running. By the time Mama was on her feet again, they'd passed the Twenty-first Amendment and the liquor stores were back in business."

"But how terrible for you," I said to Vargas. "Your new bride. When you were still so much in love."

This time Vargas was moved to pluck the cigarette from his mouth, to make his words clear in the warm, moist draft. "What else was I going to do? She was my wife. He was my son."

3.

IN ANOTHER TWENTY minutes or so, we slowed and drifted toward a slim green buoy. "First we lay the new traps," Joseph said, putting his gloves back on, "and then we pick up the ones we set yesterday."

"You do this every day?" I asked.

"Except Sunday."

Vargas put the boat in reverse and looked over his shoulder at Joseph, who was reaching over the stern with a thin metal cable, which he clipped to the buoy. The boat's wake made it bob crazily to one side and then another. Joseph turned back and lifted the first trap and clipped it to a loop on the cable.

"All right," he called forward, and Vargas touched the throttle, drawing out the cable a few yards, while Joseph clipped the next trap.

"Can I help?" I asked.

"If you like. Hand me the next trap, will you? It's already baited."

I bent and lifted the trap, which was heavier than I thought, though I wasn't going to show it. I waited until we reached the next buoy, until Vargas eased the throttle and Joseph reached expertly to snatch the cable, and I passed over the wooden cage into his large, gloved hands.

"Thanks," he said. "You're not getting your dress dirty, are you?"

"Oh, I don't care. It's an old dress."

He clipped the trap to the cable and sent it down. "You're a good sport, Miranda."

"Me? I'm just here to look pretty. Isn't that right, Mr. Vargas?"

Vargas shrugged a little, but I thought he was smiling again, sharing the joke, at least as much as you *could* smile around the cigarette stuck permanently in the corner of your mouth. The sun was really starting to get going, or maybe it was just the effort of lifting the cages, and before I reached for the next trap I drew off my cardigan and tossed it on the bow, so my arms were mostly bare. This time the trap felt lighter between my hands, and we began to develop a rhythm between us, Joseph and me, buoy after buoy, cage after cage, until I handed him the last one and said, "I think I'm ready for my ham sandwich now."

"I'll bet. Didn't eat any breakfast before you left, did you?"

"It was five o'clock in the morning. I wasn't hungry then."

"Greenhorn." He clipped the cage and committed it to the deep with a solemn splash. "Pops, where'd you put those sandwiches?"

The ham was thick and juicy, the cheese sharp. Joseph took the wheel so his father could rest his legs and eat. I sat in the bow, facing the now-blazing sun, while Vargas settled carefully in the stern, as if he wanted to keep some distance between the two of us. I asked if we were headed back to the harbor now.

"Nope," said Joseph. "Got to pick up some lobsters first."

"Oh, of course."

"Pick up some lobsters and get them back to the harbor. You don't mind if we stop at the harbor first? You get the best price if you're in early."

"Of course I don't mind. Just do your job and pretend I'm not here."

"Don't know if I can do that."

"Oh? Why not?"

Joseph popped the crust of his sandwich into his mouth and stared straight ahead. "Hate to have to tell you this, Miss Schuyler, but you smell like bait. Bait and lobster."

"So do you."

He lifted his arm and sniffed his shirt. "Blow me down. How about we go for a swim?"

"What, here? Now?"

"Why not?" He reached for the throttle. "Pops, you don't mind, do you?"

Vargas shrugged and leaned back in his seat. He'd finished his sandwich, and beneath the shelter of his hat he looked as if he might be falling asleep.

"C'mon," said Joseph, pulling off his oilskins, yanking off his boots. "Last one in."

"Last one in is what?"

"I guess you're going to find out," he said, and he climbed on the bow and dove like a dolphin into the water. A moment later, he came up again, and I cupped my hands around my mouth.

"What about sharks?"

"You just punch them on the nose, Schuyler. Don't you know anything?"

I glanced back over my shoulder at Vargas, who sat with his arms folded, watching me curiously, as if he was making a bet in his head about what I might do or not do. Swim or not swim.

"What about my dress? I can't swim in a dress like this."

"Excuses. Take it off, then. You've got a petticoat or something, right?" He was swimming in place, looking up at me, his wet hair plastered over his head. I saw the white of his T-shirt under the water, his churning legs.

"Turn around," I said.

"C'mon. I won't look."

"Turn around."

He turned. I reached back and found the buttons of my dress, and when I started to struggle Vargas came up and helped me with his gnarled, thick fingers. The dress gave way and I kicked it off, kicked off my sandals too, and I leapt in my short petticoat into the water.

It was colder than I thought, much colder than the swimming pool at Greyfriars. I came up gasping. The first thing I saw was the sun, and then Joseph's grinning face below it. I thought his hair was like a helmet, shining like that.

I called across the water. "You looked!"

"Aw, can you blame me?"

He dove back in, like something had swallowed him, and I stared at the gentle chop of the water while my heart beat and beat. A moment later he came up beside me, closer than I thought. His grin wasn't so wide now, more like a question, and I said, a little raspy, "Race you back to the boat?"

"But it's right there." He pointed.

"All right." I turned and swam away in steady strokes, like my father had taught me on the Delaware beaches before the war. *Don't fight the water, Miranda,* he used to tell me, as we trundled along past the breakers, and even though I became a strong enough swimmer, I remained grateful for his calm, muscular body—or so it seemed to me at the time, age seven or eight—keeping me company. Funny, I never thought of sharks then, and my father never mentioned them. It was my mother who liked to keep to the shallows, my mother who was afraid.

When I had gone about twenty or thirty yards, I stopped and turned, and there was Joseph right beside me. *Ready*, I said. Set.

Go.

Of course he leapt right ahead of me. I mean, I couldn't compete with those shoulders, those experienced arms, but I was glad he didn't give me any quarter. I didn't want any favors. I just stroked with all my might, strained every absolute muscle, wasting not a single speck of energy in trying to keep sight of Joseph's churning body. But I thought I was close. When my fingers touched the hull of the boat, I looked up, panting.

"I'll be damned," said Joseph, panting too. "You're pretty strong."

"I've been swimming laps in the pool all summer."

He snorted. "Pools are for kids."

"Maybe I'm still just a kid, then."

"I wouldn't say that."

We were right up against the hull, half holding the ropes that hung from the side. The boat had turned a little in the current, so the sun struck our wet cheeks, our dripping ears. I couldn't see Mr. Vargas from where I was, floating next to that wall of white paint, and I guessed he couldn't see us, and maybe Joseph had the same thought. He glanced up briefly, and his face softened, and his smile disappeared.

"Miranda," he said.

I didn't answer, just kind of kept myself afloat, holding the rope with one hand, waving my legs next to his, hanging myself on the quiet brown color of his eyes. I thought how long and dark his lashes were. His face moved, turning to an angle as he leaned forward and kissed me on the lips, salty and brief.

"Oh," I said.

"Do you mind?"

I shook my head. Under the water, he touched my waist, very lightly, and drew me closer. My legs tangled with his as I kicked them back and forth. "Hold still," he whispered, so I stopped churning and put my left hand on his shoulder to steady myself in the water. He kissed me again, just as gentle but much deeper, and the salty, silky perfume of his mouth stunned me. All I remembered of Clay was the taste of whisky; this was more real, this was like the essence of Joseph, the way two animals might know each other. The water tossed against us. For an instant, my legs found the current and slipped between his, and our stomachs met, our chests met, our lips fell apart. We were both still panting, maybe because of that reckless swimming, and maybe because of each other. Joseph's hand tightened about my waist, but only to return us to a more demure alignment, to allow a little decorous water to flood back between my stomach and his stomach, between my white petticoat and his white shirt. I think I laughed, out of nervousness, out of shock, and so did he.

"I've been wanting to do that all summer," he said.

"Really?"

"Really *really*. Are you surprised?"

"Yes! I thought—I thought—"

"Thought what?"

"Well, Isobel, obviously."

His brows slanted together. "*Isobel?* Isobel what?"

"You and Isobel."

"*That?*" He was astonished. "Oh boy. You thought that—"

The boat swung suddenly, catching us with a thump. Joseph pulled me free, but the enchantment was broken, and Vargas's anxious voice floated above us, calling our names.

"Right here, Pops," Joseph said. "Can you get the towels from the deckhouse?"

There was a noise of resignation from above. Joseph still held me by the waist, and my hand still rested on his shoulder. He turned his head back to me and kissed me again, swiftly. "We'll climb in over the stern, it's easier."

He held my hand as we half swam, half rappelled to the back of the boat. He helped me up over the side, where Vargas, looking carefully away, gestured to the towels on the bench. Behind me, Joseph hoisted himself inside, and I wrapped myself in one towel and handed the other to him, though not before glimpsing his wet shirt, plastered against his chest; not before losing my breath all over again at the audacity of what I had done. What we both had done, Joseph and me, a real kiss, not a mistake, not a drunken substitution of one woman's mouth for another's. A kiss of conscious intent. I couldn't look at him. I thought everything had changed, I would never be the same Miranda again and he would never be the old Joseph. I sat on the bow in my towel, shivering, while the sun dried my hair and my petticoat and Vargas piloted us toward the traps he and Joseph had laid yesterday. I licked my lips and tasted salt, and Joseph.

4.

BY THE TIME we had collected the lobsters and returned to the harbor, it was past lunchtime and the sun had crested the sky, and three fishing boats had already come in ahead of us.

"You had to swim," Vargas said to Joseph, shaking his head.

"Aw, it was worth it, Pops. Best swim of my life." Joseph winked at me and I turned away, because I didn't know what to say in return. I had worked silently beside him, hoping that this shared labor would cure the exhilarating awkwardness that lay between us. Now it was even worse. The sight of Greyfriars had frozen my throat as we passed it on the way to the harbor. I thought of Isobel and what she would say, what she would do if she knew I had kissed Joseph. When I had confided to her about Clay, a couple of days after the luau, she'd only laughed and said she hoped I enjoyed it, that you couldn't ask for a better boy for your first kiss than Clay Monk, and she was going to give him hell about it later. But I knew I couldn't tell Isobel that Joseph had kissed me and I had kissed him back. That was no laughing matter. To kiss Joseph was unforgivable.

Vargas brought the boat in, and Joseph jumped nimbly to the dock and wound the rope around the piling. I handed down the lobsters in their baskets, keeping clear of the snapping claws—there were forty-two of what Joseph and his father called *the little buggers*, a good haul—and when the boat was clear I jumped down too, of my own power, ignoring Joseph's outstretched hand.

"Hey," he said, in a low voice. "What's the matter?"

"Nothing."

"Are you sore at me?"

"No, of course not."

He put his hand on my elbow. "Miranda, I'm sorry if I—I didn't mean to—"

Vargas jumped down from the boat, practically between us, and went for the baskets. "Joseph, you got work to do, all right? I got to sell these little buggers."

"Pops—Miranda—give me a minute here—"

Vargas pointed to me. "You come along with me and I'll buy you an ice cream, okay?"

"Okay," I said meekly.

"Pops, wait a second."

"You clean that boat, son. That's all you got to do."

I had just enough courage to look over my shoulder as I walked down the dock with Mr. Vargas, carrying a couple of the wire baskets, but Joseph had already turned away to climb back inside the boat and put everything in order for the next day's work. Mr. Vargas's stumpy legs moved with remarkable speed. He didn't say a word until we reached the end of the dock and stepped onto the quay that ran along Hemlock Road, where he set down his lobster baskets and dug into his pocket.

"Here," he said to me, shoving a dollar bill in my hand. "Go buy yourself some ice cream while I sell these little buggers."

"But I—"

He took the baskets from my hand and picked up his own, and such was his strength and experience with these things, he trundled up Hemlock Street carrying all forty-two little buggers in their wire baskets, snapping and crawling in wholly justified panic, poor things, without missing a step.

The ice cream parlor was closed, had a little sign on the door handle that said *Back in 30 min*, so I went into the general store instead. I thought I could use some ice cream, I thought I could eat a gallon of it after tending those lobster pots all morning, besides swimming, besides kissing Joseph. Sure enough, they had a soda fountain behind a long, new Formica counter along one side of the store, trimmed in chrome, all out of place in that old-fashioned interior that smelled of must and spices. The old woman there offered me a choice between vanilla, chocolate, and strawberry. I asked for a double, a scoop of strawberry and a scoop of chocolate, and as she bent over the freezer I remembered with a shock that this was Joseph's *grandmother*. That she had lost a son to the war and another daughter in a terrible accident on the water, the night that Joseph was born, that her husband was laid up after a heart attack and she ran the store by herself.

"That'll be thirty-five cents," she said, handing me the cone.

For an instant, I hesitated, because I realized this was Mr. Vargas's money, and there was something strange about taking money from Mr. Vargas to pay his mother-in-law for ice cream. On the other hand,

I had damned well earned that dollar today, not by kissing his son but by hauling those cages and getting those lobsters in their wire baskets. I took the dollar from the pocket of my sundress and handed it silently to her, over the counter, and she pressed some buttons on the cash register and gave me sixty-five cents change.

"You're Mr. Fisher's new stepdaughter, aren't you?" she said, as she gave me the money.

"Yes," I said.

"How do you like it up at Greyfriars?"

"It's—well, it's beautiful, I guess."

She nodded. "Was that you I saw, coming in with the Vargases just now?"

"Yes. We—I went out lobstering with them today. Isobel—Miss Fisher's on the mainland with her mother, and I thought—I had nothing else to do, so I—"

"Just watch yourself, sweetie," she said. "A lot can happen to a nice girl like you, if she's not careful."

I slid the sixty-five cents into my pocket and took a paper napkin for my ice cream. "Of course," I said.

Mrs. Medeiro reached out a long, bumpy hand and took my wrist. "I mean it. You watch yourself. Don't mix yourself up with any of it."

"Any of what?"

She let go of my wrist and looked away. I thought, *Maybe she wants to protect Joseph.* Maybe she thinks I'm like Isobel, I'm no good for him.

"Don't worry," I said, stepping back, "the summer's almost over, anyway."

Oh, the look she gave me then. She shut the cash drawer with a demented ding and pushed a long, iron-colored strand of hair back into its knot at the back of her head. "That's when the trouble starts, sweetheart. Trust me."

5.

I WALKED AWAY, down Hemlock Street and around the corner to ascend West Cliff Road back to Greyfriars, devouring my ice cream as it melted in sticky rivulets around my hand. I wanted to experience the mile and a half back to Greyfriars by the pace of my own two feet, I wanted to stretch my legs and feel the sunshine on my neck, the crumbled asphalt beneath my soles. I started up the road, under the shade of the huge elms, until the houses grew apart and the sidewalk fell away and so did the trees. I started up the slope and felt the breeze strike my cheek, blowing in unchecked from the southwest, and somewhere in the middle of that zephyr came the sound of my name, *Miranda*!

I turned and shaded my eyes against the afternoon glare. For a moment, I didn't see him, and then he burst free from the sun. His face was shadowed but I knew that silhouette, those dungarees and that white shirt almost blue as he jogged to catch me. I held myself absolutely still as he approached. Only my blood moved, hurtling down my arms and legs and up into my hot face.

He came to a stop a few yards away, panting. "There you are! Why'd you run off like that?"

"I was hot," I said.

He stared at me in disbelief while the rhythm of his breathing slowed and slowed. A trickle of perspiration ran down his temple and over the bones of his jaw. "Just like that? Leave without saying anything?"

"Your father—"

"My father what?"

I held up the remains of my ice cream. "He told me to have an ice cream and get lost."

"Don't listen to Pops. Listen to *me*."

The wind came up over the nearby cliff and flattened his shirt to his ribs. He wiped his shining temple with his thumb. The heat of exertion rippled from his body and reached mine, and I raised my fingers to hide the pulse in my neck, thudding and thudding like some kind of machine, while the two of us stared at each other, unable to speak, unable to look away.

At last Joseph said hoarsely, "I'm sorry, Miranda. I apologize. I shouldn't have done what I did."

"All right." I turned back up the road and started walking. He caught up in a few strides.

"That's it?" he said. "All right?"

"I don't know what to say, that's all."

"Are you mad at me, or not? I thought you—I'm sorry if I saw it all wrong—I just thought, when you looked at me in the water—I thought you wouldn't mind. You *said* you didn't mind."

"I didn't. I don't."

He took my elbow and turned me to face him. "Is that true? Just tell me plain, Miranda, tell me straight out. Did you want me to kiss you, or not?"

"Yes," I whispered.

"Since when?"

"Since—since the morning of the wedding. Since you dove into the water and saved Popeye."

His hand dropped from my elbow. He looked up at the sky and started to laugh. "All this time? You mean *all this time?*"

"Joseph, please."

He looked back into my face. "For me, it started a few hours later. That night, when you stood up in the sand and said *Once more unto the breach*. I just stared at you and thought, I could listen to her forever. I really could."

"But Isobel!"

"Isobel. Isobel. What about her?"

"Those notes. I saw you meet her, at night, in secret."

"Oh boy. Oh, Miranda."

"What?"

"You're kidding me, right? Isobel?"

"Yes," I said, obstinate. "Isobel."

"Holy moly. You're serious. You actually think—" He broke off in a laugh. "Was that it? Was that why you kept giving me the cold shoulder? Oh, Izzy. Izzy, you little devil. Listen to me. Listen up. You can just forget that thought, okay? Forget all about it. Wash it right out of your head."

"But—"

"But nothing. I never touched her. I wouldn't touch her. We're— we've known each other since we were kids. I never—oh boy. How do I explain this? All right, I know how it looked. I can see what you must have thought, if Izzy didn't explain."

"Explain what?"

He just gazed at me, real steady, and for a moment there was nothing but the sound of the wind, the sea noises, the air in our lungs.

"You just have to believe me," Joseph said at last. "She's my friend, that's all."

"But all those notes," I said.

"I can tell you didn't read them, did you?"

"Of course I didn't."

"We're friends, Miranda. We're good friends. We talked, that's all. I swear it on my mother's soul. The only girl . . . the only girl . . ."

He took a breath like he was going to try again to finish that sentence, but while my ears strained hard for the next words, I never heard them. Only the whoosh of the breeze in my ears. We stood near the crest of the slope, where the road curved near the cliffs, and I thought that anybody could see us like this, in pungent silhouette against the sky. The sun struck the side of Joseph's face, the wind whistled through his hair.

He picked up my hand and looked at it. Turned it over and looked back up at me.

"There's only one girl on my mind," Joseph said, "and it's not Isobel Fisher, trust me. I only just met this girl, but I can't—I can't seem to get her out of my head, no matter how hard I try, no matter how many hours I kill out there on that water, and I just—I just—when I saw this girl today, this fascinating girl, kind of shy but full of brains and soul and life, when I saw her down there in the harbor today, when I saw she'd walked all the way down before dawn, just to give me some stupid note from a friend of mine, I just about—I thought maybe there was a chance, after all."

I pulled my hand away.

"Miranda, wait."

"I'm so stupid," I said. "I should never have done that."

"But you did. You did, and you can't take it back, you can't tell me you didn't want to kiss me, that kissing me wasn't the reason you went out on that boat today, the same reason I invited you."

"Isobel—"

"Isobel nothing! I already explained."

"You don't understand," I said. "Maybe she's just a friend to you, but to *her*—don't you see it? Don't you see what she feels?"

He stared at me. "That's not what she feels."

"It is, trust me. Just because she's engaged to someone else—"

"I haven't—I've never—this is crazy. Miranda, *please*. I promise you, you're seeing it all wrong. And hell, you know what? She *is* engaged to someone else. There's not a single reason on this earth why . . ."

The sentence trailed away, as if he'd lost the thought behind it. He looked away, frowning, out to sea. I thought of Isobel, what she would say if she saw us now, what she would think of me.

She's engaged, I thought. She has no right to him.

"Unless you didn't mean it, back there on the water," he said. "Unless you were just having a few kicks with the lobsterman's son. I get it."

"That's not true."

"Swell." He glanced down at his left hand, and for the first time I noticed the object contained there, which he now lifted and held out to me. My cardigan of navy blue. "You left this on the boat."

I stared down at the cardigan, which was damp and crumpled, and I thought, *I don't want this. This is not what I want.* I want the *hand*, the large, short-fingered, work-hardened, fish-scented hand. Not the damned cardigan.

"That's not true," I said again. "It wasn't a few kicks. It was everything. All summer—why do you think I kept delivering those stupid messages? Why do you think—didn't you *see* it?"

His hand dropped back to his side. He was shaking his head. "What are you saying? What are you saying, Miranda?"

"I wanted to stop, it hurt so much, but I couldn't stop—just to see you—not until I promised myself—I promised God—well, something."

Joseph's face was soft with wonder, with disbelief.

I drew in breath. "But Isobel—"

"Forget Isobel," Joseph said. "Just say it to me plain, straight out, so I can understand you."

"What do you want me to say?"

"I want you to tell me you're as crazy about me as I am about you. That's what I want."

"That depends on how crazy you are, I guess."

"I am—I am—at this exact second, Miranda? I am pretty much goddamned certifiable."

"Well, I'm crazier than *that*, believe me," I said, and Joseph moved forward then, made a whoop of jubilation as he put his arms around my waist and hoisted me up in the air, so my hands were on his shoulders and his nose crashed into the hollow of my neck.

"Saturday, the eleventh of August," he said. "She loves me. She loves me."

6.

THAT HOUR ON the cliffs, I remember it still. The innocence of it, the clean newness. The way we tumbled to the grass and kissed and laughed and kissed again, seized by a kind of giddy, childlike wonder I have never felt again. Not a single article of clothing came out of place, I mean maybe my dress rode up a little, but that was all. That was enough. Just to put my arms around his neck, just to lie there in the prickling grass and touch my mouth to Joseph's mouth, just to know the curve of his shoulder and the angle of his elbow and the weight of his knee, was enough. Or maybe it wasn't. In the middle of some delicate, heady maneuver, in which the tip of Joseph's tongue found the tip of mine, and my hips arched upward in reflex, he broke off and rolled onto his back.

"What's wrong?" I asked.

"Nothing. Just catching my breath."

"I didn't mean to—"

"It's not you, believe me. Give me a minute, that's all."

I rolled on my side and stared across the plane of his shirt to the long grass beyond, and it seemed I could see every blade, every seed and speck and insect, I perceived every detail of the world around me. How many ages ago lived the fog that had existed that morning, in the vague Before of my life! Now I lived in the After—*O brave new world, that has such people in 't!*—and my lungs breathed with Joseph's breath, and my limbs warmed with Joseph's warmth.

"It's real, isn't it?" I said. "We're not dreaming this?"

"I don't know. Feels like a dream to *me*. I mean, I've been dreaming it all summer, so what are the odds you're really there?"

"Well, what are the odds we're both having the same dream?"

"For God's sake, I'm just a fellow hauling lobsters out of Long Island

Sound. You're Miranda Schuyler, you're a Foxcroft girl, Hugh Fisher's stepdaughter, you're like—you're like one of the stars in the sky."

"No, I'm not. I'm anything but that."

"It's true. You hang there twinkling at me, and I can't even reach you."

"All right, then you're the earth. You're everything solid and real and strong."

Joseph laughed. "Jesus Mary. Listen to us, like a couple of fools. Stars and earth. How about we're just a boy and a girl, lying around an island somewhere, and the boy wants to kiss the girl again, but he's afraid, if he turns around, she won't be there after all."

I reached for his opposite shoulder and pulled him on his side to face me. "You see? Here I am."

"There you are."

"From now on, whenever you turn around, I'll be here."

"Until the end of summer, anyway. A few weeks, not even that."

"Is that all?"

"I don't know about you, but I'm due in Providence for convocation on the fourth of September."

There was a tuft of grass in his hair. I lifted my hand and picked it away. "I want it back. All that time we had! I wish we could just call all those weeks back and live them again."

"It wouldn't have gone any differently. Just be glad for what we've got."

"You'll be fishing all morning."

"You could come with me. And we have the afternoons. Evenings. At least until the happy couple returns from Europe." He took my hand and drew it away from his hair. Climbed to his feet, pulling me with him. "Come on. I'll walk you home and make you a sandwich."

"I can make sandwiches."

"Not as good as mine, I'll bet."

He plucked the grass out of my hair and my dress and helped me with my cardigan, and we walked along the deserted road, hand in hand, while the sun dropped behind us. As the road curved back away from the cliffs, the Greyfriars drive appeared, lined by rhododendrons; the distant house; the meadow bordered by a low stone wall, painstakingly maintained to a state of picturesque dilapidation. We hadn't said a word since rising, and we didn't speak now as we turned down the gravel lane. On each side of the driveway, the rhododendrons had grown in thick with stiff, waxy new leaves, obscuring the meadow and the sea cliffs, the facade of Greyfriars itself. I felt as if a great weight had descended on my chest, constricting my breath. Joseph kicked the gravel and made a noise of frustration, like he, too, was trying to lift something heavy and couldn't quite get his weight under it.

There was a particular enormous rhododendron, ancient, right on the corner, that might have shielded a small car if someone had been so bold as to drive inside the shelter of its branches. I reached out as we passed and ripped away a single leaf, an act of terrible desecration, I don't know why. I crushed it in my fingers and dropped it to the ground just before we rounded the bend and Greyfriars slid into view like an ocean liner.

Ahead of us, the house sat primly, shingled in gray cedar and trimmed in white, windows sparkling, looking so much statelier than it did from the other side. The front of the place was formal, tidy, symmetrical as could be, but from this decorous facade Greyfriars rambled every which way, trying to catch the sunshine and the sea views from every possible angle, and I never could quite get over the difference between the two sides, front and back. Either way you looked, it was beautiful, you couldn't deny its beauty and its size, its class and its pedigree, no more like my old, damp cottage at Foxcroft than a child's clay sculpture compared to the Winged Victory.

It's your home now, Isobel had told me once, as we skidded around this exact curve one night, returning from some party at the Club. She was sentimental with cocktails and cigarettes, and when we came to a stop just outside the garage, spilling happily onto the grass, she leaned down

and laid her head on my lap and gazed up at the stars. She looked so tender and happy, I hadn't wanted to bruise her with the knowledge that this
wasn't my home, didn't feel like my home, was instead like some elegant
private hotel in which I had taken up residence for the summer. And Isobel herself was like some friend you meet in a hotel like that, also staying
for the summer, with whom you strike up a passionate friendship, all the
more fierce for its unlikelihood, its mismatch, because you know that it's
not going to last. You're going to leave at the beginning of September in a
flurry of promises to write and meet up over Christmas, and though you
may both believe this at the time, you also know it's simply not going to
happen. You're not really friends. You're not really sisters. You're just
pretending. No, it's more than that. You're not pretending, you're acting
in a play, in a film, and for that space of time, it's perfectly real. And
there's your trouble, right there.

I turned to Joseph just as he turned to me, and the suddenness of his
earnest face almost made me forget what I meant to say to him.

"Isobel," I gasped.

"What about her?"

"What are we going to tell her?"

"I guess we'll just tell her the truth."

"She'll hate me for it."

Joseph shook his head. "You're wrong about that, Miranda. You'll see.
I'm telling you, you're worried about the wrong Fisher."

"You mean my stepfather? Why should he care?"

"He'll care plenty, believe me."

"It's none of his business. He's not my father, is he?"

"Miranda," said Joseph, and I looked away, toward the garage. He
touched my temple with his thumb, smoothing the skin, and went on,
"I'll just have to bite the bullet, I guess. Walk up to him, hat in hand,
like every other fellow who's fallen in love with a girl he shouldn't, and
explain myself."

"You don't need to do that. It's not the Middle Ages."

"What else am I going to do? I'm not going to sneak around with you. And if he sees me hanging about, he's going to want to know why."

"Well, they won't be back from Europe until Labor Day. Isobel, on the other hand—"

"Never mind Isobel. Right now there's nobody to worry about, not a thing to think about except you and me." He tugged my hand. "Let's enjoy it, all right? Every last minute, starting now. Come on, we'll pack some sandwiches and I'll take you sailing. There's this beach I know where nobody goes. Build a nice fire and stay out all night with the stars. How does that sound?"

"Like heaven."

So we ran down the lawn toward the kitchen door, but before we reached it Joseph just stopped and let go of my hand. Stood there arrested on the grass, staring toward the water. "What's the matter?" I said, but I really didn't need to ask. I just followed his gaze down the slope of the lawn to the dock, where a long, elegant yacht lay against the side, taking up all the space there was. The *Fisher King*.

7.

THERE WAS SOMETHING different about my mother after her honeymoon, though I couldn't quite put my finger on the change at first. She looked as beautiful as ever, maybe more beautiful, but it wasn't that. I remember how she came out on the terrace and called my name, just as I turned in shock from the sight of the yacht to absorb the meaning of Joseph's stark face.

"Mama," I whispered, and then, turning in the direction of her voice, *"Mama!"*

I ran across the lawn and up the stone steps to the terrace. We met right in the middle, hugging and laughing, and yet there was some slight reserve, some bit of Mama held back from me. I pulled back and she pulled back, and I thought she looked older—not in weeks and days, the clock hours passed since we saw each other last, but in experience. There was something worldly and mysterious in the shape of her eyes and the width of her smile, like she had finally grown up.

Before I could say anything, another voice called my name. I turned to the open French doors just as Hugh Fisher stepped across the threshold in a suit of impeccable summer wool. His pale hair instantly caught the flash of the setting sun. He smiled and held out his arms to me. "My new daughter," he said, and of course I went to him and embraced him too. Expressed my surprise, my delight at their early return. Hugh looked at my mother and she looked at him, and a thought passed between them.

"We just couldn't stay away any longer," Hugh said, and his head turned toward the lawn, where Joseph still stood with his hands folded behind his back. "Joseph. Nice to see you."

There was some faint question at the end of the sentence, a bit of upturn. I said quickly, "Isobel's off on the mainland, so I went out fishing with the Vargases today."

"Oh, what fun!" said my mother.

"That's good of you," said Hugh to Joseph. "I'm sure our girl was in good hands."

"The best," I said. "We caught forty-two lobsters."

"My goodness! Whatever did you do with them?" asked my mother.

"We sold them in the market, of course. That's how they make a living."

"Oh, of course. How silly of me. Would you like to stay for dinner?" she said to Joseph.

"That's kind of you, Mrs. Fisher, but I'd better be going home now."

I stepped forward. "Oh, wait!"

My stepfather put his hand on my shoulder, and his grip surprised me with its strength. "Joseph's got to be up early, sweetheart. Maybe another time."

"Yes," Joseph said. "Maybe another time."

I started to say something, but Mr. Fisher's hand tightened on my shoulder, and Joseph gave me a quick, hard stare that wanted to tell me something, only not just yet. "I had a wonderful time today, Joseph," I said instead. "Thank you."

"Anytime." He made a small salute and turned to go.

"Give my regards to your parents," said Mr. Fisher.

8.

HERE'S A FUNNY thing: in all our weeks here on the Island, from the wedding at the beginning of June until now, the eleventh of August, we hadn't eaten any meals in that grand, beautiful dining room overlooking the cliffs. We'd taken every single dinner at the Club or at somebody's house, and so I hesitated when we entered it, Mr. Fisher and my mother and I, wondering where to sit and also, in a larger sense, where on earth I was. Where did it come from, this acre of white tablecloth, this crystal and silver, these beautiful plates of delicate, paper-thin porcelain edged in gold? And Esther in her best, crisp uniform like it was a hundred years ago.

Mr. Fisher didn't hesitate. He was accustomed to such things, I guess. He pulled out Mama's chair and then mine, which turned out to be right in the center of the table between the two of them, but not within reach of either. And Mama sat like a princess, all dignity and decorum, selecting the proper fork and directing Esther with small, discreet, elegant gestures. A perfume wafted occasionally from her skin, when Esther's movements created the right direction of draft, and I didn't recognize the scent.

"I've sent out the yacht to fetch Isobel," Hugh said. "She'll be home first thing tomorrow, I hope."

"Wonderful," said Mama. "I can't wait to see her again. I expect you've had a wonderful time getting to know each other, haven't you?"

"Wonderful," I said.

"You did say Providence, didn't you?" said Hugh.

"Yes. The Biltmore, they told me. I have the telephone number."

Mama said, "But why didn't *you* go to Providence, sweetpea? Don't you want to buy some new things? I'm sure Hugh wouldn't mind if you bought a few things. Would you, darling?"

"Buy all you want," said my stepfather.

"You'll need new clothes for college, after all," said Mama.

"You should have gone. Why didn't you go?"

Esther came around with a large dish, from which Mama served herself. I watched the deft motions of her hands and said, "I wanted to stay here, that's all."

Hugh, who was gazing intently at my face, turned to the window. "So I see."

We ate, I don't remember what. I had a small view of the water from my seat, and I kept glancing that way, in hopes of something. Some sign of Joseph, I guess, some sign that I hadn't dreamt what happened that afternoon, that I was still living in the brave new After of my life. I'd changed into a dinner dress, and my bare arms were so lean and sunburned that Mama remarked about it.

"You're looking awfully tanned yourself, Mama," I said. "I guess Europe agrees with you."

She gazed across the table at her husband, and it's a look I haven't forgotten, because I'd never before seen that expression on her face, and I never did again. "*Hugh* agrees with me," she said gently, and I remember thinking that she could have said *Marriage*. Marriage agrees with me. But she said his name instead, because she meant one specific husband. Her new husband, Hugh.

He set down his fork and looked back at my mother the way you might look at the sun, newly risen. "Darling, shall we tell her?"

"I thought we were going to wait until after dinner."

"I can't wait any longer. I feel as if I've been waiting my life for this. I'm about to burst with joy."

"Oh, Hugh."

I reached for my wine and swallowed it. My fingers went a little numb. "Waiting for what?" I said.

"Dearest," my mother said, turning to me, stretching her long arm toward my hand, and I saw it then in the glow of her face, the new fullness in her cheeks, so she didn't need to go on. But of course she did. "Dearest Miranda. It's the most wonderful news. You're going to be a sister. We're going to be a real family at last."

9.

I WAITED UNTIL just before eleven o'clock, when the light in the master bedroom winked out. I had discovered, you see, that I could see the corner of their room from mine, such was the rambling construction of the Greyfriars rear facade. And because sometimes people turn out the light and then realize they've forgotten something—a book or a glass of water or whatever it is, and they rise again with a muttered oath—I waited a few more minutes, just to be sure. I listened for any voices, for any telltale vibrations, although of course they were really too far away from me, all the way at the other end of the house. Still, I waited, until the silence reached such a pitch as to satisfy me. Then I threw back my comforter and stole out the door and down the back stairs to the kitchen, the same way I had gone that first morning when I ran down to meet Joseph and Popeye on the dock.

Throughout the summer, Isobel had bemused me by her refusal to use the telephone to communicate with Joseph. Why bother with all that cloak and dagger business, with sending messengers and flashing lights and such nonsense, when you could just pick up a telephone receiver and speak directly? Now I knew. I considered the possibility of being over-heard, of Mama or Hugh or the housemaid picking up the extension, of Mrs. Vargas or Mr. Vargas answering the telephone in the lighthouse instead of Joseph. Impossible even to think of it. Instead I ran directly down to the boathouse and found the flashlight and made for the dock, but as I passed by the handsome Lutyens bench at the edge of the seawall, I heard my name in a voice that seemed a little amused.

"Joseph!"

I turned, but I couldn't see him, because the clouds had moved in around sunset and the moon was obscured. I just saw a movement in the darkness, a shadow pass between me and the lights of Greyfriars, and then a hand touched mine. I flung my arms around his neck.

"Ouch," he said.

"Sorry, that's the flashlight."

"Flashlight?"

"I was going to signal you."

"But you don't know the code, do you?"

"I thought you'd figure it out anyway."

He laughed. "I wasn't going to wait around for any damned flashlight, believe me."

I drew back. "How long *have* you been waiting?"

"Not long. A half hour, maybe. I figured if you were going to steal away, you'd have to wait until your parents went to bed."

"*If* I was going to steal away?" I said.

He shrugged. "I couldn't be sure."

We stood apart by only a few inches. My right hand gripped the flashlight; my other hand had somehow found his. The connection seemed both tenuous and momentous, as if the firm, intimate touch of his fingers was too good to last. "Let's go to this beach of yours," I said.

"We can't. You can't stay out all night, not with your parents home. Anyway, I don't have any sandwiches, and it's too dark to sail that far."

"Then let's go to the lighthouse. We can sit on the rocks, on that little beach there, like the first night."

"Why not stay here? Nobody's going to find us."

"No! I want to go somewhere, I want to get away from Greyfriars."

He glanced over my shoulder, almost as if he could detect the sea behind me. "Tide's pretty high right now, with the full moon. The current's going to murder someone."

"Please, Joseph. Not here, anywhere but here."

There must have been some note of desperation in my voice, because he didn't say anything for a moment, and I could just about hear the sound of his thoughts turning over, or maybe it was the sound of the blood in his veins, the blood in my veins, our heartbeats, our breath, our longing.

He cupped a hand around my cheek, and the heat of his palm surprised me. "I'll take you wherever you want to go," he said. "Remember that."

10.

FOR MANY YEARS afterward, I thought about that journey across the Fleet Rock channel, and whether I felt some kind of portent as Joseph positioned the boat inside the mighty rush of the tide. But no. At that moment, I felt nothing but exhilaration, nothing but the lightness of escape and of coming joy. I remember the breeze was chillier than I expected, as if something new and cool had insinuated itself into the atmosphere since the afternoon, but I imagined it meant only that autumn was coming, that we had better snatch our delights while we could. Anyway, Joseph had given me his thick, cabled sweater, had settled it over my head with his own hands, so the chill couldn't find me.

I certainly didn't notice that Joseph struggled overmuch with the oars. The journey toward the lighthouse was easier when the tide was rushing out—as it then did—because Fleet Rock lay a little to the east of Greyfriars, not true south. Going back was the trouble. We'd have to wait until the tide slackened; not even Joseph could haul us into the Greyfriars dock against a full spring tide. But I wasn't thinking about our return journey at all. I think, at the time, I wanted to stay on that rock forever with Joseph. You know how it is when you're eighteen, and you've fallen in love for the first time. I watched him leap to the dock with the rope and secure the boat; I moved to the bow and took his hand and leaped too. He made one of his joyful noises and kissed me, and we scrambled without words over the rocks to the small, coarse beach on the other side, nearly engulfed by the tide, where he found us a tiny resting place like a nest, and the water washed up almost to our toes.

I tucked my head in the hollow of his shoulder and spoke softly.

> *The moon shines bright. In such a night as this,*
> *When the sweet wind did gently kiss the trees*
> *And they did make no noise, in such a night*
> *Troilus methinks mounted the Trojan walls*
> *And sighed his soul toward the Grecian tents*
> *Where Cressid lay that night.*

He laughed and answered me.

> *In such a night*
> *Did Thisbe fearfully o'ertrip the dew*

And saw the lion's shadow ere himself
And ran dismayed away.

"Why, how did you know that?"

"Maybe you're not the only one who knows a little Shakespeare, Miss Schuyler. They teach this stuff in the Winthrop Island School, too."

"But they don't make you memorize it, do they?"

"I guess I always liked that bit. What comes next?"

"Dido," I said.

In such a night
Stood Dido with a willow in her hand
Upon the wild sea banks, and waft her love
To come again to Carthage.

"Poor Dido," said Joseph. "He never did come back, did he?"

"No. He never did."

The water kicked against the rocks. How strange, to be nestled here in Joseph's arms, the two of us alone in the universe, talking about Dido. Across the water, the lights of Long Island twinkled, as if from the other side of the ocean, the other side of the world.

"I used to sit on this beach and dream about sailing away somewhere," Joseph said.

"Where?"

"Anywhere. Everywhere. See the world."

"You'd need to build a bigger sailboat," I said. "And find a crew."

"That's what I used to think."

"So you gave it up?"

"Sort of. I don't know, lately I've been dreaming of something else. Like I might find some girl to sail with me." He held me in front of him, between his legs, inside the arc of his arms. His chin rested on the top of my head. "Just sail away together, without telling anyone. Maybe go to Bermuda first, just to get our sea legs, and then head south. The Caribbean, South America. If we liked someplace well enough, we'd stop and build a hut on the beach and live there. What's the matter?"

"It sounds beautiful, that's all."

"'Course, I'd have to finish college first. Work hard for a year or two, saving up to build a good, strong, sweet-sailing ship."

"Yes," I said, and a drop of rain fell on my nose.

"Wouldn't be for years yet, I guess. But it would be worth it. Just think."

I turned in his arms. "Why not now? Just leave, just elope. Borrow somebody's sailboat, if you have to."

"Because she might have second thoughts. Somewhere off the coast of Brazil or maybe Argentina, when the weather starts to turn."

"Never."

"Well," he said, kissing the top of my head. "I guess we'll have to just wait and see. You might have other ideas, after your first year of college."

"I might have a lot of new ideas, but *this* one—*this* one won't change—"

"Miranda."

He pressed his palm against the back of my head, urging me into the softness of his sweater. I breathed in the scent of wool and wondered why he stopped me, when I had so much I wanted to say, so many words cramming the inside of me.

Joseph said, "Listen to me. I want you to promise me something. Just one thing."

"What's that?"

"When you get to college—"

"Don't talk about that yet."

"No, I mean it. When you get to college, I want you to think about auditioning for something. The school play, whatever it is."

"What?"

"I'm serious. You're a natural. There's something inside you, and when it comes out—I can't explain—I just think you ought to try. Promise me."

"Maybe."

"Don't maybe. Do it. Look, I'll tell you what. You try out for that play, whatever it is, and I'll come to watch you. I'll borrow some fellow's car, I'll bring five dozen roses, we'll go out to dinner someplace grand—"

"Oh, stop."

"I mean it. I do."

"I don't want to act in front of a bunch of people."

"With you, it's not acting. It's something else. It's *you*, coming alive with something I can't even—and I don't want to be the fellow who stands in your way."

"But I don't want to share that with anyone but you."

"Miranda. Just promise me."

I didn't answer. At Foxcroft, I had never considered performing in anything; the terror of standing on a stage, of not being good enough, had held me fast. Now Joseph's arms held me fast. The world spread out before me, vast and twinkling with promise. He laid his hands on my hands and spoke in my ear.

"There's something I need to tell you."

11.

SOMETHING I NEED *to tell you*. Those were the words I heard when my uncle came to tell me about Daddy. He worked in the War Office, that's how he knew the news first. Instead of sending a telegram, they sent Uncle Harry. He wore his best uniform, so I knew something was wrong, even before I looked at his face. My mother was already upstairs, crying.

He crouched down, so that he was right down at my level, eye to eye. He was a handsome man, my uncle Harry. Blue Schuyler eyes, fair

Schuyler hair. In my hair, I take after my mother. "There's something I have to tell you, Miranda," he said, taking my hand. "It's about your father."

And I don't remember his exact words. I just remember that the walls and the floor disappeared, and I was falling irretrievably into darkness, and the only thing holding me steady was my uncle Harry's strong arms, which were scratchy and smelled of wet wool.

A week later, Uncle Harry left for Italy and never came back.

12.

SO YOU'LL FORGIVE me if I shivered a little when Joseph said those words to me, *There's something I need to tell you*. Shivered and pulled away, actually launched myself out of his arms, so that he had to take my hand and ask me what was wrong.

"You tell me," I said.

"You can't tell anybody else. You have to promise me that. Not even my father. Especially not my father."

"Why? What's it about?"

"Sort of a family secret. I've been thinking about telling you all evening, since I left you at Greyfriars. Not because I want to cause trouble or anything, but because I want to be straight with you, I don't want to hide anything, and Isobel—you had the wrong idea—I wanted to explain, so you'd understand, you'd know there's no possibility—Isobel—"

"Isobel what?"

"She's my sister."

For a moment, I just knelt there on the damp sand. A gust of wind blew against us, the vanguard of some approaching squall. I remember counting the sweeps of the light above us, though I don't remember how many passed. "Your what?" I whispered.

"You see, a long time ago, before I was born, obviously—"

"Whose—whose—so your father—"

"Is Hugh Fisher," he said. "Is your stepfather."

"He's your father."

"Yes."

I noticed, in some distant part of my brain, that the wind continued to rise, that the few tiny drops had turned into a drizzle. It struck my head, it struck Joseph's forehead and his nose. I reached up and wiped the rain from his cheek, but it was no use. As soon as my hand moved away, there was more rain behind it.

Hugh Fisher, I thought. Hugh Fisher is his father. Fathered him. Engaged in—engaged in—with some woman—with Joseph's mother. And made Joseph. And made—at almost the same time, but not quite the same time—Isobel.

My stepfather did this. Hugh Fisher did this.

"Say something," he said.

"Say what?"

"You look like you don't believe me."

"I do. I—I don't know what to think. How—your mother—"

"They had an affair, just before he married Isobel's mother. He didn't realize she was pregnant until it was too late, so they made the best of things. She married Dad, and that's why she and the aunts don't get along, because my aunt Francisca was supposed to marry him instead. And then when I was born, Francisca took a boat out to Fleet Rock, nobody knows why, and you know she drowned. So it's trouble all around, and—"

"How did you find out?"

"Mama told me, when I was about ten or eleven. She was worried because I spent so much time playing with Isobel, because we were so close, even then. She wanted to make sure I knew, so that—well, you know . . ."

"Does Isobel know?"

"She knows."

"So all that time—"

"All that time."

"Oh my God," I said. "Oh my God."

Another gust swept against us, a handful of nervous raindrops, and now I felt it. At last, I felt a premonition prickling my skin, or maybe it was just that first wave of rain, needle-sharp, promising a deluge in due course. I knelt there in the sand and stared at Joseph's anxious face, trying to comprehend the facts, the meaning of the facts, the meaning of the meaning. A whole world, a vast history of Winthrop Island I had never, in my innocence, suspected. Isobel and Joseph, brother and sister. Mr. Fisher and Mrs. Vargas—what?

"Don't be afraid," Joseph said. "It's just me. Same fellow I was a minute ago."

I shook my head and tried to speak.

Joseph started to reach for me, but his hands fell back at the last instant. His eyes were glassy with fear and moonlight. "I'm sorry," he said. "I'm sorry."

I thought, *I must do something.* I have to do something, before the squall arrives. I took his face in my hands, and exactly as my fingers touched his cheeks, the rain began to descend in earnest, heavy drops, so I kissed him. I thought if I kissed him, the rain would stop, the coming squall would dissolve harmlessly into the air, and Joseph—I don't know what he thought, just that he kissed me back as frantically as I kissed him. That his warm hands laid themselves upon my skin, under his sweater he had given me, under my pajama shirt beneath that, and it seemed to me that something of myself flowed like a current from my body into his, that something of him returned into me by the same channel. I couldn't feel the rain anymore. I pulled him down on the beach with me, and there was this moment in which the tide might have turned, the course of our history might have diverted into another strait. Joseph's hands found my breasts, my leg slid around his, and I remember thinking I would do anything, I would give anything I had to keep him there, hold him there, until the storm passed at last. I would arch my hips against his. I would slip my hands to the waist of his trousers and—and—

Joseph flung himself away, panting, and said in a hoarse voice, "You're getting soaked. Let's go inside."

"I don't care. I don't care."

We stared at each other, a couple of inches apart. The rain rattled the stones around us and coursed through my hair and my face and neck, so I felt I was drowning. Above our heads, the light made a long, eternal sweep.

"Promise me something," he said. "Don't ever let them keep you down. Those bastards, don't let them change you."

"What bastards?"

He stood up. "Let's go inside."

13.

BY THE TIME Joseph wrenched the door open and hauled me into the lighthouse, we were both as thoroughly drenched as if we'd plunged into a swimming pool. That's the thing about these summer rainstorms, so brief and potent. Two miles north, they were probably dry as a desert, had no idea of our local deluge. Just imagine if that particular squall had nudged off its course and blown elsewhere.

The room was dark and thick with the afternoon's heat still trapped inside. Joseph's hand clenched mine like he thought I might bolt away. He flipped a switch and a bulb came on overhead, illuminating a small living room, a sofa and two worn chairs, terribly old fashioned and as neat as a pin. "I'll get you some dry clothes from upstairs," he whispered, releasing my hand.

"I'll go with you."

"No, stay here," he said quickly. "Pops's asleep, I don't want to wake him."

"What about your mother?"

"She's awake, keeping the light."

"I thought it was all electric now."

"She's got this neurosis about the light going out. Just wait here, all right? I'll be back in a minute."

I wanted desperately to see Joseph's bedroom, to know this place where he slept at night, where he had grown from an infant to a man, but there was something in his expression that warned me back. I thought about what he had told me, these revelations, the terrible, merciful deceit practiced on Mr. Vargas. So I nodded. "Don't be long."

"I won't."

He hurried through the doorway at the other end of the room and I stood there dripping on the rug, afraid to sit down on any of the polished brown furniture, the clean, faded upholstery. Between the two armchairs was a table on which about a half dozen framed photographs stood in neat formation, like soldiers. I stared at them for a moment, consumed with guilty curiosity. The one in the center was a wedding portrait, I could see that much, and I stepped closer and closer until there I was, picking up the photograph in its heavy silver frame, examining the terrified couple within. I recognized Mr. Vargas instantly because he hadn't changed at all, just as stumpy and ugly as he was today, only less grizzled. He looked shocked, as if he hadn't expected to get married when he woke up that morning, and now he stood in his best pressed suit next to a voluptuous girl in a dress of pale lace—the material seemed more gray than white—whose eyes were as wide and stunned as his own. Maybe the flash had caught them both by surprise, I thought, or maybe they'd had a spat before the wedding, born of nerves, and nearly called it all off. They were standing amid rocks, next to a stone building, which I realized was the lighthouse. Mrs. Vargas carried a bouquet of flowers, and her new husband held her elbow delicately, as if afraid to touch her.

"My wedding day," said a voice behind me, and I dropped the photograph on the rug.

"I'm so sorry!" I gasped, bending to retrieve it.

"Never mind." Mrs. Vargas took the portrait from my hands and set it back in its place, just exactly so between a picture of a woman holding a baby—Joseph, perhaps?—and one indisputably of Joseph wearing one of those mortarboard graduation caps and a handsome grin. "His graduation day. He was the top of his class at the school here."

"You must have been so proud."

She snorted. "It's a small school. There were only twelve of them that year. But I knew from a baby how clever he was. I knew he must go to college, he must make something of himself."

"He will," I said.

She went on staring at the photographs, as if she hadn't heard me. "My goodness, I was so young. About the same age as you. How old are you, Miss Schuyler?"

"Eighteen last February."

She nodded. "Just out of high school. Imagining you're all grown up."

"Not all that grown up."

"Imagining you know everything. Imagining you've fallen in love."

"I don't—I don't."

She turned from the photographs, and in the dimness of the room her face looked softer than I remembered, smoother, so I could see the beauty she had possessed on her wedding day. I thought she spoke with a faint accent, much fainter than that of her husband. "I was speaking of my son," she said. "My son seems to have imagined he's fallen in love."

"*Mama*." Joseph spoke sharply from the doorway.

The funny thing was, Mrs. Vargas didn't even flinch. It was like she already knew he stood there, wet hair and dry clothes, holding a towel and a few folded garments. She smiled and turned her face in his direction. "I was just keeping your little friend company. A sweet young thing like her, Mr. Fisher's new daughter. What were the two of you thinking, getting so wet?"

"The rain took us by surprise," Joseph said. He came forward and handed me the towel and the clothes. "It's just my old pajamas. Nothing else was going to fit you."

"She could wear something of mine," said Mrs. Vargas.

"That's all right. I don't mind. Is there someplace . . . ?"

Joseph nodded to the doorway behind him. "There's a bathroom to your left, just before the stairs."

I stole swiftly through the door and found the bathroom, which was old and tiny and smelled strongly of the sea, as if the salt water tended to wash through the window during storms. I shucked my wet clothes and toweled off. My skin was pink with cold and damp. I had to roll up the sleeves and the waist of Joseph's pajamas, but I didn't mind. They were Joseph's, after all, and they smelled of him, and the soft touch of his flannel on my bare skin was like the touch of Joseph himself. I rolled up my wet clothes in the towel and went back into the living room, where Joseph stood alone at the window, staring through the glass toward the darkened channel.

"Where's your mother?" I asked.

"She's making tea in the kitchen." He turned to me. "We're going to have to wait a bit before I row you . . . back . . ."

"What's wrong?"

"Nothing. Woke up this morning thinking to catch a few lobsters. Now Miranda's standing in my living room, wearing my pajamas."

"I like your pajamas."

"I like you in them." He held out his arms. "You must be exhausted. Longest day in the world."

"You too."

"Come on. We can rest on the sofa until the tide goes down."

I wasn't sleepy, not a bit, but I followed him to the sofa and curled on my side, settling my head on his leg, not quite in his lap. "When does the tide go down?"

"Should be all right in a couple of hours. The rain's stopped, anyway."

"Why can't we use the dinghy? It's got a motor."

"Your parents might hear."

"I don't care. Why should I care? There's nothing to be ashamed of. We haven't done anything wrong. Anyway, he's one to talk."

"Who?"

"Mr. Fisher. Your father."

"Shh," he said.

"Poor Mr. Vargas," I whispered.

"It's all right," Joseph whispered back. "I sometimes wonder if he knows, anyway. You can't always tell with Pops, what he's thinking."

"Why don't you just ask him?"

"Because I can't, that's all. You can't talk about a thing like that. You just accept things the way they are. Anyway, as far as I'm concerned, he's my pops. Mr. Fisher's just a—I don't know—he's Isobel's dad. I care about *her* a hell of a lot more than I care about him."

"Doesn't he ever—haven't you ever—"

"It's the Island, Miranda. Nobody ever talks about what they really think."

I laughed a little. Curled my hand around his knee. "Well, he can't object to us. You're his son."

"Oh, he can object, all right. Just because I'm his own blood doesn't mean I'm suitable for his stepdaughter. No, don't worry." He laid a thumb against my lips. "I'm not going to let him stand in our way. Like you said, it's not the Middle Ages. It's just bad luck they came home so early."

"It's not bad luck, actually," I said. "It's good luck, the best kind of luck. Well, they're happy about it, anyway. They're thrilled to pieces."

His hand, stroking my arm, paused at my elbow. "What are you talking about?"

I turned toward him and lifted my head. "Mama's going to have a baby."

A crash came from the doorway, the catastrophe of a tea tray full of dishes falling to the floor.

We jumped together, Joseph and I, and for an instant we stared at each other—Mrs. Vargas against the two of us—while a sea of broken porcelain cut up the stone floor between us, having just missed the cushion of the rug.

Then Mrs. Vargas muttered something like *How careless of me* and bent to recover the pieces in quick, mechanical movement of her arms, and Joseph darted forward to help her. I followed him. Together we set the pieces back on the tray, not saying a word, not a whisper of dismay about the beautiful ruined dishes, the shards like razors, the massive spill of tea and milk, until Mrs. Vargas whispered something about getting a towel for the mess. As she rose, a few drops of blood splashed on the stone, and Joseph exclaimed, *Mama! You're hurt!*

She looked down at her hand. "It's just a little cut, don't worry. Stay here."

He made a move to follow her, but she repulsed him with a single look, and he went back on his heels and watched her leave. We finished cleaning up the porcelain, taking great care with the points and the edges, and Joseph took it all away to the garbage can. When he returned, he said he was going to check on his mother.

"Is there anything I can do?" I asked.

"No. Just lie down and rest, okay? I'll be back in a minute."

He turned to go, and a strange fear overtook me at the sight of his back, like the chill I had felt on the beach, only stronger. I called out his name.

"What's the matter?" he asked.

"I don't know."

He stepped toward me and put his arms around me, and as I set my cheek against his shoulder it seemed I could breathe again. "Stay here with me," I said.

"I'll just be a minute, I swear. Just go to sleep on the sofa."

"I can't sleep without you."

He laughed. "You've never slept *with* me."

"Just hurry back."

"I will. Keep the sofa warm for me."

There was nothing to do but obey him. What was a premonition, after all? Only nerves, nothing of logic in it. I went back to the sofa and curled back in the same spot, laid my head in the dent where Joseph had sat, and closed my eyes. I kept seeing the broken porcelain, the blood falling to the floor in large, heavy drops, like the rain. Maybe Joseph kept his promise and returned in a minute, but it seemed much longer before I heard his footsteps on the rug. I stretched out my arms and made a noise of relief.

"I brought a blanket," he said.

We settled on our sides, facing the back of the sofa, Joseph behind me like a wall. This was my doing; I wanted to be enclosed, I didn't want to see the place where the china had fallen, where the blood had mingled with the tea and the milk. The idea of it filled me with panic. I stared instead at the dark, immediate upholstery of the sofa cushion, and I fit my back into Joseph's chest and his stomach, my legs into the spaces between his.

"So I noticed something from the kitchen window," he said.

"What's that?"

"Isobel's home already. They must have left Providence right away. The yacht's moored at the Greyfriars dock."

"That was quick," I said softly. "You don't think she'll notice I'm gone, do you? Or row over to see you?"

"Not at this hour, no. But I think maybe you should go home soon."

His hand crept under my pajamas to rest against my stomach, and I laid my own hand over it.

"It's real, isn't it? You won't go away?" I said. "When I wake up, you'll be right here?"

"Of course I will. Your hand's like ice. What's wrong?"

"Nothing."

"Miranda, tell me. What are you afraid of?"

"I don't know."

"Is it Isobel? You're worried about her? Because it doesn't matter, I don't care if she approves or not. If Fisher approves or not. I'll come back for you, Miranda. I promise I'll come back for you."

"Don't promise you'll come back," I said. "It's bad luck."

He spread his fingers wide, spanning the soft plane of my belly between his thumb and his pinkie. "Are you thinking of your father?"

"Maybe," I said, and I tried to tell myself that this was true, that this black panic in my chest had something to do with my father's departure across the sea, my father's death on some French field seven years ago.

"I'm coming back for you, Miranda. I'm not going to leave you."

"It's real," I said. "It's happened. They can't take it away from us, can they?"

"I won't let them. I love you too much."

Those were the last words I recall hearing before I fell asleep, and I must have slept at a tremendous, subterranean depth, because I heard no voices, no commotion, nothing at all until Mrs. Vargas shook me awake some unknown time later. By then, I was alone on the sofa. I remember how I stared in confusion at her white face, and how she had to repeat herself twice before I comprehended what she said.

"There's been a terrible accident. You must go and fetch Dr. Huxley."

1969 (MIRANDA THOMAS)

1.

MY HUSBAND TRACKED me down at the end of August, the day of Tom Donnelly's party on Horseshoe Beach. The weather had turned hot, and we had moved our rehearsal to the incomplete shade of the young elms near the swimming pool. So ferociously was I absorbed in the play, I didn't notice the man in the pale suit who stood by the edge of the box-woods, observing us. It was Brigitte who pointed him out.

Brigitte was playing Caliban, an inspiration of mine. I often used to advise Carroll in his casting, even before we became lovers, and it seemed I had a knack for it, because while he freely criticized just about everything else I did, he never doubted my instinct for actors. Miss Felicity was Ariel, and Hugh was Ferdinand, and Miss Patty was Prospero, and Leonard made a perfect villainous Antonio, and Isobel—*Isobel*!—had agreed to take on Miranda, an act of cooperation that stunned me. But it worked, you know. The existing connection between Hugh and Isobel struck a mesmerizing note, when I could actually compel them to stop giggling and do the damned scene.

We were supposed to perform the first act of *The Tempest* on the beach

at Tom Donnelly's party this evening, however, and at the moment of
Carroll's appearance I was burrowed deep inside that black, echoing
cave known as opening night panic. Isobel had never troubled to learn
her lines perfectly, so Miss Patty kept feeding them to her. Miss Felicity
tended to drift into daydream and miss her cues. Hugh—well, Hugh was
never the kind of fellow to take direction, was he?

And then Brigitte. Brigitte had woken me early that morning and told
me, urgently, that she thought she'd been playing Caliban all wrong.
"He's their slave," she said, "he's their prisoner. Of course he resents
them. He says these things because they expect him to say them, because
he has decided to be their worst fear. They have invaded his world, his
island, and now they rule him. They tell him he is an inferior race, that
his mother is a terrible witch. Of course he hates them."

I sat up against my pillow, still groggy, and tried to understand her.
"But what about Miranda? She taught him language and how to read,
and he tried to rape her."

"Did he? Or is this just some Christian hysterics? This is their great-
est fear, you know, that the savage will try to impregnate the gentile."

I glanced down at her withered, bony hand, which still held my forearm, and back up at her face, which focused not on my eyes but my lips,
so she could understand me perfectly. "All right," I told her. "Caliban's
yours. You play him as you find him. Just remember it's our last rehearsal
this morning, so you don't have much time."

And now Miss Patty was thundering forth—*Thou most lying slave,
whom stripes may move, not kindness!*—when I felt the tug of Brigitte's
hand on my arm, when I followed the tilt of her head and froze my gaze
upon that figure in its pale, pressed suit, standing against the boxwoods.

I turned back to the company. "All right, let's take a short break,"
I said, in a voice of remarkable calm. "Who wants lemonade? Mama,
could you pour out some lemonade?"

My mother, who sat quietly in the nearby grass on a picnic blanket, gave me a curious stare and reached for the thermos. Hugh threw himself happily on the grass and put his hands behind his head. I stuck my paperback copy of *The Tempest* into the pocket of my sundress and walked steadily up the slope toward the swimming pool. "Miranda," Carroll said, as I approached, but I continued right past him to the gap in the hedge and stepped through. When I turned around, I saw he had followed me.

I crossed my arms and stared at the boxwoods behind him. "How did you find me?"

"Do I not even warrant a greeting, Miranda? Not even a glance?" Carroll's voice was plaintive, almost petulant. He often took that tone after one of our fights, which were my fault, self-evidently, because Carroll Goring could do no wrong. Surely I realized that. Surely I recognized that the demons made Carroll behave badly, whereas my own transgressions came from within.

I said, "I don't think we need to stand on ceremony at this point, do you?"

He made a noise of astonishment. I took in his linen trousers, his spotless leather shoes. He held a straw hat in his hand, which he spun around in slow, idle circles. His cologne was terribly strong. I had forgotten about that. The scent threw me back into his bed, into his arms, over the back of Victor's sofa. My stomach reacted in panic. I could almost see the sky's reflection in Carroll's shoes, so exquisitely were they polished, and not a blade of grass had stuck to them on the way down.

"Well?" I said. "Did somebody tell you? Was it in the papers?"

"No. I found your bank statements, when they arrived in the post. The canceled checks to some builder fellow in Winthrop Island, New York. I looked it up on the map." His hands reversed the direction of the hat, sending it around counterclockwise. "I didn't realize you kept a bank account in America."

"The Countess used to advise me to keep a bank account of my own, if I was ever so foolish as to get married."

"I see. Charming woman, the Countess."

There was a hot little pause. I stood in full sunlight, and the perspiration gathered on my temples and my upper lip. I said, "Well, now you've seen me. You know where I am. It's time for you to leave."

"Leave? We haven't said a word!"

"We have nothing to say to each other."

"Nothing to say to each other? We are husband and wife."

"But I'm going to divorce you, Carroll. Surely you understand that by now."

He swore and walked to the opposite side of the swimming pool, the shaded side, and stood there for some time, staring at the tiny green leaves of the boxwoods. I'd had them trimmed and fed, so they now sat in civilized order, although I sometimes wished I'd left them alone. You so rarely see boxwoods in a natural state. Always, always, people trim them into shape, rounded or square or something more outlandish. Poor boxwoods, they aren't ever allowed to be themselves, are they? They're forced inside the boundaries of human imagination.

Carroll turned at last. "How *are* you, Miranda?"

"I'm extremely well. As you can see."

"I mean the baby. I was so awfully sorry about the baby. I thought we might grieve together . . ."

He looked directly into my eyes and allowed the sentence to die. The temperature had soared since daybreak, and his Englishman's face wasn't taking it well. He was sixty-one, and had drunk and smoked and taken pills for at least forty of those years, had slept recklessly with every creature under the sun, and his nose was bulbous, his cheeks and eyelids and even earlobes sagging, his capillaries mapped across his skin. The trim, dapper, electric man I'd married had disappeared into some cavity within.

I said, "Grieve together? You killed my baby on purpose, Carroll. You didn't want her to begin with."

"Her?" He turned his head aside. "I did not—that was an accident, Miranda, I was angry and drunk, you'd made me so damned angry that I—"

"My fault. Of course. Nothing at all to do with your damned insecurities, your ferocious jealousy, your ugly, violent rages."

He spun back to the boxwoods.

"I owe you an apology for that," he said, and such was the well-trained timbre of his voice, the natural authority of a film director, I heard him clearly and almost believed him. "For what I did at Victor's flat. That was grossly out of line. You didn't deserve it."

"Nobody deserves that."

His head was bowed over his hands, which continued to rotate the hat between them. "I accept that, Miranda. I ask your forgiveness."

My arms fell away to my sides. He had never said such a thing before, had never approached the notion of forgiveness. Always it was for him to forgive *me* for my shortcomings, which were numerous. I was not adventurous enough in bed. I couldn't cook. I judged his friends too harshly. When I kissed another actor too passionately, even under Carroll's direction; when I accepted a role in a film he was not himself directing; when I accepted a role in a *Hollywood* film, Miranda, a prostitution for American fame and filthy American money—when I did any of these things, I committed a conscious betrayal.

He pressed the hat against his chest and said, "I went to the doctor, after you left. I underwent a few tests. It seems—that operation I had—the—er—the tube, was done in such a way that—careless—the vessel, had somehow repaired itself. So it seems—I may have been unjust—although you must admit I had reason to doubt—"

"*You*, who were faithless almost from the beginning. You, Carroll. Can you have any reason to rail at me for *faithlessness*?"

He turned. "Were you? Faithless?"

Until that instant, I had remained calm, as you see. I don't know how.

Maybe it was the coolness of the water nearby, or the shock of seeing him. I had felt panic, I had felt the familiar visceral fear of him, which I quelled by force; but I had not yet felt anger.

I stared at him in his suit of cream linen, and I thought of the carpet in his bedroom the morning after we had slept together for the first time. The same color, carpet and suit. The same man, only older now, as I was. The cluttered years, oh. Carroll's eyes had gone a little round, and his mouth made this quivering movement at the injustice of it all, at the idea of my possibly having slept with another man, loved another man except him.

I said, "I wish to God the baby hadn't been yours. I wish to God I'd slept with Victor, with Laurence, with any of your friends, with all of them. With the porter at our flat. I wish that baby belonged to any man but you."

Carroll made a strangled noise and flew toward me, and such was my anger that I didn't fall back, I took the force of his blow because I wanted to. It gave me a reason to strike back, but before I could swing, Carroll shoved me again. I lost my balance and fell back hard on the stone. By the time I scrambled up, another man leapt before me and grabbed Carroll by the lapels.

"You leave my sister alone, do you hear me?" Hugh roared. "You get off this property and don't even think of coming back."

2.

IN THE KITCHEN, I poured my brother a glass of lemonade and reflected on the curious symmetry of events.

"I can't believe I did that," he said. His eyes were bright, his skin flushed. He made me think of a football player who'd just scored a touchdown or something, not that I had ever attended a football game, or even knew what a touchdown really was. He drank half a glass of lemonade in one gulp and set the tumbler down on the table. "I can't believe I told Carroll Goring to get the hell off my property. And my sister."

"He wasn't actually *on* me."

"He was going to. I could see it in his face." Hugh spread his first two fingers and pointed to his eyes. "Why'd you marry that creep, anyway? He's a million years older than you."

"Because I was lonely. Because I thought I loved him, at the time. I thought he loved me."

"What about Vargas? I thought you were in love with *him*."

I turned away and looked out the window. "Oh, Hugh, I was a teenager then. By the time I married Carroll, I was twenty-six."

"So what would you do," Hugh said slowly, "what would you do if Vargas were standing in this room, right now?"

I whipped around. "*Where?*"

"Gotcha."

"I'm going to kill you."

He lifted the glass and tilted the mouth of it toward me. "You know what I think? I think you're still in love with him. You never forget your first love, isn't that right?"

"Of course you don't *forget*. But you cross a bridge and you can't cross back to where you stood before. You keep marching, that's all you can do." I sat down in the chair opposite him. "Anyway, isn't this the same man who murdered your father?"

He shrugged. "My father was a bastard."

"What? Where did you hear that?"

"I hear things, Miranda. I go out in the world. I go down in the harbor. Old Hugh Fisher doesn't have a lot of friends there, believe me. You get it out of them when they're drunk." He finished the lemonade and rose to carry the empty glass to the sink. "You get most things out of people when they're drunk. Maybe I should get you drunk, and you might tell me about the fellow who carried you home from the dock, the night of the moon landing."

I stood up so fast, I overset the chair. "*What?*"

"I was still outside that night, sis. I saw you."

"Why didn't you say anything before?"

"Maybe I was waiting for you to tell me. Maybe I was waiting for something exciting to happen."

"Like what?"

"I don't know." He turned to face me, leaning back against the sink, and crossed his arms. The sunlight came through the window to set his hair on fire. "You tell me."

"There's nothing to tell."

"Was it Vargas?"

I glanced down at the tablecloth. "I don't know."

"Sure you do. Where is he now?"

I looked back up and said fiercely, "I don't know."

"I'm not going to fink, I swear. I'm just curious. And I guess I want to know if my big sister needs protecting from someone other than her husband. Or whether that sweet little yacht you bought from the Huxleys isn't really for me."

I regarded his crossed arms, his fiery hair, his belligerent jaw, and I suppose I smiled a little. "When do you head back to school again?"

"The middle of September."

"Not soon enough."

"And what are you going to do when I'm gone, huh? What are you planning to do when the summer's over? Stay here? Head back to London? Back to being Miranda Thomas?"

The smile—what there was of it—dropped from my lips. "I'm going to divorce Carroll. That's the main thing. After that, I haven't—"

A knock landed on the door. We turned our heads at the same time; not toward the door, but toward the window next to it. From this angle, I couldn't see the visitor, but Hugh could. He started forward and opened the door. "What's cooking, Mrs. Medeiro?" he asked cheerfully.

"Just some lobsters." She stepped into the kitchen and held out a wire basket.

"I didn't order any lobsters," I said.

"They're a gift." She walked stiffly inside and set the basket on the counter next to the sink, while Hugh and I watched in a kind of daze. She wore wide-legged trousers and a broad hat of coarse straw, and when the lobsters were settled she continued to stare out the window overlooking the lighthouse. On the water, about twenty yards from the Greyfriars dock, Hugh's new sailboat bobbed at its mooring, white and bright in the early sun.

"A gift from whom?" I asked.

Mrs. Medeiro turned back to us, and because the sun was behind her I couldn't see her expression. But I had the impression of great anxiety. Her hands, large and reddened, twitched as they fell away from the basket.

"From a friend," she said. "I'd better go now."

She started for the door, and Hugh started for the lobsters. I followed her outside and took her arm to stop her.

"What's the matter? What's going on?"

"Those marshals. They give me a case of the willies."

"You mean the ones watching our driveway?"

She drew her arm away and glanced toward the delivery van, just visible around the corner of the house, parked near the rhododendrons. "Just be sure you watch out for their claws," she said.

"The marshals'?"

She snorted. "No, dearie. The lobsters'. Say, I hear your husband came in on the early ferry this morning."

"Came and went," I said.

"Ah." She nodded slowly. "You remember what I said to you in my store, when you came to buy ice cream, many years ago?"

"You remember that?"

Mrs. Medeiro tapped her forehead. "I remember everything. I remember you did not take my advice."

"I should have taken your advice. If I had—"

"At this age, girls do not take such advice. My girls, they did these foolish things, they were heedless for love. But you are a woman, Miss Schuyler. You will not do some stupid thing for love. You will let the dogs lie sleeping."

"What dogs?" I seized her arm again. "What dogs are sleeping?"

Mrs. Medeiro stepped away and rubbed her arm where I'd held it. She glanced up the driveway and said, "I am old and tired. Too old for this. I am done. You have your lobsters now. I am done."

"He's your grandson!" I called after her, as she hurried across the gravel to the delivery truck.

She jumped in the cab and turned on the engine.

3.

I HAD TOLD Hugh no more than the truth when I said I didn't know where Joseph Vargas was. Until my brother spoke those words in the kitchen—*you might tell me about the fellow who carried you home from the dock, the night of the moon landing*—I wasn't even wholly certain I hadn't dreamed it all, that the hour on Horseshoe Beach wasn't a drunken hallucination, that I'd simply contrived to drive myself safely back to Greyfriars that night and put myself to bed, and *that* was when my mind started twitching and scripted out some alternative, fantastic version of events. Yes, my unconscious mind, longing to return to some point in the past in which everything was simple, when you loved a boy and he loved you back, and you were going to audition for the college play and he was going to bring you five dozen roses at your premiere.

Because when I rowed myself over to the lighthouse the next morning after the moon landing—having consumed six cups of coffee to drown my hangover—there was nobody there but old Mrs. Vargas, looking pale and strained in a black housedress. She was astonished to see me, to say the least. She offered tea, then changed the offer hastily to coffee, which I refused. Instead, I came straight to the point, and she answered me without hesitation. No, she hadn't seen Joseph. She didn't know what I was talking about. Last night? She hadn't heard anything, she hadn't noticed anything at all. My goodness, she would surely know if somebody was living in her own house, wouldn't she? You could hear a pin drop at night, when the sea was calm. I asked her about those hiding places the rumrunners used to store their booze, and she said she'd never heard of them, she didn't know what I was talking about. Pascoal had never spoken of such things to her, God rest his soul. She spread her hands before me and was awfully sorry she couldn't help me. Maybe—she suggested this delicately—maybe I'd had a little too much to drink last night?

So I returned to Greyfriars just in time, as the tide began to turn, but not before I peeked inside the small covered portion of the dock that served as a boathouse, and saw that it was empty. Only Pascoal Vargas's old lobstering equipment, his lines and cages and pots, hanging on their hooks, everything in perfect order.

But now my brother Hugh had presented me with a new fact, a fact that corroborated the blurred memory of sailing for some time in a small, choppy boat, of being carried, three-quarters asleep, across a drizzly lawn, and told to make not a single sound. The smell of fish. My hair brushed by a pair of gentle hands. As I walked back into the kitchen, my head buzzed with these details I hadn't remembered until now, the way your recollection of an event sometimes returns to you in small pieces, like a puzzle that must be fit together.

"There's something funny about this lobster," said Hugh, when I walked inside and shut the kitchen door behind me. "Look at his claw."

I came up beside him and examined the lobster through the wires of its basket, and I saw that Hugh was right. There was something tied to the claw of the largest lobster, a strip of white cloth, and when I poked my fingers carefully into the basket and detached it, I thought I saw a few black marks on the inside.

"What is it?" asked Hugh.

I dropped it swiftly into my pocket. "Nothing," I said.

4.

ABOUT TOM DONNELLY'S party. Looking back, I have no doubt he'd started planning it way back at the beginning of summer—to bring together, as he said, the Families and the locals on common ground, to celebrate the end of the season. And I suppose it made sense. We were living, after all, in a more egalitarian age. There might not have been any Jews on the Winthrop Island Club rolls yet, for example, but several members, so I understood, had expressed a cautious open-mindedness to the possibility, should any Jew have felt himself tempted to purchase a house right smack in the middle of a nest of WASPs, and should he have found anyone willing to sell. But that was all hypothetical. The year-rounders already existed on the Island, and men like Tom Donnelly—owners of prosperous, well-respected businesses—made a kind of middle ground between the pedigreed summer folk and what you might call the Island's working class. And he had, after all, been entrusted with the demolition of the old clubhouse and the building of the new one.

But all that goodwill and modern egalitarianism would have been for nothing if the clubhouse hadn't closed early that summer of 1969, in order to prepare the building for its careful demise. Without the Club, the Families had no choice but to troop down to Horseshoe Beach on the evening of August twenty-fourth and join their fellow Islanders, and lucky for Tom Donnelly the weather was perfect, sunny and warm. As promised, he'd invited everybody, the lobstermen and the shopkeepers, the clergymen and the harbormen, the small police force and the volunteer fire department. He set up a tiki bar on one corner of the beach and stocked it with enough free booze to fill Lake Winnipesaukee. And then he had the nerve to ask me personally—Miranda Thomas, star of stage and screen—to get up a little theatrical production among the residents of the Greyfriars artist colony, in order to lend the evening some tone.

Now, as you might recall, there were only two ways to get to Horseshoe Beach. The first was to sail in, which most of the Families did, mooring their boats at the southeastern limit of the sand where the rocks took over. The other was to do as I'd done in July, as Hugh and I had done in June, to park your car on the edge of the field and walk across the grass and down the rocky ledge to the beach below. The Greyfriars Players (that was our company name—has a certain ring, don't you think?) chose the second route, cramming into Mrs. Medeiro's delivery van, which Hugh had cheerfully borrowed for the evening to bump along the road with our torches and our few props. I rode in front, in between Hugh and Isobel. The ride wasn't long, and we hardly spoke. Nerves, I guess. When we reached the field, a couple of cars had parked there already. I recognized a white Chevy Corvair among them.

"Oh, look." Hugh switched off the engine. "Our friends beat us to it."

"Ignore them," said Isobel.

He swung out of the cab, and for a moment, neither of us moved. We watched Hugh cross in front of the van, this brother we shared, half mine and half hers, and Isobel said, "I guess we're going to make fools of ourselves."

"At least we'll be fools together."

She reached for the door handle. "Well, that's something."

Outside, the Players were jumping from the back of the van onto the turf. I poked my head inside to make sure nothing had been left behind, nobody still sat there curled into a ball of nerves, and shut the doors. When I turned, two men stood before me. One was tall and broad, sweating at the temples, and the other was tall and thin, smoking a cigarette: the fellow I saw on the ferry in July. By now both faces were familiar to me.

I said pleasantly, "I'm sorry. I'm afraid this party is for invited guests only."

The thin man tossed the stub of his cigarette to the grass and ground it out with his heel. "You know, this is the funniest case. The funniest case I've seen in twenty-two years. The first time I've tracked down a fugitive that nobody wants me to catch."

"Really? But I understood you *haven't* tracked him down."

"Maybe I have and maybe I haven't. What about you, Mrs. Goring? You tracked him down yet?"

"Me? I haven't tracked down anybody," I said, with a little emphasis on the *I*.

"God damn it," said the broad one. "God damn it. We ought to just arrest her, Frank. She knows where he is. All of you, all you goddamned Islanders, you all know where he is. He's in the fucking lighthouse."

"Jesus, Johnny. Watch your language in front of the lady, will you? That's no way to get a lady to talk."

"It certainly isn't. Do you mind standing aside? I've got a play to direct, down there on the beach. Where you're not invited."

The man named Frank snorted. "Where *are* we invited? That's what I'd like to know. Did you know we have to board that damned ferry every morning? The early ferry, Mrs. Goring, every ever-loving morning. Why? Because nobody will rent us a place on this island, nobody will rent us a cottage or a room or a rathole or nothing. That Mohegan Inn's always full up, for some reason, the only hotel on the Island. And then there's our orders. Tell the lady about our orders, Johnny."

"It's the funniest thing." Johnny wiped away the sweat on his temples with his thumb. "Get this, Mrs. Goring. The boys in the U.S. Marshals office, my bosses and Frank's bosses, they said—once we made our initial search, mind you, turning up exactly nothing—we couldn't station more than two men on the Island until after October the first, not unless we had reasonable, specific proof that the fugitive had taken shelter in a particular location. Now, I don't know where the bosses got their orders. I guess some pretty important people spend their summers here. Don't want to have the place crawling with uniforms, spoiling the view, I get that. But for Chrissake, he's a murderer! He murdered one of your own, that Hugh Fisher. I mean, wasn't he your stepfather? The father of that blond broad over there?" He pointed to the meadow, where the Players trooped steadily across the grass toward the sea. "I mean, I don't care if you *were* screwing the kid that night—"

I lifted my arm and smacked him, huge and loud, the way Carroll had taught me to do before the camera. Except this time, I actually hit the fellow. I caught a glimpse of his red, shocked face before he reached out and snared my arm and hauled me up to his chest.

"What the fuck do you think you're doing, lady? Who the fuck do you think you're hitting? I am a United States fucking Marshal, do you know what that means?"

I stared up at him furiously. "Sure I do. It means you can't go around treating a woman like filth, when it's *her* tax dollars paying your salary, *her* safety you're supposed to be protecting—"

The rattling of my teeth cut off the rest of that sentence, as Johnny yanked me into place and lifted his fist. Quick as a boxer, or maybe a boxer's manager, Frank snatched Johnny by the shoulders and hauled him back. "Cool it, all right? Just cool it. What the hell are you doing? You want to get us kicked off the case? Stick both our careers in the goddamned crapper?" He let Johnny go, and Johnny wheeled away a few paces, running his hand through his hair. Frank looked at me. "I apologize for this fellow, ma'am. We're both a little—you got to understand, it's been the most—the craziest case, all summer long. Tempers get a little short, you know? All right, now, Johnny. Have yourself a smoke and cool off. Tell the lady you're sorry."

Johnny shook his head and mumbled into the gravel. Reached into his jacket pocket for a pack of cigarettes or something. Frank put his hand on the back of his sweating neck and watched his partner for a second or two. Without looking at me, he said again, "Tempers get a little short, that's all, ma'am. I apologize."

"That's quite all right. I understand. You've got a job to do, of course. I don't blame you for that."

"That's kind of you."

"But I really must be on my way." I tilted my head in the direction of the beach. "I'm directing a play, as I said. Things are a little hectic."

"Of course, of course. I'm a fan of yours, by the way, Mrs. Goring. Should I say Thomas? A devoted fan, ever since that—that one with the Frenchman, right?—the Frenchman who turned out to be a Nazi."

"*At the Corner of Rue de la Paix,*" I said.

He snapped his fingers. "That's it. That was some flick. Your husband directed that one, didn't he?"

"Yes, he did."

"You know, I think I saw him on the ferry this morning. I might have been mistaken."

"No, that was him, all right."

"He's not giving you any trouble, is he, Mrs. Goring?"

"None at all."

"Because I thought I saw him leaving your place in a hurry, later this morning."

"That? He'd just remembered an urgent errand elsewhere."

"I see. I guess that happens, from time to time. Well, if he gives you any trouble, you let me know, Mrs. Goring."

"I certainly will, Mr . . . ?"

He held out his hand. "Santorini. Frank Santorini."

"Mr. Santorini. Thank you. I'm so glad we had the chance to meet. Now if you'll excuse me. Mr . . . er, Johnny?"

The other man was staring in the direction of the unseen beach, smoking his cigarette in fierce, short drags. At the sound of his name, he eyeballed me over his shoulder.

"Thank you for your time," I said. "I assume you'll be watching the party from one of your listening posts, or whatever you call them? Stakeouts?"

"Yes, ma'am," said Frank Santorini. "We'll be right there on the ledge above, watching everybody get tanked. Right up there if you decide to change your mind. Something maybe jogs your memory."

"How convenient. I'll be sure to let you know. In the meantime, I certainly hope you enjoy the play."

Johnny swore and strode off toward the white Corvair.

"I'm sure we will, ma'am," Frank said softly, watching his partner go. "I'm sure we will."

5.

WE OPENED OUR scene just as the sun touched the horizon, and everybody had a drink in one hand and a smoke in the other. It's better that way, don't you think? You're prepared to like anything when you're comfortably sauced. I think Tom was counting on me to star in the play myself, but I only took a bit part in the beginning, as the boatswain. I wanted to shape the production, not perform it; I wanted to see if I could teach somebody how to act, how to be. As I gave the signal to Miss Patty and Miss Felicity to light the torches around our sandy stage, as I motioned Hugh to begin beating the baking pans with a large metal spoon, as he set about his task of turning cookware into thunder, I observed the rapt eyes of the audience and the anxiety dropped away from my belly.

Boatswain! called Doris the sculptor, in her heartiest voice, and I strode forward on my sea legs and said, *Here, Master. What cheer?*

Just like that, we sailed a ship together, caught in a terrible storm, all those hundreds of us gathered on Horseshoe Beach that evening, the twenty-fourth of August, year-rounders and Families alike. A nice way to finish off the summer, if you ask me. A nice way to end with a bang.

6.

I SPOTTED CARROLL about halfway through the performance, as Prospero and Ariel were deep in conversation. He sat in the sand near the back of the crowd, still wearing his pale suit, though he had taken off the jacket and slung it over his shoulder. From his face, I couldn't tell his opinion of the proceedings; it was too dark, the sun had nearly sunk, and anyway he always took the same intent, neutral expression when he watched a drama unfold.

I turned to Brigitte to ready her for her entrance, but she already stood by, watching Miss Patty's Prospero with her keen eyes. The magic was in full flow. I had forgotten what it was like, a live show. I had forgotten the euphoria of scenes that went on without interruption, a story told from its start to its finish without interruption. In film, you did takes. You created brief, delicate pieces of the puzzle, and the director and the editor put them together and smudged away the seams. I leaned against the rocks and whispered to Brigitte, *The game's afoot.* She read my lips, and her face lit with understanding and with something else, possibly the same joy I felt, the rapture of creation. Then she turned, and with uncanny plasticity she transformed herself into a deformed and defiant beast. Called out, *There's wood enough within.* Waited her cue and entered the light from the torches, and the gasps came forth even before she spat:

As wicked dew as e'er my mother brushed, with raven's feather from unwholesome fen drop on you both! You could not drag your gaze away from her mesmerizing hatred, her bone-deep irony, until her last words, turning to address the audience, resigned, agonized, true: *I must obey. His art is of such power, it would control my dam's god, Setebos, and make a vassal of him.* She lifted her right arm to the sky, fingers spread, and the sleeve fell back to expose the long, dark tattoo along the inside of her wrist. I don't know if anybody saw it.

Because I didn't want to tax my actors or my audience, I clipped our show at the first act. Always leave them wanting more, Carroll used to tell me, and maybe it was a cliché but it was true. After Caliban's ferocity, there came Ariel's song, and then the enchantment of Miranda, seeing Ferdinand for the first time. I held my breath, because that last rehearsal had been awful—Isobel so restless and cross, I thought she wasn't going to turn up for the performance at all, and I would be forced to take over a role I had avoided my entire career.

But you know, when all the lights and the eyes fall upon you, something particular transforms you, according to your character—either you freeze up like a Fudgsicle, or you come to life. And Isobel. I don't know what came over her, whether she'd planned it all or whether she discovered this thing at the same time as the rest of us. She was competent enough in the early scenes, even forceful in her exchanges with Caliban, and then Hugh sauntered into the glow of the torches, the compleat Ferdinand, too princely for words, and it was right bang when she breathed out, *I might call him a thing divine, for nothing natural I ever saw so noble*—those precise words—when she came to life, utterly. I remember turning my head to search across the audience, to where Clay sat near the rocks with a dull-faced Livy, and how the longing there in his face—in the shape of his jaw and the reflection of the torches in his eyes—made my chest ache, nearly overcame me, so that I would in that moment have given the rest of my life to be able to live the past eighteen years over again, and especially that day in August, the eleventh, the best of those days and the worst of them.

7.

ANYWAY, LIKE ALL scenes, this one reached its end. Hugh brought the tears brimming to their eyes when he gazed nobly into the phosphorescent surf and said, *My spirits, as in a dream, are all bound up. My father's loss, the weakness which I feel, the wreck of all my friends, nor this man's threats, to whom I am subdued, are but light to me, might I but through my prison once a day behold this maid.*

The torches went out. For an instant, there was precious silence, and then a half-drunk roar of appreciation, echoing off the rocks, and in the enthusiasm, in the breaking up of audience and actors, in the violet twilight that now engulfed us, I slipped away to the rocks at the southern tip of the beach and found the little sailboat waiting for me, and the man made of shadow who stood next to it, knee-deep in the tide, holding a rope.

8.

WE DID NOT touch, we said not a word until we rounded the point on which Greyfriars stood and crossed the bottom of Fleet Rock channel to approach the lighthouse from its eastern side, the most forbidding, an almost vertical face of rocks.

I called, "Watch out! You'll hit the rocks!"

And he didn't reply, but simply brought her in neatly to a gap I hadn't seen before, disguised by the rocks. Snagged the rope neatly on a hook, lit a small, old oil lantern, and said the first words I had heard from his throat in nearly two decades: "They carved this out in '21, to land in the boats from Rum Row."

Of course his voice had grown deeper and rougher, a man's voice. I supposed my voice had changed too. He drew down the sail and un-shipped the rudder, and when he had finished all these things he lifted the lantern and held out his hand to me.

"There's a ledge to your left. D'you think you can climb it?"

"Of course."

I took his hand and leapt from the boat to the ledge, a few feet above us. The tide was on the rise, and I imagined that when it peaked, the step would be nearer level. As Joseph prepared to join me, I looked around the tiny cave, just large enough for the boat and a few pieces of equip-ment. The damp, rough-hewn walls flickered in the light from the lan-tern, and I thought we might have slipped back into another age, crossed some barrier of time where we would be safe. But of course that was only an illusion. Joseph stepped to the ledge by my side and nudged me to the open doorway, up the long, steep stairs, until we reached the closed door at the top. He stretched an arm around me and unlocked it, and we came inside a basement of the ordinary, non-rumrunning kind, fitted with a masculine workbench and shelves of tools, an oil furnace, a boiler, the smell of mildew and kerosene.

"It's the bottom of the lighthouse," Joseph said softly, almost a whis-per, as if he didn't want to wake somebody. "The actual lighthouse, I mean, not the living quarters."

"Can we go up?"

"Sure we can."

He crossed the room and opened another door, and I perceived that the walls were built to a slight curve. I followed him down a cramped corridor until we reached a ladder that disappeared through the ceiling. Now I smelled iron and rust, the peculiar tang of salt meeting metal. I put my hands on the cool bars and climbed, rung by rung. I felt the groan of the ladder as Joseph started up beneath me. I seemed to be climbing entirely into darkness, climbing on faith alone. My head passed through the hole in the ceiling, my chest, my waist, and then the blinding path of the light crossed the air above me. I made a little gasp and climbed the last few steps to emerge in a round, tall room, perhaps fifteen feet in diameter, dominated in the center by the great electric light and the gears on which it rotated.

Behind me, Joseph stuck his head through the opening in the floor and said, "Wait here for a moment, will you? I'll be right back."

"But—"

He'd already disappeared, and I spoke to blank air. The room was hot, having taken in a day's relentless sunshine, having absorbed the glittering incandescence of the enormous Fresnal lamp. The light passed over my head, but the space was otherwise dark, and I thought of Mercury—the planet, not the god—existing in such proximity to a sun that the whole of your experience was nothing more than the swift, brilliant contrast of light into dark.

Still, somebody lived here. There was a narrow camp bed on the other side of the light, neatly made; a shelf with books, an old kerosene lantern like the one Joseph lit in the cave below. At the bottom of the bed sat a small wooden trunk, and I resisted the urge to inspect the contents of either trunk or bookshelf. Instead I went to the windows that surrounded the room and stared into the black sea until I understood I was looking at the tip of Long Island, twinkling with tiny lights, each one signifying some house, some family, some lives, some little world I knew nothing about. Slowly I walked the circumference of the room, dragging my hand along the glass as I went. I saw the emptiness of the gap between Long Island and Rhode Island, where the ocean lay; I saw Winthrop Island return to view, and the faint light glowing from the vicinity of Horseshoe Beach, though I couldn't see the beach itself from this angle. I continued walking until Greyfriars intruded, black and still except for a single lamp shining in my mother's bedroom. Mama alone had not gone to the beach this evening. Everybody tried to convince her in turns, but she was resolute. She said she had seen the rehearsals, that was enough. As she folded up the picnic blanket that morning, she said, "I've enjoyed watching you at work, Miranda. I'm sure everything will go wonderfully tonight." That was all.

The room was not quiet. The metal gears ground as the lamp made its circuit around the night sky. Above it, I almost thought I could hear the movement of the light itself, the beam as it whooshed through the air, but of course that was an illusion, too.

"In the olden days, it was an oil lamp."

I jumped and turned. Joseph's head and chest were visible from the hatchway; his hands lay flat on the floor. As I watched, without speaking, he climbed to his feet and continued.

"The lighthouse keeper had to stay up here all night, every night, to make sure it didn't go out. Actually, there were several lamps set against reflectors, in order to create the necessary candlepower. And when there was a bad winter, a lot of storms, and the oil began to run out—well, it would get pretty desperate, because the keeper could go to prison, could even lose his life if the light went out and some ship wrecked on the rocks."

He ran out of words and stared at me. I stared back. In the space where our eyes met each other, there was no other thing, no molecule of even air, not ether or electricity.

"Then I guess he would have done anything to keep it lit," I said.

"Yes. They were almost like lovers, the keeper and his light. They couldn't exist without each other."

The light passed just over Joseph's head, then mine, then around again in an eternal pulse. He looked the same, which surprised me. Oh, his skin was tougher, as you might expect, and his face was leaner, spare of flesh, the bones fixed in place. But his hair remained thick and dark, brushed the same way. He moved with the same lithe grace. Maybe his shoulders were stockier, I don't know. Maybe he carried more muscle. But the shape, the frame was just as I remembered it, just exactly filled the hole in my memory. His eyes were the same soft, wise brown, only narrower, as if he'd spent most of his time squinting into some bright sun.

"Where did you go?" I asked.

"Just checking on Mama. She's asleep."

I reached into the pocket of my dress and pulled out a small strip of white cloth. "Why did you send me this? Why now?"

He glanced at the cloth and then away, out the window, toward Greyfriars. "Because I need your help," he said.

I don't know what I was expecting him to say. I don't even know what I hoped he would say. He was a fugitive, he was going to get caught sometime, that was inevitable. The first of October, Frank Santorini had said. Once the summer was over, once the Families left, there was nobody to protest if a hundred United States Marshals landed on the Island in an amphibious invasion. Well, nobody important, anyway. Joseph Vargas had a small, pitiful future, and that future was shorter still if he elected to remain near Winthrop like some kind of homing pigeon, some species of fish that must forever return to the waters in which he was spawned. So why should I think to figure in that nonexistent future of his? Of course I didn't.

Still, there was that hollow feeling in my stomach. That bitterness I swallowed back in my throat, which tasted of disappointment. "What kind of help?" I asked. "You know we can't hide you at Greyfriars, they'll certainly see you there."

"Not me." He turned his head back to me, and his expression—which a moment ago, gazing at me gazing at him, had been animated with something like hope, or longing, anyway *life*—had turned dull. "My mother. She's dying, Miranda."

"Oh! Oh."

"It's cancer, I think. She won't see a doctor, she won't leave Fleet Rock."

"Why not?"

"Because she won't, that's all. It doesn't matter why. She just won't. When Pops died, there was no one left to take care of her."

"What about her family? The Medeiros, don't they care?"

Joseph moved a few feet away, around the side of the light, and turned his back on me to gaze at the black water outside, the same tiny lights of Long Island I had observed a moment ago. "They care, in their way. But she won't speak to them."

There was a hoarseness to his voice that hadn't existed before. I wondered if he'd started smoking—a natural thing to do, one presumed, in the state penitentiary—but I couldn't smell cigarettes, fresh or stale. So this additional timbre, this low, ragged edge must constitute some natural evolution that occurred in the years we lived apart, the way my own voice had been shaped and sculpted by Carroll and by various professional dialect specialists. The glow of the light passed across his face, and for the first time I noticed a bump on the bridge of his nose. A scar along his jaw. And yet his hand, pressed against the glass, was so gentle.

"That was why you escaped, wasn't it?" I said. "For her."

"Two more years before I went up for parole. I couldn't wait that long. She'd be dead by then."

"Oh, Joseph."

"Don't say that. Don't pity me. I made a choice, that's all." His hand loosened and dropped. "Anyway, I figured if there was one place in the world I could hide in plain sight, it was Winthrop Island."

"To the eternal frustration of Frank and Johnny."

"Frank and Johnny?"

"The two marshals trying to catch you all summer. You do know they were watching the party, don't you? They might have seen us."

"No, they didn't. I made sure to moor outside their line of sight."

"You saw them?"

Joseph glanced over his shoulder with an expression that suggested my question wasn't worthy of an answer. "Frank and Johnny," he said.

"Nice names."

"If they don't catch you tonight, they'll catch you in the autumn," I said. "Once the summer's over, they can send as many agents as they want. The Coast Guard. You can't just live here forever."

"I'll be gone by autumn."

"*Where?*"

Joseph turned and leaned back against the window, crossing his arms. "Mama can't last much longer. Not even a week or two. Can't get out of bed anymore, won't eat anything. Not even soup. Wants to starve herself, I think. She just wants to die."

I bent my head and tried to say I was sorry. But how could you say such an inadequate thing? I wasn't sorry. I was something else, I was so full of pity and rage I could hardly breathe.

"What will you do?" I asked instead, leaving out the unnecessary end of the question: *When she dies.*

"I'll turn myself back in. Finish my sentence."

There was nowhere to sit except the bed. I crept there and sank on the ancient patchwork quilt. "But they'll extend your sentence. They won't let you out for parole. You might be in for life."

"What else was I supposed to do? She's my mother. She hasn't got anyone else."

"By her own choice!"

"It doesn't matter. *How* doesn't matter. It's just the way it is, Miranda. Some things you have to accept as they are."

I sprang back up. "*No!* No you don't. You do the opposite. You *fight*, Joseph, for God's sake! Don't let them win. Isn't that what you told me, once? Don't let the bastards keep you down."

"I was a kid, Miranda. Anyway, that wasn't what I meant."

"Then what *did* you mean? Was that only about me? Because I'm Miranda Schuyler and you're just some fisherman? Because I've got a right to fight and you don't?"

"That's got nothing to do with it."

"I fought and I fought, Joseph. Every time I got knocked down, I rose again and I kept fighting. And now I'm here, and you're here, and I don't understand . . ."

"Understand what?"

"Why you won't fight, too. Why you never fought for me the way I fought for you. When I loved you so—I love you—"

Joseph turned his back on the sob that escaped me. He braced his hands on the window frame and said, "Because I loved you more."

"You didn't answer a single one of my letters, not one."

"I kept them, though. I read them a million times. For years, the only thing that kept me sane was you."

Because of the grinding gears, I thought maybe I hadn't heard him. I stood there next to the bed, staring at the back of his head, his broad back in its dark shirt. Camouflage, I guessed. For a man who moved about only in darkness.

"And then?" I said.

"And then I had to stop. Turned the corner and started to go crazy, thinking about you. There are just some things you can't accept, I guess, and one of them is when the woman you love gets married to somebody else."

"Carroll."

"Don't say his name."

"You have no right," I said. "What else was I supposed to do?"

"I know I've got no right, believe me. I wanted you to live. That was the point. But it still ripped my guts out."

I felt sick. I actually shook as I stood there, trying to inhale in slow, deep breaths, the way Carroll had shown me to calm my nerves. I said, "Well, it ripped my guts out, too, being married to him. If that's any consolation."

"It's not."

"I left him. I left him in April. That's why I came here, so he couldn't find me."

Now Joseph straightened and turned. "Why? What did he do to you?"

I opened my mouth to tell him about the baby, about Victor's sofa, about the tree on the Bath Road. His raw expression stopped me. "He didn't treat me as I deserved," I said instead. "I think it's because he knew I didn't really love him. Not the way he wanted to be loved."

It was the right answer, I thought, and also a true one. Joseph relaxed back against the window. "I'm sorry," he said.

"Sorry for what?"

"Because it was my fault. If it weren't for all this, you'd never have met the bastard."

"No, I wouldn't. But then I wouldn't have made all those films, either. I wouldn't have become what I am."

"Yes, you would. You'd have found a way. Anyway, if you ask me, those films weren't worthy of you."

"You saw them?"

He nodded. "Some of them. They show flicks in prison, you know. I saw *Four Roads to Paradise* and *The Fox*."

"Those weren't my best."

"Maybe not, but I also saw *Shrew*."

"That wasn't Carroll's film."

"I noticed. I noticed you were a different woman in that one."

"He was so furious. He told me I was selling out, making a film for Americans, for Hollywood, but I wanted . . . it wasn't just the script, which was wonderful . . ."

"What?"

"I wanted to make a movie *you* might see. Some way I could speak with you. That was the reason I started acting to begin with."

"Not for me."

"Yes, for you. What else? I made you a promise, didn't I? Don't you remember?"

The gears ground and ground. Joseph's face, illuminated in vast pulses by the light, was stricken. "I remember," he said.

"And you kept yours. Those roses—there were more than five dozen, I counted."

He turned his head and stared out the window. "It was a dumb thing to do, I guess."

"You might've been caught."

"No, not that. There was no point, that's all."

"They made me happy. Isn't that enough?"

He made a noise in his throat and leaned his palm on the window ledge. The light sent odd shadows streaking across the side of his face. For a moment, we kept vigil, waiting for something to return to us. I remember wondering what he was looking at, wondering what he was thinking, wishing he would turn his head back to me and say something, say something, before the tide went slack and the minutes ran out. But he didn't move, and finally I opened my own mouth.

"Joseph, can't we just—"

He turned then. "So promise me something else."

"What?"

"I need you to promise me, if they happen to catch me before Mama dies—"

"Don't say that."

"But if they do. She's got nobody else. You're the only one I can trust. Everyone else . . ."

He let the sentence fall. My breath came easier now, my hands steadied against my sides. The duskiness of his skin entranced me. I said, "I promise."

Joseph leaned back against the window frame. His head bowed. I started forward, and though the sound of my footsteps was swallowed by the noise of the mechanism, Joseph must have felt my approach. Just before I reached him, he looked up. "Don't touch me," he said.

My hand, which had just risen to find his shoulder, fell back. "Why not?"

He made a dry, sad little laugh and stepped away. "I'll bet you can figure that out yourself."

"You touched me on the beach," I said. "Last month, you held me in your arms."

"That was different."

He was staring out the window again, but I knew he wasn't looking at anything. I felt the scintillation of his nerves, and the scintillation of mine. I moved forward without fear and laid my hand on his back. He flinched and went still.

"Just give me one thing in return," I said.

"I can't."

"Not that." I slid my hand along his shoulder and came to prop myself on the edge of the window frame, exactly to his left. I took his hand and held it in my lap. "Remember what you told me that night? Sailing off around the world?"

"That was the old dream, Miranda."

"Promise me you won't turn yourself in. Promise me you'll take a boat—my boat, Hugh's boat, the one I just bought from the Huxleys—and you'll sail away from Winthrop and never come back. You'll find some island or some village somewhere—"

He pulled his hand away. "It's a fantasy."

"Promise me."

"It's not a promise I can keep, is it?"

"Yes you can. It's simple. If they don't catch you before your mother dies, you won't turn yourself in. You'll sail off this island and never come back."

"Miranda—"

"You've served your time! Whatever debt there is, you've paid it. You've suffered, my God." He started to pull away, and I rose and caught him by the shoulders. I said fiercely, "Whatever happened that night, I don't care what it was, you don't deserve to suffer for it anymore. You deserve to live."

"It doesn't matter what I deserve or don't deserve."

"Damn it all! Don't you care? Don't you *want* to live?"

Joseph pulled my fingers from his chest, where they had made fists in his shirt. "I wish I could make you a promise, Miranda. But I can't. I've got nothing to give you. I'm asking you for something, and I can't give anything back."

For some time, we didn't move. We stood there absorbing the points of contact between us—my hands in his hands, our gazes laid upon each other. The heat of the room was like a crucible, was like a forge, and just as noisy. I wanted to ask if he could open a window or something, but I couldn't seem to move my lips.

"I'll row you back to Greyfriars," he said at last.

I roused myself. "You can't. The tide."

"What do you know about tides?"

"I learned how to sail for *The Devil and the Deep Blue Sea*," I told him.

He started to smile. I thought about tides, how you might say that everything in life moved according to an eternal ebb and flood, ebb and flood. How famine turned to feast and back again, and dark returned to light returned to dark. I thought my own tide was turning. I thought, *We are in flood again at last, we are bathed in light for this one hour*. I lifted one hand and touched his cheek. He flinched and drew away, but I pulled him back. "What are you afraid of?" I said. "It's only me."

"I've got nothing. I don't have anything left to give you."

"Yourself."

"It's gone. That's all gone."

"No, it's not. It's still there. You're still there, and I want it—I want *you*—"

"Miranda—"

"Joseph, listen to me. I didn't have any letters, I didn't have a photo or one thing from you. All I had was the thought of you. I had the knowledge of you. That you were *there*, just that you existed."

He leaned his face into my hand and closed his eyes. I thought how pale he must be, hiding from the sun. He had been so tanned that summer, almost brown. How I had adored the nut color of his skin, the smooth, young texture of him. All that had changed, too, but this skin was still Joseph's skin, and Joseph lay underneath.

"I don't know how," he said. "I don't know how to touch you anymore."

"Yes, you do."

"Eighteen years. Eighteen years in the fucking pen. You don't know. Things I can't tell you."

"Maybe there's things I can't tell you, either."

We stood without moving. I thought, *Maybe this is enough*. Just to touch him. To have his waist under my hands. His heart beating a couple of inches away. In the ordinary course of things, I was supposed to forget him, this first love of mine, but I had not, and he had not. Whatever it was that connected us, it still existed. Between my chest and his chest ran some force of understanding, some kind of magnetic current that could not exist without its opposite pole.

Joseph said my name. His hands, having left mine, had found their way to my back to rest along my spine.

I drew his shirt from his trousers.

He pulled the zipper of my dress.

The bed was narrow and the room was hot. It was a relief to take off our clothes, a relief to touch Joseph's bare skin. He was lean, my God, too lean. There was a hungry concavity to his belly, and the muscles of his chest and shoulders were hard and compact and useful, not like those of actors, just for show, the muscles I was used to. He shied from my touch, but I made him bear me anyway. I laid my fingers and my lips upon his skin until he got used to the sensation of being felt. What he really wanted was to touch me, but he didn't dare, he stood there trembling until I actually took his hands and brought them to my belly and my breasts. I sat on the edge of the bed and he knelt to face me. The passing light lit his shoulders and shadowed his face.

"I don't know how to do this," he said hoarsely.

I put my arms around his neck. "Yes, you do."

9.

WE LAY TOGETHER afterward in a damp, naked knot upon the sheets. The quilt had long since slipped to the floor. I was thirsty, and Joseph rose to bring water from the sink downstairs. I asked what was the source, and he gave me a strange look and said it was Greyfriars. A well on Greyfriars land, piped along the sea floor to Fleet Rock, because the water table was too low out here, the rock too deep and solid.

The water gave me life. I set down the empty glass and wandered about the room, picking up books and inspecting the lamp, while Joseph lay on the bed and watched me. I loved his avid gaze, his silence. Eventually he called out to me and I returned to settle myself against him, my back to his front.

"What if I go with you?" I said. "What if we sail off together?"

"No."

"Why not?"

"Because you have a life. You have your films. You can't go back to being nobody. You have to keep going."

I stared at the mechanism of the lamp before me. "The trouble with acting," I said, "is that the scripts are all written by men."

"So what?"

"So characters only say things, they only *do* things that the writers think they would do. A woman in a film, she only thinks and speaks and acts the way a man imagines she thinks and speaks and acts."

The light swept above us. The metallic noise of the gears rose and fell and rose again. I smelled the woolen blanket, the heat, the human perspiration. The familiar scent of Joseph's skin, only more intimate now, more thorough.

"Yeah," Joseph said. "I see what you mean. Like in *Four Roads to Paradise*. He was posing you like a doll, it was like you weren't even a woman. You were some man's fantasy."

"I know."

"And *Deep Blue Sea*. Don't get me wrong, you made them live and breathe. Only you could have made those girls human. But the only movie that—I don't know, the only role that I really loved you in was *Shrew*."

"Carroll was furious with me, taking that role," I said. "Not just because it was a big Hollywood movie. He hates that director, he hated that he took Shakespeare and made it something new. And he especially hates Kate. He hated the way I played her."

"Subversive. You had this rage."

"Yes. I had that rage."

"But wouldn't the same thing happen, the other way around? Women writing scripts and directing films? You'd just have men doing things that women think they would do."

"Maybe. Maybe it wouldn't be so bad, for a change."

"So do it. Make your own flicks."

I laughed. "Oh sure. It's that easy."

"None of this was easy, but you did it anyway." He drew the hair from my temple and laid his fingers along the side of my face. "One thing's for sure, though. You can't do anything from a sailboat off the coast of Argentina."

"Why can't I?"

"Your face. Everybody knows that face. And maybe nobody's going to rat you out on Winthrop Island, but everywhere else . . ."

"Then I'd wear a disguise."

"See, I don't want you to wear a disguise. I want you to be just who you are. And you can't be Miranda on a sailboat with Joseph Vargas."

Now I turned in his arms, so we faced each other. "I disagree. I maintain that I am more Miranda on a sailboat with Joseph than anywhere else in the world."

"That depends on who Miranda is, I guess."

"This," I said. "This is who I am."

He touched his forehead against mine. The cot was so narrow, the edge so close, I thought I might tumble off if it weren't for Joseph's hand on the small of my back, Joseph's leg gently pinning mine in place.

"How did you do it?" I whispered. "How did you survive? Being locked up in that terrible place."

"I just did. How did you survive being married to that bastard?"

"That was my choice."

"Well, maybe prison was my choice."

"How could you *choose* prison?"

"Because the alternative was worse. Because I figured nothing in my life could ever be so bad as what happened that night, so I might as well go away somewhere where . . ."

"Where what?"

"Where nobody knew a thing about me. Where I didn't know anybody. Because nothing hurts more than that, nothing ever hurts you more than the people you love."

"I would never hurt you."

"Not on purpose," he said quietly.

We were so close on that pillow, our noses nearly touched. Our lips moved side by side. We were stripped of everything that did not belong to each other, our clothes, our vanity, our misery, our secrets. There was just warmth and breath and skin. A scent that was not his or mine, but ours. I still remember it, the smell of us that night.

"You didn't answer my question, though," I said. "How you survived."

"I don't know. I just did. Kept my head down. Got in a few fights at first, that's how they say hello. But the rage, the tough guys, that's not the worst part of prison. The worst part's the boredom. Boredom makes you hopeless, makes you insane, makes you do stupid things. That's what you have to fight. You have to find something to care about again."

"Yes." I moved my head, so my face was buried in his neck and he couldn't see what was in my eyes.

"So I read. Read everything I could get my hands on, taught a few guys a few things. I thought of you and your dad, and I got some of us together to read aloud, all kinds of books."

"What else?"

"Exercise," he said. "Exercise keeps you sane. And boats. Taught myself draftsmanship. I must have designed about a hundred of them, racing yachts mostly."

"What did you do with them? The drawings, I mean."

"I left them all behind."

I looked up at his chin. "How did you do it?"

"How did I leave the drawings?"

"No, I mean escape. How did you escape?"

There was a pause, about the length of a single circuit of the light. I was about to ask him again when he spoke, in a voice that only just rose above the noise of the gears.

"It was so damned easy. They trusted me." He moved his hand in my hair. "They trusted me."

I waited for him to say more, to tell me the specifics, the planning and execution, but he didn't. I said, "That's why you're going to turn yourself back in, isn't it? Because they trusted you."

"Just stop talking, all right?"

"Don't do it," I said. "Don't go back. You don't owe them a thing. We've got a sailboat. I bought one for Hugh. It's stocked with food and everything. We can leave whenever we want."

"And do what, Miranda?"

"Your old dream. We'll sail the world."

"That was a boy's dream."

"Well, what do you dream about now?"

"Nothing."

"Yes you do." I struggled out of his arms and sat up. "What about your drawings? You could start a business, building ships."

Joseph made a sound of exasperation. "Building ships? Are you kidding me? Where? How? I'm a goddamned fugitive."

"Somewhere. Anywhere. We'll find a harbor on the other side of the world and settle down together, and you can do what you love."

"But *you* can't. You can't be a movie star on the other side of the world."

"I've done that already. I don't need it anymore. I don't want it anymore."

"Then what *do* you want?"

I put my hands on either side of his head and bent to kiss him. "You. That's all. We'll live in a hut somewhere. I'll pick up a hammer and you'll show me how to build a boat."

"Miranda—"

"We'll make our own paradise." I slid my leg over his hips—he was already aroused, he had been stiff for some time as we lay there against each other—and I watched his expression soften into rapture as I drew him back inside me, so deep as he could reach, so deep as I could take him. For a moment, I held him there, while his hands made fists against the mattress and his head swung back to expose the pulse underneath his jaw. I kissed his throat and his jumping artery and said, "We'll make *this*—"

"Jesus Mary—"

"—make our own island, make our own children—"

Joseph grasped my waist and flipped me on my back.

"Lord Almighty," I said.

"You all right?"

"Yes."

He took his time, as if we had any of that left. I felt the might of his discipline, the pendulum beat of union as if there might be no end to us, an infinity of Joseph and Miranda, until somewhere in the middle of that infinity I went straight out of my mind and off this sheer, vertical cliff into oblivion. I must have made some kind of howl that caused him to stop and ask—again—if I was all right. I assured him I was. So he lifted himself high on his palms, threw back his head, arched his back for several long seconds then crashed against me like a shipwreck, a total loss, and the sexual ecstasy was nothing to that of his weight on mine, his sweat, his emission like a purifying balm on my womb. Our skin touched at every inch, every knob and plane, every junction. There was no part of me that was not married to some part of his. I remember wondering what time it was, whether we had made love for hours, whether it might be dawn. At some point, he rolled us on our sides. This time I faced the metal wall just beneath the windows, lit intermittently by the passage of the light. I loved the messiness of the bed, the wild state of my hair, the wetness between my legs, the chaos. I thought in wonder, *Joseph*.

"If they come for you," I said, "you have to sail away. Even if you leave me behind."

"I can't just sail away from you."

"You can. You will, because you love me, and that's what I want from you."

"You want me to leave you?"

"I want you to be free."

He didn't answer, and I must have fallen asleep, because I remember waking at the jump of his body.

"What's wrong?" I asked.

He was already out of bed, yanking on his trousers. "It's Mama," he said, and he dove for the hatch in the floor.

I didn't know what to do, whether to rise and dress and follow him, or to stay where I was and wait for some kind of signal, wait for him to return. I looked out the window and saw that it was still the middle of the night, and the tide was reaching its slack. I might now safely depart, but I didn't move. The pillow smelled of Joseph, the sheets. I leaned to the floor and found my dress, and the strip of white cloth in one of the pockets. The light was too uncertain for reading, so I just ran my finger along the small, neat black letters, over and over, while my nerves strained for news from below. When I couldn't stand the incessant noise of the gears any longer, I pulled the dress over my head and started down the hatch.

I banged right into Joseph halfway down the corridor that led to the living quarters. He grabbed my shoulders to steady us both.

"What's wrong?" I asked.

"She wants a priest."

"Oh God. What about a doctor?"

"She won't see a doctor. I'm going back out to the beach. Everyone's still there, the sky's lit like the Fourth of July."

"But you can't! They're out there, Frank and Johnny. The marshals."

"They won't notice me in the crowd." He set me aside and continued down the corridor in long strides until he reached the ladder, and I was astonished at his strength as he hauled himself up like an acrobat. He called, "Wait there, I'll be right down."

In less than a minute, he dropped back down the ladder, using only his arms. He wore his shoes and his shirt, which he tucked into his trousers as he spoke.

"I need you to stay with her, Miranda. Can you do that?"

"You stay with her. I can go instead."

"No. You'd have to row. You can't sail it, and they'll hear a motor. Miranda, please. Stay with her. Stay with her. I'll be back before you know it."

The corridor was dark, and his face was shadowed. When was the last time I saw Joseph Vargas in full daylight? Not since that afternoon on the cliffs, eighteen summers ago. I was seized with terror that I would never see the sunlight on his face again. I took his arm. "Don't go."

"I should've been with her. Downstairs all alone while you and I— while we—aw, hell."

"She was not all alone. We were right here, you went to check on her."

"I have to go. I have to go now. Don't argue, I don't have time to argue."

"Is it that bad?"

"I don't know. I'm no fucking doctor, God help me. But she wants a *priest*," he said, in a terrible voice. He wasn't even looking at me, he was looking at the ceiling, as if he could see God through it, brandishing some thunderbolt because he, Joseph, had been upstairs enjoying sexual intercourse with some woman while his mother lay dying, *this* woman who stood before him, flushed and unwashed, and he was damned.

So what choice did I have? I followed him down the corridor and through the doorway into the living quarters. Ahead, I glimpsed the old sofa, the entrance to the kitchen, but Joseph turned away from these, to the right, up an old staircase that creaked under our feet. The landing was dark and windowless. I grabbed Joseph's hand and he led me to her room, Mrs. Vargas's bedroom, where the bedside lamp was lit next to a woman I hardly recognized. Her gray hair was spread across the pillow, brushed and dull, and her face was like a skull's, though her eyes were closed. There was a peculiar smell in the air, not of body fluids but something else, sour and dreadful. Joseph went to the bed and smoothed the skull's forehead. "Mama, I've brought someone to sit with you while I fetch the priest."

In the gap beneath Joseph's arm, I saw her eyelids move, and for an instant, as she looked into Joseph's face, she seemed almost human. I could have sworn that her skin smoothed out, that the blood rushed into her face and revived her. I stepped closer as Joseph stepped back.

"Don't go," Mrs. Vargas mumbled.

"I have to go, Mama. You want me to fetch the priest, right?"

"Yes!" she burst out.

"Then I'll be right back. Miranda will stay with you." He dragged a chair next to the bed and turned to me.

"What if something happens?" I whispered.

"Then it happens. Done all we can." But his eyes were glassy with tears. He leaned down and kissed my cheek. "Thank you."

He was gone so fast, I didn't have time to think of a reply, not even *You're welcome*. I was too stunned. I stood there behind the chair and heard the sound of the door. For an instant I thought of bolting. Going after him. My God, she was like a corpse lying there, and I didn't even know her. The corpse of a stranger. And here *I* was, some stranger, some strange woman, standing in her bedroom. Her son's lover. His handprints still fresh on my skin. And she was dying, this was possibly her dying day, her dying hour, and I was all she had.

I crept closer and sat quietly in the chair. She lay with her eyes closed. Her hands twitched on the bedclothes. There was just the single lamp, and beneath its light her skin looked too delicate and too papery for life. The sour smell was strong, though the bed was immaculate. I saw the

pitcher and glass on the nightstand, and I asked if she wanted some water. She didn't reply. The twitching went on, stilled, and resumed.

I thought maybe a prayer would comfort her. I knew the Hail Mary
from one of my films. I leaned next to her ear and said it now. *Hail Mary,
full of grace, our Lord is with thee; blessed art thou among women, and blessed
is the fruit of thy womb, Jesus. Holy Mary—*

Her eyelids flew open and settled down again.

*Holy Mary, Mother of God, pray for us sinners, now and at the hour of our
death. Amen.*

Her lips moved. "Thank you, Father."

"I'm not—"

"Say it again."

*Hail Mary, full of grace, our Lord is with thee; blessed art thou among
women, and blessed is the fruit of thy womb, Jesus—*

Her hand shot from the blanket and scrabbled for mine. I hesitated an
instant, looked at her bony witch's hand in horror, and then I was ashamed
and laid her fingers in my palm and closed my other hand over it.

She whispered, "Bless me, Father, for I have sinned."

"But I'm not—"

"It has been many years since my last confession. I don't know how
many."

She spoke slowly, littering pauses between the words, but her voice
was remarkably clear. When Carroll's mother had died a couple of years
ago, at the end of a long decline, I couldn't understand anything she said.
Not a word. It was as if her voice had sunk deep into her chest, and her
tongue, attached to her shuddering throat, had lost its will and couldn't
quite shape itself around the necessary sounds.

I squeezed her hand and said, "The priest will be here soon. Joseph is
bringing the priest."

"Joseph. My son."

"Yes. He loves you so much. He'll be back soon."

Her fingers curled into the back of my hand. "Not yet!"

"No. Not yet. Maybe an hour."

"An hour, an hour. We have no time. Bless me, Father."

"I'm not—"

"Bless me!" she shouted, lifting herself from the pillow. "Father!"

"I—I—bless you, my child," I said helplessly. "Lie back, now. You need to rest."

"Joseph cannot hear this, Father. You must never tell him."

"Just rest, Mrs. Vargas. You need to rest. Close your eyes."

"I don't need to rest. I need to confess."

"Not to me!"

"And who else, Father? Who else is there to absolve me?" She clutched at my hand, lifted herself again and leaned over and kissed it. "Hear my confession, please. Grant me absolution in the name of the Father, and the Son, and the Holy Spirit—" She crossed herself.

"Please stop." I rose from the chair. "Please stop."

"Father! Father!"

"I'm not—I'm not the priest! I'm Miranda! Miranda Schuyler!"

She shook her head. "Miranda's gone. She's a movie star now. My husband showed me the magazines."

"No, I came back. I'm here. It's me."

Mrs. Vargas stared at my face, and the strangest feeling overtook me, of being seen but not understood. Maybe it's the light, I thought. Maybe she can't see me.

"Please, Father," she said. "Please, Father. I don't know why you won't hear my confession. Is it because I haven't been to church since then?"

There was something mesmerizing about the way she looked at me, the way she spoke, in that pitiful, halting voice that was not quite a whisper. I said, without thinking, staring at her lips, "Since when?"

She said, "Since I killed him."

10.

I REMEMBER MANY details about the night of my stepfather's murder, but I can't remember the whole of it put together, if that makes any sense. From the moment I woke up on the sofa until many days later, maybe even a month, my memory is more like a kaleidoscope than a linear, cinematic recollection.

I remember watching Mrs. Vargas speak on the telephone, in her low, calm voice. I remember wondering whom she was speaking to, and what she was saying. She turned away, so I couldn't pick out the words. I asked her what had happened, where was Joseph, was he okay, and she put down the receiver and said Joseph was just fine. It was my stepfather. He had been injured.

Naturally, this confused me.

"But Mr. Fisher's at Greyfriars," I said. "He's gone to bed already."

Mrs. Vargas stared at me without expression, holding the telephone receiver to her chest, which was covered by a dressing gown of dark red flannel. "You're mistaken," she said in a flat voice. "He's not in bed with his wife. He is here with me."

She then returned the receiver to her ear and turned away, and I rose from the sofa. I think I wanted to find Joseph, to get this terrible misunderstanding cleared up, to steady this quaking world around me. To wake me up, if I was dreaming, or having some hallucination, some curious psychological visitation of the moment I heard of my father's death. But Mrs. Vargas snared my arm as I started across the room and shook her head sternly, so I just stood there until Joseph himself appeared through the doorway, a minute or two later. The front of his shirt was wet with blood, and so were his hands. He didn't seem to see me. He just looked at his mother and said, in the same flat voice, "He's dead."

That's when the memory snaps—possibly I fainted or something, although I never faint—and other memories appear. The police and Isobel and my mother's screams outside, because they wouldn't let her in. The noise from all those motorboats, the Coast Guard, whatever.

And also the smell, a peculiar, putrid sourness in the air, the smell of death.

11.

AN ODOR I recollected now, as I stared at Mrs. Vargas's lips, although I couldn't decide if it originated from inside my own head, in the region of memory, or whether it actually existed, floated in the air, connecting me to that terrible night eighteen years ago. I said to her, "This is a grave sin, Mrs. Vargas."

"I can't tell anyone but you, Father. Not my husband, not my son."

"But Joseph—"

"He will never understand. Only God understands."

I found the chair again. My mouth was dry; I reached for the pitcher with my right hand—Mrs. Vargas still clutched my left—and poured a glass of water. A little of it splashed over the edge, because my hand was unsteady. I drank a sip or two, and when I looked back at Mrs. Vargas, she had sunk back on her pillow. Her eyelids were drifting shut.

"Why would God understand?" I asked.

"He knows how I suffered."

I picked up the glass and drank again. My heart thumped so hard in my chest, I was almost afraid of my own fear. I wiped a trickle of water from the corner of my mouth. "How did you suffer, my child?"

"You know. You remember how they hated me. My aunt and my cousins. Then when Francisca was killed, and they blamed me for that, too—"

"But Francisca was your sister."

She opened her eyes and looked at me with suspicion. "Francisca was my *cousin*. I am an orphan, Father, don't you remember? An orphan who belongs to nobody."

"Of course. Of course. But Francisca. What did Francisca do?"

"Father, please. You remember all this."

"I—it's been so long. She died so long ago. Right? It was when— when—"

"When the baby came, Father, when the baby came and she got in the boat to visit, to kill me probably, and then God sent the storm to drown her so she could not reach me and my son."

"Why—why would Francisca want to kill you?"

"Because I took her husband from her. She would not forgive me because I married her Pascoal to give my baby a name. But you know this already, Father."

"It was so long ago. It was—it was many years ago. Why would you do—why would you commit such a sin, Mrs. Vargas?"

"I had no choice, Father! I was so young. I was in love with him. I thought we were married. I thought we became man and wife, when I lay with him."

"With whom?" I bent closer. "With whom? With Joseph's father?"

"Don't you know," she whispered. "Don't you know, his soul contains a piece of mine, and mine contains a piece of his. We have a son."

"Joseph."

"Our son, a gift from God. *She* gave him a daughter. But a man wants a son, don't you think? A man needs a son to carry his blood into eternity. I gave him his son."

Now I rose from the chair and walked to the door and then to the window. I stared at the shore beyond, the tiny light in the bedroom at Greyfriars, where my mother lay awake.

"Father?" said Mrs. Vargas.

"Yes, my child?"

"I am already absolved of these sins. You have already absolved me."

"Yes."

"Tia Maria has not forgiven me. My cousin Laura has not. But I am innocent before God. He's forgiven me."

"*Holy Mary,*" I muttered, gripping the windowsill. "*Holy Mary, mother of God—*"

"He has made me suffer for these sins. He has made me do penance. When I gave birth to my son, I nearly died."

I turned my head over my shoulder—not quite looking at her—and said, "What about Mr. Fisher? He sinned too. He—he did this to you. What was *his* penance?"

"To die," she said simply.

I couldn't hold myself upright any longer. There was nowhere to sit except the bed or the chair, so I went to the chair. Mrs. Vargas had stopped talking. For a moment, I thought she had stopped breathing, but her fingers still made spasms around the edge of the blanket, and I perceived a slight movement at her chest, by the shift of the shadows cast by the lamp. Her mouth had fallen open. I wondered what else might come out of it. What new horror. I wanted to know, and I didn't. I couldn't even quite encompass what she had already said.

She had killed Hugh Fisher, she said. Or had she?

Of course she hadn't. What mother would allow her son to go to prison for a crime she herself had committed? What woman would kill the father of her son? It was impossible.

But I had known, I had always known in my heart that Joseph couldn't kill anybody. Could never, ever kill his own father. I hadn't mentioned that fact—the vital clue of Joseph's paternity—to the detectives, because I knew without being told that this fact was not mine to disclose. But I *had* told the detectives that Joseph was innocent. Over and over I'd insisted that Joseph couldn't kill any man. No, I hadn't seen it happen. No, I hadn't heard anything. No, I had no idea how Hugh Fisher ended up on Fleet Rock that night. I'd fallen asleep on the sofa with Joseph Vargas, and when I woke, Hugh Fisher was mortally wounded. But Joseph could not have inflicted that blow, not willingly. If he *had* killed Hugh Fisher, it was an accident.

I don't know how I long I sat there, staring at Mrs. Vargas. She seemed to be asleep, but restless. Her hands kept twitching. She thrashed her head from side to side, as if trying to avoid the blows of a persistent opponent. I went to touch her, to soothe her—God knows why, because I had promised Joseph, I suppose—but she batted me away with peculiar strength. At last I rose and went back to the casement window. I took hold of the handle and forced it open, and the gust of fresh, salty air surprised me. The tide had turned and was rushing fast, a fearsome current. Ahead, Mama's light was still on; I tried to look to the northeast, in the direction of Horseshoe Beach, but even when I stuck my head around the glass and into the open air, the angle was wrong, and all I saw was a faint, blazing glow. The party in full swing. I thought I could smell smoke from the torches, from the bonfires, but maybe that was just my imagination.

I heard a noise behind me. I pulled myself in and turned back to the bed. Mrs. Vargas's eyes were open, her eyelids quivering. "It hurts," she said.

"What hurts?"

"Everything. I need my pills."

"Where are your pills?"

"Joseph has them."

"Joseph will be back soon."

"No," she moaned, "no. You need to absolve me, Father. You need to hear my confession. Why won't you hear me?"

"Because I'm not him. I'm not the priest."

I had drawn closer to the bed, and she lifted herself up, groaning in pain, and reached for me. "Father, please. Are my sins too terrible?"

"I can't hear them, that's all."

"I'm dying, Father. You must give me the sacrament."

I cast another desperate glance out the window. Mrs. Vargas's fingers raked my palm, the back of my hand.

"Bless me, Father. I have sinned, I have sinned. I have not been to confession for many years."

"Why not, Mrs. Vargas? For God's sake, why not? Why haven't you confessed?"

"Because of my son. What if my son heard of it? He would never forgive me."

"But he *does* know! Don't you realize? He went to prison for you."

How bewildered, her face. Her rheumy eyes. "To prison? You're crazy, Father. He's not in prison. He's right here, he's staying with me. How can he know the truth? I never told him, my God, how *could* I tell him that I killed his father? Father, listen. Kneel with me."

Her hand was insistent. I thought, she's dying, for God's sake. Give her what she wants. She's dying. She's Joseph's mother, and she's dying.

I went down on my knees, on the soft rug underneath the bed.

"Father, I have killed a man, the father of my son. I killed him with a knife, which I held in my two hands."

"God have mercy," I said. "God have mercy."

"He had broken his vow to me. We had made a vow together, and he broke it."

"What vow?"

"He married her. He married her and started a baby in her."

"But he didn't know. He didn't know you were going to have a baby, too."

"No, no. Not the first one," she said. "His *new* wife. Francine. She seduced him, I don't know how, she took him away from me. They went to Europe on his boat. For two months they were gone. For the summer, like me, a summer wife. I heard her daughter telling Joseph—"

"Her daughter. Miranda."

Mrs. Vargas nodded. "Her. The movie star. She said to Joseph that her mother was going to have a baby. So I knew what I must do."

"God have mercy," I whispered.

"Then God sent me a sign. Father, it was a sign. I went to my bedroom and looked out the window and saw Hugh Fisher in his boat, rowing to me, rowing to this house. He came inside the back way, the cave, the way he used to visit me, and he went right upstairs to Joseph's bedroom. So I waited for him there with my knife from the kitchen."

"God have mercy. God have mercy."

"Joseph heard the noise and went upstairs, but it was too late. I said to him, *There was a fight, Mr. Fisher tried to kill me*, and somehow the knife—a terrible accident—but how could I tell him his mother had done murder? It would kill him."

"God have mercy."

"Will you absolve me, Father?"

"I can't, I can't."

She made a noise of agony and fell back on the pillow. Her lips moved, she was muttering something. I climbed to my feet, trying not to touch the bed itself, and stumbled to the window and the pure, salted air. Outside, a purring noise stretched across the water. I braced my hands on the window frame and searched the black water until I saw it, an old, handsome speedboat, lights ablaze at bow and stern, louder and louder, making a foamy arc through the current toward the Fleet Rock dock.

12.

BY THE TIME I ran down the stairs and out the door, the boat's engine had already slowed to a putter as it eased into place against the dock. In the darkness, I couldn't see who was aboard. I called out, and Isobel answered.

"Here comes the rope!"

The white line snaked through the beam of the bow light. I caught it at the last instant and hauled it tight around one of the rotting bollards. There was a clatter of feet and Isobel's voice again.

"Come on, Father. I'll help you out."

I didn't dare ask about Joseph. I moved forward and reached out my arm, while the priest grabbed hold of us both, Isobel on the left and me on the right, and heaved himself out of the boat, dragging a thick, unmistakable atmosphere of Scotch whisky in his wake.

"Whose boat?" I asked.

"Donnelly's. He let us borrow it."

"What about—"

"Not now," she snapped. "Where is she?"

"Upstairs, in her room. I'll show you."

The priest said, "How is the poor girl?"

"Not well, I'm afraid." We were already starting down the dock, Isobel and I, half-running. The priest made some noise of protest. I turned and saw his white hair, his large frame unrecognizable in a Hawaiian shirt and secular trousers, like any other fellow enjoying himself at Horseshoe Beach that evening. Tom Donnelly's end-of-the-year bash, his gift to the Island. I went back and took the priest's arm. "I'm sorry," I said. "I'm afraid I don't know your name."

"McManus," he said.

"She's been asking for you. She has—she has something she needs to confess."

He spoke with remarkable precision—remarkable, I mean, when you considered his state of inebriation. "I imagine she does. It's been eighteen years since I last took that poor girl's confession."

"You know, she's hardly a girl anymore."

"She was. We were all young, Miss Schuyler."

I didn't ask how he knew my name. I didn't know if this was the same man who had blessed the fishing boats eighteen years ago, now older and fatter and drunker, or somebody else. Mrs. Vargas spoke of him as if she'd known him forever, but Mrs. Vargas was dying, she'd said a lot of things that made no sense, and how could you pick out what was truth and what was confusion?

Ahead of us, Isobel held open the door. The lights in the living room were dark; all the lights were off except for the upstairs hallway and the lamp in Mrs. Vargas's bedroom, and I couldn't see her face. But I felt her impatience. I felt my own, boiling beneath my skin. But you can't hurry an elderly, portly priest, a man of God, thoroughly drunk. You can only hold his arm firmly and help him along the rickety wooden boards and up the stone steps, wondering how the hell he managed to keep himself from falling out of Tom Donnelly's speedboat for the entirety of the half-mile run between Horseshoe Beach and Fleet Rock.

We reached the door. Isobel allowed us past and closed the door behind us. The bang made me jump. I didn't look at the furniture as we hurried across the living room to the stairs. I didn't see the sofa, or the table with the photographs. I stepped off the rug and over the place where Mrs. Vargas had dropped her tray full of porcelain. Where those drops of blood had fallen to the stone. We climbed the stairs, one by one, Isobel trailing behind in case Father McManus missed a step or lost his balance altogether. Already my shoulder strained, my arm strained under his weight. When we found the landing, I panicked. I thought maybe she was already dead, I had left Mrs. Vargas to die alone when I had promised Joseph to stay with her. I hauled poor Father McManus down the short hall and through the doorway, into the lamplit bedroom, Mrs. Vargas's deathbed, her confessional, Greyfriars framed neatly in the window with its single light burning.

"Here she is." I dragged Father McManus to the chair. "Mrs. Vargas, he's here. The priest is here."

To my relief, she turned her head. "Father? Where did you go?"

"I was at the beach, my child."

"I was waiting—was waiting—"

"Yes, my child?"

"For the blessing. For my absolution."

I backed away from the chair. I could see Father McManus's bemusement as he tilted his head—or maybe that was drunkenness, who knew—and reached for her hand.

"My dear, let's start from the beginning," he said, because of course he knew how to deal with a dying soul, with people who bemused him. He was a trained professional, a man of God, howsoever soused with whisky, whereas I was a mere, imperfect human who judged and railed. I stared at Mrs. Vargas's withered face on the pillow, her hands both clutching the single palm of Father McManus. The reek of whisky overcame the sourness of death, and it was good.

Isobel's hand clamped around my elbow. She hissed into my ear.

"Come with me."

13.

I FOLLOWED MY stepsister back down the hall and the stairs. Instead of turning right, into the living room, she turned left, toward the lighthouse tower itself, moving so swiftly on her long, athletic legs I had to run to keep up.

"What's going on?" I called. "Where's Joseph? Is he safe?"

She didn't answer, just kept hurrying down the corridor. She knew where she was going. She found the ladder and climbed the rungs in a series of lithe, easy movements, the way I remembered her. Her legs disappeared, her feet. I made a noise of frustration and followed her.

When I emerged into the warm, shifting space, she had turned her attention to the walls beneath the windows. She was pacing along, looking for something. The air was heavy with the scent of human coition. I wondered if she noticed that. I crossed my arms and asked her what the hell she was doing, but by the time I finished the question, she had reached the bed. She came up short and stared at the wet, crumpled sheets, the discarded quilt. The light streaked across the top of her head. She spun around.

"You fucked him," she said. "My God, you fucked my brother."

"What's going on? Where's Joseph? For God's sake, tell me!"

Isobel resumed her pacing. "I'm trying to find the damned switch. Where's the switch?"

"What do you mean, the switch? The switch to the light?"

"Of course, the switch to the light. What else?" She turned to the mechanism in the middle of the room and fell to her hands and knees. "Don't just stand there, help me!"

"Why? What's going on?"

"Can't remember, can't remember. He showed me once. Christ! The floor!" She crawled around the base of the light like an overgrown baby, and somewhere on the other side she made a noise of triumph. I sprang after her. She was opening a panel in the floorboards. She reached inside. An enormous screech of metal came from within the light's mechanism, gears grinding against gears, and the light snapped out. The darkness dropped over us like a blanket.

"What have you done?" I cried.

"If they can't see the light, they can't find Horseshoe Beach."

"Who?"

"The Coast Guard! Those damned marshals, they called in the Coast Guard."

"Oh God! They caught him?"

"Yes, Sherlock. They caught him. Just when he was about to get into Donnelly's boat and head out here himself with Father McManus. You'll never guess who ratted him out."

"I can't—who—I thought the Islanders were—"

"Not an Islander, you nitwit. Your husband."

"Carroll!"

"A real prize, that ball and chain of yours. A twenty-four carat rat. The only sober man on the beach." Her voice had moved to my right. I thought she was looking out the window, and I followed the sound, followed my sense of her, the smell of her, until I bumped right into her shoulder. "Watch it," she said.

"We have to go. We have to take the speedboat back to Horseshoe Beach, before the Coast Guard can land there."

"And do what? They have guns, those two. You can't just snatch a man away from a United States Marshal. We'll all end up in prison."

"I don't give a damn! He's innocent, don't you know that? He didn't kill his father!"

"Did he tell you that?"

"No. His—" I bit off the sentence, because I didn't know, didn't know if I could say this thing that had been told to me within the sacrament of confession. Didn't know if I could even believe it. "Damn it, Isobel, you're *here*, aren't you? Why are you here if you don't want to save him?"

"Because it's my fault."

"Your fault? What's your fault? I thought Carroll was the one who—"

"No!" She took me by the shoulders. "*I* was the one who saw you here with Joseph that night. *I* was the one who woke up Daddy and told him."

There was only the faintest amount of light in the room. Isobel's face was like a shadow, a manic shadow, leering over mine. Her fingernails bit into my skin.

"You," I said.

"Me." She released me with such ferocity, I fell back a step. "He was mine. My brother. The only person in the world who understood me. You can't just take a girl's brother, Peaches. It's not right."

"Clay. Clay understood you."

"No, he didn't. He wanted something else."

"Maybe he did, but he understood you anyway. He loved you."

"Oh, shut up. It's done, it's finished. Daddy's dead, he's gone."

"Why—" I couldn't seem to make my voice work properly. I tried again, and I was not myself, it was some other woman's throat that made these sounds. "Why didn't you say anything?"

"Because it didn't matter! I wasn't the one who killed him, was I? I wasn't the one holding the knife. And if Mama knew—oh God, if she knew—"

"You mean *my* mother."

"*I* was more a daughter to her than you were. I was daughter and husband to her. We raised that boy together. There was nobody left but us."

"You," I said. "*You.*"

"No, it was you. You were the one who—"

A flash of light caught my gaze from outside the window, startling me out of the stupor of shock. I ran past Isobel, stumbling over my own shoes, toward the sight of the sea, the shadows, the minuscule light of the stars, the pure bath of full moonlight. The flashes came from a pair of boats, large ones, and I couldn't see their shapes or colors, but I knew what the hell they were, all right, and where they were headed.

"The Coast Guard," I said, and just as I was about to turn and dive for the hatch, I saw something else, glowing somewhere over the cliffs to the north. An angry orange blaze, a massive cumulonimbus of smoke illuminated by the moon. "My God," I whispered. "What the hell is that?"

Isobel joined me at the window. "Jesus Christ. He's gone and done it."

"Who? What?"

"Tom Donnelly. He's burning down the clubhouse. While everyone's drunk on the beach—the firemen even—"

I turned and dove for the hatch on the floor.

"Where are you going?" called Isobel.

"Where do you think?" I yelled back.

14.

ISOBEL FOLLOWED ME down the ladder, the corridor, out the door to the dock. I climbed in the boat and she tossed me the rope and jumped in too.

"I'll drive," she said. "I know the way."

Between the motor and the current, we hurtled down the Fleet Rock channel and around the point, converging on the area of Horseshoe Beach at an acute angle to the path of the two Coast Guard cutters, bent on the same destination. They must have seen us, because one of the boats—the foremost one—made a loud, electronic noise like a horn, and somebody yelled at us through a megaphone or something. Isobel didn't seem to notice. For the first time, I wondered how much she'd had to drink that night. She reminded me of the old Isobel, swerving along the road between the Club and Greyfriars. Her face was ruthless, her hair white in the moonlight. Her hands gripped the wheel and the throttle, and mine gripped the side of the boat, praying to God we wouldn't hit somebody's wake, because we'd be goners. I saw the southernmost point of Horseshoe Beach, the rocky finger stretching out into the sound, and how swift and how near Isobel meant to clip it.

"Watch out!" I gasped.

"Shut up. This was your idea, Peaches."

We came within a foot of catastrophe, I think, and then the bowl of Horseshoe Beach stood before us, the sandy shore coming up so fast I stopped breathing. The surf had kicked up since I'd left a few hours ago.

There were now unruly breakers crashing and rolling over the sand, and Isobel plowed right through the lines of white, threw the boat into reverse, and shuddered us up to the edge of the beach where she jerked the wheel, so we came in sideways. I jumped out and splashed through the foam. The torches were still lit, the bonfire. Everybody was milling around the tiki bar, still drinking, a drone of conversation and music from a brave band performing on the stage. I ran toward them and opened my mouth to scream Joseph's name.

But Isobel had a better idea. From behind me, she shouted, *"Fire! Fire! There's a fire at the clubhouse!"*

Funny thing, the word *fire*. Hits you right in the gut, doesn't it, right bang in the middle of your human viscera. The band stopped playing so abruptly, it was like somebody had pulled a plug. All those Islanders, drinking restlessly, overthrown by the bizarre turn of events yet determined to remain on the scene until the night's conclusion, they just shut right up and whirled around.

"Fire!" she screamed again. "The clubhouse is on fire! Somebody help! Don't you smell the smoke, you idiots? Get in the boats, the cars! Where are the firemen?"

Somebody roared, "Donnelly, you goddamned fox!"

And then pandemonium, absolute melee, as the Islanders ran for their boats, scrambled up the cliffs to their cars, clumsy with vodka. I don't know if they meant to fight the fire or just take in the once-in-a-lifetime spectacle of the Winthrop Island clubhouse burning to the ground. Only Isobel and I stood still in the center of this panic, searching for the other people likely to remain where they stood on this beach, until we saw them, on the opposite point—three men, signaling in the Coast Guard cutters by means of a flashlight.

I made a noise of despair and launched across the sand. Ahead of me, a few of the Islanders ran for their boats, moored on the sand near the rocks. I thought I saw Clay Monk and his wife. Here on the beach you could really smell the smoke, a different smell altogether from the torches and the bonfire. This was thick and heavy and filled with the ominous reek of other things, the things that burnt along with the wood, the metal that was melting and the paint that was scorching. The fire roared a few miles away and still you could smell these poisonous things. I ran straight past the boats and onto the rocks, my bare feet slipping, my breath coming in gasps. I lost a step and cut my knee, and I just picked myself up, though the blood trickled down my leg. "Joseph!" I cried. "Joseph!"

The three men turned at the same time. One of them took a step forward, and was yanked right back.

"Stay where you are!" came a shout. I think it was Frank.

I kept going.

"I said stop! I'll shoot!"

"Don't you dare shoot me! He's innocent! He's innocent!"

A gun fired, *CRACK*. I thought I heard the bullet whizzing past, a warning shot, and I kept scrambling forward, borne by I don't know what tide of courage.

Then Joseph's voice, agonized. "Miranda, stop! For God's sake!"

So I stopped. I was about fifty yards away, maybe closer. I could see their figures in the moonlight, Johnny's stocky frame and Frank's thin one. Joseph between them, dark and tensile.

"Let him go! Please! He's innocent. His mother—"

"Doesn't matter," Frank called back. "Not my business."

"About as innocent as goddamned Lizzie Borden," said Johnny.

"He didn't do it! Don't you care? Don't you give a damn?"

"I don't, as a matter of fact," said Frank. "I ain't no court of law. I give a damn about getting him on that goddamned Coast Guard cutter and getting the hell out of Dodge, that's what I care about. That's my job."

I made a noise of rage and started forward again, while the noise of the propellers thudded closer, and somebody yelled through the megaphone.

Another shot cracked out and whistled past, splintering against the rock behind me, and in the shock of noise I cried out.

"Miranda!" Joseph shouted. I saw him struggling to break free from Johnny's arms, and I realized he wasn't wearing handcuffs.

"Run!" I screamed. "Just run!"

"Don't be stupid, ma'am!" said Frank. "Jesus Christ, he'll get killed."

"I'm not running, I'm not running," said Joseph. "Miranda, I'll be all right. It's all right."

I dropped on my knees. "You promised. You promised me."

"No, I didn't. Let me go."

"But you didn't do it. Your mother—"

"Just let me go." He had to shout, because the first cutter was chopping up the water about twenty feet from the point, and they were dropping a boat from the side.

"I can't!" I screamed.

"Trust me, all right?"

You know, they teach you how to scream in the movies. It's true. Because an ordinary, instinctive human scream doesn't cut it; you have to scream a certain way, primal, not the way you would if you were actually terrified, actually in some kind of agony, when your throat doesn't work and your lungs don't work. What came out of me, in that moment, as the Coast Guard fellow sprang up from the boat and scrambled to the rocks, and Frank and Johnny jerked Joseph down between them, was just a strangled noise, caught somewhere between a yell and a sob, the noise you make when something terrible unfolds before you and you can't do a thing about it, you're helpless, you're just one woman with no voice, no gun, no way to stop the goddamned injustice of it all. Just to watch a piece of your soul torn out of your body, to watch it climb into a boat and spurt off toward a monstrous Coast Guard cutter and God knew what after that.

I climbed to my feet and started to scramble again, down the long finger of rocks to its very tip, matching the progress of the boat. The Coast Guard man was piloting the outboard motor; Johnny sat in the bow, Joseph next, Frank behind Joseph. I reached the last rock and stood there with my hands in my hair, raging, and when the shot rang out I almost didn't hear it.

I just heard Johnny cry out. I saw him pitch forward into the water while the boat cruised past, I saw Joseph stand up and dive in too, and I screamed out, "Swim, Joseph, swim! Go!"

But he wasn't swimming away. Oh no. How could you expect Joseph Vargas to just swim away from a drowning man? His dark head disappeared in the foam, and for a long minute there was nothing, nobody dared to shoot because of Johnny, there was just shouting and panic and the pilot circling back, trying to find them both.

And then Joseph burst up from the water, holding something, holding Johnny, and even though Johnny must have weighed fifty pounds more than Joseph—most of it around the middle—Joseph hauled him toward the cutter, two heads bobbing against that rough surf, until they reached the side of the boat, under the sweep of the searchlight, and Joseph grasped the bottom of the entry ladder.

"You fool," I whispered. "Just go. Just *go*."

One of the Guardsmen came down and grasped Johnny by the shoulders while Joseph pushed him up from below, and another Guardsman, reaching down from the railing, grabbed Johnny's arm as the first Guardsman hauled him up. They managed to get him over the rail, but for that moment, those thirty seconds, they forgot about Joseph. I was the only one who saw him disappear under the water, surface again, and dive once more, and I didn't say a word, I just stood there with my hand over my mouth, waiting for them to look back down.

By that time, Joseph was gone.

15.

CLAY WAS THE one who drove Isobel and me back to Greyfriars, an hour or so later, right past the frantic Coast Guard helicopters sweeping the water with searchlights.

"They won't find him," I said. "They can't find him."

"At least he's got a sporting chance," said Clay.

I turned and stared at his profile. "Why, that was you. You fired the gun."

He shrugged his shoulders, reached into his jacket pocket, and pulled out a gun. "My service pistol," he said, and he stuck it in the glove compartment. "I keep it in the boat in case of sharks."

16.

I WANTED TO take out the dinghy and look for Joseph, but Clay said there was no point. "If we find him, the Coast Guard will find us finding him. Best off letting him go his own way. He's a tough nut. Strongest swimmer I ever knew."

"But the current," I said.

"Maybe he went the opposite direction."

I stood on the Greyfriars driveway; Isobel had already hurried into the house, without a word. Clay sat impatiently at the wheel of his car, eager to get home. I bent to the window. "They're going to search the Island, every rock. He can't hide forever. They'll search the lighthouse, no one can stop them now."

"Look, I'll keep an eye out for him, all right? That's your brother coming out of the house. Isobel's with him. I'd better get going. Take care of yourself, all right?"

"All right," I whispered, and then, as he pulled away down the drive, aiming for the marshals guarding the entrance, "let me know if you hear any news!"

He waved back, and I turned toward Greyfriars, which was now ablaze from every room. A strobe of flashlights crisscrossed the driveway, and Hugh and Isobel marched swiftly down the lawn toward me.

"They're here to search the house," said Isobel. "Every goddamned corner."

17.

THEY SEARCHED FOR hours while all of us sat in the living room—Mama, me, Isobel, Hugh, the Greyfriars artists—wearing our clothes and our dressing gowns, whatever we had on at the start of the invasion. Mama offered to make tea, but they declined. They were all from the United States Marshals office, grim and determined, just doing their jobs. I have no doubt they went through our underwear drawers with perfect integrity.

By now, I existed on nerves alone. I kept rising from the sofa and pacing the room, looking out the window at the moonlit water, the searchlights, the darkened lighthouse. The Greyfriars dock, Hugh's new yacht at its mooring, the boathouse, the bench. I thought, *He's out there, he's out there.* Every last atom of my body strained to fly through the French door and down the lawn, fly across the water and find Joseph, help Joseph. *He's a tough nut,* Clay said, but to swim so far, in darkness, against current and tide, helicopters and boats—it was impossible, impossible, impossible.

Be alive, I thought. Be alive somewhere, but not here. For God's sake, not here. Not down by the water, where the searchlights swept and swept over all those dear patches of lawn. Not the bench where Joseph had met me in the night, not the dock where I had helped him carry Popeye from the boat. Not the lighthouse, already searched, under surveillance from above. The marshals had a dog with them, a German shepherd, and to this day I can't quite love a German shepherd, however much I love dogs. I think of menace, I think of that terrible night when I wanted Joseph to be alive, but not nearby. Anywhere but Greyfriars.

By the time the telephone rang at four o'clock in the morning, Brigitte was asleep on the rug, Otto and Leonard snored from the window seat, and Miss Patty was sketching something on the back of a newspaper. Mama rose from the armchair and answered the ring, under the gaze of one of the marshals, the one who had been left to keep watch on us.

"Yes, I see," she said. From across the room, she met my gaze briefly, and then turned to the wall. "How awful. Yes. Yes. I'll have Hugh come to help. Yes. Yes, right away."

She set down the telephone and said, in a voice of tremendous calm, "That was Father McManus. I'm afraid poor Mrs. Vargas has passed away. Hugh, would you mind taking the dinghy across with Dr. Huxley? He's on his way here now."

I jumped from the sofa. "I'll go with him."

"No, darling. You stay here."

"She's got to stay here," said the marshal. "Him, too."

Mama turned to the marshal. "Sir, there's been a death. An awful tragedy. Poor Father McManus is stranded at the lighthouse with a— with a corpse. Surely you can allow my son to ferry the doctor over the channel."

The marshal shifted his feet. "I'll ask."

He disappeared, and I looked at Mama, who returned to her seat without a glance at me. Picked up her crochet and resumed the steady, even stitching of a doily or something. Brigitte stirred from the rug and sat up. "What's the matter?" she asked.

"Mrs. Vargas died," said Hugh. "I'm taking Dr. Huxley over to lay out the body."

"God rest her soul," said Brigitte, stretching, and she laid herself carefully back on the rug and fell asleep again, curled up like a fetus.

The marshal returned. "All right. But we got two men going with you."

"Sounds fair." Hugh rose from his chair. "I'll go get the dinghy on the water."

"Not you," said the marshal. "One of the women."

"Aw, you've gotta be kidding me. It's heavy."

"That's what they said."

Isobel stood up. "I'll do it."

There was just the smallest pause. "Are you sure, sis?" said Hugh.

"Sure I'm sure."

"You know where it is, right?"

"Jesus Christ, Hugh. Of course I do. Miranda, can you give me a hand? It's in the boathouse."

There was absolutely nothing in her voice that suggested she needed anything more than a hand with the dinghy. There was nothing in her face, as she searched me out from across the room, except the half-bored weariness of a woman kept up past her bedtime for the sake of a few more irritating chores.

"Can't you get it yourself?" I said.

"Come on, Peaches. It's heavy."

I sighed. "Fine, then."

We trooped down the lawn. The bright, full moon had sunk deep in the western sky, casting our faint shadows on the grass. Behind us came the two marshals, who made heavy footsteps that seemed, in that hour before dawn, to echo off every rock and tree and bush, every object in the universe. So we didn't try to talk, Isobel and I, in the center of all that racket. We just walked in exact step with each other, down the long, damp slope toward the boathouse, Isobel in her white nightgown and robe, me in my clothes I hadn't yet changed. I thought she looked like a ghost. The ghost of the old Isobel, the Isobel I used to know, who ran down often from Greyfriars in the middle of the night, wearing nothing but her nightclothes.

As we got close, the marshals patrolling the shore approached. They addressed not the two of us, but their colleagues behind. The dog whimpered and jumped toward me.

"Look," I said, "can you keep that mutt under control, please?"

"He smells something on you."

"Of course he does. I spent the evening with the fugitive, didn't I? Trying to get him to turn himself in."

The dog leapt and snarled, and the marshal drew in his leash.

"Just go get the boat, ma'am," said one of the marshals from the house, and he turned and explained the situation to the man holding the dog on its leash.

Isobel started forward to the boathouse, and I followed her. The dinghy, I knew, would be resting upside down on its horse at the back. There would be Hugh's scull, and the oars on their hooks along the wall. The door stood open. There was no light inside, because the Fishers had never run the electricity this far out. Just the flashlight on the shelf, which Isobel picked up and switched on. She shone the beam toward the back, where the dinghy sat in place, and together, without a word, we started forward and lifted the boat from its horse and set it, right-side up, on the wooden floor.

Then Isobel handed me the flashlight, climbed on the horse, and pulled down on a small, rusted hook stuck in the ceiling, practically invisible. A hatch swung out, and a man silently leapt downward to land on his bare feet before us, wearing nothing but a pair of trousers, still damp and reeking of the sea.

18.

THE DINGHY WASN'T large. Joseph had to curl in the middle, between the two bench seats, while we laid the oars over him. Nobody said anything. It was like we did this kind of thing every day, like we were accustomed to smuggling fugitives from hidden compartments on the premises. Like we spent a hundred years practicing how to carry a dinghy with a full-grown man hidden inside, in such a way that you couldn't tell how damned heavy he really was.

As we reached the edge of the dock, the dog wheeled on his leash and let out a series of desperate barks. I heard the handler swear and take him in. The other two marshals saw us, adjusted their vests, prepared to start down behind us. Now we hurried, Isobel and I, trying not to look as if we were hurrying. I thought my arms might fall from their sockets. Tiny starbursts popped before my eyes. We reached the end of the dock and grabbed the ropes and made to lower it down the three or four feet to the water, which was now rising again from its ebb.

Two feet into this operation, Isobel swore loudly and let the rope slide right through her fingers, so the dinghy dropped into Long Island Sound with an almighty splash, and nobody knew, nobody saw the man who rolled neatly into the water and swam under the shelter of the dock.

19.

BY MORNING, HUGH'S beautiful yacht was gone. The water search had been curtailed by then, the fugitive presumed drowned or ashore, and nobody noticed the boat's departure except me, sitting in my window seat while Brigitte snored from her bed. I nestled there with my binoculars, the binoculars I bought for ten dollars from Mrs. Medeiro's general

store, and observed Isobel's return from the lighthouse with the marshals and the body and the priest and the doctor—she had to make two
trips—and all the attendant confusion, while the dawn grew silently on
the eastern horizon and a breeze gathered up from the northwest.

The sun appeared, new and brilliant, and in the middle of this blinding
light, the mainsail went up, the rope slipped from the mooring, and the
mighty spring tide carried the sailboat silently down the Fleet Rock
channel and out into the open ocean.

AFTERWORD: 1931

HUGH FISHER COMES to visit her while Pascoal is out in his lobster boat, tying his own vessel brazenly to the landing where anybody can see it. In March, however, nobody will see it, except possibly Pascoal. And what can Pascoal do? He has no power over Hugh Fisher.

Bianca saw him motoring across the channel toward her from the window at the top of the lighthouse, and she waits for him now in an atmosphere of great composure, just outside the door, though her heart beats in quick, mighty strokes. He springs up the stone steps with all his old athleticism, and she notices that he doesn't wear a wedding ring. Most men don't, of course, but she looks for it anyway.

As for Hugh, he's not looking at her left hand, which naturally bears the slim gold band that Pascoal placed there in October, but at her belly and breasts, curving like huge summer melons against the material of her dress. He stops a few yards away, one foot on the step above, his gloved hand resting on his thigh. His eyes meet hers painfully.

"So it's true," he says.

"Yes."

"He's mine. You know he's mine."

She shifts her feet. "It might be a girl. You never know."

Hugh makes a noise of agony and turns away.

"How could you?" he gulps. "How could you let him?"

"Because I had to."

"You didn't have to. I would've taken care of you. Don't you think, if you'd told me, I would have—my God, I've have moved heaven and earth for you, I'd have given you everything."

"Would you? Everything?"

She sounds terribly wise, even to her own ears, but then she's aged about a thousand years since last August, has lived through a number of lifetimes, it seems, has been an enraptured teenager and a wronged lover and a cold, calculating seducer and a hasty bride. Now she is an outcast. Her family won't own her, nor will the rest of the Island. Only Pascoal is loyal to her. When she went to him and told him tearfully that their love had borne fruit—this was three weeks after Francisca's return, she couldn't wait any longer than that—he looked horrified and then fearful and then determined. He was expecting some kind of retribution, after all. He had done a terrible, sinful thing, taking her virginity—Bianca, the pure young cousin of his own fiancée!—and now he must pay his debt manfully to God. In two more weeks they were married, and they moved into the lighthouse that very afternoon. Pascoal worships her, and the more he worships her the more she despises him, and so great is her revulsion that any day now, any minute she's afraid she's going to do the very worst thing possible—more awful than copulating with him while pregnant with another man's child, more awful than betraying Francisca and her aunt and uncle, who had taken her in and raised her almost as their own—and tell him the truth.

But now an even worse possibility stands before her, in the person of Hugh Fisher.

He stands as straight and beautiful as ever, his hair as golden, even in the iron-gray light of a March afternoon in New England. He is so perfectly groomed, so fine and fair and crisp at the edges, smelling of masculine soap—a scent she tries to recall at night, but can't quite capture anymore. Inside her womb, his child kicks and grows. She stares at his bare, pink neck and her heart pours from her body and flows across the dank air into his, the way it poured across that July swimming pool on the morning after his father died, the way her heart always pours between them as he stands before her, even when she hates him.

There is no escape, she thinks. We are bound, just as he said, bound together always. We can't help it. It is God's will I shall bear his child. It is God's will we shall live and die because of each other.

She says sharply, "I hear your wife is expecting a baby."

"Yes. In June."

"Good. They can grow up together, then. My child and hers. They're almost twins."

"Don't, Bianca."

"Why not? It's your doing. You made my baby, you made hers. You did this."

"How was I supposed to abandon her? There are things you don't understand, things you can't understand. I had no choice." He turns, and his face is streaked with tears. "Anyway, you left me. I thought you were gone for good. And I was angry, and then I saw you were right and I should try to make the best of things, and then I heard—I learned—and I can count, Bianca, believe me, I can apparently count better than any of—well."

"If it makes you feel any better, everybody hates me here. Except Pascoal." She laughs bitterly at the sound of her husband's name and she glances out to sea, as if expecting to see his boat, his gnomish figure dragging the wooden traps from the water, one by one.

"No, it doesn't make me feel any better. I've been out of my head with worry for you. I love you. Just to look at you now, carrying my child, my son, you're the most beautiful thing I've ever seen. I want to—right now, God forgive me, I could—"

. He stops and looks down at the rocks. Bianca tries to think of Pascoal—her husband who worships her, who willingly faces down her shame before the world—tries in desperation to think of him lovingly, as a wife should, but all she can summon up is the fishy smell of him when he comes home in the afternoon, a smell that clings to the oil of his skin and fills her nose when he sits across from her and eats his dinner in juicy, purring mouthfuls, when he reads his newspaper in the chair by the lamp, when he climbs into bed and sticks his gnarled fingers under her nightgown. How she turns her face away when he tries to kiss her, because she's afraid she'll gag on the taste of his mouth, so they make love without kissing, without even looking at each other, a silent and graceless humping that's no more than a parody of the sacred union between husband and wife. Afterward, guilt and remorse, because she cannot love him, cannot even like him, not while Hugh Fisher walks upon the earth like a god.

"And you live two hundred yards away from Greyfriars," he says. "For the rest of my life, years upon years, you'll be just out of reach, you and my boy. Inside a tower. A *tower*, Bianca! It's like a cruel joke. Lamp flashing always at my window. And I can't just sell up and move away. I can't do without you, that's the goddamned pity of it. I can't think of any woman but you."

The wind howls softly around the lighthouse walls and whips his hair. For an instant, Bianca imagines that Pascoal's boat will be caught in a squall, hurled upon the rocks, a terrible tragedy. She crosses herself.

"Do you love me, Hugh?" she asks.

He looks up, and his beauty stops her breath.

"Do you need to ask?" he says.

"I think I do."

"Then yes, Bianca. I love you."

"Always, Hugh?"

"I swear before God, Bianca, if I ever stop, if I ever love another woman before you, you can kill me with your bare hands."

Bianca balances delicately on the point of a rock, in the middle of the roiling sea.

She turns and opens the door behind her. The warm air rushes past her cheeks, smelling of smoke and the soup she's making for supper. Above their heads, the light swings in its mighty arc, pulsing in time with the universe, making her young blood rise at last and clamor in her veins. She places her hand of the curve of her gravid belly.

"Come inside, then," she says, "and we will keep your promise."

This she believes with all her heart.

AFTERWORD: 1970

THE WEEK BEFORE Hugh's graduation, the weather turns warm and fair. After dinner, when the dishes are washed and put away and the bridge table is set up in the living room, I open the back door and slip out to wander across the gravel, around the side of the house and down the long, grassy slope toward the sea.

Behind me, Greyfriars is ablaze against the indigo twilight. Every bedroom is now occupied. Miss Patty and Miss Felicity stayed through the winter, and so did Brigitte. Otto and Leonard arrived at the end of April. A couple of new residents introduced themselves nervously in March, having heard of the new Greyfriars theater residency through some circuitous connection, and after a brief trial period they seem to be getting on well. Through the open French doors, the chatter and laughter float from familiar throats, and the sound of it chases me all the way down the lawn, fading and fading, until the lapping of the water against the sea wall absorbs them all.

For some time, I stand and look out over the water, toward the empty lighthouse and the steady, anodyne electric glow from its tower. There was some talk of tearing it down entirely over the winter, but the Islanders objected on historic grounds, the lighthouse was duly declared some sort of monument, and while the old mechanism was cleared out, along with any sign of human habitation, the structure still stands while the Department of the Interior decides what to do with it. Lighthouses are an anachronism, you see, a relic of the past, built for an age before charts and radar and all those modern gadgets that keep ships out of trouble. Built before a powerful electric lamp could just sit there and glow for weeks and months, putting out steady, faithful candlepower without needing any human being to attend to it.

Still, there's something so beautiful about a lighthouse bathed in the light of a full moon. It breaks your heart, almost. This brave, lonely, silvery thing standing tall in the middle of a hurtling tide. I've come here often in the evening, when the weather could stand it, when I wasn't on the mainland attending to business. Sometimes I perch on the end of the dock, sometimes I sit on the bench. These past couple of months, I have mostly sat on the bench. Always my gaze searches the horizon, searching for a particular sail, and sometimes I think I perceive it. But it turns out to be an ordinary sailboat, of course. One of hundreds, of thousands plying these populous waters. Isobel tells me I'm crazy to keep looking. Isobel, who now spends a great deal of her time in the guesthouse at the Monks' place at the other end of the island. I'll let you decide for yourself what that means.

Since the beginning of April, there have been no more postcards. They never did arrive at regular intervals to begin with—sometimes twice a week, sometimes once a month, four in one day on Christmas Eve—and contained no message at all, just my name and address, Miranda Schuyler, Greyfriars, Winthrop Island, New York, in neat, black letters. And postmarks, of course. Bermuda. Cumberland Island. Belize. If the Winthrop Island postmaster had been inclined to cooperate with the United States Marshals office, I suppose some useful information might have made its way up and down the chain of command. But the Winthrop Island postmaster happens to be Mrs. Menzies, a close cousin of Mrs. Maria Medeiro, who runs the general store, and at her age, she isn't inclined to cooperate with anybody, trust me.

But the postcards have now ceased altogether, and their absence has been a blight on my soul. Just the sight of that handwriting warmed me for days during the chill, miserable pit of the Winthrop Island winter. Mama set them aside for me when the mail came, along with all the legal correspondence related to my divorce, the legal correspondence related to the case of Mr. Joseph Vargas, the legal correspondence related to the formation of the Greyfriars Players, Incorporated. All of which is sometimes more than I can stand, which is why I like to come down here in the evenings and stare at the lighthouse until everything becomes clear again. Sometimes I doze off, bundled in my wool coat and scarf, and Brigitte has to wake me up and scold me. To tell me that rascal will return in his own time or not at all, and it was no good catching my death of cold out here waiting for him.

But tonight I'm not catching my death of cold. Tonight I'm wearing not a wool coat but a cardigan. Tonight the air is mild, the moon is out, the drunken scent of late May viburnum drifts past now and again, so faint it's almost my imagination. The night birds stir in the nearby trees. Summer is so close, so real, so within reach, the whole world is alive with anticipation, and I could no more doze off than I could fly to the moon. The dear, familiar moon. I stare down at its reflection on the calm sea, and I say to myself, sort of a murmur:

> *The moon shines bright. In such a night as this,*
> *When the sweet wind did gently kiss the trees*
> *And they did make no noise, in such a night*
> *Troilus methinks mounted the Trojan walls*
> *And sighed his soul toward the Grecian tents*
> *Where Cressid lay that night.*

It turns out you can't just walk into Washington and demand a presidential pardon. Clay Monk helped me. He put in hours and hours. He constructed a perfect case, calling in evidence from me, from Father McManus, from the forensic report of the murder itself. Even then, it helped that Joseph was presumed drowned. It helped, as Clay put it, arguing eloquently before his president, that Joseph—an innocent man—had sacrificed his own life to save the life of the United States Marshal who was arresting him. Find the hero, as Carroll used to say. People need their heroes. And even then, it helped that Clay's father had known the president personally, that Clay's daughter—I don't remember which one— had once bounced from the knees of Richard Nixon in the Oval Office itself. These things matter, after all. It seems the Monks and Fishers of the world are maybe not entirely irrelevant, yet.

And in April we won our pardon at last. The newspapers were full of it. I made sure of that, believe me. I made sure that my name was connected to the case, my celebrated name that was always good for a headline. I made sure that anyone in the world—anyone who could overhear a conversation in a café, anyone who could read a newspaper, anyone who could listen to the announcer on a radio—would learn of this extraordinary tale of heroism and sacrifice and redemption. Anyone in the world, wherever he might be. In whatever harbor he might have found shelter.

Shortly afterward, the postcards ceased.

The water slaps against the wall and the dock. A breeze drifts off the water, smelling of the peculiar tang of Long Island Sound, fish and brine and green, living things. Beyond it, the open ocean, the unforgiving Atlantic, over which my father sailed away from me, and Joseph sailed away from me. Over which I myself sailed away, and then returned, to this arcane little island, *this little world, this precious stone set in the silver sea, which serves it in the office of a wall*—oh God, my father's voice again—*against the envy of less happier lands* . . .

I rise awkwardly from the bench and walk to the end of the dock. There are moments when I wonder how he did it—slipped past all those Coast Guard boats, past the tip of Long Island and into infinity. Maybe it was luck. Maybe it was the tide, turning at last in Joseph's favor. Maybe I'll never know. Maybe, when our child asks about his father—her father— I'll simply say that the ocean took him away and never gave him back.

I lift one hand to my belly and speak again, more clearly. Unless I'm just saying the words in my head. Sometimes, when you're alone like that, it's almost the same thing.

> *In such a night*
> *Stood Dido with a willow in her hand*
> *Upon the wild sea banks, and waft her love*
> *To come again to Carthage.*

The baby moves beneath my hand, a soft kick, and in that instant a sail appears around the edge of the lighthouse. One of hundreds, of thousands plying these populous waters.

An ordinary sailboat, carrying an ordinary man, beating its way past the edge of Fleet Rock and up the treacherous channel toward me.

AUTHOR'S NOTE

Few people outside the Long Island Sound area have heard of Fisher's Island, and that's exactly how residents of this small, discreet enclave like it. As a result, I expect that most readers won't recognize Fisher's in my fictional Winthrop Island, and in fact, the two are not identical in geography, history, or population. But the unique and somewhat secretive microculture of Fisher's Island inspired the writing of this book, and I'm grateful to a few longtime Fisher's residents—primarily John Talbott and his daughter, Thayer—for sharing their stories and reflections with me. Thanks are also due to my husband's parents, Sydney and Caroline Williams, who provided additional details that enriched my understanding of this era and the social classes depicted here.

While some episodes taking place in this novel have their basis in actual events, the characters and the plot are entirely my own invention.

ABOUT THE AUTHOR

Beatriz Williams is the bestselling author of eight novels. A native of Seattle, she graduated from Stanford University and earned an MBA in finance from Columbia University, then spent several years in New York and London as a corporate strategy consultant before pursuing her passion for historical fiction. She lives with her husband and four children near the Connecticut shore, where she divides her time between writing and laundry.